Dirty Geese

LOU GILMOND

Armillary Books

First published by Armillary Books 2023
This hardback edition first published by Armillary Books 2024

Armillary Books
Summertown Pavilion, 18–24 Middle Way, Oxford, OX2 7LG

A CIP catalogue record for this book is available from the
British Library

1 2 3 4 5 6 7 8 9 10

ISBN 978-1-914148-74-3

www.fairlightbooks.com

Printed and bound in Great Britain

Cover Design © Nick Castle

FSC
www.fsc.org

MIX
Paper | Supporting
responsible forestry
FSC® C013056

For Kathy

Prologue

As dawn broke over London, Mrs Joyce Newbury, principal private secretary to the Minister for Personal Information, hurried into her Whitehall department's little galley kitchen, shrugged off her overcoat and put some fresh coffee on to brew. In her bag were two chocolate muffins. Good, she thought, pulling them out. They were still warm. Just how Percy liked them.

She placed them lovingly on a tray next to his coffee, and with a smile shook her head to see his mackintosh thrown on the floor. Poor darling, Joyce thought, picking it up and hanging it over her arm. He must have come in early to work on his speech.

'I thought I might have beaten you in,' she said, backing into the ministerial office and placing the tray onto the nearest console table, only to find it wouldn't sit flat. Joyce lifted the tray and found the problem to be a strange gelatinous blob that lay on the polished mahogany. She peered at it, curious.

'Did you want me to go through your speech with you, Per—?' But, looking up, she noticed more gelatinous blobs in front of her. She turned slowly, her eye following them as a child might study a picture of the Milky Way painted on the schoolroom wall. They led to the minister. He was at his desk where she had first seen him out of the corner of her eye, but she hadn't expected to find him slumped forward, hadn't thought to see an antique pistol peeping out beneath his neck, or a great hole in the back of his head.

As Joyce Newbury sank to her knees, the tray of coffee slid to the floor. A chocolate muffin spun across the room and came to rest beside an armchair.

The minister's office was large, grand even. As well as his vast partner's desk and the green rayon armchair, there was a walnut board table, another armchair and a slightly mismatched sofa. On the other side of the room from where Joyce knelt weeping, a line of tall windows looked out over Whitehall. Beyond the window, a delivery drone, one of many being trialled in the city, rose from the ranks of its fellows, and hovered there, turning its silent eye towards the room. With a howl of rage, Joyce Newbury snatched up the wayward muffin and hurled it at the window. The drone flinched away. But after a moment, like a pigeon doggedly hoping for titbits, it inched slowly back.

*

Henri Lauvaux, VP of regulatory affairs for Alcheminna Systems, was interrupted at his desk by a call informing him that Percy Dvořáček, the UK Minister for Personal Information, was dead.

He leaned back in his chair and reflected on the news. Through his windows he could see the town of Sevrier sweeping up the opposite shore of Lake Annecy, its villas and mansions dotted among the trees and a light morning mist hovering along the shoreline.

'Suicide?' he said, bringing the handset of an old-fashioned desk phone back to his ear. 'How terribly sad.'

After a few more questions, Lauvaux ended the call, picked up his e-pad and turned back to the view, shaking his head. He was a tall man, his height due to long legs which today were trousered in dark brown corduroy. He wore a cream shirt open at the collar and above that his hair was wiry and grey around a mountain-weathered face.

Dirty Geese

He wondered who they might find to replace Dvořáček. His system suggested several names, some of which he knew, some of which he didn't.

Outside, the sun had risen over the hills behind his building, bathing the opposing massif of rock with a sharp light. He worked for a while, jotting down strategies on a calf-skin notepad until a motor launch crossing the lake reminded him he was to take his wife and daughter into town for lunch at La Ciboulette. Just as he remembered it, his daughter danced into the room.

'*Papa*,' she said. '*Tu m'emmèneras skier cet après-midi?*'

'In English, please,' Lauvaux replied.

'Will you take me skiing this afternoon?'

Lauvaux beckoned his daughter over and took her hand.

'Not today, *ma chérie*. I have to go to London for work.'

The girl frowned, her lips pursing together and her eyebrows coming closer, just as her father's had during his call. 'Again? But you didn't say so at breakfast.'

'I know, but something has changed. I'm sure your mama will take you.'

Lauvaux went to kiss the top of his daughter's head, but she turned away.

'I don't want to go with Mother. She doesn't ski very fast. I don't run a business. Why should I have to change my plans?'

Lauvaux pulled his daughter towards him, and with his thumb smoothed away her frown.

'Alright, you win. We'll ski. Now go and get changed, and find your mother. See if she is ready to go into town. You know how busy the restaurant gets.'

'But they always keep a table for you, *Papa*.'

The girl raised herself onto a toe, and with her arms outstretched performed a series of ballerina twirls out of the room, calling as she went, '*Maman! Papa dit, dépêche-toi!*'

7

Lauvaux called for his secretary to come in and a young woman appeared in the doorway.

'I'll fly to London tomorrow afternoon. Tell them to make sure the plane is available, would you?'

'*Oui, monsieur.*'

When his secretary had gone, Lauvaux picked up his e-pad and swiped it open again, pursing his lips in thought once more as he studied the list of potential candidates. A thought or two fell into place. Suddenly, he saw who they were likely to appoint as the new Minister for Personal Information, and Lauvaux gave a small chuckle of delight at his own cleverness. A certain Harry Colbey. Lauvaux had never heard of the man, which meant he was nobody of importance – at least not until now.

After a few jabs of his finger, an image of Harry Colbey appeared on his screen.

'Tell me what matters the most to you,' Lauvaux asked.

'To be honourable,' was the reply. Lauvaux thought Colbey's voice was confident but with a tired note, the last syllable dropping away with the hint of a sigh.

Lauvaux nodded, swiped the e-pad closed, and slapped the cover shut with a satisfying flick. So... an *honourable* member. His frown returned once more and then he smiled.

Honour, thought Lauvaux, usually has a price. It's just a question of discovering what it is.

PART ONE

I.I

The joy of another bright spring day in London, with last year's half-remembered sun cutting through the plane trees and streaming bright onto the paving stones of Westminster. Up in the canopy, the new leaves were just budding and the seedpods hung heavy, ready to carpet the streets with untidy yellow dust. Not that Harry Colbey cared about such things, for he was in disgrace and woefully late.

He parked his car beside Westminster School as the boys in their blazers came pouring out of an archway like a pack of newborn puppies, clad in grey and climbing over one another in their excitement to be out. Colbey wished he could share in their exuberance, but today he could not.

So, instead, he straightened out the creases that had gathered in his suit over the long drive, checked for the third or fourth time that his shoes were neatly polished and hurried off towards Parliament Square. It was cold, despite the hint of summer to come, and when Colbey reached the Cenotaph, within sight of his destination, he tried hard not to break into an unseemly trot.

'Come here,' the prime minister had growled, but it might as well have been 'Come here so I can skewer you with my ornamental letter opener', Colbey thought grimly as he waited at the gates for the duty officer to validate his ID and permit him through to the scanners. The message was the same: Colbey was in for a roasting.

It looked like the whole thing was his fault, but that was hardly fair. Yesterday, a private member's bill containing some of his own department's legislation had nearly been passed without the government knowing anything about it, without *him* knowing anything about it. As his wife had pointedly told him that morning, the fact that he had been minister of the department for only six hours at the time was no excuse. Nor the fact that at the time of the debate they had been flying home from a hastily cancelled city break following Number Ten's unexpected call offering him Percy Dvořáček's new department.

As Colbey scurried from the security shed to that famous front door, his jacket tails catching the breeze and showing off a flash of expensive blue lining, he hoped that the prime minister's temper was already fading. Apparently, Esme Kanha, chief whip, had taken the first brunt of the PM's anger, and his chief of staff, at least one permanent secretary and even the Speaker of the House had been hauled in for their share.

Colbey surrendered his mobile phone, placing it in one of the slots in the hallway designed for the purpose, before being directed upstairs. Perhaps Ewan MacLellan might even be opening up to the chief whip's first tentative jokes on the matter, and letting out a hearty and much welcome guffaw. For the whole thing had not, in the end, been the disaster it might have.

Outside the door of the PM's office, Colbey paused and caught his breath. How strange it was to be standing there, he considered. How unexpected. Just a few days ago his life had pottered along with its rather stale routines – his week filled with committee meetings and parliamentary votes, his weekends with his surgery work, perhaps a dinner or two with the neighbours or even a little badminton. And yet, now, this. The PM's diary secretary, sitting at her desk, was looking up at him.

'How's the weather?' he whispered. She was an old school friend of his daughter's and usually referred to him as Mr C. He hoped she wouldn't do it here. Colbey patted empty pockets and after attempting to wipe his glistening forehead with a corner of his sleeve, took the tissue Anastacia offered him and did the job properly.

'Squally but turning to fair,' she said softly. 'I heard him laughing a minute ago.'

Colbey heaved a sigh of relief. The worst thing about potentially being fired on his first full day as cabinet minister was the prospect of having to go home and tell his wife. Clarissa would not have taken it well.

'You should probably go in. They've been waiting ages.'

Colbey came round the desk and dropped the tissue in a bin at the girl's knees.

'Crash on the M40. Got stuck behind it. What a nightmare. Thanks, Anastacia.'

He tapped at the office door. It was opened by Kanha, who was dressed as always in her sombre uniform of dark suit and towering court shoes. She waved him in with a stern look and went and stood by the window, her arms crossed over her chest. The prime minister was perched on the edge of his desk. There was a smell of coffee and stale biscuits in the room which nearly but didn't quite mask the aroma of whiskey drunk late at night and sweated out through a gentleman's aftershave.

'So,' said Ewan MacLellan. 'You're here at last.'

Colbey glanced at Kanha. Her face was inscrutable.

The PM went to sit behind his desk. Now that Colbey was closer to him than ever before, he saw how their leader's skin was shiny across his forehead. The old man must have had work done over in the States.

Colbey sat opposite the PM following the directions of a carelessly waved hand, but Kanha remained standing by the window, her arms still crossed and a fingernail tapping soundlessly against the sleeve of her jacket. Today, her thick black hair was swept into a tight bun at the back of her head. There was an empty silence that Colbey dared not break.

'Right...' said the prime minister, looking into his blotter and then peering up at first Kanha and then Colbey, '...so what I'm led to understand is that before Percy Dvořáček went into his office and... and... well, you know... he had placed a piece of government legislation into a private member's bill and then gone on a drinking binge, ringing up members of our party asking them to vote for it.'

'Yes,' said Kanha.

'Did he call you?' the PM asked Colbey.

'Yes, he did,' Colbey said. 'My daughter, Chloe, took a call on Friday, but forgot to pass the message on.'

He saw out of the corner of his eye that the terrible Kanha was smirking, but her smile disappeared when the PM laughed and said, 'Chloe, eh? More interesting things to think about I expect.'

Hah! Take that, Esme Kanha, Colbey thought. You didn't know the prime minister and I were socially connected, did you?

'And why do we think he would do such a thing?'

'He was very drunk,' Kanha ventured and Colbey hurried to agree, for surely it was Dvořáček who should take the blame in all this. After all, it wasn't going to affect his career now. It was terribly sad, and altogether rather unexpected.

The PM grunted. 'That may well be, Esme. But I *still* haven't got to the bottom of why your department didn't notice the switch in legislation. It's an utter embarrassment, I tell you...'

Kanha frowned and said, 'If you must know, it's my belief Dvořáček deliberately worked the whole thing to keep it a secret.'

'A secret?' said the PM, his eyebrows rising.

'Yes, a secret.' She glanced at Colbey, and he got the impression she was uncertain whether to speak in front of him, but seemed to make up her mind that she would. 'He was sneaky about it,' she said. 'Switching the papers at the last minute, telling the clerks it had my approval, not sending the new papers to the lobby press.'

The PM made a growling noise. 'Well, which was he? A nonsensical drunk or a cunning fox? But our members voted for it! That's the really embarrassing thing. Not a single person had read that bloody bill, not even you whips. Percy hadn't even given an opening speech for the bill, being... well... you know... dead.'

Kanha relinquished her place by the window and came over to them, her famous temper finally showing, and said, 'None of it makes any sense, Ewan, but we did manage to stop the bill going through, didn't we?' When she stood up straight like that, she was taller than the PM, and Colbey saw that she was not afraid of him. He felt a little stab of admiration for her, but the PM was not to be daunted.

'Not a single person had read it,' he repeated, his eyes opening wide. One side of Kanha's mouth turned up in what looked like the beginnings of a smile and she said, 'It was a private member's bill, after all,' and suddenly she and the PM were both laughing heartily.

The prime minister picked up his reading glasses from his desk.

'So what's to be done, then? Mmm? Esme, why don't you get your team to speak to our members and remind them that any drunken phone calls from colleagues should be reported straight to you.'

'That's already been done,' she said, and her arms folded and the tapping of her fingernail began again.

'And you, Colbey. The Department for Personal Information is *your* department now. Get a bloody grip on your brief.'

Colbey tried hard not to let what felt like a breath he had been holding in come out as a sigh of relief.

'I mean, we might only be a month or two away from an election. You do know that, don't you?'

'Yes, of course, Ewan.' Colbey realised it was the first time he had dared use the prime minister's first name. Was it too much? No, the PM didn't even notice. Colbey was not only safe, but a little step closer to the inner circle. Clarissa would be pleased.

The prime minister began polishing his glasses. 'And in all this, let's not forget about poor old Dvořáček, eh? Terribly sad when a man takes his own life. Left behind a wife and two children, you know. It's a damn shame, I tell you. A damn shame.' Colbey mumbled his agreement, but Kanha looked away. 'Anyway, enough of all that. Now where's that home secretary? She's always bloody late. Kanha, go and see Anastacia and find out where she's got to.'

The PM put his spectacles on, shuffled some papers around and, seeming to wait until Kanha was out of the room, took them off again and looked directly at Colbey.

'Yes, indeed, poor Dvořáček. Do something for me, will you? He had a black book – a notebook or diary, that sort of thing. Often carried it about with him. Old dinosaur he was. Everything on paper.' The PM got up and came to place a hand on Colbey's shoulder. 'If you come across it in his department – I mean *your* department, of course – bring it to me, would you? Don't take a look, if you know what's good for you. Just bring it straight to me. There's a good chap.'

'Of course,' said Colbey. 'I'll have a search later today. See if I can discreetly track it down.' He tapped the side of his nose and then felt foolish for having done so.

The PM stood lost in thought, so Colbey waited, uncertain whether his audience was over. Out of the window he could see swings and slides in the garden and wondered why the elderly PM and his wife had not arranged to have them cleared away. But, of course, it was said that the pair had pretended to embark on a lengthy renovation of the apartments above Number Ten and Number Eleven, so that they could instead move into what should have been the foreign secretary's grace-and-favour residence in Carlton Gardens. In the bars of Westminster, it was rumoured the PM preferred living at Carlton Gardens because from there he could more easily slip into his favourite club in St James's without the press noticing. Arrogance, the opposition called it, while the sympathetic press bayed in return that he was a strong leader who knew what he needed to best run the country. The sign of a healthy majority, Clarissa had said.

The PM spoke at last. 'Do you know, I agree with Kanha there's something fishy about it all, but I don't want that sentiment gaining traction. Particularly don't want those gossipy whips using it as an excuse for their monumental cock-up. So don't repeat that you heard that, mmm?'

Colbey nodded as Kanha came back into the room.

'She's isn't due until this afternoon, Ewan.'

'Oh. My mistake. Off you go then, Colbey. Run along to your new department. Get them all jumping through hoops for you... mmm?'

Feeling flushed about the secret mission the PM had given him, Colbey couldn't help saying, 'Oh, prime minister, Clarissa wondered if we should bring anything for dinner this evening?'

'What? For dinner? Shouldn't think so. Zandra will have it all in hand.'

Colbey dared a smile at Kanha and a cheery goodbye, but seeing her stony face he was left with the bittersweet realisation that needling Kanha was a stupid thing to do.

At least his ministerial position was still intact, for the moment at any rate. He left the room to be greeted by Anastacia's grin. 'Still in one piece then, Mr C?' she whispered, and he made a fist in mock celebration, making her laugh.

'Do you happen to know,' he asked, 'whether a car is coming to collect me?'

Anastacia shook her head. 'You could check with the doorman? Perhaps your principal private secretary has arranged for it to fetch you.'

'Right oh,' said Colbey, not wanting to admit he didn't know who his principal private secretary was.

As he made his way back down to the front door, he took a moment to have a proper look about him. He did it shyly, so that it wouldn't be obvious. So he was to keep his position as the Minister for Personal Information, was he? He felt a little frisson of excitement at the opportunities it would bring – the right to walk unaccompanied about the famous corridors of Number Ten being one. Yet the prospect of his new job didn't entirely fill him with joy. He would be running a department that had only recently been formed, whose previous minister had just shot himself, and with a key piece of legislation to be shepherded through parliament before the country went to the polls: the much-lauded Personal Information Bill.

He considered – and it was not the first time he had considered it since he had received the call from Number Ten – it wasn't going to be much fun at all. In fact, it would involve heaps of paperwork, late nights entertaining, the management of civil servants whose entire focus was on trying to reverse manage their minister instead, plus all the political shenanigans and... bullshit... that came with being a cabinet member. All things considered, he didn't have the energy for it and had actually been hoping to coast his way towards a gentle retirement somewhere in the South of France, where the light was soft, the air was warm and the rosé wonderfully chilled. Why his name had been plucked from the hat, he had no idea. It wasn't as if he put himself about in that eager way that the ambitious ones did. But at least, he thought, as he arrived back at the front door of Number Ten and collected his phone, it has made my wife very happy.

I.2

After Harry Colbey was gone, the PM turned to Kanha and said, 'What do you think, then?'

Kanha found her coat on the rack by the door and, picking up her bag, said, 'He'll do.'

'Good. We could do with a steady head in that department for a while. Speaking of which, would you go over there and speak to Morland?'

'The permanent secretary? Why?'

'Something to do with a painting in the ministerial office that was damaged. He wants a decision from us. Why he can't figure it out for himself, I've no idea.'

Kanha turned to the door and with her back to the PM, said, 'Can't Colbey do it?'

'I don't want to rattle him,' was the reply. 'Rather you handled it.'

'Alright,' Kanha said, and closing the door behind her found Harry Colbey still in sight, making his way down the stairs. He was taking his time and looking about him, so she dawdled, waiting and watching as he recovered his phone from the pigeon-holes and spoke with the duty officer. The doorman shook his head in response to whatever Colbey had asked.

As soon as he was safely away, she followed him out onto Downing Street where her pool car was waiting. By now, Colbey was down by the gates that opened onto Whitehall, peering sheepishly out. From the Jaguar she watched him through the anonymity of her car's tinted windows as he tentatively set off down the strip of no-man's-land that separated Downing Street from Westminster Palace and the House of Commons. No minister in their right mind would willingly cover that ground on foot – a sitting duck for every zitty blogger with journalistic pretentions. Particularly one in so newsworthy a state as Harry Colbey, newly summoned to Number Ten after a disgraceful embarrassment – or so she had discreetly briefed her favourite lobby hack. Better that the press run with the story that *he* was in hot water for this fiasco with Dvořáček's private bill than *her*. But now that she had met Colbey, she felt a little stab of guilt at having done it. Of course, it was exactly how the PM had taught her to act, so he wouldn't be surprised to learn of it, but Colbey was just so... so green.

As her car turned in the opposite direction, Kanha leaned forward and tapped on the privacy screen that separated her from the driver and the intercom crackled into life.

'Mick, where's Harry Colbey's car?'

Her driver's voice came through the speaker beside her. 'Harry Colbey? The new Minister for Personal Information?'

'Yes, that's right. Where's his car?'

Holding up a finger he said, 'Give me a minute.'

The gossip of the ministerial and pool car drivers came through the still-open intercom while she waited for the answer. A car had been sent to Wales to collect a secretary of state's dogs and ferry them to London, and somewhere in Surrey, a minister's daughter was having a meltdown about a dead hedgehog in a swimming pool. When the language turned blue, the driver cut the intercom and when it crackled back into life the radio had been discreetly turned down.

'It's with the previous minister's widow, Chief Whip.'

'Why does she still have it?'

The driver turned his head and pulled a face. 'She's been given permission to keep it for a day or two for the arrangements. Know what I mean? They're off to the undertakers.'

Kanha nodded and sat back as the grey turreted columns of the Department of Personal Information loomed in front of them. They swung into a side street and down a ramp to the car park below.

Damn it all, she thought, dwelling on the car sent to fetch the dogs jealously. She needed to work her way into a ministerial position that came with a designated car, as well as a grace-and-favour flat. Enough of this pool car nonsense; it was a fresh bunfight every day, and unlike them, the other cabinet ministers, she had the expense of running a car for her journey home and the rent of her constituency house, yet she got the same salary as the rest. For her there were no trust funds or inheritance on which to fall back; there were no bank accounts stuffed with cash from an earlier career at the bar or in the City.

Wiping the condensation from the window, Kanha mulled over whether she should make a play for the Home Office or Treasury, and whether it would be better to do so before or after the election. She was in the PM's favour at the moment. Such things did not always last.

*

Inside the department, Kanha met the permanent secretary, Gerald Morland, by the lifts and the two of them went up and across to the minister's office.

'Are you sure you want to see this?' he asked as they stood in the corridor outside the room. 'It isn't necessary, you know.'

Kanha hesitated. Going into the room where Dvořáček shot himself was the last thing she wanted, but without admitting it was so, she couldn't avoid it, so tugging aside the police tape she opened the door. Although she had known what she would find, she felt an involuntary jump of her heart, which beat so loudly it seemed that Morland might be able to hear. She crossed the room, weaving between the armchairs to the desk at the far end. The interior was darkened by its oak panelling, despite the line of tall windows on one side and the wide diagonal patches of sunlight that lay on the floor. It was a space she was familiar with, which added a macabre edge to what was before her.

On the wall behind the desk was an oil painting of an aristocrat standing before a velvet red curtain, a crown on a table by his hand. About a fifth of the way down the painting was a ragged hole. By some horrible quirk of fate, it fell in line with the head of its kingly subject, so that his nose, chin and his neck were missing. Just his sad brown eyes were all that was left of his face, gazing serenely out at them.

Was it by chance? But that was too fanciful, to think that someone in such a distressed state should try to calculate how best to pass the bullet not only up through his own head, but across the space behind him and into the head of this ancient gentleman. There was blood and debris across the upper part of the canvas, and splayed in a neat halo on the wall at both sides. The whole messy affair could have been transferred to the Tate as modern art, with some comment about the inhumanity of man to man, or an exposition on sovereignty or some such.

Kanha felt light-headed and pretended to be taking a moment's reflection while she tried to breathe slowly and count down from ten. She felt calmer and the beating of her heart had slowed to its normal rate by seven. She would not get upset in front of this particularly sly permanent secretary, not for all the tea on all the rattling trolleys in Whitehall.

'Who is he?' she said at last, not wanting to go closer.

'Frederick V,' replied Morland. 'A king of Bohemia.'

'It looks old.'

'It's dated 1632, by a Dutch master, or so it says on the panel at the bottom.'

'I'll take your word for it.'

She turned her back on the painting and walked over to the windows.

'How did Dvořáček get a gun past the door scanners?'

'He didn't. A flintlock pistol has hung just there for a century.' Morland pointed at some empty hooks that stuck forlornly out of the wall, a line of unfaded wallpaper between them; Kanha saw and remembered how beautifully manicured Morland's nails were. He was a meticulous man – precise in manner, dress and speech.

'We believe he brought the shot in. It would have looked to the scanners like coins in his pocket. Apparently, he was a member of an antique arms club. They would dress up in old military clothing and—'

Kanha sighed. 'So... the problem in question.'

They both turned and gazed at the painting again. The effect of the precision was even more striking from this distance. Morland rose up on his toes and gave a little harrumphing noise before speaking.

'The GAC say it's not salvageable.'

'The GAC?'

'Government Art C—'

'And that's a problem because?'

He gave her a look that suggested he was surprised she didn't know, but which she suspected was just him being patronising.

'The cost of a write-off, following damage to a government artwork, is allocated to the department in which it hung when the damage occurred.'

'And how much was this one worth?'

Morland told her and Kanha swore quietly.

He smiled. 'Yes, the problem in question... You look a little pale, Esme. Perhaps it would be better if we had some air?'

As he spoke he rather deliberately took his telephone out of his pocket and placed it on the console table that stood beneath the empty gun hooks. Kanha hesitated, and then did the same. She followed him over to the nearest window, where he fussed with the knob of one of the French doors and pushed it open with a little brute force. Kanha followed him out onto a narrow balcony, a few feet across. He pulled the door to behind them. Cold air swept between the stone balusters and flew up Kanha's skirt. It made Morland's hair rise out from his head, but Kanha knew hers, in its tight bun, was not affected. At the enquiring lift of her eyebrows, Morland said, 'I hear those phones are still not as secure as GCHQ suggests. We – the senior civil servants, that is – think this is best practice until they get on top of the issue. We can speak more freely this way.' Although for a while nothing was said.

A delivery drone lifted up from a stream of them below and hovered close by. Morland picked up some loose gravel that had crumbled from the masonry and flung a piece of it into the drone's propellors. It spun off, out of control and out of sight. 'Bloody things,' he said.

Kanha rested her hands on the cold grey stone and looked at the buses passing below. In her head she read out the numbers painted on the tops as the rumble of the traffic served to fill the new silence.

'When is Colbey due in?' she asked eventually.

Morland waved a hand in the air. 'Oh, sometime this afternoon I expect.'

'You haven't told him a time?'

They both smiled and Kanha turned to lean back against the balustrade, absently chewing on a fingernail.

'What do you think of his appointment?'

Giving a little mock bow, he said, 'It's not for me to say, but to serve.'

'Come on. I'm due a little more than that.'

Morland hesitated. 'I'm uncertain how it will be, because of his... reputation.'

'Reputation? What reputation? He's always seemed a bit of a nonentity to me.'

'Ah, well, I suppose I'm going back a bit. We, who stay, while others come and go...'

Kanha pursed her lips, not wanting to play the game of teasing it out of him. She knew he would tell her and would take pleasure in doing so. 'It's going to be a busy day, Gerald.'

Delighted, Morland said, 'Before your time. There was such a thing, you know.' He smoothed down his tie. 'When Harry Colbey first arrived in Westminster, he was very green in the ways of politics, but remarkably capable. He was promoted quickly – to a junior minister within a matter of months, but, alas for him, it only lasted three weeks. He fell back to earth as quickly as he had been raised.'

Kanha waited patiently while Morland picked some lint off the front of his jacket.

'He was found to be... difficult to manage.'

'By his permanent secretary?'

'Very droll. No, his minister found him difficult to manage.'

'And?'

'And... also his permanent secretary.'

Kanha frowned. 'I thought he had a reputation for being honest?'

'Exactly.'

'Oh... I see.'

Morland held his palms out. 'Of course, we don't want dishonest junior ministers, do we? That wouldn't do, but there has to be a little... flexibility.'

'So what happened?'

'Oh, it was all rather dull. He was in DECC – Energy and Climate Change as it then was. Kept insisting we tell the public they couldn't have cheap electricity *and* green electricity. Kept saying they had to be aware that there was a trade-off. He was on about transparency and honesty, even back then, you see.'

'He didn't want green energy?'

'No, no. He was all for it. Just wanted to be sure that the public was apprised of the facts.'

'So what did you do?'

'Well, we explained to him that the green electricity will be cheap, it will be cheap compared to a future brown price when there's war in the Middle East and the oil price goes sky high. He wanted to know what if there wasn't war in the Middle East and the oil price didn't go sky high. Well, I mean, really. There's always war in the Middle East... eventually, mmm?'

Kanha waited for Morland to tell all.

'Not that any of that matters now, of course. But he wouldn't accept it, so in the end he was discreetly managed out and back onto the backbenches. It must have taken the wind out of his sails somewhat because he ran away to his constituency and threw all his effort into being a pain over there instead.'

'Hence the huge majority?'

'Yes. Better placed locally, that sort of energy. He wasn't really suited for the bigger pond, at least not then. But he's a changed man now, of course, I'm sure.'

Kanha leaned forward and looked down at a group of businessmen getting into a taxi. She ran her fingers over her hair and squeezed the hard tuck of the bun for no reason other than that she liked the feel of it. 'Don't you think so?'

'What do I know?' said Morland. 'Why did you give him the job if you didn't think he would be a good boy this time round?'

'I didn't give him the job,' Kanha said, trying not to sigh. 'He was the PM's choice. And... it served other purposes.'

'Linked to his Honest Politicking Bill, perhaps?'

Kanha smiled. The civil service's intelligence division was quicker to the truth than the MPs' gossip train.

'Yes, his idea for an Honest Politicking Bill was getting too much support outside Westminster. The only way to kill it would have been to throw him out of the party or...'

'Promote him?'

'Exactly. We needed something to keep him busy.'

'Well, he will certainly be that here.'

Kanha turned to the door, but then paused. 'One last question. Do you know why Dvořáček... did what he did?'

Morland considered, weighing each word carefully as if he were a barrister giving his summing up. 'He led a complicated life, Esme. I don't think he was a bad man, but he did try to keep a few too many people happy – colleagues, friends, women. Perhaps it all became too much. And he was very drunk after all.'

'So they say.'

'Indeed he was. I saw the CCTV footage of him entering the building Monday evening. He couldn't even walk straight. By the way, are you happy to take his personal effects and see they are given to the widow? Assuming that's the appropriate thing to do?'

Morland pointed through the windows at a storage box that sat on the floor by the door of the office.

Kanha couldn't hold back a grimace.

'Don't worry,' Morland said. 'I've given everything a thorough wipe down.'

She wrinkled her nose. 'Oh.' Then she sighed and said, 'Jesus. Poor Percy.'

Morland opened the door and held it for Kanha to step through. He followed after her, across the room, and handed the box to her. She lifted her head in the direction of the portrait.

'Ah. Good point,' said Morland. 'We nearly forgot the reason for your visit. As we are between ministers, so to speak, what would you like me to do with it?'

Kanha thought for a moment. Then she said, 'Get someone to clean off the, er... you know. Put it in a storage room somewhere in the basement and have it revalued at the next inventory audit.'

'Which is not until August?'

'Mmm.'

'An excellent solution, Chief Whip. A small parting gift for the opposition, should you not be returned to office in a few months.'

Kanha pretended she hadn't heard him. 'And don't leave Colbey sitting on his thumbs for too long.'

'Of course not. I shall rally the welcoming committee and put out the bunting as my very next task.'

Kanha paused at the door, shifting the heavy box onto her other arm. 'It's been a long time since you worked with Colbey,' she said. 'Maybe he's mellowed with age. I think he'll make a good minister this time round.' Taking hold of the sleeve of Morland's dark suit and, barely realising she did it, gauging the quality of the wool between her thumb and forefinger, she said, 'Try and look after this one better than the last, eh?' Then she kicked aside a trailing strip of blue tape and walked as briskly as she could to the stairwell, relieved to finally be out of the room.

1.3

Harry Colbey hurried into his office, turned on the television that hung on the wall opposite his desk, and swore out loud. 'Bloody hell, bloody hell,' he said. Two Mouth of the Mob hacks had cornered him at the junction of Whitehall and Parliament Square.

'What, no car, Mr Colbey?' one of them had shouted, phone held out.

'They're not expecting you to be in the job long, then, that it?' said the other.

Beyond the door, in the outer office, his researcher's desk was empty. With a sigh, Colbey picked up the phone to the internal administration team.

'I've had an email to say my researcher resigned. Do you know why?' He realised as he heard the answer that he was clenching his teeth. 'This is a really awkward time for her to leave, you know. Do you realise I've just been made minister and there might be an election in a couple of months? Oh, you do, do you? Well, why did she leave?'

Colbey snorted. 'Personal reasons – what nonsense. What were they? What do you mean, they were personal? Well, I was her boss, surely I should be told. My secretary? You mean my wife. What has she to do with it?' Colbey raised his eyes to the ceiling. 'Yes, I'm sure it is very awkward for you, but I'd like to know all the same, so that next time… Oh, never mind. Just send me over a new researcher, will you?

'I know we're weeks away from an election, I just said that. Just send one over when you can, will you? Thank you.'

Colbey slammed the phone down. His researcher had been quite hopeless, so he couldn't entirely blame his wife for ribbing the girl, but really, now he had no one. How was he to find out where his car was?

With relief, Colbey heard his wife arrive. She tutted loudly at the empty desk and then came into his room without knocking. For what had to be the hundredth time, Colbey said, 'Clarissa, would you please knock before coming in? I could have been with someone.'

'I could hear you were alone,' his wife replied, taking off her gloves and perching on the end of his desk before leaning over to be kissed on the cheek. 'I could hear you thinking. And you, my darling, are in a very grumpy mood considering you've just been made a member of government again, at long last.' A waft of cold air from the street emanated off her as she held her hands out to him. He took them in his and rubbed them. They were cold despite the gloves she had been wearing.

'It's not gone brilliantly so far.'

'Yes, I heard about this morning.'

'Already?'

'One of the bloggers has you coming through the gates of Number Ten looking a bit ginger.'

'Damn it, I didn't even see that one. I can't seem to track down my car, and I'm sitting here with nothing to get started on, waiting to go over to the department, and Gloria's just buggered off and left me in the lurch. Did you know about that?'

'Of course.'

'Why didn't you tell me?'

'I haven't had a chance. Does it really matter?'

'Yes. There's no one left they can send. I might have to wait weeks for another researcher.'

His wife blew a little air out with rounded cheeks and said, somewhat insincerely, 'Oh, poor you.'

Seeing the picture the blogger had snapped come up on the screen, Colbey picked up the remote for the TV. Then he put it down again thinking it might be better not to hear the commentary. 'Right, thanks. Only HR said...'

'Said what?'

'Said... oh, nothing. But perhaps you can find me a new researcher from somewhere. Maybe one you approve of, so you won't be getting at her the whole time.'

'For goodness' sake, darling. I'm your secretary, not your HR manager. If you've managed to upset your researcher so she left, I don't think there's much I can do about it.'

'I didn't upset her. HR said...'

'What? What did HR say? If you won't spit it out, then do shut up and stop getting at me. She was as useless as a chocolate teapot, as you know perfectly well. I'm sure you can find a new one from somewhere.'

'From somewhere? Clarissa, you can't pick up researchers in the supermarket, you know—'

'Harry, would you please lower your voice.'

'Alright. I'm sorry. It's just I'm sitting here waiting to be called to go over to the department, and I've got no car and I can't track it down and at least she would have been able to have a go at doing that.'

'Yes, you are a poor thing, aren't you?' Clarissa jumped off the desk and came round behind him and rubbed the back of his neck.

'That's nice,' he said.

'Yes, you used to like that.'

'I still do. Look... I wouldn't normally ask, but would you just stay this morning and fill in for her? I'd love to find out where my new car is and need to get my hands on Dvořáček's diary.'

'Why do you need Dvořáček's diary?'

'Just because. Please, would you do that?'

Clarissa lifted her hands from his shoulders and walked over to the television, picking up the remote from the desk as she passed. She flicked through the channels until she found his face again. 'I can't believe you just asked me that.'

Colbey groaned inwardly as he realised they were about to have a huge row. He sighed. As if he didn't have enough to deal with right now.

1.4

The whips' underground domain, though cavernous, was loud with raucous high jinks as Kanha carried the box of Dvořáček's personal effects through it and towards her own office at the far end. As ever she felt her heart sink at its sight. It was really just a corner of their communal cave, partitioned off with a glass screen and furnished with the same drab filing cabinets, the same prefab desks and the same plastic wastepaper baskets as the larger office.

Kanha had once been told that her predecessor's department moved here when its original home was no longer large enough to hold their extended whipping team, which these days included an ever-growing circus of moderators and well-being coaches. Gone were the days when the whips could coerce and bribe, blackmail and nag as they saw fit; now they had also to nurture and support.

Pursing her lips, she made her way through the melee. The whips' assistants were involved in some form of joint packing effort, which for some reason was hysterically funny. Bubble wrap was strewn everywhere and there was a strip of kitchen foil that had rolled off a desk and unravelled down the length of the floor. Kanha had to step over it and tutted her disapproval as she did so.

The assistant of her vice-deputy whip, a chap with small glasses and a long thin nose, was standing on a chair and reciting what sounded like Homer's *Odyssey*. Not for the first time, Kanha cursed the fact that she had arrived at her office to find it staffed by a bunch of kids parachuted in by their influential parents. But as she stood and watched the quoting of the Greek epic, she knew that much of her feeling was born from jealousy.

Her own education at St Vincent's had been patchy, but that was a long time ago. Since then, she had pulled herself up by her bootstraps, as her favourite saying went. Yet there were some things she would never be able to compete with – a public schoolboy on a chair quoting Homer from memory being one such.

The assistant saw that she was watching him and his *Odyssey* faltered. Oh, yes, she thought. You look at me, looking at you. The boy got down from his chair.

Indeed she was jealous. This lot would not face the circuitous snakes and ladders that had brought her a senior role in government at the grand old age of forty. These kids rolled the right number from the start and landed on the ladder that went all the way to the top. God knows what they were up to today.

Elliot, her own assistant, was sitting at her desk using her office phone and giving thumbs-up signs through the glass partition to the others. He stalled when he saw her there but recovered quickly, acknowledging her presence with a flirtatious grin before giving a final thumbs-up sign and putting the phone down. A half-hearted cheer arose around her, but it fell away quickly.

'Sorry, Chief,' Elliot said as she opened the door and went in, dumping Dvořáček's box on her desk.

'And what part of the whips' role is this contributing to, exactly?'

'Security for MPs. Trying to find the best way to shield their phones, should they be hacked.'

'And what have you discovered?'

'Cardboard, to some extent. Bubble wrap is much more effective.'

'And your plan is?'

'Well, if we can figure out how to shield the phones, the MPs will be able to use them in meetings.'

'When they're encased in bubble wrap?'

Elliot frowned. 'Mmm. I see your point.'

'Any chance we could get on with some real work and leave that sort of stuff to MI5?'

'Right, of course. Sorry, Chief.'

Elliot relinquished her chair and Kanha went and sat in it. A large majority breeds a lazy whips' office, she thought. Perhaps it was as well they'd had a scare before the election with that Dvořáček bill. Things might not be so easy next time round, what with the Whigges unbelievably gaining momentum in some sectors despite their ludicrous policies. Reports of Number Ten business being carried out at Ewan's gentlemen's club in St James's were not endearing him to the young women of the country, an increasingly influential and politicised group. Where were the women who voted as daddy did? Gone, all gone. To Peckham of all places. For soya lattes and meditation classes and woke Whigge politics.

Elliot was still hovering.

'Anything else?' she said, dropping her bag at her feet.

'Nope.' Elliot turned away and then turned back again. His shirt was almost out at the back. What a scruff he was.

'What do you want?' she said.

Elliot frowned. 'Did you... I mean to say—'

'No,' she said.

'But did he... did he...?'

Kanha looked at him wearily. 'No, the PM didn't ask which idiot in my team failed to spot that the members' bill had been changed to a piece of government legislation. And no, I didn't tell him that the idiot was you.'

Elliot's features softened in visible relief and he turned to the door. She really should have fired him, or at least moved him on in disgrace. Why hadn't she? Why did she always cover for them?

'Not that you didn't deserve it,' she said. 'And for the record, if you cock up like that again, you're out of my department, do you hear?'

As he backed out of the office, Elliot said, 'Of course. Thank you, Esme. I totally appreciate it.'

He gave that smile that Kanha hated. Hated because he was a charming, good-looking sod, and fifteen years her junior, and she knew he didn't seriously fancy her. But he gave just enough of a hint as often as he could that, heh, you know, she's pretty fit for her age, and yeah there was an age difference, but he'd go there given half a chance and fuck what the rest of the office thought. *Fuck it, let's face it.* She might go there too. In a different world.

'That's Chief Whip to you,' Kanha said.

'Sorry. Thank you, Chief Whip.'

As he walked out he must have given a discreet thumbs-down sign to the others, because they all scuttled back to their desks. She sat and watched as they got back on the phones along the length of the long office.

On first becoming chief whip and moving into her new quarters, Kanha had gazed in horror at the grey stone walls, their recessed arches cut off abruptly by white Styrofoam panels dotted with flickering fluorescent lighting, considering it rather like a dungeon. She wondered what colossal cock-up the previous whipping team must have made to have been sent down here. The irony that it was the whips who doled out the offices was not lost on her. If she sat here for too long at night without moving, the sensors determined everyone had left and plunged her into deepest darkness until she waved her arms around to wake them up again. Sometimes in winter a whole week might pass when she didn't see daylight.

To her annoyance, Kanha realised Elliot had closed the door behind him, despite the fact she had told him at least a dozen times not to, and she decided once more that he really was an annoying cocky little shit. They liked the door closed so she wouldn't hear them going on about what they found on their social media feeds. She'd told them a million times 'That's not real news', but still they would exclaim 'Ooh! So and so's trending,' and then they'd sit there going 'Why? Why?' about something that had been all over the mainstream newsfeeds hours ago. Or they'd follow the gossip that came from those Mouth of the Mob hacks and believe it, however ridiculous it was.

She tilted the box of the old minister's personal effects towards her. Inside, at the top, a framed picture of Dvořáček and his wife on their wedding day smiled up at her. Sarah had been a stout little lady even when she was young, but it was his shock of red hair that surprised Kanha. Dvořáček had been follicularly challenged as long as she had known him, his ring of grey tufts around his ears being his signature look that the papers played upon. She felt her own bun and thought of the grey at the edges beneath the dye.

Kanha pulled her phone out of her bag and started to scroll down to the Dvořáček home number, but decided she couldn't face it. Would the widow want to be disturbed today, when she was making funeral arrangements? Kanha had already left a message with her condolences and she would give them again at the funeral in a couple of days' time. Someone else could arrange to get the personal effects to the widow.

Through the glass, she looked at her team, tapping away and making calls to promote the whip to the party's members in a now subdued fashion. Beyond them were those ancient cabinets, full of files left behind by previous whips that no one could be bothered to go through, to scan the contents or even just throw away. She was determined; soon she would move on to another department. She would speak to Ewan and insist. A new role when they started the new term. Either Treasury or back to the Foreign Office for the top job, no more of this whipping nonsense.

From where she sat just a hum of the phone work reached through the partition. She moved her desk phone back to its usual position, then toyed with its cord, thinking. After looking up to be sure no one was about to come in, she lifted the receiver and pressed to replay the saved messages. No one ever called this phone any more, they always called her ministerial mobile – but for some reason Dvořáček had tracked down the number of this phone in her office. She didn't even know what it was herself.

Had he been wanting to catch her alone there, late at night? It could only have been shortly after he called her that he took himself into his own office and... She pressed play.

Esme. Dvořáček's voice was soft at the edges like a block of ice cream left in the sun. *Esme, I've had*— There was a bang, a long pause and a rustling as if the phone had been dropped on a table and retrieved.

I've had enough. Enough, Esme. They're telling me... Telling me what I should and shouldn't do. I've had it for years. How many years? I'm sick of it, you hear? I won't do it any more. I won't. And it isn't right what they want. And now this. Oh, my poor Sarah.

There was another scraping sound, muffled, like maybe Dvořáček was rubbing his hands across a chin rough with stubble.

Kanha. She'll know what to do. She's always so clever. Always so fucking clever. Tell me, mmm? Could you believe they would do that to me? To me? To Sarah? They're listening, you see. Watching, following. They're inside my head. Talking to me, inside my head. But what should I do? Come find me, Esme. I'm going to my office. You'll know what to do. I need—'

The message ended and Kanha reached her thumb to her right eye and wiped away a tear before the mascara on her eyelash could touch it. There was a second message, but Kanha saw that Elliot was heading back in, so she quickly put the phone down.

This time he crossed more tentatively over the threshold into what was once again her domain. A piece of paper, which she assumed was a draft of the next few weeks' Order of Business, was in his hands.

He put it on the desk in front of her and then stood back, pushing his thick fringe off his forehead.

'Draft Orders of Business,' he said.

Kanha glanced down at it. 'I know. I've seen them before. I'm chief whip.'

Elliot gave a weak smile, and sensing her change in mood, hurried out.

She looked at the paper he had given her. Headlining was supposed to be the Personal Information Bill – the government's official one – and it was to be triple underlined, a three-line whip, all party members to vote in favour. There wasn't much other important business due, just the usual Prime Minister's Questions, likely to be well attended. After all, there wouldn't be too many of them left before the House rose and all sides dispersed across the UK for electioneering to begin in earnest.

She sighed and was about to sign to approve them when she saw that the privacy bill was entirely missing. The thing was turning into a farce.

Kanha's stomach rumbled and she felt queasy. When had she last eaten? Not since yesterday lunchtime. Last evening's nutrients had been taken in liquid form in the Red Lion.

Where had Dvořáček been when he was on his bender? Morland had seen the minister come into his office on the department's CCTV footage of Monday evening, but his wife had said he'd left home Friday morning and that she never saw him again. Where had he been all that time?

Kanha picked up her bag, took the paper over to Elliot and put it down on his desk.

'Where's the Personal Information Bill?' she said, cutting through his phone call.

Elliot looked up, startled. 'I understand it's ready to go,' he said, hanging up. 'Just waiting on the new minister to push the button.'

'Colbey took office today. Get on to Gerard Morland and chase for it, will you?'

'Gerard Morland is…?'

She didn't really hear him because at that moment a morass of nagging confusions crystallised into a properly formed thought. She stood and dwelled on it for a moment and the buzz of the office faltered as her mood travelled like a scent through the room. Kanha had been chief whip for nearly three years now and in that time she'd seen the worst of human behaviour: drink, drugs, corruption, how secrets and affairs of the heart could cause men and women to take peculiar risks. But there were always common themes driving their behaviour; usually lust or greed, sometimes plain laziness. But this business with Dvořáček... What had 'they' been trying to make him do? And who exactly were *they*?

If only she had heard his message in time, she might have been able to do something. Instead she had failed him, her colleague, her charge, and... yes, she had to admit, to some extent at any rate... her friend.

'Sorry, Chief. Gerard Morland is...?'

Was Percy Dvořáček delusional at the end? But even as the thought occurred, she dismissed the idea. There was something off, something rotten behind all this.

An image of Harry Colbey came to her: dawdling down the stairs of Number Ten, looking at the paintings on the walls beside him with a wide-eyed stupor. Why had the prime minister really chosen him, and why so speedily? Kanha felt a sudden fear for the new minister, combined with an annoyance that something was going on that she wasn't part of. How to get to the bottom of it? There was only one place to start.

She looked down at Elliot and found him still waiting for an answer to his question. He'd figure it out. 'I'm on my phone,' she said and headed for the door.

1.5

Several floors above the basement office of the whips, Harry Colbey prepared himself for a row with his wife. It was a familiar skirmish between them, and one that these days he would usually, wearily, turn aside from – but for some reason today he was feeling stubborn. It wasn't every day he was made a minister, after all.

'I wouldn't normally ask you to help out here, darling, but these are exceptional circumstances. You are supposed to be my secretary, after all.'

Clarissa turned sharply to him and her lips tightened a little. She was petite, with fair hair, blonde over grey. 'Good for age' was their running joke after she was once classed as such after a half-marathon.

'How dare you throw that in my face?'

'Yes, but—'

'When I agreed you could become an MP, what did I say?'

'That you didn't ever want to be sitting in some dingy parliamentary office surrounded by dusty paper and typing like some lowly temp, but be reasonable... this isn't—'

'Exactly. And today you were handed three hundred and twenty-six staff on a plate, so I don't see why I should start now, and in that pokey little office out there. There isn't even a window.'

'That's ridiculous. You can't have a blanket ban on your work location just because there isn't a window.'

'You've got a window.'

It was true. His office had a window behind his desk, which looked down onto New Palace Yard. He loved to stand and gaze out of it, to reflect on what a privilege it was to be a member of parliament. But he'd worked hard to get there, whereas she...

'You do take the *London* salary, remember,' he said. These thoughts had been brewing in him for some time. It was a relief, finally, to be given a chance to voice them.

'Why are you always so mean?' she said in reply. 'I do work as your secretary, you may recall, just not from here.'

And not very well or very often, Colbey thought. But then appraisals and formal reprimands were tricky when your secretary was your wife. So as usual he said nothing, realising with a sigh that he not only had a new department to take on and his Honest Politicking Bill to further, but he had no researcher months from an election and a secretary who was difficult to manage. Thank god he had Tom, his campaign manager – at least he was the full shilling in his camp.

'Look, I don't want an argument today,' he said, thinking it best to be rid of her and sort out a new assistant himself. Perhaps he could find someone from the new department, and now that he had spoken his mind he felt less angry about it in any case.

'Nor do I,' she replied. 'Not on this special day, when I'm so proud of you and so excited, and it's everything we've worked towards finally again.'

Colbey softly realised it was perhaps everything *she* had worked towards, but for him it was just a further load of stress and late nights. But then he thought of her sitting hours into the evening, putting letters into envelopes when he had first stood for parliament. Of her tireless networking at the tennis club to work her way into the PM's set. It had to be the cause of his sudden reversal of fortune. That and his Honest Politicking Bill. He was really getting somewhere with that.

'I'm sorry,' he said. 'It's just the waiting that's driving me crazy. I can't seem to concentrate on anything. Why don't you head off and do whatever it was you came up to town to do?'

Clarissa reached for her gloves. 'Alright, darling. I'll get out of your hair and leave you to it. That sounds like Tom's voice. He'll take your mind off it. In here, Tom!'

As they stood waiting for Tom to come through the door, she said, 'I'm not just being a cow, darling. I would love to help, you know, but I've an appointment, and if I cancel at the last minute, I'll never get another one there again. You do see that, don't you?'

Colbey failed to see, but as usual he just said, 'Alright, darling.'

Clarissa picked up the car keys from his desk. 'Where is it parked?' she asked without appearing to have so much as a qualm of guilt. That morning they had agreed she could have it for the day.

'Over by the school in the usual spot.'

'Right. And good luck today.'

'Thank you, darling.'

Tom's chubby fingers appeared around the edge of the door, tapping to announce his arrival, and Colbey called him in.

'Hello, Tom,' said Clarissa, reaching up on tiptoes to kiss him on both cheeks. An ex-rugby player, Tom was broad, his body turned to that solid sort of wall of flesh where you couldn't quite tell what was muscle and what was just plain fat. He bent down to make the job easier for her.

'Hello, Clarissa. You just coming or going?'

'I'm off. I'll leave you important men of government to it. Goodbye, darling. Good luck again.'

Colbey stepped forward to welcome the arrival of his campaign manager and felt the gloom that had descended upon him during his wife's brief visit lifting.

'So where is your researcher?' Tom whispered theatrically as he closed the door behind Clarissa.

'She left.'

'Why?'

'Personal reasons.'

Tom raised one of his black bushy eyebrows. 'Oh, what were they?'

'Personal, apparently.'

The two men smiled and Tom threw himself into the chair at the low coffee table and leaned back, linking his hands behind his head.

'You heard about that job yet?' Colbey asked, sitting back at his desk.

'Yes, I'm in. Head of Campaign for the entire party. Won't stop me looking after you, though, don't worry about that – in fact it means you'll have your own man sitting at the top table when it comes to the election.'

'Congratulations. When do you start?'

'Started already. There's a meeting tomorrow of the volunteers for the Taunton by-election. I'll be running it. Me and some company HQ have hired. They've a cutting-edge campaigning system, AI-machine learning, the works.'

'Sounds great. You can rely on me.'

Tom gave a broad grin. 'You, Minister, will have much more important things to attend to. Not expected at all.'

'Well, good for you.'

'Hey, look, there's you on the television.' Tom leapt up and looked around for the remote. It was out of sight under the set where Clarissa had set it down. He was an ebullient man, always rushing to kiss female acquaintances and giving Colbey the impression that he'd just arrived from the Gents after stuffing god knows what up his nose, which unfortunately was often the case. Tom made a little cash on the side, keeping the young spads supplied with their running powder in the House of Commons Gents, or so the rumour went.

Colbey kept quiet about the location of the remote because he could already see the subtitle: *Newly appointed Colbey's position in doubt one day after his appointment to...*

Tom threw himself back down again and put his foot on the coffee table, but seeing what it was resting on, Colbey made a point of lifting the toe of Tom's shoe between his finger and thumb. Revealed was a picture of Dvořáček on the front page of *The Times*.

'Oops,' Tom said as he tried to smooth out the crumpled cover. 'So, when are you heading over to the new department?'

'Waiting for them to call me.'

'What? Why don't you just go over?'

'They told me to wait. Want to arrange a welcome gathering or some such.'

Tom pulled a face. 'Harry. I've been looking after you for years. You're great at managing constituents and local government, playing by the rules, being respectful. But these civil service chaps... You've got to show them who's boss. Pick up the phone, tell them you'll be there in ten minutes. That'll get them jumping.'

'Thanks, Tom, but I'm perfectly capable of handling this side of things on my own. Why don't you save all that cleverness for tomorrow, eh?'

'Alright.'

The two men sat in silence for a moment, then Tom twisted the paper to face him and looked at the picture of Dvořáček and his wife, dressed up for an evening event. They were holding hands and Dvořáček's wife was looking shyly at the ground, obviously unaccustomed to being papped. Colbey guessed it was taken a few years ago, when Dvořáček had still been in the Foreign Office.

'Poor old Dvořáček,' Tom said. 'The question is, why on earth did he do it? I mean, kill yourself, yes, it happens – but why would a man choose to spend the last forty-eight hours of his life trying to sneak some god-damn boring privacy bill through parliament? Oh, sorry, no offence.'

'None taken. I guess that's what a few people want to know right now.'

'Really?' Tom asked. 'Who?'

Colbey faltered, realising he had said too much.

'Ho ho,' said Tom, spotting Colbey's minute hesitation. 'On a need-to-know basis, eh? Right you are, Minister.'

After that, Tom got down to business and ran Colbey through their plan for his re-election campaign so they could get ahead of themselves before the date was set.

'OK. We'd better call it a day,' said Colbey when the meeting tailed off into gossipy talk about his constituency's administration team. 'They'll probably call soon to invite me over.'

'Alright, do it your way. But I still think you should just go down there and get them jumping. Catch you later.'

Tom left, tapping the door again with his chubby fingers on his way out, and Colbey went and stood by the window.

What a privilege it had been to be the allocated owner of this room for all these years, he thought as he heard the outer door close behind Tom. Not one of those flat-pack offices over the road in Portcullis Place, but here, in the heart of Westminster. I bet this room has been used by members for over seven hundred years, he thought. Dwelling on the idea, Colbey imagined London changing while this room and the house in which it stood, its committee rooms, bars, restaurants, its corridors and ways of working remained largely unchanged.

Once, a month or two ago, Colbey had gone down to the library and asked if they kept a record of who had been housed in his rooms before him, but the question had caused confusion. It wasn't the role of the librarians to keep such household records. That would be the domain of the whips, for as everyone knew, good offices were given out as favours for loyalty or as bribes. In Colbey's case, his office had been a 'shut up and go away' consolation prize after he had been thrown out of government for not saying what they had wanted him to say. But he couldn't have approached the whips with such a fanciful question. They were a terrifying bunch, Kanha the worst of the lot, and most likely would have told him to bugger off and stop wasting their time. Or worse, they might have wondered what a nobody like Colbey was doing with such a prime piece of real estate and promptly taken it away.

That was all by the by now, of course. For now he was to be forced to hand over his beloved couple of little rooms in return for something far grander. A huge office in his new department, a minister's office, no less, along with three hundred and twenty-six staff. Yes, three hundred and twenty-six. His head spun at the thought of them all. It didn't really make him happy. For what could be more noble than his role now? Serving his constituents' interests, arguing in parliament for the things that mattered to them.

Colbey lifted a box from the floor and started to put his personal effects into it. First in were the photographs from his noticeboard; he gathered them into a pile and picked the drawing pins out. Then went in a print of the House of Commons from the eighteenth century that had been hanging on his wall. Colbey paused as he picked up a framed photo of his wife from his desk. He had always felt a picture of one's wife on one's desk to be an embarrassment. Clarissa had put it there herself. Perhaps he could accidentally leave it behind, he mused, but with a sigh he realised that would cause trouble, and into the box it went along with a stapler that for some reason he had an inordinate amount of affection for, and a set of pencil tubes that must have started with him during his banking career. He scooped out the pens and laid them flat in the box. Next he tore out and shredded the few remaining pages of his current Black and Red notebook and threw the cover in the bin. Finally he tenderly placed in the box a clay plaster rabbit that his daughter, Chloe, had made for him when she had been little – she was twenty-five now. That was all there was, really. They were encouraged to have a paperless office these days.

Colbey picked up the phone and swiped through its screen to find the switchboard number of his new department. He was surprised to find it answered almost immediately. It was a good sign that the permanent secretary, Morland, ran a tight ship.

He coughed to lower his voice. 'Harry Colbey's researcher here. Would you let Gerard Morland know that Colbey is on his way over in a cab? Yes, a cab, that's right. Should be there in ten minutes.'

He hung up and tucked his box under one arm, took one last look at his home of twelve years, and with some foreboding and a heavy heart, pulled the door open and left.

1.6

By the time Colbey's taxi hit the down ramp, Gerald Morland was already waiting in the building's underground car park, obviously fuming that his orderly plans for the day had been disrupted. But by the time the taxi rolled up, he had modified his features to a welcoming mask of beneficence. He stepped forward and with a smile fixed to his face pulled the taxi's door open so that Harry Colbey could climb out.

'Wonderful timing, Minister,' Morland said, shaking the hand of Colbey that was not clutched to the box he carried. 'The department is now gathering in the canteen to await your first address.'

'Very good,' said Colbey.

Morland reached into his jacket pocket and pulled out a slim paper which he offered to the minister. 'Did you have anything prepared? In case not, you should find this one—'

Colbey took the speech, and saw that Morland appeared annoyed but slightly impressed to see that the minister just glanced at it and then passed it back.

'I'll be fine off the cuff,' he said, striding towards the stairwell, leaving Morland to hurry to catch up with him.

'Wonderful, Minister. After the address to the staff, you can meet with your senior team and we can hand over your red boxes so you can see to the most urgent business.'

Colbey grunted his agreement and, on the way up the stairs, paused and permitted the permanent secretary to pass in front and lead the way. As they reached the door to the ground floor, they were passed by a young man, his sleeves rolled up, carrying a large canvas down the stairs. Colbey couldn't help but notice on glancing back that there was a ragged hole in it, but Morland hurried him along with a warning that they were working to a tight deadline.

The departmental staff looked a friendly enough bunch, gathered around the canteen's silvered tables. Colbey kept it short, his box on the table beside him. The truth was he didn't entirely know what they all did, but afterwards, Morland gave an overly long speech about consistency and solidity and longevity, a sort of civil servants' rah, rah, rah, until at last they made their way up to his ministerial office – or his new penthouse suite, as Chloe had joked – up on the fourth floor.

Morland opened the door and presented the room with a wave of his hand as a hotel bellboy might, hoping for a tip. It was indeed a huge room, with a desk at one end, a long walnut table in its centre, and a collection of soft furnishings at the other.

Colbey eyed the bookshelves at the far end and the smaller ones arrayed beneath the tall windows that ran along one side of the room and thought of the quest the prime minister had given him. There was a little painting between two windows that was crooked, and as Colbey dumped his box on the desk, Morland went and straightened it with a delicately raised finger and said, 'I hope everything is to your liking.'

Colbey agreed that it was, but remembering Tom's advice, he pointed at the garish canvas behind his desk and said, 'Is there any chance we could change that for something a bit more...'

'Colourful?'

'Traditional.'

'If you wish. I'll get someone to bring you a catalogue of what's available.'

Sitting down at the long table, Morland made a neat little note in a pocketbook he pulled from his jacket pocket. There was a timid knock at the door, and the four members of Colbey's senior team arrived, each offering up a limp handshake and a whispered name before dropping themselves down, plop, plop, plop, plop, in a row along one side of the conference table opposite Morland. Just as Colbey took his place at the top of the table, the young man from the stairwell hurried in too, rolling down his sleeves and buttoning the cuffs distractedly as he took the seat beside Morland.

'Well,' said Colbey. He looked from the permanent secretary dressed in his Saville Row suit to the four civil servants opposite, who were the most shabbily dressed bunch he had ever seen. Then his eyes tracked across to the young man and immediately identified him as the most competent person in the room on the basis the man was able to dress himself without looking like he had done it at a charity shop or in the last century. He was an intelligent-looking chap with cropped dark hair, and he was composed, unlike the others who either fidgeted and fussed or slumped in upon themselves.

Earlier, Colbey had been offered a choice of departmental refreshments, but he knew, as it was in all government departmental offices, that it would be a choice between tea that tasted of coffee or coffee that tasted like piss and had stupidly chosen the former. It sat, even now, in its white plastic cup, the scum on the top slowly floating across the surface, theoretically cooling, but actually too terrible to drink.

'Tell me...' he said to the room in general, 'what direction had Dvořáček given you?'

One of the four went to open her mouth, found there were no words to come out and closed it again, so Morland stepped in.

'There are a number of consultations ongoing, which you can review at your leisure. Obviously, with the restriction period a matter of months or even weeks away, we won't get much progressed before the election, but the Personal Information Bill is an urgent matter that needs immediate ministerial authorisation.'

That didn't sound too bad, thought Colbey. To the group before him he said, 'So who took the lead on the bill?'

When no one answered, Colbey looked at Morland with a frown and then back at his senior team.

'Who's been working on it the longest, then?'

The four debated the issue. Finally, it was determined that the lady farthest from him, who was too frightened to speak above a whisper, was the one, because her tenure in the department had been for an entire eight weeks.

Colbey turned to Morland. 'Is this usual? To not have anyone on the senior team who has been here for more than two months?'

'Civil servants rotate, Minister. It makes them more effective as administrators. But your principal private secretary has been here for two years and she knows all about the department's coming legislation.'

'And where is she?'

'Taking leave of absence due to ill health, unfortunately.'

Colbey looked across at the bag carrier.

'And you...?'

The young man glanced at Morland as if to see whether he had permission to speak, and Colbey caught the faintest glimpse of a nod.

'Mani.'

'So, you, Mani, how long have you been here?'

'Six months.'

'Ah,' said Colbey and smiled. So he could dress himself and he might also know something.

'And do you know anything about the bill?'

'Yes,' Mani said. 'I drew up a summary for you. I can talk you through it if you'd like.'

Morland raised his eyebrows in surprise, which Colbey thought rather rude, so he sent the other four off, telling them to get up to speed on their brief – it felt good to pass the PM's orders on to someone else, made him feel like he was beginning to achieve something already – and after once again shaking four sets of limp hands, he asked Mani to talk him through the briefing note.

Afterwards he said, 'So what is your job?' to which Mani replied that he was an associate.

'Not any more,' said Colbey. 'You're now my acting principal private secretary, if that's OK with you?'

Mani gave an eager nod and out of the corner of his eye, Colbey saw Morland's chin jut out a little. 'I'm not sure that Mani is vetted for that grade, Minister.'

'It's only acting, Morland. In the meantime, why don't you vet him?'

Mani looked down modestly, and Colbey instantly knew that he liked him. 'What next, then?'

Morland said, 'I suggest you sign off the Personal Information Bill now, and then tomorrow you can start with the red boxes.'

Colbey was tired of the meeting. There was a lot of reading to be done, and sitting here was just wasting time.

'I'd like to read the bill before I authorise it,' he said.

Morland looked surprised. 'Are you sure that's necessary, Minister? Dvořáček was ready to authorise it in *his* role as minister.'

'I'm not going change the bill. But I would like to know what I'm authorising to be passed to parliament. It will be the first piece of legislation to be made under my ministerial guidance, after all.'

Morland held out his hands, palms facing out. 'Of course, of course. We have a little time. A day, perhaps. Why don't you look at it this evening and you can sign it off tomorrow morning. It can be the first thing you do in your new office. What a wonderful start to your time as the minister, Minister. Protecting the privacy of millions of UK citizens with a new bill.'

Colbey thought of his dinner that evening and wondered whether it was possible to cancel a date with a prime minister – as if Clarissa would let him.

The permanent secretary turned and tapped a slim red box that stood beside some surplus polystyrene cups.

'All the documents can be found in your red e-reader along with their appendices and supporting documents.' He spoke in a crisp, plummy voice. Permanent secretaries were still the poshest people on the planet, Colbey reflected. He wondered where they came from because rank and file were obviously not so. 'If you could take a look at as many as you can,' Morland said, 'and let us have approval for your recommendations by tomorrow morning, that would be enormously helpful.'

Then he turned to Mani. 'Do you have the other boxes?'

Mani bent down below the table and lifted four heavy red boxes onto the top. 'We weren't sure if you'd prefer to work on paper,' he said, 'so I printed all the documents out in case.'

Colbey glanced at the deceptively thin red box beside the polystyrene cups with its scarlet government e-reader inside. The papers would all be there – screen after screen of words that one could scroll through, never knowing when the end would come, not knowing if there were a hundred words in a paper or a hundred thousand.

He sighed again. 'I'd better take both.'

Mani slid the boxes across the table to Colbey, but they were intercepted by Morland who slid them back to Mani. Then he reached and took the slim e-reader box by its handle and passed it to Colbey.

'Policy, Minister. We're a paperless office, remember. Please ensure you are only ever seen carrying a slim box. Never an old-style one.'

'Right oh.'

'So that just leaves the press call.'

'Press call?'

'Yes.' Morland looked down at his phone. 'Number Ten's press officer is just arranging it for you now. They were keen for it to be done as soon as possible, otherwise they'll only hound you.'

'Hound me?'

'Yes, but not if we do the press call now. Let them have a chance to ask their ridiculous questions and then their flurry of postings will be over and done with. Number Ten thought they would arrange for it to happen outside the department as you leave to go to the House for the afternoon's vote.' And turning to Mani, he said, 'Take those other red boxes across to the minister's Westminster office.'

Colbey thought of the PM's warning that he should get a grip on his department as quickly as possible, as well as the search he was to carry out for Dvořáček's black book. He looked again from the cupboards at one end of the room to Dvořáček's desk at the other. 'But I don't have a Westminster office right now. I'm to be allocated something in Portcullis House.'

Morland just smiled pleasantly and rubbed his hands together and Colbey inwardly growled with annoyance. The sooner he was in charge of his own day, the better.

'I'll go home after the vote, then,' he said. 'They can come with me to my London flat, Mani. Oh, and Morland?'

'Yes?'

'Would you see to it that I get access to Dvořáček's electronic diary as soon as can be arranged? I'd like to understand who he had been meeting with and get up to speed on who has been lobbying us.'

'Certainly,' Morland said. 'Obviously your principal private secretary would usually arrange that for you, but as Mani won't have the clearances yet, I can find someone else to speak to the IT department for you.'

'Thank you.'

And with that, Morland escorted him back out into the corridor and ushered him to the lift, leaving Colbey with the distinct impression it was his audience with Morland that had come to an end, rather than the other way round.

1.7

Kanha stood in the central lobby of the Houses of Parliament and enjoyed its momentary silence.

It was a small octagonal hall, bequeathed grandeur by the chandelier that hung from a domed ceiling, a dignity diminished somewhat by the numerous doors that led off to who knew where: labyrinthine stairways, long-forgotten bathrooms and storage cupboards so full of fold-up chairs and dusty royal standards that their doors could barely be opened. Only the post office window on one side gave hint to the bustle that would soon arrive when the House filled with members gathering to vote.

But now... for now, it was empty – a dull and poorly attended debate rumbling on in the chamber being the only point of attraction – and as always for Kanha that calmed her. As she turned left, the clip of her heels echoed off the bleached stone walls and announced her arrival into the members' lobby to no one but the Serjeant at Arms who stood lost in thought in front of its doors. Beyond him was the room in which it all happened, government members on the benches of one side, the largest opposition on those of the other and the smaller parties bundled together near the doors.

'Everything alright?' he said.

He was a good sort. Not for him sarcastic comments about whether her whip was in order today. Even as she nodded with a note of recognition, she tutted to think of what might be said when the ongoing debate wound to its conclusion and the members of all sides of the House arrived to vote.

For in a few minutes' time, one of the doorkeepers would push a button and make the division bell sound out across parliament and ring also in many of the restaurants, pubs and bars of Whitehall, giving the honourable members eight minutes in which to gulp down their gin and tonics, wolf down their cheese and pickle sandwiches and make their way to where Kanha and the parliamentary official now stood.

As chief whip, it would be her place to be here with her team, scowling and glaring and generally putting an uncertain fear into any recalcitrant member of their party who was thinking of voting against the whip. But she knew well enough that at that time every weaselly oik from the other side and quite a few of her own would be making snide remarks about yesterday's vote. For regardless of what she and the PM had said to Colbey, everyone knew that the previous day's fiasco with Dvořáček's bill had been down to her department's cock-up. Why had Dvořáček put government legislation into a private member's bill? No one seemed to care about that. But she did. So, before then, before she faced them all, she had work to do if she was to find out who really was to blame.

Kanha hurried over to her little whips' office in the corner and went into the empty room. Under one of the desks she found the recycling bin, lifted its top and pulled out a stack of papers. It didn't take too long sifting through them before she found a crumpled copy of Dvořáček's bill.

The light in the office there was poor, so she carried it out, through the members' lobby, nodding again at the Serjeant at Arms, and into the central lobby. She studied the paper for a while by the light that fell from the chandelier, then looked up and frowned. Off to her right, one of the narrow doors led to the little used bathroom where she had taken herself off in grief at the news of Dvořáček's death. That was the one thing no one knew: that when the division bell had sounded to call the members together to vote on the ill-fated lately deceased member's bill, she, Kanha had been in the toilets crying. That was where she had been. Not in her team's little box room off the members' lobby where she should have been, checking through the order of the day and flicking through the bill that was to be whipped.

Yes, her. Killer Bitch Kanha, as they called her. She had been in the ladies' bathroom up there snuffling and pinching her nose and trying to stop the tears from making a mess of her mascara; thinking of Dvořáček and his head shot wide open; thinking of his wife and the phone call she had just had to make, when Sarah had simply said, 'But why, Esme? Tell me why?'

What had she replied? She couldn't remember. What a fuck up of a morning it had been. And if she had been tougher, if she had been at her post despite what had happened, she would have noticed that Dvořáček had secretly changed the content of his private member's bill and had forged her signature on the document he had sent to the clerks the day before. If she had been tougher, she would have had a better team in place, not that bunch of self-serving, back-scratching, social-climbing bougie wannabees that they had jettisoned into her office.

Kanha thought back on the chaos of that day. She had pieced it all together now, all that had transpired while she was sitting in the toilets weeping.

It had happened like this: around three o'clock on the day after Dvořáček shot himself, a small number of members from her side of the House had arrived to vote on Dvořáček's private member's bill. Apparently, they had stood undecided which way to vote. They had hovered by the entrance to the No lobby, where they had been prompted to go by the party's relaxed one-line whip recommending a rejection of Dvořáček's bill. They hadn't been present at the official debate, which had lasted all of ten minutes, a barely quorate number of members in the House, with no one having read the papers. They stood there and debated why a private member's bill should have been changed to cover something that looked like government legislation. She knew who they were. 'Why is it only a one-line whip against?' they had apparently asked one another. Perhaps the government had some new tactic for passing legislation?

Where was her trusty assistant Elliot at the time? Who knew? She suspected he was canoodling with her deputy whip's assistant, Tabitha, in some other nearby cloakroom, since Paddy knew nothing about the switch either.

Some of the group had asked those friendly on the other side if they knew what was going on. Some had even turned to the lobby journalists to find out what they knew. 'No more than you,' was the response to both enquiries.

Then one had shrugged his shoulders and thought of the last conversation he'd had with the tired and emotional Dvořáček, in which he had replied to the old boy's drunken ramblings about how sometimes one had to stand up for what was right, rather than what one was told to do by one's supposed betters. 'Stuff and nonsense. Go to bed, Dvořáček,' he remembered he had said. And so, standing at the doors of the two lobby corridors, the member had said 'Poor old Dvořáček', turned towards the Aye door and entered. Emboldened, so had another.

The opposition party members had accompanied them, wondering why there was a division at all, for they had a two-line whip Aye and the other side seemed inclined to agree, despite their whip to the contrary.

As the trickle of MPs arriving from around the palace grew to a steady stream, the sound of voices in the Aye lobby would have given those arriving the confidence to ignore their one-line whip and also divide as Dvořáček had drunkenly begged them to just the weekend before, to join the growing numbers in the Aye division. Few even looked at what the bill was. It was a private member's bill, after all, Kanha thought, not able right now to smile at the recollection.

And so there she had been, not really caught with her pants down because she had been sitting fully dressed on the toilet, pinching her nose, holding her breath, anything to stop the tears falling and pull the red away from her eyes before she stepped out to face the House and follow her own whip into the No division lobby, unaware that few of her colleagues were there.

We're all dirty, aren't we, hmm? Even you. Even clever Kanha. Dvořáček's last words, which she had just discovered in the message on her desk phone, kept going round and round in her head.

Then her phone had rung and she had jumped to her feet as Paddy, her deputy whip, had told her the news that there was government legislation hidden in a private member's bill, stumbling in his panic, blaming her assistant Elliot who had not even bothered to check its contents, his voice shaking, panicking, asking her where she was and what he should do. She shuddered now to remember it as even now the division bell sounded clear and loud in the central lobby.

'What the fuck?' she had said, and leaving her bag forgotten on the floor, she had ripped the cubicle door open and run, puffy nose, streaming eyes, down the rickety staircase and into the central lobby.

She had fought her way through the stream of members heading towards the lobby for the division. Everywhere she heard the name Dvořáček.

'Shot himself,' she heard. 'Terrible mess.'

'For god's sake, get out of the way,' Kanha had said to a dithering old MP who was refusing to yield to her hand on his back.

Finally she got to the head of the stream of ambling idiots, and there she had heard it – the buzz of members in the Aye lobby, a terrifying quiet in the opposite corridor. She'd run into the whips' little office and grabbed the order papers, desperately paging through the contents of the bill to confirm that what Paddy had told her was true. Its topic really had been changed. What the hell was the vote about? She knew nothing of it. It was pages and pages of legislation about data privacy. It was supposed to be about a one-way system in Minehead.

She had turned to face the oncoming members, picking out those of her party.

'Three-line No!' she shouted and then repeated it over and over, pushing them physically in the direction of the No lobby corridor when needed, when they were ambling towards the babbling sound of their flock like dumb sheep. She shook her head at Ewan as he approached her looking confused and concerned, asking her what was going on. He tried to stop to speak to her, but she even pushed him away with the words 'Three-line No!'

The Serjeant at Arms had stared at her in horror and surprise.

Finally the stream of members had died to a trickle and both of the lobbies became alive with the roar of disbelief, of gossip spreading like wildfire through both ranks, amusement and laughter at the government's predicament from the other side.

The Speaker called out from the chamber, 'Lock the doors.' One last member came running up, but was denied entry.

Kanha had never known such terror in her life as she and the entire House filed back into the chamber. She saw now how many members of the opposition were present and realised they had been part of it, had spotted what her team had missed, had taken their chance to embarrass the government by making the private member's bill a two-line whip in support. It took the Speaker a moment or two to be heard but as soon as the chamber knew that they wanted to summon the count, silence fell, an uncharacteristically deep silence. Both sides of the House realised the importance of the moment. Those first ones who had voted against their party's whip to a bill that contained content it shouldn't have were coming to their senses, waking up as if from some drunken escapade that they realised with horror might have involved dancing girls and women of the night. They glanced at each other. Who had they followed into the Aye lobby? Why had they done so? He or she was surely to blame, not them. They had only followed where others had gone before, had only carried out the wishes of a dying man. It had been a one-line whip, after all. Surely that would be in their defence?

Those who had been caught in time by Kanha were gripped by the delight of something perhaps terrible befalling the government, on which they had been found to be loyally on the correct side. Their daydreaming thoughts would have been of promotions, of ministerial posts, of red boxes and departments with secretaries and researchers galore. Meanwhile the opposition members smirked and grinned in delight as if they had knowingly had an involvement in an embarrassment for the government that might be at hand, rather than unwittingly contributed to it, as confused as those on whom they turned their teeth, displaying mock smiles. Only the opposition chief whip stood proud like Machiavelli surveying his handiwork. Through quick work and cunning, it was he who had seized the moment, hurriedly increased their support of the bill to a barely noticeable two-line whip *for*, had refused to answer the lobby journalists' queries, and had helped bring this situation into being.

The House held its breath. The tellers were called by the Speaker to come forward. They handed the results to him. As the Speaker grazed his eyes across the paper in his hand, the tellers stood poker straight, their faces turned still towards him, their backs to the chamber so no clue could be garnered. The Speaker himself had a stake in all this. Should he have stopped the proceedings? Was there a precedent for a member's bill when the member in question had suddenly become deceased?

The Speaker took a breath, a deep inhale to be sure that his voice would carry to all corners of the room, though no foot shuffled, no floorboard creaked; there was no mutter or whisper of gossip. All sat or stood on both sides of the House, cramming themselves by the door where there was no seating room, hands on phones, thumbs ready to flutter across electronic pads.

'The Ayes to the right,' he had called. 'Two hundred and sixty-four. The Nos to the left...' He seemed to hold on for a fraction of a second longer than usual, as if perhaps interrupted by the knowledge that his image would be prime-time news fodder that evening. 'Two hundred and seventy-one.'

The memory of it made Kanha shudder and brought a dry sickly feeling to her throat. Now, as the division bell sounded again, she heard sniggers around her as the first few honourable members gathered for this day's vote. Kanha hurried through the members' lobby, made sure her whips were where they should be, were doing what they should be doing, and that the papers were as they should be. Then she walked into the correct division lobby, made for its darkest, furthest corner, and buried her face in her phone.

1.8

Through the security door bubbles Colbey looked out at the pack of journalists gathered together and was washed with a thrill of nerves. The day had lost its promise of spring and above the waiting hacks the stone walls of the surrounding government buildings were shadowed with grey, and so too was the sky.

According to the press officer's arrangements, Colbey's taxi was waiting at the far end of the pack. 'Always be on the way somewhere,' Sampson had said. 'Somewhere important.' He was out there now, making a final check that everything was as he wanted it, and he grimaced when he came back in. 'They're an odd lot today,' he said and muttered about loiterers.

Colbey clutched his red e-reader box. 'I'll be fine,' he said and Sampson brought him up to the doors and pointed out what he called the respectable journalists: *The Guardian*, *The Telegraph*, the *BBC*. There was something of a crowd, more than Colbey had expected.

'There's a lot of them,' he said.

Turning to him, Sampson frowned. 'Anything you want to tell me?' When Colbey shook his head, the press officer hesitated and looked into his eyes as if waiting for Colbey to fill the silence with tales of affairs, embezzlements or a rent boy secreted away in Shoreditch.

Colbey thought of how Esme Kanha had looked at him that morning with a similarly appraising eye, and thought of how he would shortly see her again when he went to attend the afternoon's vote. He signalled for the receptionist to slide open the security bubble, and with a pat on the back from Sampson, he stepped through and down the steps to the pavement, a confusing babble of voices rising into the air as he did so. Clinging to Sampson's instructions, he picked out his man's men and women: 'Yes, you...' he said, and then, 'you,' and they led him where he wanted to go – how excited he was to have this opportunity to protect the privacy of everyone, our children, our friends, our families, our businesses.

To another question he was able to say how pleased he was to be able to continue with and build upon Dvořáček's excellent work, but that out of respect to his widow he would say no more on that for today.

It's going to be fine, Colbey thought, and moving towards his waiting taxi, he took a first official question from one of the Mouth of the Mob hacks. Field three, four at the most, Sampson had told him, and at the time he'd wondered how he would know them, but the Mobsters were easy enough to pick out with their ponytail hairstyles and their funny little Tintin clothes. So this was why his wife's nephew dressed as he did. It made him feel old to see them. He singled out one with a gesture of his finger, not a point, certainly not a point.

The question was shouted across the barriers and a hooting began. 'Is your party worried about the rise of the Whigges?'

'Not at all,' Colbey replied, answering as much to the hack as to the forest of phones before him, the TV cameras that sat behind, and as he moved along to the next question, he had a feeling that although it ebbed and flowed with his responses, the level of the noise of the crowd had grown.

He need only answer two more questions, however many spectators might stop and join in, he thought, but even as he did so he was bothered with an idea that people were gathering behind him. He wanted to turn and look but knew it wouldn't do well for the cameras and phones to see him glancing over his shoulder. He was not so green; this was his moment and if like last time they thought him no good, probably his last. He took another step towards the taxi and invited a second Mobster to speak.

'Are you planning to defect to the Whigges?'

'I'm happy to say, most definitely not.' He looked to see the reaction from Sampson's respectable men and women, but could no longer find them.

Hunting for the sanctuary of his black cab he found that those behind him had spilled to his left as well as to his right, muddying his path to it. He tried not to frown. They were certainly a mixed bunch, just as Sampson had said. Were they Mobsters? But they didn't look it. Where had they come from? And what did they want? Keep calm, keep smiling, keep moving, Colbey thought, although he had become disorientated. He spied Sampson off to his right trying to make his way over, but the pack behind the barrier had swollen also, and when one of their number refused to let Sampson through, he saw his press officer demand to see the interloper's press pass.

With relief, Colbey caught a glimpse of black and chrome between the bodies of those milling about on his left-hand side, and saw a young Mobster, saw her excited face, heard her eager call, and realised that stepping towards her would halve the distance to his waiting taxi. Let her ask her question, let him answer it and then he could be away without it looking as if he had panicked and fled.

'You! Yes, you,' he said, reaching her. The young Mobster herself was being jostled now by the crowd and Colbey instinctively put an arm out to protect her as she pushed forward her phone and said, 'Is there a tunnel from Carlton Gardens to the PM's private members' club?'

'Gosh, I've no idea,' he said. 'That sounds a bit fanciful.' But even as he looked anxiously about him, knowing that he was doing so and yet not being able to help it, she laughed excitedly and he saw that this was the moment that she had waited for – her first question to a minister answered with something worthy of click-bait that would make her ranking soar. But even as they shared that moment, she was knocked in the face by a woman waving something around, something black.

'Fuck all that,' the woman said with a sudden snarl, and turning to Colbey she said, 'Minister! How many CCTV cameras in the city now have listening devices?'

Colbey turned for his cab but the woman took hold of his shirt collar and called out, 'Tell us, Minister. How many CCTV cameras in the city have listening devices?' She tried to push the black thing in his face again and he wanted to step back from whatever it was but found himself pressed up against bodies behind him. He heard his shirt tear, he trod on someone's foot, and as he turned to apologise, the young Mobster in front of him said, 'Hey, be careful with that.'

'Fuck you, you filthy Mobster,' the woman spat out, a little spit falling onto Colbey's face, and at last it became clear what she held in her hand as she pulled the balaclava over her head.

In that moment everything changed and, as it does when we are confronted with the agonising pain of a life possibly about to be snatched away, time slowed down so that everything seemed to happen at once and yet also to happen in a long series of unconnected events. He saw intense flashes of images and sounds, like an old-fashioned slide show.

For sure there was a look of fear on the face of the young Mobster, for sure he had turned to find a crowd transformed into a chequerboard of covered and uncovered faces, for sure he had felt a shoving in his back and found himself pressed up against the same barriers that were supposed to be there to keep people away from him. Standing out sharp and clear was the image of a Guy Fawkes mask, its insouciant smile, its mischievous upturned moustache, and the sound of the girl crying 'Let me through, for god's sake, let me through'.

'Filthy Mobsters. Filthy Mobsters,' someone was chanting over and over, and even as Sampson reached him and pushed people aside and bundled him into the taxi, he thought, But I'm on their side. If they are privacy campaigners, I'm on *their* side. Why are they mobbing me? Did he say it out loud?

As he was hustled into the taxi, he said, 'Sampson, the girl...' but the door slammed shut behind him. As the taxi moved off he lost sight of her, and then it was over.

They drove perhaps five yards down the road, no further than that, and they were already beyond the crowd, the multi-backed beast not even realising that its target was no longer at its core. He looked back and saw that the crowd had not been as big as he had thought, twenty or thirty people at the most, and Colbey felt a fool for having panicked and for the fact that he was now shaking.

In a neat ring a few paces behind the mob were Sampson's so-called respectable journalists. They had known it was going to happen, he thought bitterly, and he wondered whether he should have stayed and reasoned with both sides, asked them to talk to one another in a rational way. Should he have done that? But of course it was he himself who had been the catalyst used to spark the reaction. The wail of a police siren sounded at the same moment his phone rang. At his feet were his red boxes, placed there by Mani, and he instinctively put a leg against them to stop them sliding about as he answered the phone.

It was Sampson, telling him not to post about the flash mob or make any comment, but even as Colbey mumbled his agreement, he heard again the wail of a siren and their progress was blocked by a police van skidding to a halt across the road. For a moment, Colbey was sure it would slam into them and he flinched. When he opened his eyes again, he found the pavement on one side and the road on the other to be streaked with fleeing protestors who fell like skittles to the knees in their backs, their black masks ripped off and held aloft here and there by their pursuers, as Perseus might have held up the head of the slain Medusa. One was pressed up against the side of the taxi, his cheek smeared against its window, an officer tight behind him, and Colbey instinctively slid across the seat and away. He heard the policeman shouting to see the protestor's phone, to see his ID app. From his new position, Colbey saw with relief that beyond them was the young Mobster of earlier, cross-legged in the centre of the pavement, her phone held aloft and a trickle of blood rolling down from a cut in her cheek.

Then the taxi was moving again. The protestor who had been pushed up against it cried out and Colbey saw him fall to the ground through the back window, the police officer tumbling after him. The taxi driver said nothing, Colbey said nothing, and they turned onto a Whitehall that was ignorant of mobs and masked protestors, and gentle with a little early afternoon traffic. He put his hand on one of the red boxes and looked out the window, aware that his breathing was ragged and trying to hide the fact. He watched the tourists and office workers pottering along its shining white paving stones, saw how they weaved like slalom skiers around the newly installed listening eyes, how the new delivery drones hummed along above them. Colbey craned his neck and peered up into the dark globe of one of the listening posts, wondering where the data was sent and what was done with it – probably for that great all-sweeping term 'analysis'. Colbey pursed his lips in thought and looked up to see they had arrived at the House.

1.9

The vote was not so bad after all. As Kanha had her face buried in her phone in the farthest corner of the lobby, she had seen an email from central office warning that there had been a flash-mob attack on Harry Colbey, and looked up to see him across the long narrow room, mobbed this time by his colleagues eager for the gory details. He was smiling, but she thought he must have been shaken by it. What a day he was having for his first in office.

After the vote, she realised she had not eaten in twenty-four hours, so she took the tunnel across to Portcullis House with a plan to pick up a sandwich from one of the cafés there. Ascending into the marble atrium she heard the hum of a hundred conversations punctuated by the freshening timpani of cutlery on china. Good things happened here: constituents were listened to, businesses allowed to lobby in an open and transparent forum, while the members of the House were sustained in their noble task of running the country by tea in thick white mugs and cellophane-wrapped deli sandwiches.

Kanha used her House card to buy a sandwich and a small carton of milk from the counter with the shortest queue, then went and stood at the edge of the circle of tables, discreetly stretching her sore calf muscles by slipping one shoe off after the other. It took several minutes for the milk to do its work and ease the vice-like pain in her chest.

Around her, members were going about their business. How many of them had been called by Dvořáček, she wondered. Perhaps they were even here when it happened, nodding uncertainly as he spoke his nonsense. Why had he done it? Why? Why? Drunk as a skunk, many had said.

Alison Appledew, member for Cambridge East, passed nearby, a tall glass of latte in one hand and a packet of crisps and a croissant clutched to her breast with the other. She was scanning for an empty space, a fawn drifted to the edge of the herd. Kanha went over and took her elbow.

'Alison. A word.'

'What have I done?' The diminutive MP jumped at the presence of Kanha. There was some dirt here to be uncovered, it seemed, thought Kanha, but that would have to wait.

'Did Percy Dvořáček ring you last weekend?'

Appledew said that he had.

'And where were you when he rang?'

'Nowhere. Here.'

'In the atrium?'

'Yes.'

'So that would have been Friday, right?'

'Yes, lunchtime.'

'Lunchtime? On a Friday?'

'Maybe earlier.'

'And what did he say?'

'That there was an important debate on Tuesday for his private member's bill and could he rely on me to be there. Said could he rely on my support.'

'And you said?'

'Gosh, I don't remember. I didn't agree to anything... He wasn't drunk, you know. People have been saying he was drunk.'

'But you probably said yes to be polite, didn't you?'

'Probably, yes.'

'Did you ask what the bill was about?'

'It was a private member's bill.'

'Indeed it was. Can you find the call for me?'

The member did as she was asked, giving her latte to Kanha to hold.

'Oh, it was eleven o'clock.'

That was more likely. So Dvořáček called Appledew at eleven on Friday morning, starting off sober. He slurred down the phone at Karson on Saturday afternoon and in the same condition called Michaels on Sunday. By the time he rang the member for Portsmouth, Piers Williams, on Monday afternoon, he was barely lucid. Dvořáček had worked his way through a list from the central phone book during his four-day drinking binge, then when everyone else had gone home he must have wobbled into his departmental office with a decision to shoot himself. But then... when did he get the shot for the pistol? Had he already determined his course of action before he started his drinking binge? In which case, why wait until Monday evening? And why ring around all the party's members to encourage them to attend a bill's opening speech that he never intended to give? Kanha remembered Appledew's elbow was still in her grip, and thinking of how Dvořáček had called her desk phone rather than her mobile, a thought occurred to her.

'What number did he call you from?'

Looking about her as if hoping an escape route might open up, Appledew read out the number and Kanha tapped it into her phone. After that, to the MP's relief, Appledew was allowed to scuttle back to the safety of the crowd.

A search provided the answer Kanha was looking for easily enough. The phone number was that of a hotel on Piccadilly, one of a chain of fancy establishments around fifteen minutes' walk away.

Throwing her half-eaten sandwich into her bag, where it found itself in company with that of the previous day, Kanha headed for the exit tubes.

I.IO

After the vote, Colbey hurried back to his waiting taxi and told the driver to take him to his London flat. After a while he wiped the condensation from the window to see where they were. Stuck at Knightsbridge. He should have told the driver to take the Victoria route.

Colbey called Clarissa to see if she was at the flat, but she didn't answer and when he stepped into the apartment, he knew at once that she wasn't there.

It was a cramped first-floor conversion within a Chelsea town house, the original rooms having been halved and quartered and arranged into several dwellings – interior walls rising in odd proportions, the rooms too narrow, too tall, decorative cornices ending at abrupt angles that made no sense. He had wanted to get something bigger, something cheaper in Westminster or Victoria, but the idea had been pooh-poohed. Nobody lives *there*, Clarissa had said.

Colbey carried the heavy boxes into the flat as his phone rang, and thinking it might be her, he hurried to put them down. But it was just Mani to say he had tracked down the ministerial car.

'Well done,' said Colbey, but on hearing it had been with the widow, he felt ashamed of his agitation to locate it and renewed annoyance at Morland for not telling him so. He hung up, filled the kettle for two cups in case Clarissa should arrive any minute and flicked it on. He thought he would call her once more and leave a message with the good news about the car, but when there was still no answer, he suddenly didn't want to leave a message at all and hung up abruptly.

Colbey held the tip of the phone to his lips and frowned. Then he rang again.

'Trying to get hold of you. Call me back.'

He listened to the Chelsea traffic rumbling away outside. Mondays and Thursday, and sometimes Wednesdays too – the romantic routine of the unfaithful. Was it so predictable as to be laughable? Or was it all in his mind, those hours in which she disappeared from the face of the earth? The conversations when he tried to pin her down without it sounding as if that was what he was doing: Darling, I called you, but your phone was switched off. 'Was it?' a breeze in reply. 'I was probably at the gym. I expect it was in the locker with no reception.' Or, 'I left it in the car. What a bother it was to be without it all afternoon.'

And often as not she'd walk out of the room as she was saying it as if she'd always been heading that way to retrieve something – some scissors for the tag of a dress, or a magazine she had just remembered needed straightening in the hall.

Could he blame her? Would it be so wrong if she had taken a lover? They were rarely intimate now. His touch seemed to leave her cold where once even the thought of it had excited her. And on the odd occasions when they were forced by good manners to make love – on birthdays and holidays, he had to confess even he felt as if he were going through the motions. Their lives were just so disparate now; that was the problem, and perhaps their personalities had grown so too. If they went to the Lake District, he wanted to climb a mountain, whereas she wanted to walk around the lake. He suspected she no longer loved him, but that she kept up an overly jovial pretence of it.

The kettle bubbled and he saw the red boxes behind him reflected in its chrome surface. He didn't mind hard work, but he was tired. He had needed that break. Had been looking forward to it for months. They had only just arrived, not even unpacked their bags when the call from Number Ten came.

On the countertop in front of him was a sketch pad. Colbey flipped the cover open and looked at an outline of his daughter, Chloe, sitting on their sofa at their Gloucestershire home. She had refused to sit long enough for him to finish, and instead had taken a photo of herself on her phone and sent it to him even as he sat across the room from her. Then with a laugh she had leapt up and told him to use that instead. He smiled at the memory of it. The picture, the part of her he had managed to capture, her face and shoulders and one arm dangling down wasn't bad. He picked up a pencil and idly chewed the end of it.

What he really wanted to do was to sit in a garden somewhere in France, with lavender-edged lawns, where there were grey metal tables and chairs with curly backs, teetering on gravel in the dappled sunshine. When he couldn't sleep at night, he would picture this place and imagine himself retired, sitting and practising his sketching. Across from him in the fantasy was a woman who laughed at his jokes rather than raising her eyes to heaven. Concentrating hard, Colbey tried to draw the woman's face. She was trying not to laugh, but her eyes had already crinkled, the laughter lines sinking into the skin. He wanted to capture that image that was so often in his head and put it on paper. The point of the pencil flicked into the outer corner of a right eye; he drew the lines out—

But no, it was no good. The lead broke; he was pressing too hard, his hand still shaky after what had happened. He scribbled the drawing out with the blunt stub just as the kettle clicked itself off. With a sigh he made a single mug of tea and set another up, ready to be poured out should she return. He felt guilty at the realisation that although he was preparing for it, Clarissa's home-coming wasn't something that he looked forward to. Was this how it would be from now on?

At least soon he would have his car and a dedicated driver. That was the one luxury he looked forward to. Mani had arranged for it to collect them for the drive over to the prime minister's house in Carlton Gardens. It was bomb proof, something that he had considered a silly luxury; now he was not so sure.

Colbey turned on the spots and grimaced as the living room was flooded with an overly white light. He hated the apartment. Hated being here. He picked up the top box and carried it to his easy chair, and as always with a disposition that one must get on with good spirit, forced himself to remember what a privilege it was to hold a job in the government, and with his brain engaged upon turning the first page, got down to work.

After a couple of hours, Colbey threw a document as thick as a Yorkshire cob onto the floor. He thought of Clarissa somewhere turning off her phone, leaving it in a locker, in a car, in a handbag, under a bed. He wondered what she would say if he called her once more and howled and screamed into her voicemail, and begged her not to do it. Not today, on this dreary March afternoon with the sky overcast and the threat of a little light rain to come.

Perhaps he would go for a walk. A brisk trot around the nearby streets might shake out the adrenalin that seemed to have settled in his nerves, like an unwelcome guest hinting it planned to stay the night. He left a note for his wife to say where he was and that he would be back before they had to leave for dinner in the ministerial car. Reading it back, he thought it a bit terse, so he underlined the words 'ministerial car' and added some jaunty exclamation marks, then he hurried out, trying hard not to look out for ambush at every corner.

I.II

Kanha decided she would go to the hotel via the river and swing around the south side of Trafalgar Square, circumventing any hacks who might be loitering on Whitehall with their persistently annoying phones. But to her dismay, she found that the city had installed seeing and listening posts every few hundred yards along the Embankment too now. She tutted as she stopped at a notice below one of them, which said they were part of a smart city trial for the West End: part information points, part connectivity, partly security against street crime. There would always be someone to hear you call for help, was the theory. Kanha shook her head. What with them and the drones... She looked up at them streaming above her.

At least these were visible. The rumour went that the Mobsters had started hiding listening eyes in the bars of Whitehall. These days they might be nothing more noticeable than a camouflaged sticker attached to a column or wall. *I suppose you can't hold back progress,* Kanha mused, though it probably meant the days of wild drinking and gossiping were over for the Westminster crowd. One had to be so careful what one said in a pub these days – anyone or anything could be listening. What a boring old world it was turning into, she thought, and made her way onto Piccadilly.

Of course Dvořáček was well known for his extra-curricular activity. It was impossible to sleep around in Westminster without it becoming common knowledge. Seeing eyes or no seeing eyes, as chief whip, it was Kanha's job to know the details, yet Dvořáček's affairs had always been hard to pin down. He was a wily operator, not one to get caught with his hand up a woman's skirt by some phone camera in the Clarence. Not he.

Thoughts of Dvořáček's wife came to Kanha, though she wished they would not. Sarah was one of the better other halves of Westminster. She was sensible, worked hard at campaigning, and never made a fuss unless she really felt strongly about a constituent's problem.

Widow... Kanha corrected herself as she reached the hotel and pushed through its circular door, weaving her way through the seats of its ornate entrance lobby, past its bar, and on to its reception area at the back of the hotel. Here there was another entrance, a more discreet one, as well as lifts up to the rooms. A clever choice for Dvořáček, she thought. Far enough away from Westminster to reduce the chance of bumping into someone from the parliamentary estate, and if one were to use the back door, the short distance from the hotel entrance to the bedrooms minimized that chance even further.

The uniformed receptionist behind the counter gave Kanha a bored smile.

'Checking in?'

Kanha ran her finger along the marble column beside her and said, 'Actually, it's a little delicate.' The receptionist tucked a loose strand of hair behind her ear and indicated they should step a little to her right, even though the lobby was empty apart from the two of them. 'Aren't you...?'

Kanha raised her eyebrows and indicated the woman should come closer. 'Yes, a cabinet minister. And... how can I put this... it's delicate. I think perhaps a member of parliament spent the weekend here?'

'Oh, he did.'

'And that he might have left behind an unpaid bill?'

The receptionist blushed and moved back to her original position where she started tapping on the keyboard. 'Oh, yes, he did that too. When we saw the news that Mr Dvořáček was... Well, we weren't sure what to do. So we...'

Kanha followed her over and gave her time to speak up.

'Well, his belongings went into lost property. And the bill – gosh, I'm sorry, we were about to pass it to a debt agency. That's the company policy. They trace the customer to a home address, and... So I guess his wife would have to...' When the girl trailed off, Kanha put a reassuring hand on the counter.

'The thing is, the government would like to pick up the bill so as not to upset his widow.'

'That would be wonderful.' The receptionist tapped again at her keyboard and a bill came spewing out of a printer behind her. It was several pages long. 'There's a lot of charges for all the telephone calls. And I'm terribly sorry, but there was also a television that was smashed...'

Seeing Kanha frown, she said, 'But I tell you what I'm going to do. I'm going to mark that down as accidental damage and take it off.' She tapped at her keyboard again and replaced the bill with a new one.

Kanha fingered some of the pages apart and saw the long list of itemised calls. There were several bottles of vodka too.

'Would you mind if I ask you something? Was he alone?'

'I couldn't possibly tell you that. It wouldn't be right.'

Kanha felt a stab of amusement as the receptionist said it, a prim look on her face. Oh, to be high-principled and twenty-five again.

She took her credit card out of her purse and handed it over, gritting her teeth as she looked at the amount to be paid. She wouldn't be able to claim it back on expenses. What code would the clerks put it under? The cabinet secretary might consider refunding her, but she couldn't ask. It would only remind them all of her impoverished background. It would only *other* her. Shit. What she would have given to spend four hundred pounds in a fancy hotel in London with room service on tap.

When the receptionist went off to search lost property for anything Dvořáček might have left behind, Kanha slipped the bill into her bag and, as she did so, a woman came in through the back door and made for the lifts. Though she only caught a glimpse of her, Kanha felt sure it was someone she recognised. She moved softly to the end of the counter, and as the lift pinged to announce its arrival and its doors slid open, Kanha leaned out the last few inches and peered around the marble column – just in time to see Clarissa Colbey stepping into the lift, followed by the swish of the doors closing behind her.

Kanha groaned. Why was everyone's love life so much more interesting than hers? Poor old Harry Colbey, what a day he truly was having, did he but know it.

The receptionist returned to say there was only a toothbrush and a razor and did she want them.

Kanha said no and thanked her for her help. 'That was the only room bill, wasn't it?' she said.

'Oh no, I mean yes, Mr Dvořáček had always paid before.' Then the receptionist leaned forward and said, 'Look, it wasn't usually the case, but I'm sure he was alone that weekend.' She sighed. 'If only I'd...'

Kanha thanked her and left by the nearby door, finding herself in a narrow alleyway that led back onto the ever-frenetic Piccadilly.

So, the taking of the room was a regular occurrence, was it? Kanha threaded her way through the stationary black cabs of Piccadilly, skirted the Tube station and dropped down into Green Park, thinking that it might be better to walk back through the royal parks. The drones were banned from crossing them, so there was a little privacy left there.

As soon as she reached the first of the avenues of plane trees, a cloud passed over the sun and, tucking her hands into her pockets against the cold, Kanha picked up her pace. Although this was also a more scenic route, which would pass by Buckingham Palace, Horse Guards Parade, the Churchill War Rooms and the back end of Downing Street – not that she would really see them – it had the negative aspect of arriving at Westminster via Parliament Square with its irritatingly permanent fixture of camped-out hacks from the Mouth of the Mob. As Kanha walked, she studied the hotel room bill, holding it in one hand while flicking through her phone with her other. Dvořáček had done just as she suspected – he had worked his way through the directory of members' phones, missing her out only to call her not on her mobile but her desk phone. It was indeed the last call he had made. From the hotel room at any rate.

Lost in the thought of it, Kanha tucked the bill safely away from sight in her voluminous handbag and got ready to hurry past the Mobsters with a well-practised 'Not today, thanks.'

1.12

Harry Colbey sat fuming on a chair in the hallway, not having noticed that dusk had come upon him and that the room was in near darkness. His wife had still not returned. She had rung an hour ago to say she was on her way, yet there was no sign of her. Without doubt they were going to be late and now he couldn't find his phone. He groaned with the realisation that it meant he would have kept the prime minister waiting twice in one day.

With relief he heard her key in the lock.

'For god's sake, Clarissa, we're going to be late,' he said.

She struggled through the door, a serried line of bags hanging from her arm.

'That's not much of a welcome, Minister.'

'I don't know if you noticed, but the traffic's terrible and we've got to get back through it to Whitehall.'

'I'm ready to go.' She turned on the light. 'I changed into my outfit in the shop. I just need to find the right shoes. Why are you sitting in the dark?'

She ran off into their bedroom and when she returned she'd obviously decided that attack was the best form of defence. Her lips had sealed into a thin line and she would no longer look at him.

'I can't find my phone,' he said tersely, speaking to her back as she turned away to fix her lipstick in the mirror.

'Where did you lose it?'

'Obviously I don't know, or I'd be able to find it. Just bloody ring it, would you?'

After she had finished with her make-up, taking longer than he thought necessary, she threw her lipstick into her bag, pulled out her phone and made a call. There was the sound of ringing from beneath a scarf on the console table, and with raised eyebrows she extracted his phone and handed it to him. 'Hidden beyond wit of man,' she said.

Colbey took the phone from his wife and slipped it into his pocket. 'Thank you, darling.'

Like a white flag of surrender, she offered him a cheek and, his temper cooling, he apologised for being short with her, tenderly putting his hand behind her head to kiss her. His fingers touched damp curls at the nape of her neck. She had taken a shower wearing a cheap plastic cap.

Considering whether to say anything, Colbey pulled away. Now was not the time, so instead he said, 'I just don't understand you. One minute you're desperate to have me in the cabinet, the next you're off somewhere not answering your phone and couldn't care less if... if we turn up at the MacLellans' late for dinner.'

'I couldn't hear the phone because I was at the hairdresser's,' she said, the thin lips returning. 'And I couldn't care less about your sorry excuse for a career, as it happens.' She picked her way down the steps to the street and he slammed the door behind him.

In the car they sat in silence at a set of roadworks, Colbey breathing heavily through his nose, unable to calm himself.

'Do stop fretting,' she snapped, 'it won't make the traffic go any faster. And anyway, who cares if we're late?'

Colbey considered she was being deliberately blasé to make the point that these were her friends, so she was absolutely fine with arriving late; she wanted to make it clear that it was he who was nervous about having dinner with his prime minister.

As the car turned into St James's, Colbey breathed a sigh of relief. They were going to be late, but only by fifteen minutes or so, which for a dinner party was probably not such terrible form. He put his hand tentatively on Clarissa's thigh. He didn't want them to be in a bate with each other all the way through dinner.

'Was it really just under that scarf?' he said.

Clarissa softened, and he saw a half smile in the dark.

'It was a true man-search,' she said.

Now that they were speaking again Colbey took her hand in his and she let him. 'Do you think we should bring the bottle of wine?' he said.

'I don't know,' she whispered. 'What do you think?'

The car was waved through the temporary security blockade that had been constructed at the end of Carlton Gardens, a double-ended cul-de-sac that ran alongside Pall Mall.

'Well, we can't turn up empty-handed.' Like her, he was uncertain whether the internal intercom to the driver was still switched on or not.

'You decide,' she hissed. 'You were the one who forgot to pick up the chocolates.'

They decided to bring the bottle, but then just as they got out of the car, she said, 'No, leave it there,' and he realised the whole thing, all her sanguine nonchalance, had been bravado after all. Colbey didn't want to catch the eye of the police officer who escorted them from the car to the house in case he had overheard the discussion.

Number One Carlton Gardens was a classic piece of St James's architecture with its white stucco and Doric columns, and Colbey could not help a quick glance up to the third floor, where the prime minister and his wife were said to have their apartment. They were received by another officer and ushered up the steps and in through the front door. Here was the same arrangement as at Number Ten, with a scanner and pigeonholes into which electronic devices were to be surrendered. When they got to the third floor, they were deposited at an unmarked door and he and Clarissa looked at each other and smiled. 'Go on, then,' she said.

It was Zandra, the PM's wife, who opened it. Although she often played tennis with Clarissa, it was the first time Colbey had met her. She was more petite than he had expected, and was swathed in what seemed to Colbey to be a rather lurid designer dress, and he watched to see whether the two women were really as close as his wife had made out.

'Come on in, darlings, out of that draughty corridor,' she said. 'Do you know, they only let us heat our private rooms. As if the government can't afford its own fuel bills!'

Colbey was about to say it was likely to be part of the government's green drive, but Clarissa's eyebrows came together in warning. They followed Zandra through a series of over-decorated rooms of gold and red stripe, and into a dining room where a table was laid for six. A casually dressed prime minister was deep in conversation with Jonnie Whitwell-Thrupp, the owner of the Mouth of the Mob. Standing by was someone he assumed to be Thrupp's wife. Colbey shook the PM's hand and was introduced to Jonnie, although the two had met long ago, at a charity dinner.

'Good to see you again, Harry,' Jonnie said.

Mrs Thrupp poked her head out from behind her husband's back and said hello. She was very beautiful, very thin, and, Colbey suspected, somewhat surgically enhanced.

'Juliana,' she said. 'Lovely to meet you.'

'Oh, yes,' said the PM, 'and this is Clarissa. Terrific backhand.'

Jonnie kissed Clarissa on the cheek. 'We know each other already, don't we? How are you? It is a terrific backhand, you know.'

'Never play myself,' Juliana said. 'Prefer horses.'

Zandra walked off, saying as she did so, 'Come to the kitchen, girls, I just need to put some strawberries on the dessert.'

'Likes to make the dinner herself,' the PM said. 'God knows why, she's a terrible cook.'

'I'm still in earshot!' his wife called over her shoulder, but the PM was already focused on fixing the men a drink and didn't seem to hear.

'Jonnie owns that god-damn awful Mouth of the Mob website,' the PM said.

Colbey nodded. 'Yes, of course. Very impressive.'

The PM poured each a large glass of red and ushered them over to the table. 'Where do you want us, Zandra?' he called out.

When there was no reply, Jonnie found his name on a place card and sat down. 'Here's your lovely wife between me and Ewan, Harry. And there's you, next to mine.'

Colbey went round and sat as directed and the PM came and took his own place at the head of the table, bringing the wine bottle and another with him. Looking at the silver cutlery, Colbey wondered whether it belonged to the MacLellans or to the apartment, but the women returned, their conversation continuing unabated. Jonnie Thrupp frowned with open annoyance when he saw the huge glass of wine in his wife's hand and she made exaggerated wide eyes at him to show she didn't care.

'What are you girls talking about?' asked the PM.

His wife came and planted a kiss on her husband's head. 'Kitchens, darling,' she said and he gave an exaggerated yawn.

Seeing it was just the six of them, Colbey couldn't help but feel a little proud of Clarissa. An ambitious young minister couldn't want for a better wife. It wasn't Clarissa's fault he was neither ambitious nor young. At least he was a minister now.

Zandra smoothed Clarissa's hair in a motherly way as she passed to take her seat, asking her what she had been up to that week, and Colbey was shot a look that said *I told you so*.

Jonnie was fidgeting with a spoon, tapping it on the table. 'Any chance I could borrow your phone?' he said to Ewan as Zandra lifted the covers of several pots. They really were late. Dinner had already been set out. Colbey didn't dare look at his wife.

'What do you need that's so important?' the PM said. 'You just run a rag. I run the country and you don't see me needing to look at my phone, do you?'

'Just my headlines.'

The PM fished his phone out of his pocket and handed it over while Zandra gave Juliana a serving spoon and told her to help herself. 'Gentlemen, please. We have house rules, remember, this week?'

'Sorry, I forgot,' the PM said. 'You'd better hand it back. No phones allowed at the table.'

'Hang on a second,' said Jonnie, 'Woodward is breaking something big.'

'Who's Woodward?' asked Clarissa.

'One of the Mobsters,' replied Juliana.

The PM growled a little. 'Hand it back,' he said, and as it was returned, Colbey saw him take a sneaky look at the headline himself before he put it in his pocket and frowned.

'Bad news for you lot, was it?' Jonnie said.

'Morons,' said the PM and seeing, as they all did, that her husband was on the verge of being thrown into a bad mood by whatever headline he had seen, Zandra said, 'It's to set an example to the grandchildren. Do you know what Isabelle said to Ewan this morning?'

There was a moment where everyone except Jonnie held their breath to see if the ploy to distract the PM might work and Juliana played ball by saying, 'No, what?'

'She asked Ewan whether he had to wear a crown at work now that he was the king again.'

The PM chuckled and everyone breathed a sigh of relief. 'Her grandmamma put them straight on that,' he said.

'I certainly did,' said Zandra.

'So do they stay here in the apartment?' Juliana asked, looking round as if the children would jump out from a corner at any minute, and Jonnie chuckled.

'Maybe Ewan has them hidden in the basement, darling.' He tucked his serviette into his collar and reached across to help himself from one of the dishes.

Taking a mouthful of food and talking through it, the PM said, 'Actually, you're eating them.' He laughed at his own terrible joke accompanied by the false trill of Clarissa.

'It is a good rule,' she said. 'We tried it in our house, but then the children left.'

'Oh. Can you get rid of them that way?' asked Jonnie, and Clarissa laughed louder than ever. Colbey looked at her in amazement.

'Any chance I could see that Woodward headline?' Jonnie asked, but the PM pretended he hadn't heard and told everyone instead that Zandra's sauce was a secret family recipe.

Jonnie made a joke of taking an extra spoonful at the news. 'You should put the recipe on the web so that all of us plebs can enjoy it.'

The PM scowled, but Colbey saw that it was a pretend scowl. By now the wine had done its work and he along with everyone at the table, Colbey included, was in a jovial mood. 'You are beginning to sound more like a Whigge every day, Jonnie old boy.'

'So? I've never promised you had my vote.'

At this the PM snorted into his pork and Clarissa squawked. 'Is he allowed at the table if he's not one of us?'

The PM put a hand on her arm. 'Of course he is, Clarissa my dear. We welcome all sorts here. Even private equity.'

'Private equity? Who are you calling private equity?' Jonnie puffed himself up and rubbed a hand up and down his chest, a pleasant smile on his face.

'What are you then, if you're not private equity?' the PM said loudly.

To which Jonnie put a spoon in his mouth and with it dangling out, said, 'We're economic generation these days, if you must know.'

'Hogwash.'

'No, don't be like that, my dear Prime Minister. You must get with the new anti-hate branding. We specialise in the generation of jobs and opportunities.'

The PM turned to Colbey. 'What do you think, Harry?'

Colbey smiled slowly. 'And a little wealth along the way as well, perhaps?'

Jonnie rubbed his chest again, and agreed with a vigorous nod. 'Well, just as a sideline,' he said, and the PM roared. Zandra told him to calm down or he'd wake the grandchildren who in fact really were asleep a few doors down.

One hand beneath her chin, Clarissa said to Jonnie, 'But your Mouth of the Mob site is doing rather well, isn't it?'

Jonnie agreed that it was so. 'Just topped six million users.'

'Is that a lot?' asked Zandra.

The PM snorted again at his wife's stupidity, a little red wine coming out of his nose. He was forced to wipe it with his napkin.

'Ewan. You really *are* going to wake up those children if you're not careful.'

Ignoring his wife, the PM carried on at exactly the same volume, if not a little louder. 'It's more, my darling Zandra, than all the other news sites put together.'

'Yes, but what we do is very different,' said Jonnie. 'They're news outlets. We're a gossip sheet, and transparently so.'

'But everyone looks to you for the news, my darling,' Juliana said.

'No, that's not true, Jules. The reality is that we embrace the concept of fake news. Totally the opposite of your honest politicking thing, Harry.'

'You know about that?' Harry said, excited at the thought that the news outlets had picked up on it.

'I mean, what's the difference between gossip and fake news? Not much really. Anyone can set up as a bone fide hack on our site. They can put whatever they want on their page, any nonsense they make up or hear in a pub or on the street.'

'Yes, on the street,' said Zandra. 'But that's the problem, isn't it? All these people hiding listening eyes everywhere.'

'Oh, please let's not talk about that,' Juliana said dramatically, and Colbey considered she might already be a little drunk.

'No, let's be clear,' said Jonnie, seeming serious for a moment. 'Mouth of the Mob is the home of fake news and unsubstantiated gossip. There's no confusion there.'

'Except, it's not, is it?' said Zandra. 'People follow your top hacks as if they provided real news. Those with the most golden shovels at any event.'

'Scoops,' said Jonnie. 'They're golden scoops. Every time a hack is found to have broken a genuine news story rather than just churned out a load of made-up nonsense, they get awarded with a golden scoop.'

'It does look a bit like a shovel,' said Clarissa.

'Scoop, shovel, it doesn't matter,' said the PM. 'It's an annoying site filled with all sorts of balderdash, rude insinuations and downright lies.'

'And some very clever reporters,' said Colbey. 'A lot of Woodward's copy, for example, does turn out to be true...'

'That's my point,' said Zandra. 'But all the same, it's very clever of you to have started it, Jonnie.'

Jonnie seemed now to be the most sober person at the table. 'Well, the cleverness of the idea, I can't take credit for. I was just jettisoned in with the equity funds.'

'Private equity!' roared the PM to Zandra's glare.

'It was a bunch of kids who came up with the idea, but they didn't have the wherewithal to make it work. They were doing alright, but they needed some grown-ups to take over.'

'Do you say that in front of them?' Clarissa asked.

'All the bloody time. They used to get a bit antsy, but they've so much money now they barely bother turning up these days. They seem more interested in checking out the world's Victoria's Secrets models.'

Everyone laughed at Jonnie's impression of a Victoria's Secrets model, except his wife, who said, 'Mother and I think he was just lucky that finally one of his investments turned into something resembling a gold mine.'

'A gold mine?' Clarissa said, barely audibly.

'Alright, alright,' said Jonnie. 'Better to be lucky than good, eh?'

'Not every time you get lucky enough to be an early investor in a company whose shares go stratospheric,' said the PM.

'Stratospheric?' said Clarissa, and Colbey thought that if she were a cartoon character there would be slot machine dollars in place of her eyes.

Probably to change the subject away from money, Zandra said hurriedly, 'But it is left leaning, isn't it?'

Her husband gave a great guffaw, drawing a very stern look from her.

'We're partisan,' Jonnie said, and as the PM slapped the table with great whelps of laughter, Jonnie asserted it was true, but then said, 'Well, with the odd bit of directional educating in the choice of top-ranking Mobsters...'

The PM banged his hand on the table again and said, 'No more of that Whigge nonsense, please! You've drifted too far that way in your desperation for clicks.'

Juliana tried to cut in again, her voice overly loud and slurring slightly. 'Can you believe it? My mother's terribly embarrassed. She hates the name of the paper. It makes you sound like plebs, she said to me.'

Colbey couldn't help but laugh along with them.

'It is ironic, though, isn't it?' continued Juliana, clearly enjoying having the floor. 'Jonnie as the voice of the plebs.'

'Not really,' the PM boomed. 'He did go to Rugby after all.'

'Ha ha,' said Jonnie loudly and sarcastically. 'Well at least I don't wear a belt with a suit.'

'What's wrong with that?' said Clarissa.

'Exactly, Clarissa, my dear,' the PM said. 'Spot on. What's wrong with that, eh Jonnie?'

And Colbey said, 'I think, darling, Jonnie is suggesting Ewan wearing a belt is an affectation because one wouldn't normally wear a belt with a suit.'

'Oh, you think that's what it is, do you?' the PM said, and Colbey feared he'd overstepped the mark. He imaged Ewan and Esme Kanha discussing tomorrow how he would not do, how he must be sent back to where he came from, but then the PM laughed and slapped the table loudly one more time. 'Alright, alright. I do have a responsibility to look approachable to my countrymen, you know. Man of the people and all that. If it's what the PR girls say will do it, then... you know... I'm big enough to be able to sacrifice certain things for my country. It's not like it hasn't been done before.' Ewan waved his glass around as he spoke and those closest to him watched it nervously.

'Oh, do stop talking nonsense,' his wife said wearily, and seeing her face, the PM calmed down for a moment.

'Alright, alright. Let's change the subject, shall we? How's it going over in West Oxford, Harry?'

'I think we're safe there, Ewan, belt or no belt.'

'And how about you?' The PM turned to Clarissa. 'Holding up under the strain of being a new minister's wife? You do a very good job, my dear.'

'Indeed she does,' said Zandra.

Clarissa smoothed her hair back, letting her diamond ring sparkle in the candlelight.

'We're old hands at this now, Ewan, aren't we, Harry?'

Colbey felt happy for his wife, watching her bask in the joy of those words from the prime minister and his wife. She really had made it.

Ewan declared he was away to fetch a bottle of Madeira and Zandra cleared some plates.

'I *was* lucky, you know? I'll admit that,' Jonnie Whitwell-Thrupp said to Clarissa and Colbey. 'Not often you get to be in on the ground floor of something like that, is it?'

Clarissa nodded and got up to help Zandra bring in a pavlova. Juliana was going to help too, but she sent a pepper pot flying and sat down again. Jonnie reached across and took her wine away from her.

'Anyone want a little shot of Madeira? I've been saving it all day,' the PM said, returning.

'No you haven't,' said his wife, also coming back into the room. 'Some of it's gone already.'

'Well, I just wanted to check it was alright for everyone.'

After the pudding, Zandra wanted to take everyone into their sitting room to see a Lowry they had recently purchased, but the PM told Colbey to stay behind and join him for another glass of Madeira.

Colbey thought of all that paper sitting in those red boxes back at the flat as he unsuccessfully tried to prevent the PM from filling his glass to the brim.

'So what do you think about these young Whigges then, mmm, Harry?'

'Seems a bit of a jumble of policies,' he replied. 'Something for everyone.' And seeing his chance, Colbey added, 'Though they do have something akin to an honest politicking policy.'

'Honest politicking, eh?' The PM grunted and put his hand on Colbey's shoulder. 'Not on my watch, old boy.' Then he tried to top Colbey's glass up again before saying, 'Look, you're smart. Wait for the right time. I'm not hanging around forever. Keep your powder dry on that honest politicking malarky for now. Be close to me. Learn from me. Be useful to me. Oh, which reminds me, have you found that book yet?'

Colbey told him that had hadn't, but that it was not forgotten, and seeming not to listen to his reply, the PM continued regardless. 'And when the time is right, I'll give you the nod. Then you can shout from the rafters about your Honest Politicking Bill and get a ticket based on that. Go for the top job if you dare. Then, once you're in and I'm safely back at my house in Palo Alto, you can try running the country with your bloody honest politicking.'

'What about Esme Kanha?'

The PM looked genuinely surprised. 'Kanha? Don't be a fool. She's, you know... Hadn't you noticed? Might even be a Muslim for all I know.'

'I don't think she is...'

'She's very good. Smart young lady. I'll give you that. But between you and me – and God above, don't say anything to Zandra – but well, on top of everything, she's a woman, isn't she? I'm all for equality, but it never works out in the end, does it? A woman prime minister? They're too soft, liable to cry when they get angry. Not really made of the right ingredients for that sort of job, in my opinion. Good lord. I mean, they're not even allowed in the bar of my club. At least they didn't used to be. Some bloody fool had to go and make a name for himself, so they are now, of course. But I might see if I can get that changed back. Are you a member?'

Colbey thought how it rarely worked out for any prime minister in the end, and as his head spun from the wine, he thought again of the bill and the fact that he still had to finish reading it before morning.

'But that's just my opinion,' Ewan said. 'I know I'm not with modern thinking any more. It's all very well, but some of us have to run the county. At least for now, but I'll be gone at some point.'

The PM insisted on filling his glass again.

'Go on, help me drink it. Otherwise Zandra will think I drank it all. Yes, I've got this little place over in the States. Waiting for me. Waiting for when I'm ready. And I'll not go before I am. You mark my words on that. You try and take it from me before then, and it will not go well for you. Have another. Go on, drink up. It's on the ocean. Lovely little place. When I get over there I'll take over the management and shipshape it up a bit. Can't wait. You sit at the bar there and look at all the beauties in their swimsuits. The children can come out with their families, my secretarial staff too, you know? Lots of family rushing around, and the beauties in their swimsuits. Ah, Harry, Clarissa would love it, I know. You'll have to come out and visit us. But not till I'm ready, I tell you. Not till I'm ready. Right. Look, your glass is empty. Nonsense. Nonsense. Let me fill it up.'

1.13

Back in the Houses of Parliament, the long whips' office was dark and silent, its senior members having taken themselves off to their clubs in St James's, while their various assistants, researchers and spads had scurried off to engage in the political sport of Whitehall in more down-to-earth establishments: the likes of the Westminster Arms, the Red Lion, the Marquis of Granby.

Only at the far end of the room was there some light, where Esme Kanha sat bathed in the glow of her monitor, her ghostly reflection looking back at her from the glass partition. She was keeping to one corner of her desk to avoid catching the room's motion detector and being plunged into the harsh reality of the fluorescent lighting.

The box of Dvořáček's personal effects was gone, and in its place was a message on a Post-it note confirming it had been delivered into the hands of the widow. Beside that was a draft of the bill that Dvořáček had tried to sneak through parliament, which Kanha had pulled out of the recycling bin in their little lobby office.

Carefully, Kanha opened her desk drawer and pulled out a bottle of wine, drained her tea mug of its residue into a nearby plant pot, and after swilling the mug out, poured herself a good measure.

Dvořáček's bill looked like a copy of the official privacy bill that was due for its first reading in a week or so. So why try to push it through early? Had Dvořáček been afraid his official government bill might get talked out by an opposition member before the House rose and not become legislation this session? But it didn't make sense. The other side of the House had signalled their support, it was popular with voters, particularly the extremely vocal privacy nutters that were beginning to get momentum behind their campaigns. It wouldn't do any party any good to be seen to be blocking it. Was he worried the Whigges might gain in number and block it? There were rumours of coming defections, but that couldn't be the case; with such a majority, the government had no difficulty getting its business through the House at the moment.

But perhaps Dvořáček wasn't thinking straight, and who would be during a four-day drinking binge that was to end in suicide?

Kanha reached for the mug and took a few mouthfuls of wine. She waited for the blur to come and soften the edges of her anxiety, flood those neural pathways and break thoughts loose from their moorings. She let them come at her sideways, backwards, in a weaving random fashion. During the day she knew she could be too rigid; logic assailed her and forced her into straight lines. Only at night when she fell to the wine could she think outside the grooves she had worn down during the day.

She went once more over Dvořáček's bill, thoroughly this time, but this was not her area of expertise and there were pages and pages of thick incomprehensible passages. Kanha was better at people than bills. She lifted the handset of her phone and tabbed through to the second message saved on its ancient system.

Esme. It's me again. Percy Dvořáček. Do you know what I think, mmm? I think we're all just stupid old geese. Greedy. Waddling around pushing our stupid fat chests out, squawking across the House at one another, as if we mattered. As if we were important, but we're not. None of us are. We're too far behind. And we're all dirty, aren't we, hmm? Even you. Even

clever Kanha. So what are we, eh? Just stupid, useless, dirty
fucking geese. We don't know anything, but they're watching
us, listening to us. And they're inside my head, I tell you. And
I don't want them there.

There was a frightful noise, like a car crash that went on and
on. Now Kanha knew what it was. It was the television screen
shattering as he repeatedly lifted it up and smashed down again
and again. The message cut out and that was the end of it.

Kanha put her head in her hands and thought of facing
Dvořáček's wife at his funeral. The tears welled up and her nose
stung, but she refused to let them fall again. Had Ewan shed tears
over Dvořáček? Did Harry Colbey? Damn it.

She reached for the wine bottle and found it empty, so she
turned to the terminal and found her way to a staff directory of
the Department for Personal Information.

Who did she know whom she might pin into some dark corner
and interrogate? There was Morland, but he would be tight-lipped
however many whiskey and sodas he'd had in the Stranger's Bar.
Dvořáček's PPS was marked as off as long-term sick. No... no...
She scrolled through, discarding options until her finger stopped
on an entry.

Could it be? Kanha picked up the handset in front of her
and with a small gasp of delight rang the number. When it was
answered, she knew at once it was not just the coincidence of a
shared name.

'Newbie,' she said, 'what are you doing here?' She toyed with
the wire of the desk phone, smiling. 'And when exactly were you
planning to call me and let me know you'd landed in town?' Then
she interrupted the answer, snapping, 'I can call you Newbie
for as long as I like. Anyway, where are you? It sounds like the
Westminster Arms.' She smiled again. 'Yes, you're right. I can still
name a pub in one. Get me a rum and coke and I'll be there in ten.'

Kanha stood and the strip light above her flickered on, making her shield her eyes as she picked up Dvořáček's bill, folded it into four and slipped it into her handbag. As she hurried through the cavernous office, the lights switched on one by one in her wake. So her old friend was not only here, but ensconced in Dvořáček's department. If there was anyone who might know what had been going on there, it would be him.

1.14

Shortly before midnight, Colbey sat in bed, a pen in his hand and a copy of the privacy bill on his lap. A lamp shone over his shoulder onto the page before him and there was a cup of strong coffee cooling on the bedside table. Clarissa lay beside him. He could see the knot of her eye mask at the back of her head, where she had twisted the stretched elastic to make it tight.

'He told me he's going to run a restaurant,' Colbey said.

'A restaurant?' she murmured. 'Ewan?'

'I know, strange, isn't it?'

'I can't see him running around with an order pad.'

'I don't think that's what he had in mind. I think it's more that he wants to *live* in a restaurant.'

Clarissa sat up and pulled her eye mask up onto her forehead.

'Why was he telling you? Was he talking about retiring?'

'No, not really.'

A silence lingered.

'Look. We've been through this. Let's just keep our focus on the election.'

'Rubbish, Harry. If the party don't do well this time round, he could be out in a flash, and you've got to have laid the groundwork before then. Let them know you want it.'

'What if I don't want it?'

'For god's sake, Harry.'

Grumpily, she pulled her mask back over her eyes and lay down with her back to him again.

He put his hand on her shoulder and she reached up and put her hand on his.

Perhaps I was mistaken, he thought. She was rushing. She was carrying those bags. It was cold out, and she had been running in and out of all those shops with the heaters blowing over the doorways. Perhaps it was just sweat.

With that thought, Colbey set his alarm for four in the morning and turned off the bedside light. He would get a few hours' sleep and go through the documents before dawn. Nothing could be done with his head spinning the way it was. A moment later, he drifted off, one arm still resting on Clarissa's shoulder, the other tucked under his pillow, finding the combination of claret and Madeira to be a potent sleeping draft.

1.15

Henri Lauvaux arrived at a private airfield a few miles to the west of London on a Legacy 500 light aircraft. While the plane was taxiing to a halt, Lauvaux put away the book he had been reading, stacking it neatly in an alcove by his knee, and went and peered through the front-most cabin window. A customs official was standing by the mark where the steps would be lowered and the man gave a friendly wave of recognition. Behind him, Lauvaux could see a car waiting to ferry him the short distance to the terminal building and from there it was a moment's walk to the car park where his London driver usually parked.

Although the traffic had subsided, the speed limit of the main arterial road into the centre of the city had been lowered once more, so it took just as long to reach the city as if they had arrived in rush hour. Soon they will have people walking with red flags in front of the English and their cars, Lauvaux thought with a tut of annoyance.

He called home to say goodnight to his wife, and finding his daughter was up and being given a glass of milk, he asked her nanny to bring her to the phone.

'*Oui, Papa?*'

'English, my darling.'

'*Papaaa,*' she remonstrated.

'I only want to say goodnight.'

'Thank you for taking me skiing again. Were you very late getting to London?'

'You skied very well today.'

'I know. I'm the fastest.'

'And when is it you come for your ballet lesson?'

'In a few weeks' time. Will you be there to pick me up?'

'Perhaps. We'll see.'

'Good night, *Papa*.'

'*Beaux rêves, ma chérie*.'

When they hit a little late-night congestion on Piccadilly, a thought occurred to Lauvaux, and deciding that the delay was irritating him, he told the driver he would get out. It would be as quick to walk the rest of the way and those who habituated St James's were usually an interesting study. As they waited for a chance to pull over, Lauvaux opened his bag and dug around for a small hard case. Finding it wedged at the bottom, he tugged it out and balanced it on his notebook. Inside was a pair of contact lenses. By the time he had them in, the car had pulled over to the kerb.

'You sure?' asked the driver. 'The traffic will clear just up here.'

'Yes, yes,' Lauvaux replied, brushing a pool of spilled sterilised water off the calfskin notebook and tucking it back into his bag. 'A little stretch of the legs is a good thing after a flight, don't you agree?' He didn't really listen to the driver's long answer, just murmured something vaguely polite in response as he got out. The driver shrugged his shoulders and drove off, with no obvious complaint that his day's work had finished a few minutes earlier than expected.

For Lauvaux, meanwhile, the landscape of London took on a slightly crystalline sheen. After weaving his way through the midnight cabs of Piccadilly, he stood in his tailored Neapolitan suit beneath the awnings of the Ritz, his overnight bag gripped in his hand. He felt like a rocky outcrop in the centre of a fast-flowing river, as a stream of party-going and party-returning pedestrians parted about him. Words appeared before Lauvaux's eyes like so much white foam. They read such things as *William Secker, Coutts banker*: a portly gentleman in a beige mackintosh; trotting behind him was *Judith Colliard, race-horse trainer*, in tweed, with hair scooped back into a scallop-shell shape. Off in the other direction, with a brown bag tucked under her arm, went *Carole Browne, sex worker*, petite, demurely dressed, and only identified when she glanced back at Lauvaux with mild curiosity.

To Lauvaux's left, *Mr and Mrs Hopkins, retired schoolteacher and blank* did not realise that upon climbing out of their taxi and tipsily staggering to their hotel, they brushed shoulders with a member of the extended Thai royal family, who crossed in the other direction coming out of the hotel and jumped into their empty cab, its orange light flicking on and off again, but of course Lauvaux did.

He thought for a moment of how he was like a god. No, not *like* a god, he *was* a god – omniscient, all-knowing. He pulled his phone from his pocket and listened to the audio for a while, but decided he preferred the words that flashed up around him. He would let the inner-circle wizards know his feedback.

Not favouring the Ritz, Lauvaux was booked to stay at the Stafford, a more discreet hotel, tucked away a few streets behind it. As he passed a champagne bar on the corner of St James's, Lauvaux saw the German ambassador and the French national security advisor huddled together, unaware that luxuries such as privacy were over.

Even as Lauvaux thought to make a note of his sighting of the meeting, he remembered his system would already have assimilated the fact. For the connectivity of name tags that floated before his eyes were fed into it along with everything else that could be scraped by fair means or foul: texts, emails, conference calls, apps, traffic cams, GPS phone locators, health trackers, smart speakers, motion detectors, CCTV internal or external. There was no end to the list these days. Now his company was also adding in the live feeds they received from the listening eyes that they had kindly donated to the city's councils as well as those they had provided to the Mobsters for their own entertainment and fun. Not to mention the drone footage.

The system was called Alcheminna – a world of people and everything about them – and now it was all about joining up the dots. Only their system could do it; so far only their system had mastered the power that quantum computing brought, and everyone who was anyone knew it. It was all about first-mover advantage, and Lauvaux was on the winning side.

In fact, he mulled, taking the thought further, they had already won and now were moving to consolidate. The system used voice recognition to pick out individuals as they passed the listening eyes or spoke to friends and family in front of any accessible microphone – any mobile, television, drone, or smart speaker that had an app with permission to listen in, and of course many that did not. Now that they were gaining momentum, now that the system was live, they could allocate any speech they heard to the right individual, and that was just the start. They were starting to work on mannerisms and facial expressions learned from millions of hours' worth of video calls, matching expressions to words, and words to thoughts…

Lauvaux looked at his reflection in the bar window and realised with satisfaction that there was no tag attached to it. He walked as a ghost through this digitally enhanced landscape. He was a founding member. Not *the* founding member, but an early investing member. Soon he would be a truly wealthy man, and not necessarily just in monetary terms. For it was not necessarily just money that mattered to him. Being a part of it was what mattered. The wealth just brought a comfortable life. After all, though a god, he must still live in human form.

Lauvaux decided to take a quick turn around the little park of St James's Square before going to his room. He was not sleepy yet. As he walked on the pressed gravel path under the plane trees, he took his e-pad from his bag and dialled into the system. After a few stabs of his finger, and a glance at the camera to allow the security system to scan his retina, an image of Harry Colbey appeared on the screen.

'Can I help you?' Colbey asked.

Lauvaux saw how calm Colbey was and thought he might not have needed to be so hasty coming to London.

'Have you signed off the bill yet?'

'Not yet,' Colbey replied.

'What might you be waiting for?'

'I want to study it first.'

Lauvaux nodded his understanding. 'Are you reading it now?'

'I'm sleeping right now.'

'Then you'll read it and sign it tomorrow when you awaken?'

'Yes. The prime minister has asked me to. My alarm is set for 4 a.m. I hope I don't miss it. I'm sleeping right now. I'm sleeping right now. I'm sleep—'

Lauvaux pursed his lips, stabbed a finger to log out of the system and put his e-pad back in his bag, making a mental note as he did so to add that additional glitch to his feedback list. Perhaps his journey here was wasted after all, but there were other things he could attend to.

As he turned back towards his hotel, Lauvaux looked absent-mindedly into the branches of the plane trees. They rose up from their great grey pyramid bases like the legs of so many giant elephants. He was used to the prim little trees they planted around Lake Annecy or the evergreens of the mountains where he skied, but he loved the plane trees of London, particularly in the summer when they grew thick and huge in leaf.

Lauvaux realised his vision had cleared. He was seeing the world as it was. No name tags, no importance ratings, not for a tree, not for the night sky. Alcheminna was a system of people, a world of people. It was not a toy or a game, as some suggested. No, no, far from it. For a moment he felt light-headed.

He knew so much of the world was at a tipping point; he had read his Orwell. He wanted himself and his family to be behind the giant eye that read 'We are watching you' on the bridge between London and his airport, not in front of it.

Was that a star there? Grudgingly, he thought that it might be a nice feature to add to the system – so that one could look up at the night sky and see the names of the constellations written out, the lines drawn between them: Ursa Major, Cassiopeia, Orion the great archer with his bow. In which case, why not have the trees named too?

But of course there were no stars visible here in the middle of the city, and it was too early for leaves, though he could see them budding above the hanging seedpods of the previous year. He thought of what they would look like when they were in full leaf, with the wind blowing through them, the canopy dropping some light rain that had collected here and there, setting the sky shimmering as the leaves danced in the wind.

'Think of it,' he said softly. They could add a feature that would show the tree in full leaf, even as you stood there looking at its bare branches. There would be a thousand leaves, a hundred thousand, a million even. One small breeze and they would all flutter and dance. What a thing it would be to recreate. A million leaves dancing, each to its own tune.

When it happens, Lauvaux thought, *when the wind blows through the branches of a tree, it looks like chaos.* But if he wanted to, he could arrange a program to be written that would follow every leaf and record its dance. Then he could make his own breeze blow through the square and know for every leaf which way it would twist or flutter or strain; would know how much wind could be withstood before it broke off and fell to the ground, a sad forgotten thing, left to rot, its days of dancing over. For then it would lie, waiting to be trodden underfoot, turning to a skeleton of white strands, until it finally disappeared and became part of the earth.

PART TWO

PART TWO

2.1

On his second full day as minister, Colbey woke around eight o'clock with a small sense of contentment. In the early hours he had risen to the sound of his alarm and read the privacy bill along with Mani's briefing document before returning to bed. His first bill, ready to be signed off.

Chloe had arrived unannounced sometime around midnight, and although he had not heard his daughter creep in, she was even now fighting with his wife for the bathroom. The fact of it made him happy. As Colbey sat hunched over his paper at the kitchen table, he reflected on how the two women treated the apartment as if it were one contiguous space, their conversation continuing from room to room, bathroom to bedroom, bedroom to hall. He didn't really listen to what was said, most of it being, to his mind, fatuous, but the sound of their chatter warmed him and he felt, as he always did, a little leap of joy when he heard or saw that his daughter was overnighting at the flat with them.

There was a squeal that registered out of the white noise. 'Daddy,' she said coming into the kitchen, phone first, 'you're trending.' She turned the screen for him to see but he declined to look, giving a grunt of acknowledgement as if it was not news to him. In fact, it was not – he had seen it was the case already. Yesterday's flash mob was picking up momentum, and though he had tried, he couldn't seem to watch the footage without getting strangely upset, so he hoped Chloe would not dwell on it.

'And they caught some terrorists.'

Again he grunted. That he had also seen on the early feeds.

Clarissa was in still the bathroom. He could hear her humming and wished she would hurry up and come to clear the breakfast plates so that he could unfold his paper and lay it flat on the table. Of course he could do it himself, but long ago they had divided the chores between them and now there was some hideous stand-off where face was lost by doing the other's work for them. God, was everyone's marriage like this?

Evidently bored with her phone, Chloe put it down. She was going to try and talk to him although she knew he needed to read his paper in the morning.

'So what do you think about Ricky, then?' she asked.

He thought of ignoring her, but instead glanced up. 'What about Ricky?'

'Hah,' she said triumphantly, pulling her hair up into a pile on the top of her head. 'Don't you know?'

Colbey sighed. 'Know what?'

'That Ricky's standing for parliament.'

'Is he?'

Chloe smiled to see him confused. Sometimes he wondered why she got pleasure from that. Ricky was Clarissa's nephew. Her sister's son.

'Who for?'

'Who do you think?'

Colbey leaned on his paper. 'I have entirely no idea. I didn't know he was even political.'

'Well take a guess.'

'Tell me,' he said.

Chloe sniffed. 'Not you lot, of course.' She took a cold piece of toast and started to spread it with jam. 'He's not a dinosaur like you. He's a new socialist.'

'A Whigge? He's standing as a Whigge?'

'That's what I said, Daddy.' And she picked up her phone again, evidently pleased at the bombshell she had left in her wake.

'Since when?' Colbey asked. But Chloe was already as lost to his words as he had been to hers when he had been reading his paper.

Clarissa's humming grew closer and ceased as she came into the room. 'Since last week,' she said.

'Well why didn't you tell me? Why hasn't *he* told me?' Colbey lifted the edge of his paper and pushed the empty toast rack in his wife's direction in the hope it would spur her into action. He picked up his phone and looked to see if there were any messages from her nephew. There were not.

Clarissa expertly swept up the plates, balancing them on one hand while she reached for a cloth to wipe the table. 'I expect he wanted to tell you himself when he sees you at the cricket match.'

'They don't need to come to that,' Colbey said unfolding his paper and turning the page, trying to make a point that he had been waiting too long to be able to do so. 'Please tell your sister she really doesn't need to.'

He wanted to know how long Clarissa had known about her nephew standing for parliament and why she hadn't told him, but he knew somehow to ask would lead to a row and it was such a good morning, he couldn't bear the thought of it.

Clarissa made herself a coffee and, pulling a magazine from a pile on the countertop, joined them at the table. With a sigh, Colbey refolded his paper in two to make space for her.

There was a moment's peace where Colbey managed to get nearly through an interesting article about some Silicon Valley billionaires who had bought an island nation in the Pacific and were renaming it Nirvana when he realised his wife was holding up a picture of a strip of white sand beside a turquoise sea.

'Look at that, darling, *that's* Bequia.' She had perhaps been talking in detail about it for some time. He nodded as if to signal he had seen and had heard, while really he was waiting for her to stop talking so he could ask her about the article he was reading. A US senator was trying to argue that the billionaires' purchase of the island was illegal under international law, and that the US shouldn't recognise it. He wanted to know what she thought because she remembered the law she had studied at university remarkably well.

When it seemed she had finished telling him about the beach, he said, 'What makes a country a country?'

Clarissa frowned. 'Like Bequia?'

'Yes, like Bequia. But any country, really. If you want to start a country, what do you need for it to be legally recognised?'

She frowned. 'There was a treaty… What was it called now? It lays down the requirements: land of a certain area, population of a certain size, some sort of institution for government.'

'So, any island that has a government of its own could claim to be a country?'

'No. It also needs to be recognised by the other countries of the world. So… some countries that you might think are very obviously countries might not be recognised by the whole of the world. I think that's right? But I think Bequia is part of Antigua. I don't think it's a country in its own right anyway.'

That made sense to Colbey. 'And if you bought an island that was already a country? Would that make a difference?'

Clarissa looked concerned. 'Is someone buying Bequia?'

Colbey looked at her in surprise. 'Why do you keep bringing Bequia into it? No, not Bequia, any country.'

'But we're talking about Bequia.'

Colbey noticed his daughter glance up from her phone. She was a good conversational weather vane though he doubted she had heard a word said since her phone had been picked up again.

'Why would I be talking about Bequia? I'm talking about these men, these billionaires who have bought an island.'

'But not Bequia?'

'No, not Bequia,' Colbey said, unable to not sound exasperated and immediately regretted it as his wife flushed red. He tried to parse back through what she might have been saying about the beach in the magazine. Obviously it was a beach in Bequia, wherever that was.

'I think sometimes when I talk,' said his wife, the clenching of her jaw visible from where Colbey sat, 'you pretend to listen, but don't actually have the faintest fucking interest in anything I've got to say.'

There were two paths open to Colbey. Mollifying, which he doubted would work because his wife was entirely correct and it would be difficult to claim that he had been listening when he didn't know what all this Bequia nonsense was about or brazen it out. He opted for the latter.

'For god's sake, Clarissa. I'm trying to read the paper so I'm up to date on what's going on in the world before I go into the office as a bloody minister and sit in bloody cabinet meetings and help run the bloody country. I haven't time to be sitting talking about beaches in the Caribbean that we are never, *ever*, likely to go to.'

He knew from the fact that she said nothing that he had made a fatal mistake somewhere in that speech.

He folded his paper up. 'What?' he said roughly. 'What now?'

But his wife rose and left the room.

Colbey turned to his daughter, who, without looking up from her phone, said, 'It's where Mummy wants you to go on holiday with that fat old lump of a prime minister and his wife.'

Colbey groaned. 'I thought that was Mustique?'

Chloe looked up from her phone in shock. 'Daddy, don't be ridiculous. Nobody goes to Mustique any more except reality TV stars and wannabes.'

Clarissa came back into the room and started to throw the plates from the countertop into the dishwasher. 'I suppose you think we're wannabes, do you?'

'Look,' said Colbey. 'I misunderstood. I thought it was Mustique you wanted to go to with Ewan and Zandra. I didn't know, or I had forgotten, it was Bequia.'

'And Jonnie and Juliana, and all of their set, including—'

'But we've been through this. We can't keep up with these people. We can't afford it, and we'll just make ourselves unhappy trying.'

'No. You'll make yourself unhappy trying. And I'll be unhappy if we don't try. And in any event, we *can* afford it, there's the money in the savings account.'

'That's for emergencies. This isn't an emergency.'

This was better. This was familiar territory. Next they would be on to the fact that he would prefer to holiday somewhere that she considered 'dull as ditch water', and he would argue that dull wasn't bad, dull was a chance to recharge one's batteries, to sleep, to read, to paint, to wander around some out-of-the-way backwater in torn dirty clothes with no chance of bumping into a neighbour, a constituent, a colleague. Certainly not one's boss. Certainly not the owner of a tabloid rag who might sneak up and take a photo of you snoring with drool coming out of your mouth to be useful for when you fell out of favour with such a set.

He stood and folded his paper and he knew he was in the right at the essence of it – they couldn't afford it, but still he felt shitty. Whose fault was it that they couldn't afford it? His, of course. For if he had been and become all she had hoped of him when they had married, then they would have been able to afford it.

'I'm sorry, darling. We really can't afford it,' he said planting a kiss on her cheek which she didn't try to evade, but stared stony-faced at the egg spoons soaking in cold water in the sink. 'Let's get some lovely villa in Provence, near the Killeys' place, again. You loved that last year. Big enough for us all, a couple of Chloe's friends and your sister's lot too, if they want.'

'Don't drag me into this,' Chloe said, also getting up from the table and pushing between them to make for her bedroom.

Clarissa nodded and said, 'Whatever. Whatever you want, Harry.' She smiled weakly and, sad that another morning had started with a row, Colbey left for the office.

As he sat in the car, he thought of his father. 'Family is everything,' he used to say. 'You stick with your family come what may, for better or worse.' Colbey wondered what advice he would give now if he were around. He wanted to ask his father 'But what if *she* won't? What if she continually thinks everything is for the worst, for the poorer? Even when it's not? Even when they were in health, in richer, in better? What then? Wouldn't she be happier in a different family? With some other man sticking with her come what may?'

Eventually, Colbey realised his driver was knocking on the interconnecting window to draw his attention to the fact they were already in Whitehall. He called Mani to ask him to send someone down to help carry the red boxes as they drove underneath the building, and getting no reply asked the security guard to arrange it instead. Then, with his unfinished paper still tucked under his arm, and just his slim red box held in his other hand, he hurried towards the lift. At least up there, in his giant new office, there would be some peace in which he could finish his paper.

2.2

Kanha woke to a dry mouth and the sound of someone tapping softly at a keyboard. The bed was unfamiliar. She braved one eye open. Through an open doorway, she could see a black leather sofa, chrome standing lamps, a polished floor of neat wooden chevrons. She levered herself onto an elbow with a moment of rising panic, but the sheets smelt freshly laundered and the figure hunched over a desk in the far corner was familiar. Mani. She lay back down again.

Hearing her stir, Mani turned round and smiled. 'Kettle in the kitchen. Ibuprofen on the counter. Peppermint for me, please, and I'd go for another slice.' He turned back to the screen.

Checking what she was wearing – her silk shirt from yesterday and not-too-small knickers – Kanha gingerly got out of bed and stumbled out of the bedroom. An expanse of sky presented itself. Beyond the window was a small balcony with a round table and a couple of fold-up chairs. There was a pleasant smell of toast in the room.

A few minutes later she put Mani's tea and a slice of toast beside his keyboard and then sank gratefully onto the soft dark sofa, a steaming cup of coffee clutched in her hands, a plate with two thickly buttered brown slices, the glossy whirls already melting and slipping, balanced on her bare thighs, and the painkillers safely consigned to her stomach. She could see her skirt and jacket arranged on a hanger up against the back of a door, with her tights carefully laid over them.

'What time is it?' she said.

'Just gone six.'

'We didn't…?'

There was a pause in the tapping. 'Subject didn't even come up. I slept on the sofa. Happy to enter into a conversation now if you'd—'

Kanha picked up a felt coaster from the table in front of her and threw it at him. It bounced off his back unremarked upon. 'What are you doing?'

'Buying drugs.'

She inhaled the too-hot coffee. 'I feel like a cat threw up in my throat.' Banks of grey cloud stalked between the buildings of the city skyline.

'What are you doing now?' she said.

'Still buying drugs.' He held up a finger to indicate he wouldn't be much longer and she wondered if she could be bothered to get up and put her skirt on for the sake of decency.

'It's early for you to be up,' she said. 'Did you even go to bed?'

On the coffee table, alongside the soft felt coasters, was her handbag and the crumpled copy of Dvořáček's privacy bill. Trying not to make a sound she used a finger to turn it to face her, but the papers rustled when they caught on the edge of a TV remote. God, had she been talking about it with Mani last night?

Finishing what he was doing with a flourish of his fingers, Mani turned round. 'I have a breakfast meeting with the new boss. Which is apparently like an ordinary meeting, except I have to bring coffee and breakfast.'

'Aren't you the brown-noser these days?'

'Don't call me names.'

'Don't be a millennial.'

'Don't be a dinosaur.' Mani smiled and swivelled his chair over to join her. 'And it's *acting* principal private secretary, you might remember if you had any recall of last night.'

'Ah yes. The celebratory promotion drinks.'

'Which you drank a lot of, if I recall. Am I right?'

Kanha sipped at her coffee and shrugged. 'Someone had to.'

The previous night when she had found him, Mani had been celebrating a surprise promotion with a bunch of geeky civil servant chums who drank like… whatever the opposite of fish was. She vaguely remembered missing her last train home. They had walked here after stopping off at her office for some reason. She frowned as she tried to remember why. God, she hoped it wasn't anything inappropriate.

'Where exactly are we?' she said.

'Vauxhall.'

'Oh.' Kanha nodded, and the memory of staggering across the bridge came back to her.

'It was good to catch up,' Mani said.

Kanha blew a little harrumphing noise. 'Yeah? If I hadn't happened to see your name in the directory, we never would have.'

'Don't start all that again.' Mani got up and fetched the hanger with Kanha's skirt and tights and brought them over to her, and she peered at the screen behind him.

'Are you really buying drugs?'

He ran a thumb over his lips. 'Just a little marijuana. Safer on the net than from a junkie in the street. They deliver like Amazon these days. Even use Amazon boxes.'

'You haven't changed.'

'Have you?'

Kanha shrugged. 'Fair point. And are you still into all that hacking business? As I recall you wouldn't give me a straight answer last night.'

Mani turned his back on her, logged out of the computer and pulled its plug out. 'Hacking? No, I was never into that.'

'Yes, you were, you liar.' She took the empty plate off her lap and started to get dressed, pulling her tights up and smoothing down her skirt. 'Anyway, where have you been all this time?'

Mani grinned. 'We did this last night.'

'Did we? Well, let's just say I'm a bit fuzzy on the details. Let's do it again.'

'Just here and there, you know.'

'No, I don't. One minute you were there, my partner in crime. My cool-as-fuck intern, us against the arsehole senator. The next you were gone. I was worried, you know.'

'I sent you a postcard.'

'I think I still have it somewhere. Hawaii, right?'

'Yeah, well, the surfing career never took off, so here I am. General political dogsbody again.'

'But why Britain?'

'Why not, right?'

They were quiet for a moment.

'Mmm,' she said, unconvinced. 'So acting PPS for Colbey, eh? Well done, you.'

'He's a good man, isn't he?' Mani said.

'Who, Colbey?'

'Yes, Colbey.'

Kanha considered for a moment. 'Maybe. I don't know him that well. Why hasn't he signed off the bill?'

'He wanted to read it.'

Kanha pulled a face and walked into the hall to find her shoes. 'It's due for debate. All very laudable, but... Can you make it a priority of the breakfast meeting please? Hey, did you polish my shoes? God, you really haven't changed, have you? How many hours sleep a night do you get these days?'

Mani picked up her handbag and the bill from the table and brought them to her in the hall. 'Have you read it?'

'The privacy bill? Of course not.'

'Tut tut, Chief Whip.'

'Jesus. You sound like a pompous old civil servant already. I've read the summary, same as anyone else with a life.'

Mani shook his head. 'It's awesome stuff. I helped draft some of it. See here—'

'Yes, yes,' said Kanha, not really listening. She knew perfectly well what was in the bill.

'What's this, though? This isn't the bill.'

Kanha said, 'So why exactly does Colbey have a department full of newbies?'

'Bad luck, I guess. Still...' Mani grinned.

'Lucky for some?'

Mani grinned wider. 'Lucky for some.'

'And what became of the department's real Private Secretary?'

'She's off with stress.'

'Really?'

'Was very close to Dvořáček...'

Kanha groaned. 'Not another one. I don't even have her on my list. Where did you hear that?'

'Off the grid.'

'The man was a machine. What does that mean – off the grid? Is that some sort of hacking term?'

'I mean someone in a pub told me.'

'You're such an arse. You really haven't changed.'

She pointed at the bill. 'Well, this will be good for Colbey's career at any rate. Giving the people what they want – privacy. It's very popular with the voters.' She looked around for her phone and, not finding it, went back into the bedroom to look around the bed and on the floor. She came back, a note of worry in her mind.

'But this isn't the bill, Esme,' Mani said.

'I've lost my phone.'

'We dropped it off at your office, remember?'

'Ahh, yes, I do now.'

'What is this?'

'It's the legislation Dvořáček tried to sneak through in his private member's bill before he shot himself. Shit, I've got a cabinet meeting this morning. What time is it now?'

'Seven. Last night, when we got back, you said you thought Dvořáček was being blackmailed.'

Kanha bit her lip. 'Did I? I was probably just talking shit. Don't mind me.'

'So you think his extramarital escapades were spied upon? With his phone perhaps?'

'It was a government phone, secured by GCHQ,' Kanha said, thinking out loud. 'But he'd smashed the TV in his hotel room.'

'What hotel room?'

Kanha didn't answer and turned to a mirror. She twisted her hair up into its bun, watching Mani scan through the papers behind her. Then he faltered. His eyes went wide and his hand flew to his head. She saw it distinctly. He swallowed and wiped an imagined piece of sweat from his brow.

'What is it?' she said, turning to face him.

But by then he had recovered and shrugged, no feature of concern on his face. Had she imagined it?

'It's just an earlier draft of the current bill,' he said. 'Typos corrected, probably a few little legal nuances cleaned up.' He folded the paper back into four and put it in her bag, which he handed to her. Kanha turned away again to watch him once more in the mirror. No, she hadn't imagined it. He was composed now, but that wasn't what she had seen a moment ago. They looked at each other in the glass, and she felt sure he must realise, knowing now that she had been able to see him in the mirror as he was reading the bill, that she must have seen him falter. He seemed to be searching her face to find out for sure.

They had been so close when they had both found themselves like fish out of water in the wild west of Washington, two hopeless

'A Whigge? He's standing as a Whigge?'

'That's what I said, Daddy.' And she picked up her phone again, evidently pleased at the bombshell she had left in her wake.

'Since when?' Colbey asked. But Chloe was already as lost to his words as he had been to hers when he had been reading his paper.

Clarissa's humming grew closer and ceased as she came into the room. 'Since last week,' she said.

'Well why didn't you tell me? Why hasn't *he* told me?' Colbey lifted the edge of his paper and pushed the empty toast rack in his wife's direction in the hope it would spur her into action. He picked up his phone and looked to see if there were any messages from her nephew. There were not.

Clarissa expertly swept up the plates, balancing them on one hand while she reached for a cloth to wipe the table. 'I expect he wanted to tell you himself when he sees you at the cricket match.'

'They don't need to come to that,' Colbey said unfolding his paper and turning the page, trying to make a point that he had been waiting too long to be able to do so. 'Please tell your sister she really doesn't need to.'

He wanted to know how long Clarissa had known about her nephew standing for parliament and why she hadn't told him, but he knew somehow to ask would lead to a row and it was such a good morning, he couldn't bear the thought of it.

Clarissa made herself a coffee and, pulling a magazine from a pile on the countertop, joined them at the table. With a sigh, Colbey refolded his paper in two to make space for her.

There was a moment's peace where Colbey managed to get nearly through an interesting article about some Silicon Valley billionaires who had bought an island nation in the Pacific and were renaming it Nirvana when he realised his wife was holding up a picture of a strip of white sand beside a turquoise sea.

'Look at that, darling, *that's* Bequia.' She had perhaps been talking in detail about it for some time. He nodded as if to signal he had seen and had heard, while really he was waiting for her to stop talking so he could ask her about the article he was reading. A US senator was trying to argue that the billionaires' purchase of the island was illegal under international law, and that the US shouldn't recognise it. He wanted to know what she thought because she remembered the law she had studied at university remarkably well.

When it seemed she had finished telling him about the beach, he said, 'What makes a country a country?'

Clarissa frowned. 'Like Bequia?'

'Yes, like Bequia. But any country, really. If you want to start a country, what do you need for it to be legally recognised?'

She frowned. 'There was a treaty... What was it called now? It lays down the requirements: land of a certain area, population of a certain size, some sort of institution for government.'

'So, any island that has a government of its own could claim to be a country?'

'No. It also needs to be recognised by the other countries of the world. So... some countries that you might think are very obviously countries might not be recognised by the whole of the world. I think that's right? But I think Bequia is part of Antigua. I don't think it's a country in its own right anyway.'

That made sense to Colbey. 'And if you bought an island that was already a country? Would that make a difference?'

Clarissa looked concerned. 'Is someone buying Bequia?'

Colbey looked at her in surprise. 'Why do you keep bringing Bequia into it? No, not Bequia, any country.'

'But we're talking about Bequia.'

Colbey noticed his daughter glance up from her phone. She was a good conversational weather vane though he doubted she had heard a word said since her phone had been picked up again.

'Why would I be talking about Bequia? I'm talking about these men, these billionaires who have bought an island.'

expats, her a Brit, him an Aussie. They had kept each other sane with heavy drinking sessions in a grungy hockey bar, laughing at the madness of it all. She frowned and he saw her frown, but said nothing.

'Don't be late for cabinet, Minister,' he said eventually.

'Nor you for your important breakfast meeting, *acting* principal private secretary.'

Mani pulled the door open.

They looked at each other awkwardly, then he said, 'Hey, let's be careful out there.' It was a reference to an old cop series that she'd introduced him to, that he'd subsequently become hooked on.

Kanha smiled and nodded. As he closed the door behind her, she realised she would need to scour every inch of Dvořáček's bill to try to figure out what Mani had seen. And then she would need to figure out why he had tried to hide it from her.

2.3

After he had finished reading his newspaper, Colbey walked the length of his office, then came back and stood by the windows. He tried hard not to feel proud or elated, or at least to not let the fact that he felt proud and elated be obvious should someone come into the room. The thought prompted him to remember the task the PM had set.

He started with the bookshelves at the far end of the room, but there was nothing there that might be Dvořáček's black book, just a few dreary law texts and some stationery. He picked up a notepad and a pen.

The low cupboards dotted beneath the windows were not only empty, but smelt faintly of furniture polish. That just left the desk, but Colbey found that its drawers had been similarly cleaned out, even of those odd crumbs of dirt and dust that usually collect in the corners. Someone had been thorough.

Morland came into the room, and Colbey closed the drawer quickly, feeling a rush of guilt as if he had been caught snooping into someone else's affairs. But it was his office now, he reminded himself. Crouching down, the permanent secretary worried at a loose edge of the rug. 'I'll have someone come and fix that,' he said as Mani knocked and came in carrying a plate of pastries and a tray of takeout coffees, and Colbey said, 'Right, let's get down to it, shall we?'

He looked across the room. The conference table took up most of it, beside which were the two sofas and three – he counted them – three armchairs. A surfeit of choices for where to take his meetings. What was the protocol? Was it soft furnishing for one's PS and PPS? Colbey hesitated at the division between the two, but Mani came and laid the breakfast down at one end of the table, so Colbey pretended he had merely been pausing for a moment's reflection and hurried on over to sit at its top.

'I have arranged access to Dvořáček's diary as requested, Minister,' said Morland. 'You will find a tab labelled "Previous Minister" in your email app.'

'Thank you.'

'Did you have a chance to read the bill? Are you in a position to sign it off?'

'I certainly have. It's a very good bill.'

'Thank you, Minister.'

'I commend it to the House.'

While Mani helped himself to a pain au chocolat, Morland smiled his thin smile that wasn't really a smile. 'Excellent. To sign it off just log into the departmental system, navigate to the bill and you'll find an authorise button available only to you. It's very straightforward, but let me know if you have any difficulties. Shall I call the rest of the senior management team in to join us?'

'God, no,' said Colbey, taking a croissant and dusting the sugar off his as yet blank notebook. 'It's ridiculous they're all so new. I think I might have to speak to the PM and suggest the issue is looked at.'

Ignoring not only Mani's plate of pastries but the coffee too, Morland said, 'The rotations can be frustrating, but the belief is it makes us better civil servants.'

'But nobody gets a chance to develop any real expertise.'

'The argument is they gain expertise at being good civil servants.'

'But it's a ridiculous merry-go-round. I bet they get promoted every time they rotate.'

'As they gain a broader depth of experience...'

'So they just spiral their way up, not really knowing anything about anything, other than how to be a good civil servant, until...'

'Yes, Minister?'

'Until...' But Colbey didn't say out loud the last thought in his mind, which was *until they bang up against a ceiling made of the leather soles of posh Loakes jettisoned in from above.*

Morland smiled his non-smile again and said, 'Well, once the bill is signed off, we can all move on to other matters.'

Mani, helping himself to another croissant, said, 'Was there something that you wanted to change, Minister? I could look and see if we have other versions, perhaps an earlier draft to compare with?'

Did he want to see earlier drafts? Maybe, but Colbey knew himself. If he looked at earlier drafts, he would no doubt find something that might be improved upon. It was too late to go backwards at this point. At dinner, the PM had been clear the bill needed to be passed before the election date could be announced.

'No,' Colbey said. 'It's a good bill and well drafted. It's about time we had more robust laws about data privacy. The voting public are very concerned, you know. This bill will stand as the first major leap forward in protection for the privacy of the British people for over twenty years. We have to guard against invasion of privacy not only by private enterprise, but by government institutions. Here at last we have – this is good. Mani, would you note this down?'

Mani picked up his phone and sat ready to type Colbey's words.

'Here, at last, we have legislation designed to ensure the British state will never be allowed to use technological advances to invade the privacy of its own citizens – Are you getting this? – Britain will never be China, it will never be an Orwellian Big Brother state, no Ruritania here. Is that right? Ruritania? Well, anyway, you get the gist.'

'Yes, I think we get the gist,' Morland said. 'Mani, would you work something up and send it to us both this afternoon?'

'Will do,' said Mani. 'Minister, don't forget you have a cabinet meeting at eleven this morning.'

Colbey laughed inwardly at the thought he might forget to go to his first cabinet meeting, but thanked his new PPS for his efficiency.

As soon as his two public servants had left and the door closed behind them, Colbey got up and walked the length of his conference table, softly repeating the start of his new speech.

'In any democracy,' he said as he wandered over to his collection of armchairs, 'there is a sacred trust between a government and its citizens...' Was citizens the right word? Staring at the soft furnishing Colbey lost his thread.

Each of the chairs and sofas were upholstered in a green fabric faded to a slightly different hue. He suspected they had been in entirely different rooms exposed to differing amounts of sunlight, a few in a bright office, others in a dingy one, until some junior needing to refurbish the minister's office on a tight budget had noticed on some document somewhere that the department owned three green rayon upholstered armchairs and two sofas, and had scoured the building to reunite them.

Colbey thought they made the office look like a care home for the elderly. He would have been ashamed had he not known that every departmental minister's office was the same. Apart from the Treasury and the Foreign Office, of course. One had to keep up standards in front of the bankers and Johnny Foreigner.

'I will stand firm against a technological slide to a Big Brother state,' he muttered as he moved over to his desk, sat down, put his phone into the system's holder and waited for his monitor to load up the department's welcome page.

It was a moment's work to find the bill, and, as promised, there was the authorise button – bright red with the words *Minister*

Authorisation written in oversized lettering upon it; the programmers had obviously decided that ministers were either poorly sighted or very stupid.

'No other government has taken such leaps forward in protecting and ensuring the privacy of the British public...' Had he said 'British public' too many times now? Should it be 'UK'? He would ask Mani to check.

Colbey emptied the box containing his personal things, which was still sitting on the desk where he had dropped it the day before. He stood the photo of Clarissa up, but then after a moment's reflection, opened one of the empty drawers and put it in there instead. She would not be able to saunter into the departmental building as easily as she could wander through the Houses of Parliament with her staff pass.

The stapler, pencil tub and plaster rabbit were given carefully chosen positions on the huge blotter inlaid on the surface of the desk. Colbey opened up his new notebook and began to write down his speech.

'No other government...'

It was dingy at this end of the room. There was a brass desk lamp before him so he switched it on. By its light, he saw a spot on the desk that shone a little. He touched the mark with his fingertip, and it came away with scarlet dust that he realised must be blood, if not worse. He took his handkerchief from his pocket, wiped his finger and then scrubbed at the mark. The worst of it came away, leaving a pink smear on the white cotton.

As he wrote down his speech, his eyes kept returning to the mark that remained. Finally, with annoyance, he picked up the heavy brass lamp and moved it to cover the stain. But in doing so, he uncovered something else.

Beneath where it had stood were some words carved deep into the wood. The letters were ornately stencilled, curlicue depressions, through the centre of which ran a line of blue ink like a stream at the bottom of long looping canyon: *Quis custodiet ipsos custodes, Minister?*

Although he was only a grammar school boy, his education had included a little Latin. *Who guards the guardians, Minister?*

Colbey reflected for a moment. He heard the door handle turn and quickly moved the lamp back to its original position as Morland came into the room. His permanent secretary held a few sheets of paper in his hand.

'The directory of the departmental paintings, Minister. I'll leave it on the table here for you.'

When Morland was gone, Colbey lifted the lamp again and peered underneath. No, he had not imagined it.

For the next hour, he composed his speech for the bill's second reading, writing it by hand over and over in the notepad until it was good enough to dictate. The words appeared on his screen as he spoke.

When he was done he emailed it to Mani with a copy to Morland, adding that he had included some further suggestions, just in case they hadn't entirely got the gist earlier. Then he reached up with his finger hovering over the privacy bill's *authorise* button. He looked at the lamp and put his hand down again.

Colbey flicked over, found the email system and clicked into Dvořáček's electronic diary, but there was nothing of interest there. What Mani had said about older versions of the bill nagged at him, and he had a sudden thought.

He pulled his phone out of the holder, the screen folding to black as he did so, and took his coat from the stand by the door. He determined that after the cabinet meeting he might get his driver to take him over to the House to get a copy of this private member's bill of Dvořáček's and see what it had contained.

2.4

Cabinet meetings were something of a farce these days, thought Kanha as she pushed her way through the milling circus thronging the corridors of Number Ten, waiting for the doors of the cabinet room to be opened. When at last they were, she drifted like everyone else into the room and saw with the usual stab of relief that her name tag was on the main table where it should be, opposite the prime minister who sat with his back to the fireplace. Others had not fared so well and the usual complaints could be heard here and there.

Annoyingly, the prime minister's national security advisor, Anthony Tirrell, a thoroughly unpleasant man, had been seated to her left, which was not usual. She had noticed that the man had been worming his way into Ewan's affections of late. As an advisor, rather than a minister, he would normally be consigned to an off-table seat at the back of the room. Perhaps it was thanks to that morning's successful dawn raid on a terrorist cell, which had, according to the Mouth of the Mob, been triggered by a tip-off from someone in Tirrell's team, that he had made the leap to the inner circle. If it were true, it meant the website once again knew the facts before they, the cabinet, did. The usual owner of the spot taken by Tirrell, the foreign secretary, arrived with an expression of disgust.

'What the hell's this?' she said. 'Where the fuck am I, then?'

Kanha pointed to the space on her right. Not a bad position, but a slightly inferior one. As the foreign secretary sat down, the defence minister arrived and was even more put out to find that his usual spot two on from Kanha's had been given to the home secretary, who had been shifted to make room for the foreign secretary's move.

When he finally found his name tag on an off-table seat behind him, he deftly scooped it up and switched it with that of the home secretary, muttering 'Disgraceful' as he did so, much to Kanha's amusement.

'William, you can't do that,' the foreign secretary protested.

'Why not?' he said. 'Tirrell's already made a fool of her this morning. I hear her MI5 heads are furious.'

At that moment the home secretary herself arrived, puffing and out of breath. 'Thought I was going to be late,' she said. 'Say, why am I over here at the back?'

She waved a folder at the cabinet secretary.

'Jerry, what's going on? Why am I over here?'

Turning his back on her, the defence minister leaned into Kanha and the foreign secretary and growled, 'What I want to know is where Tirrell's getting his intel from.'

As he spoke, Kanha's deputy chief whip, Paddy, passed by to take his usual seat behind them, and settling down threw in a cheery bombshell. 'Our lot are saying he's been given access to GCHQ's listening systems.'

Kanha rolled her eyes at him, but it was too late to stop him.

'Is that true?' said the foreign secretary and home secretary simultaneously, the latter still waving at the cabinet secretary to try to get him to come over.

'It's true that they're saying it,' Kanha said carefully. It wouldn't do to upset either of these two women. The home secretary, a big blousy woman, was highly strung – Kanha and the PM had spent

many hours trying to keep her focused since she was appointed –
and the other, the foreign secretary, known for her lavender suits,
was a formidable political beast that Kanha thought best to keep
on side.

'Surely, *you'd* know if it's true, Sheryl?' she said to the foreign
secretary, whose department encompassed GCHQ.

'Well, I never authorised it,' Sheryl said. 'But that doesn't mean
someone else hasn't.' She raised her eyes wearily in the direction of
the prime minister.

'It's a disgrace,' the defence minister growled again, and Kanha
saw that he was glaring at Tirrell who had entered the room and
was making his way over. His progress was slowed by the toadying
congratulations of bag-carriers as he passed. The defence minister
curled his lip like a dog that sees its enemy across the street, but
it was only noticed by her as everyone else had turned to watch
what would happen now that the cabinet secretary had arrived in
response to the home secretary's persistent yoo-hooing.

'Finally, Jerry,' she said. 'Now what an earth is all this?'

The cabinet secretary took one look at the mood of the defence
minister and seeing immediately what had been done, picked up
the home secretary's name tag and moved it back to the table by
demoting the education secretary to the off-table seat instead.

'Well, she's late,' he muttered, hurrying off. 'So she only has
herself to blame.'

This time Kanha smiled openly.

The foreign secretary had waved her own special advisor
over from his corner seat and loudly whispered to him, 'Find out
whether Anthony Tirrell is cleared for access to GCHQ's listening
systems, will you.' The advisor nodded and started to make a note
on his pad, so she pushed at him. 'Now, I mean. Find it out it
now.' He stumbled back only to find he had bumped into the prime
minister who had come round to pour himself some coffee, and
with a series of strange bows and apologies, the assistant scurried

off. Finding him suddenly there, Kanha saw that the foreign secretary was not able to hold back from asking him herself.

'Did you give Tirrell access to GCHQ's systems?' she said. 'Did he use them for the tip-off he sent to the Met last night?'

'Goodness,' the PM said as he pumped coffee into a cup from one of the portable dispensers and looked round for the sugar. 'Not now, Sheryl.'

'So it's true then, is it?'

The defence minister leaned back. 'Is he using it to listen to my phone?'

Finding a nearly empty sugar bowl at last, the PM emptied its contents into his cup, then peered round the defence minister to look at the line of name tags on the table and frowned. *Not much gets past him,* Kanha thought.

'Let's take this to another meeting, shall we?' he said.

The defence minister growled audibly. 'What, like the National Security meeting?'

The PM looked round nervously at the number of bag-carriers and researchers that sat nearby. 'Esme, set up a meeting to discuss this, will you? And let's all focus on the good news for today, shall we?'

As he moved off with his coffee, he muttered to Kanha, 'It's like herding bloody cats.'

Tirrell finally arrived as the defence minister completed a negotiation with the health secretary to switch places so that he could sit even further from Tirrell. As that was an upgrade closer to the centre of the table, the health secretary was more than happy to oblige. Tirrell dumped his papers next to Kanha and as he sat down she couldn't help but agree with the PM that managing this lot was like herding cats. Tirrell smelt faintly of mothballs and sweat.

The home secretary leaned across both the foreign secretary and Kanha and said to him, 'Anthony. I wish you had told my lot about that terrorist intel before you told the Met police. I've quite a few unhappy campers in MI5, you know.'

Tirrell gave her a grin that showed a set of remarkably yellow, crooked teeth. It was a strange expression, which Kanha found he used wherever the conversation was heading.

'It was only a little tip one of my boys picked up from his sources,' he said. 'Nothing to get excited about.'

'People are saying you got it from GCHQ's system.'

'For god's sake, Helen,' the foreign secretary snapped, her eyes fixed front. 'Of course he didn't. If it had been intel from GCHQ, then *we* would have given it to the Met police.'

'And to us.'

'Yes, and to you.'

Tirrell said, 'I can reassure you, Helen, that it definitely wasn't from GCHQ. You can sleep easy there.'

'But do you have access to our system?' the foreign secretary said, turning at last to Tirrell.

'Our department has only the resources we've been authorised to have.' He smiled again and Kanha decided it was not unlike the smile of a deranged terrier.

Both the home secretary and foreign secretary turned away, and Tirrell leaned into Kanha and said, 'What a lot of fuss about nothing.'

With an involuntary motion, she found herself leaning away. '*Do* you have access to GCHQ's listening systems?' she said.

Tirrell moved to close the gap between them again, and the smell of mothballs became overpowering. 'Who doesn't, my dear?'

There was another row going on at the other end of the table, where a junior minister and the spad of a senior minister were arguing over who had the most right to sit on one of the last few chairs at the back of the room. Kanha saw Colbey arrive and promptly sit in it. She couldn't help smiling, but while they were waiting the interminable time it took to get these farcical meetings under way, Tirrell insisted on continuing to talk to her.

'I hear your team have been experimenting with bubble wrap?' he said. She wondered who he had heard it from. Surely he was too busy to be listening to her phone all day.

'The MPs are concerned,' she said. 'They think their phones are being used to spy on them.' Then she added, but not in an overly friendly way, 'I don't mean by you.'

'Well, they probably are. Not by us, I mean.'

'Shouldn't GCHQ give all our MPs protected phones, then?'

'What, so they can have carte blanche to creep about having their seedy affairs without anyone knowing? Perhaps if they acted more honourably, they wouldn't have anything to worry about.'

But the foreign secretary had overheard and hissed in Kanha's ear, 'He's stark-staring mad, you know. William said he was a bloody liability in the SAS, and he's a bloody liability to the PM, I tell you.'

But Tirrell whispered in her other ear, 'What they don't understand is that every Tom, Dick and Harry who wants to track them or listen to them can do so at any time. Why do you think we make everyone leave their phones downstairs? Even the ministers?'

'And who are Tom, Dick and Harry when they're at home?' Kanha said.

'These days? Could be any number of parties. And it's not just the phones. That's only the beginning.'

'Is that so?'

'Come on. You know better, surely? What can see watches, what can hear listens, what's written is read, what can be followed is tracked. The internet of things is everywhere, and anything can be hacked... that is if it doesn't already have open access from a nation state. Look around you – the conference phone, the security camera above our heads.'

'The camera on the television over there?'

'Goodness, yes. Any fourteen-year-old hacker with a few gizmos from the dark web could get into that if they wanted to.

Probably on it right now.' Then his top lip curled up just as the defence minister's had, and he glanced down the line of the table. 'Such a joke. These women and that fool need to get real.' He spat out the words. 'They're putting people in danger with their regulations and rules. The wicked world doesn't care about rules and regulations, you know. Like to see what they'd think if they were locked up in a cupboard for a year and fed nothing but rice. Bloody rice. Can't stand the stuff now.'

Kanha looked at him and realised that the foreign secretary might be right. Anthony Tirrell was not all there. Feeling uncomfortable, she reached and took a mint so as not to have to answer. She stuffed it in her mouth quickly, nodding slowly. The cold freshness took the edge off her alcohol-dehydrated gums.

Tirrell took one too.

'A little dusty, Esme?' he said. 'You look a bit tired. Almost like you spent the night in your office.' And he grinned at her with those terrible yellow teeth.

As the meeting began and the room fell to order, Kanha realised that while she had not spent the night in her office, her phone had.

2.5

Colbey's first cabinet meeting was something of a let-down. He no more felt like a critical part of the government there than he had as a lowly backbencher with no invite. Nothing was covered or discussed that wasn't already known from the newsfeeds. It seemed to him they were just going through the motions in the fancy cabinet room of Number Ten for the look of it. He had not spoken, had not been called to speak, and had not felt the need to push forward to do so. In fact, he had not even had a place at the table, had been forced to fight for one of the seats at the back.

He was surprised to find himself so disappointed. Now that he had agreed to take on the post of minister, surely he should have some say in the running of things? Otherwise wasn't he really nothing more than a glorified pen-pusher? What separated him from Morland?

Afterwards he headed over to the clerks' office to ask for a copy of Dvořáček's bill. They were an amiable bunch, the clerks. Colbey waited patiently while the MP for Suffolk asked a series of rather obvious questions and the clerk answered them equally patiently. It made Colbey think of Tom and how his friend had known so little when he had first started working for him. Colbey determined he would go over to Tom's meeting after all. He could just show his face, didn't need to stay long.

With that decision made and a realisation it meant he needed to get a shift on, he tapped on the counter beside him to show his starting impatience and the MP, seeing it was a minister waiting, took the hint and told the clerk he'd return later. Colbey admitted to himself that there were a few benefits that came with his new job.

'Do you happen to have,' Colbey asked the clerk, 'a copy of the private member's bill that Dvo—' He caught himself in time. 'That private member's bill of earlier in the week?'

The clerk raised her eyebrows. 'Of course,' she said, handing him a bound copy from the stacks behind her.

'That was quick,' said Colbey.

'It's a popular bill,' she said.

He flicked through the document and gave it back to her. It looked identical to the official one.

'Actually, you wouldn't be able to do me—'

'A comparison between the member's bill and the draft of the government's coming privacy bill?'

She looked rather pleased with herself, but couldn't help giving the game away, saying, 'As it happens, I did one just this morning for Esme Kanha. Let me print it off for you.'

Colbey thanked her and took the printout. On a quick flick through, jumping to pages where the red line caught his eye, he could see that most of the differences were minor drafting changes, but there was a large clause in Dvořáček's bill that wasn't in the government's version. He frowned and thought about the implications of Dvořáček's additional clause as he rolled the document up and put it in his pocket. It made his coat bulge out, so he pushed it down deeper to stop it working its way out, left the parliamentary estate and made his way across the square to the Queen Elizabeth II Exhibition Centre. He was ignored this time by the Mobsters who huddled together on the corner. They themselves were looking uneasily towards a group of protestors gathered at an opposing corner, blowing whistles, banging a drum and waving banners that Colbey could not read.

The room Tom had hired for the event was easy to find, marked on a noticeboard for visitors in the lobby.

The meeting had already started, so Colbey slipped in and sat on one of the few empty seats left at the back of the room. A well-groomed American woman's presentation was already under way, a slide of Taunton broken down into quadrants on the screen behind her. She was loud, confident, fast talking. Tom sat beside her, and Colbey had a sudden fear that his friend might not cope with the pressure of his new role.

The audience of party volunteers were the usual ragtag of retired folk and worthy students. When Tom spotted Colbey, he raised his eyebrows in an exaggerated show of surprise as the presenter clicked on to a slide showing generic people: a young boy with a skateboard, a harassed-looking mum with small children. Caricatures, thought Colbey, clichéd voting profiles. Glancing down at the papers he had picked up from his empty seat, he wondered if this was the exciting development that Tom had talked about. The woman presenting was a Ms Olivia Powers. He frowned to see there was a legal document in the pack, and he opened it up and flicked through it – a non-disclosure agreement, and a pretty restrictive one from the look of it.

Colbey only half listened to the presenter as he thought of the differences he had seen between the bill his department had prepared for its first reading and the version that Dvořáček had tried to sneak through. For that was what it was, he saw now. Dvořáček had tried to pass a different version of the bill, one that looked on the surface to be similar, but which had a rather important difference. Get up to speed, the PM had said.

'So, before knocking, take a moment to familiarise yourself with the starting question for each member of the household who might answer the door. There'll be photos of them on your tablets, so they should be easy to recognise.'

The presenter held up an earpiece. 'After you receive a response to your opening question, your next suggested question, response or statement will sound in the earpiece for you to repeat. The system is dynamic so it listens to the constituent's response and suggests something that the AI knows is likely to resonate with them.

'We'll hand the tablets and earpieces out when you go out canvassing, and I'm sorry to say, folks, we will be collecting them back at the end of each canvassing period. But when we finish for lunch today, we have a few sets here that you can all have a play with.'

An old gent with white hair, who was dressed up in a suit for his trip to town, raised a wavering hand. Ms Powers indicated he should speak and he stood slowly and deliberately.

'May I say how impressive this all is. You've made it very straightforward for us. I was just wondering – how many scripts are there? Would it be better if we had the electronic pads and earpieces a few days before so we can learn the scripts? That way we could talk more naturally, rather than look as if we're repeating from the computer like dull automatons.'

Ms Powers smiled. 'It's a great idea, there. Thank you for that. But the truth is there are too many different possible responses to memorise. Each one is personalised to the voter you're talking to and the AI dynamically adjusts the approach as the voter responds.'

She came around to the front of the desk and said, 'When we've used this technology in other countries we've found it increases—'

Tom said, 'Could you show them the graphs, Olivia?'

Olivia Powers obliged, clicking the presentation forward to a slide with some bar charts. 'Sure thing, Tom.

'When canvassers stick to the suggested responses, we've found it increases positive voter outcome by up to three hundred per cent compared to situations in which the canvasser ad-libs or uses a set script for every household. Keep the tablets open when you're talking to your constituents, stick to the responses given to you in your earpieces and we'll have this by-election in the bag, folks.'

Colbey thought the old boy looked like he might follow up with another question, but he pursed his lips and sat down again. A lady in a big blue coat a few seats away from him spoke up next, calling out her question. 'How does the computer decide what to suggest?'

Ms Powers smiled. 'Good question, there, thank you for asking it. The categories are based on what we know about voters from surveys they've completed and information they've offered up.'

'I see,' the lady called. 'But surely not everyone will have filled in a survey.'

'You're very right. So sometimes the information about voters will come from their spending habits or information gathered through lawful means using their internet searches and the placement of regulated cookies.'

'Cookies? Like biscuits?'

But the question was not heard by anyone other than those around her because the old gent, standing once more, said, 'So you spy on people and then tell them what you know they want to hear?'

'Everything we do is strictly regulated, and we only use information that people have agreed to provide.'

Someone stuck up their hand and said, 'What is AI?' and someone else from the audience jumped in to say, 'It means artificial intelligence. Machine learning, you know, computer intelligence.'

To this there were some gasps of awe and a few *oohs*.

'Anyway,' said the man from the audience who had spoken out. 'Who cares where the information comes from? If it helps us talk to people about the issues that matter to them, it'll save a lot of time.'

'Exactly. Any other questions? No?'

'So, is this micro-targeting?' the older chap persisted. 'Isn't that illegal?'

'Absolutely not,' said Ms Powers. 'Everything we do is one hundred per cent lawful. And we make sure of that. Now, if there are no other questions—'

Colbey raised his hand and saw a lick of worry pass over Tom's face as he stood. 'Could I just ask, when you say "we gather the information through lawful means", legally speaking, who is *we*?'

'Sorry, who are you?' asked Ms Powers and after peering at him she said, 'Harold Colbey.'

'That's right,' said Colbey.

She swiped through her tablet. 'I don't have you on my list.' She looked at Tom, who looked down at his hands.

'You shouldn't be in this meeting. It's for a pre-approved audience and you have to sign an NDA to attend.'

Colbey felt his face flush red. 'Ms Powers, forgive me, I should have introduced myself. I'm the Minister for Personal Information.'

'I know that.' She gestured at her e-pad. 'But you shouldn't be here.' Then she said briskly, 'Now that you are, you'll need to sign the non-disclosure agreement.' She looked down at Tom who frowned and looked at his hands again, and Colbey thought they probably shouldn't continue this in front of the volunteers who were looking excited at this sniff of in-house drama.

'Perhaps we could discuss the matter later...'

Ms Powers gave a strange little laugh and said, 'You can discuss whatever you want whenever you want, but you do have to sign that NDA now that you've attended the meeting.'

Colbey felt his temper rising and knew he was going to struggle to control it if this ridiculous woman didn't stop saying that.

'I don't need to sign an NDA, Ms Powers. I'm a member of the cabinet and to be honest I'm not sure I understand who agreed that our party volunteers should be signing NDAs with –' he looked down at the papers he had picked up '– Voter Services, anyway. And if we're asking our volunteers to sign NDAs, they should be governed by English law, not...'

At this the woman herself flushed red, but before she could respond, from somewhere off to the side of the crowd, a clear and polite voice rang out. Colbey looked across to see a well-dressed man with wiry hair and a tailored grey suit sitting alone on a chair, his back to the wall and one long leg crossed casually over the other. He was not part of the audience, nor part of the presentation team.

'Can I just interrupt there, Ms Powers, and pick that one up?' He apologised to Colbey politely and formally on behalf of Voter Services for any confusion. 'Some of the technologies we are developing have been worked upon with some of your senior party members, in fact your PM himself was involved, and he would prefer them kept confidential. They were keen for there to be an NDA, and the terms of it were agreed specifically with them. I'm sure he'd be happy to reassure you on that when you next speak to him. But of course there's absolutely no need for us to have one from yourself, Minister – after all, you are, as you say, the Minister for Privacy, are you not?'

There was a titter from somewhere in the crowd, but Colbey thought only that there hadn't been any confusion and that they still hadn't answered his question about who exactly Voter Services was.

However, the stranger's polite pitch at once made Colbey feel a fool for raising his voice to match Ms Powers'.

He thanked the Frenchman, agreeing that perhaps he was not up to speed and would catch up with his party leaders after the meeting to raise his concerns, and then he sat down, trying not to let his worry show. Ms Powers asked if there were any more questions, but at a stubborn silence from the audience, no one wanting to speak after the unexpected quarrel, she called the meeting to a close and invited everyone to attend the buffet, which was shortly to arrive.

Tom still looked intently at his hands, and Colbey thought how tired he looked. No, not tired, old – old like the rest of them – and Tom had once been his and Clarissa's young friend. Now that was a depressing thought.

The meeting broke up and the volunteers took to cliques to drink coffee and eat their floppy free sandwiches while they gossiped about their new candidate, declaring she would never be able to fill Dvořáček's shoes.

Colbey tried to leave as quickly as he could, but the party volunteers closest to him were delighted for a chance to pin down a minister to let him know where they thought the party was going wrong. He listened politely to a few as he inched his way towards the door, giving the old lie about being needed in a debate. When he reached it, he turned to mouth an apology to Tom, but couldn't see him. As far as he could tell, the Frenchman was no longer in the room either. When Colbey finally did manage to escape, he caught a fleeting glimpse of him disappearing down the corridor.

The meeting papers were still in his hand. He glanced through the attendee list, but only the volunteers, Tom and Ms Powers were named. There was no mention of the Frenchman.

Colbey looked at the worrying gagging order. Could Tom be being unduly influenced by this company, he wondered? Why would Tom allow such a thing?

Colbey found he could ask his friend the question himself, for he came across him in the Gents, coming out of a stall with wide eyes.

'Christ, I'm sorry for the scene,' Colbey said.

Tom washed his face in the sink. 'Not a problem. The whole thing's fucking dodgy as hell. It's why I didn't want you to come.'

'Who are they?'

'Voter Services?'

'Yes.'

'Nobody. Some nonsense company from Switzerland with about five employees.'

'So why are we using them?'

'They have access to a system that belongs to another company. Though they think I don't know that.'

'So how do you know?'

Taking a paper towel that Colbey offered him, Tom said, 'Ms Powers and I had a few drinks one night. She was pretty indiscreet, but,' Tom grinned, 'also pretty good.'

'So who's really behind the system?'

'It's some tech company called Alcheminna, or at least their system's called Alcheminna – based out of a Pacific island. Anyway, I'd better go back in,' Tom said, patting him on the back. 'You'll have set the cat among the pigeons. I'd better go and calm Ms Powers down.'

Colbey stood by the sinks after Tom was gone and tugged Dvořáček's red-lined bill from his pocket. Then he pulled out his phone and searched for anything he could find out about Alcheminna. It was a tech start-up that specialised in quantum computing and artificial intelligence. There wasn't much else out there.

It was raining outside. As Colbey watched the drops that blew onto the window merge into rivulets and flow down the pane, the pieces of it all suddenly fell into place and he took out his phone again.

'Anastacia? Would it be possible to get an audience with the PM this afternoon? He asked me to look into something, and I think I have the answer to it.'

Anastacia said she would see what she could do and minutes later called back to say the PM was in his club having lunch and would see him there. Shoving the document back down into his coat pocket, Colbey made his way down the escalators and out of the building into a sleety drizzle. He turned his collar up and wondered why he had not brought his umbrella. Like yesterday, the day had started with such promise.

*

Half an hour later, Colbey stood beside the reception desk of the wood-panelled lobby of the PM's club, lush dark curtains discreetly shielding his view of its interior while they sent word of his arrival. He wasn't a member here, nor ever likely to be invited, to Clarissa's shame.

When word came that he was to be admitted, the girl on the desk fussed over whether she might take his coat, and her black dress, long glossy hair and heavily made-up eyes distracted him. She was probably a sweet girl, somebody's daughter, but her uncalled-for glamour at this time of the day in this dark establishment made Colbey uncomfortable.

He followed her through a hallway and into a members' lounge of green and gold furnishing, barely registering those who sat, clichés of themselves, behind broadsheets as he went over in his mind what he should say to the PM.

At the end of the room were gathered the prime minister's security detail. The girl took him as far as them, asked if he would like a refreshment of any sort, which he declined, then pointed in the direction of an open doorway. Colbey was left to make his own way there, the security detail nodding their approval.

He found Ewan quite alone in a small dining room. Before him were the remains of a late lunch, or perhaps it was an early supper. As Colbey hurried over, fighting the urge to shout his revelation across the room, the PM was using a pair of tongs to lift sugar lumps out of a bowl and drop them into his coffee. From the looks of it he had demolished a bottle of Bordeaux that stood nearly empty on the table. Of the two crystal glasses laid out, only one was stained with a blood-red sediment at its base.

'Harry Colbey!' said the PM. 'I like a man who takes me at my word. So what news?'

Colbey sat down and then after a moment of hesitation got up again to clear some of the plates to a nearby side table.

'Terribly slow on the service, here,' Ewan said. 'But you can't beat their prawn cocktail. I refuse to put up with those cooks back at base. It's kale this and spirula that. Trendy apparently.'

Making a brave attempt to wipe away the worst of the crumbs, Colbey pulled the bill out of his pocket. 'I think I've figured out something important.' The words came tumbling out, one upon the next in his haste.

'So this is what it's come to,' said Ewan, 'ministers hiding paperwork about their person like illegal contraband. I'm going to tell the cabinet office this paperless rule is a farce. Mmm?'

Colbey put the bill on the table and tapped it with his fingertips. 'I know what Dvořáček was trying to do.' The PM raised his eyebrows and lifted his chin, waiting for Colbey to spit it out. Calm down, Colbey told himself, and stop acting like such a bloody fool. He felt like a school snitch rushing to tell the head boy what high jinks the first years were up to.

Pointing at a few sections of the paper and then at the red-lined clause of Dvořáček's private bill, Colbey said, 'There's a difference, you see.' The PM glanced down but that was all. 'Dvořáček wasn't trying to get the bill through early. He was trying to force a bill with different wording through to the House for debate.'

The PM nodded and Colbey continued. 'Our bill, our official bill, that is, does all sorts of wonderful things to stop data being taken without the person's permission, and specifically prohibits a communication services provider or even a government body from reading or listening to private correspondence or conversations, at least not without a court order. Otherwise, everything has to be encrypted.'

Colbey faltered, because looking up at Ewan's frozen face, it seemed to him that the PM was waiting. Not waiting to find out what he would learn from Colbey, but waiting to find out what Colbey had to say. He ploughed on, for what else was there to do?

'That's what we promised voters in our manifesto, it's what you promised in the last election. No more spying on people. Not by governments, nor businesses. But...'

Still the PM's face was inscrutable. Colbey swallowed and continued. 'But it's missing one important thing. It doesn't stop computers from reading the messages or looking at the data. Our intelligence agencies don't have people reading messages any more, of course. That's so twentieth century. Now it's computers that read them. Machine learning, artificial intelligence, whatever you want to call it. Our bill doesn't preclude computers from reading people's private correspondence, listening to their calls, or sifting through their health app data and so on. And crucially... it doesn't prevent an AI system gathering together all the data it can to create an individual profile of a person, but the clause Dvořáček added – Dvořáček's clause – does.'

Although Colbey said it triumphantly, inside he felt flat. 'Did,' he said, trailing off.

The longer this speech of his had gone on, the more he realised he wasn't telling the PM anything he didn't already know. But he thought he might as well finish what he had come to say. Otherwise, he was really making an accusation against the PM.

So he ploughed on. 'What I'm saying is this. Dvořáček's bill added this in. Just one clause. If you didn't understand the bill thoroughly, if you hadn't studied it, you might just think the differences were old drafting or a different way of saying the same thing. But here, look, and here, these changes to the definitions that Dvořáček made preclude *any* form of intelligence, human or otherwise, sifting through a person's intimate data, their emails, phone calls and so on, and using that to build a detailed profile of the person.'

There was silence between the two men for a while. The PM took a sip of his coffee, and moved to put another lump of sugar in it. He seemed to think for a while, the sugar tongs hanging over the cup. Colbey thought that in many ways the chosen sugar lump might represent him – the PM was undecided whether to drown him or return him to the silver pot from which he had been drawn.

The lump was released and a splash of coffee leapt from his cup and onto the white sheets of Colbey's document.

Then the PM nodded slowly. 'What a clever fellow you are,' he said.

He seemed to consider some more. Then he said, 'I've come to a decision, Colbey.'

Colbey thought, *He knew. He knew all along. He knew exactly why Dvořáček changed the bill.* Was he to be fired for knowing too much? He thought of Clarissa and how disappointed she would be. He could already hear her words in his head – *What an idiot you are, Harry. Couldn't you just play the game for once?* It was really most unfair on her.

'I could do with a clever chap like you in the Security Council,' the PM was saying. 'You don't have the clearance, that's the problem. There's so much I want to tell you. So much help I need from clever chaps like you. And for the future, don't you see? We must think of the future!'

Colbey wasn't sure that he did see, but he said nothing and resisted the urge to blot the coffee stain that was growing and eating into Dvořáček's clause.

The PM got up and collected another cup and saucer from a laid table, brought it over to Colbey and filled it with coffee. He pushed the milk jug and the pot of sugar towards him.

'I'm going to tell you something that is strictly outside your pay grade, but I'm going to trust you, for now, and then we can sort all that out when you become a fully signed-up member of the council. And it's this: if we don't allow AI, that's artificial intelligence – you see I'm well briefed, I'm not such a dinosaur – to have open access to our citizens' correspondence and video calls, some of our international friends would not be best pleased. Many countries' entire intelligence programme is based upon using AI to identify terrorists. Take that away and what have you got? An unprotected society. Think of that, Harry. Unprotected. And you don't know half the terrors that are coming for us right this very minute. You haven't the security clearance. But if I gave it to you. Well... It keeps one up at night, I can tell you. Dvořáček couldn't bear the burden – that's why he did what he did. You have to be strong enough to bear it. But it's up to you, of course. It's up to you.'

He looked sharply at Colbey, waiting for an answer or a sign in one direction or another. What answer was he wanting? What was Colbey supposed to say? He understood the line of argument, privacy versus security. It was not the first time he had heard it, and he understood what the PM was offering. He was offering inner circle in return for his silence. In return for his complicit agreement to allow continued spying on the British public even though they had specifically promised the electorate they would put a stop to it. Even though he, personally, was going to be given the credit for putting the bill through. His first piece of legislation.

But his thought process was interrupted by a polite knock. One of the security men hovered in the doorway. 'Your next meeting, sir,' he said.

The PM nodded and then stood. Colbey stood also, taking the stained bill; he rolled it up and pushed it back down into his pocket. The PM put a hand on his back and walked with him to the door, patting him gently as one might do with an old relation one was fond of and who was getting on a bit.

'I can see you're undecided,' he said. 'But that's because of the things you don't know. Get the bill passed, Harry, let's get through this election and then in the new term, I'm going to make you a member of the National Security Council, the Privy Council, the works. Then you'll see, mmm? If you have the stomach for it? If you have the strength to make some of the decisions we have to make. Their lives depend on us, you see? On the decisions we make.'

Colbey could see the logic. Did he have the stomach for it? Again he could hear Clarissa's response. *Of course you have the stomach for it. What are you, a man or a mouse?* Perhaps she should take his place on the Security Council. She would certainly have the stomach for it.

So lost in this quandary was he that he didn't notice the next visitor had already entered and stood before them in the doorway. Looking up, Colbey saw with surprise that it was the man from the meeting that morning, the smooth Frenchman who had stepped in and agreed that a gagging agreement was not required from Colbey. If he was concerned to find Colbey with the PM, he did not show it.

Ewan swayed a little on his short legs, and now that they stood close together, Colbey could smell the sweet cloying scent of Bordeaux on his breath and knew for certain that the bottle had been shared with no one but himself. 'I understand you two met this morning,' Ewan said, and Colbey had to think for a moment to be sure he had not mentioned it, even though he had meant to, given time. So the Frenchman must have been concerned enough about the disagreement to tell the party's head office, who must have told Ewan. Or perhaps Tom felt himself forced to tell head office.

Not until the two men shook hands in a way that suggested the relaxed informality of long-term acquaintances did it occur to Colbey that it might have been the Frenchman himself who had told the PM.

'Forgive my earlier rudeness,' the Frenchman said to Colbey. 'I was obliged to leave in a hurry and didn't get the chance to introduce myself. I am Henri Lauvaux. President of regulatory affairs for Voter Services.'

Colbey took the hand that was offered and looking up he instantly knew the face. It was one of those who dined discreetly in the corners of expensive restaurants in Nice and Courchevel, or in that chichi harbour restaurant in Mallorca where he and Clarissa had coughed up an arm and a leg to eat apple pie. The sort who would sit with a serene wife and polite young children dressed in shorts and light blue shirts with stiff little collars, while his own would be squabbling and dropping food on the floor and Clarissa was becoming garrulous from too much wine.

In reply he said, 'It's very nice to meet you.'

As Colbey walked through the members' lounge, he resisted the urge to look back. Outside he found his driver's shift was over and his car had returned to his department without him. So he took the black cabbie's shortcut along Marlborough Road and made his way on foot through St James's Park back to his department. The temperature had dropped and there was a crisp stillness to the air.

As he walked along the avenue of plane trees, he thought of terrorists lurking with dirty bombs and vials of virus mutations in bedsits across the city. He thought of the things he had put in letters to lovers of the past. Words of anger, despair. Silly, embarrassing, personal things.

He suspected he would do as he always did; he would ask Clarissa what she thought, but suddenly he doubted whether he should.

After all, when he joined the Security Council, come the new term, he would be required to sign the Official Secrets Act. It would become illegal and most certainly immoral to tell her anything that was discussed in those meetings.

Perhaps *that* was what he should ask her. 'Clarissa, is it OK if I stop asking you for your opinion because I have to sign to agree not to?' But he knew she would say 'Sign it and tell me anyway'. And therein lay his answer.

*

Back at the PM's club, after Colbey was gone, Ewan MacLellan invited Henri Lauvaux to join him at the table, but he declined, saying, 'I haven't long. I've to be in Berlin for dinner.'

'How did the meeting go?' the PM asked. 'Any problems from the volunteers, your gatecrasher aside?'

'Nothing we weren't prepared for.'

'Good.'

Lauvaux pushed his wiry hair out of his eyes. 'I don't understand why you chose him to replace Dvořáček without consulting with me.'

'What's wrong with the man?' the PM said gruffly. He rang a little bell that sat on the table and a waitress came in, but Lauvaux declined a drink, saying again that he was pressed for time.

'Anyway,' the PM said when the girl had gone, 'I don't have to run my decisions by you, you know.'

Lauvaux conceded it was true.

'And you don't know everything yet, do you? You didn't know that Dvořáček would get a gun and shoot his bloody head off.'

Lauvaux said nothing.

'You did know?' the PM said.

Still Lauvaux said nothing.

The PM turned away. 'Well, it's done now, anyway. Colbey, I mean. His appointment was for my own reasons.'

'Yes,' said Lauvaux.

The PM turned back to look at the taller man. 'So what does the great and powerful Lauvaux think will happen next?'

Lauvaux transferred his briefcase to his other hand and said, 'He will sign off the bill because you've asked him to. You are his prime minister, after all. And he is an honourable member of parliament.'

'Yes, he does seem to be,' the PM muttered.

Lauvaux agreed again and after they had finished with the business he had come to discuss, he took leave of the PM and made his way back to the club's entrance.

He checked his watch to see how late he was running. He didn't like these fusty old places. Found them suffocating, with their dark panelling, their wine-sodden curtains and dreary brown furniture. He suspected it was kept deliberately dark so that you couldn't see the dirt of centuries.

On coming out into the street he waved his driver over. So, to Berlin, where a new set of different but similar problems awaited him, but nothing he couldn't master. In the car, he would use the Alcheminna system to speak to the profiles of those who he would be seeing, and by the time he met with them, he would already know their secrets, all of their hopes and dreams, their likes, their dislikes, their friends, their hobbies. But, of course, he wouldn't need to know any of that. He would just find them in the system and ask them, the people themselves, what was the best way to get around them. And, of course, they would tell him.

2.6

The next morning saw an unexpectedly large crowd gathered for Dvořáček's funeral, which was to be held in his local church. The inclement weather had worsened overnight and now a cold and blustery wind drove raindrops under the umbrellas of the mourners, mingling with the odd tear here and there as the congregation queued patiently to enter the church.

Attendance at the funeral was something of a three-line whip for quite a number of their party members, and although she preferred not to set foot in a religious establishment if she could avoid it, Kanha felt obliged to attend. She had liked Dvořáček, and his ever-forgiving wife.

It was even colder inside the stone church than outside and, walking in, Kanha turned her collar up and fumbled in her pocket to find her gloves and put them back on.

The pews were full, the collected whisperings of those seated merging to a sibilant hum that rose and dissipated in the void. She could see the widow at the end of the aisle speaking to the vicar. It was terrible to see even from this distance that she was crying incessantly, her hand clutching that of one of her children.

The pews were full, but Kanha's deputy whip, Paddy, waved an order of service card over his head when he spotted her to indicate he had saved her a seat. A few of their junior team were huddled in the row behind, and they gave polite little waves to Kanha upon seeing her.

'Jesus. It's like an old boys' reunion in here,' she said to her deputy, once she had shuffled her way along the politely folding up knees of those already in the pew.

'Thought you weren't going to make it,' he said.

Behind them their assistants were discussing whether there would be any kneeling, and if so, whether they might be allowed to use the cushions that hung on the back of the pews. She turned around and frowned at them.

The service was painfully long for Kanha, for whom religion brought back bad memories. At one point a loud bout of sobbing broke out from first one corner and then another. It seemed as if a couple of Dvořáček's lady friends were competing in their despair. The widow, her back to them all, gave no sign of recognition.

Kanha discreetly looked round at those from the top level of the party who were in attendance. They could be picked out by their heavy overcoats, their signet rings and the way they would turn their heads to glance and pass acknowledgements of greeting between one another.

She looked at the stained-glass windows. Her quest to discover what had been going on in Dvořáček's department had come to nothing. His bill looked to be a close version of the official bill; a few drafting differences, perhaps just an earlier version, but perhaps she was missing something. Should she forget it and move on? Certainly, Ewan had. And looking at the party leaders, it seemed they too thought nothing amiss.

Behind them, her team were still whispering inappropriately. She raised her eyes to Paddy, who pursed his lips. As a hymn started, Paddy's researcher Tabitha whispered something to Elliot, something about a little black book, and some of the cold air made its way into Kanha's throat.

'What did you just say?' she hissed.

Tabitha attempted to profess that it was nothing, but Kanha gave her a look that said *don't you dare*. So Tabitha said, in too loud a whisper, 'I was just wondering what became of his famous black book.'

Elliot swallowed and caught Kanha's eye. As idiotic as he seemed sometimes, he wasn't stupid. Neither was Paddy, who beside her softly said, 'Fuck.'

'Oh shit,' Elliot said. 'Do you think…?'

Kanha heaved a sigh and hissed, 'Was it in the box you sent to the widow?'

'What box?' whispered Paddy. By now several heads were turning with disapproving glances.

Elliot turned pale. 'I didn't look. I just put the lid on and…'

As anger overwhelmed her, Kanha knew the fault was hers, not Elliot's. Why should he look in the box? Why should he not do exactly as she told him and send the box of Dvořáček's personal effects from his desk straight to the widow unopened?

'What's wrong?' said Tabitha, and Elliot whispered in her ear. She pulled a face and as the hymn came to an end, in the rumble of everyone sitting, Kanha told both of them not to breathe a word to anyone. But it was too good a story not to go flying out of their mouths the moment they hit the bar of the Sports and Social that evening.

'Do you think Elliot gave Dvořáček's little black book to his widow?' whispered Paddy.

Kanha raised her eyes to the heavens in response. Just please let her get it back before Sarah saw it. Who knew how many women's names and details of assignations might be contained within it? That it existed was in no doubt. Why had she not thought of it before? He was known for his notebook that he carried everywhere with him and it was widely whispered he used it to keep up with all his various liaisons. It had been a running joke in the Red Lion for the last year or two.

The rest of the service was agonising as Kanha debated how best to get her hands on the book. To think it had been sitting in a box on her desk and she had glibly ordered it to be delivered to the widow. What cruelty. What thoughtlessness. Kanha felt a wave of shame and misery wash over her.

They were to transfer to the Dvořáčeks' house for the wake. Perhaps she might see the box sitting in the hallway, but that was unlikely. The house would have been tidied and prepared for the visitors. There was no other way – she would have to confess the error to Sarah and say that some confidential government notes had been accidentally placed in the box and needed to be retrieved. She would just have to hope the widow had not yet had a chance to open it and sift through its contents. Perhaps she would not have felt strong enough so soon and thought she might wait until after the service when she could look through it in peace.

But that thought about confidential notes made Kanha think of something else. Perhaps Dvořáček had also made notes of what was going on in his department that had made him do what he did. There might be some insights into who was blackmailing him, if her hunch on that was correct. He had been an old-style politician. Perhaps as well as his romantic dalliances, he had kept notes of his political affairs in his book.

As the organ music signalled the move to the graveyard, Kanha threatened Tabitha and Elliot with the end of their careers if she heard so much as a peep about it from any quarter. Then she trailed along after the congregation, peering when she could at Sarah, but she was now veiled again, and what could be gleaned in any event from the face of a widow at her husband's funeral?

'What are you going to do?' Paddy asked as they filed out.

'Try and get it back,' she said.

2.7

The Paddington train rattled through Hungerford, Bedwyn, Pewsey and Westfield. Then it crawled, in a stop-start fashion, from Frome to Castle Cary so that by the time it finally picked up speed and arrived at Taunton, Colbey knew he would be late; the funeral would be over and the wake well under way by the time he arrived. So much for his plan of swishing down in an empty first-class carriage, dark plump seats, with tea and cookies trundling by on the quarter hour. Down on their uppers, the service provider had replaced every other train with old rolling stock and it had been his misfortune to pick such a one. First class was just a few designated seats at the end of the carriage, no plush cushioning, no complimentary trolley service, in fact not even a table to rest his notes on. The heating was set too high and there was something wrong with the panini he had bought at the station and stupidly eaten even though it looked like it was the previous day's offering warmed up. It was gurgling its way through his digestive system and making him feel queasy.

Last night, he had got little sleep, tossing and turning, and waking every couple of hours as his dilemma went round and round in his head – shouldn't the public know the bill wasn't as comprehensive as it could be? Shouldn't the House debate the matter? What might Clarissa say if he woke her to ask?

In the morning, the one thing he knew was that the decision was his to make. What Clarissa would say was known fact – *for god's sake, do as you're told*, she would say – but when he woke he was as unsettled on the matter as he had been when he had gone to bed. Finally, coming in to find the girls at breakfast, a decision found its way to him.

Chloe was fussing about how exciting it was to see him on her newsfeeds every morning. Clarissa had come and kissed him on the head and said that he was right – they didn't need to go to Bequia, that Provence in the summer would be just lovely – and he thought what a privilege it was to be a member of parliament, and that he must trust his prime minister, and made up his mind there and then.

With relief that the decision was made, he wished them all good morning.

'You look tired, darling,' Clarissa had said as she kissed him goodbye. He left her sorting through the constituency post, which always trebled in size as an election approached, the paper correspondence being the worst; it was only the crackpots left who couldn't use email.

He had gone straight to his office and signed off the bill before he could change his mind. Afterwards, he had expected a word of pleasure from Morland, but for some reason the man looked a little disappointed. It was a classic bait and switch technique used by civil servants to keep their ministers on their toes, he assumed.

Mani had been splendid, though – a fine choice of hire. He was already up to speed on all the decision documents that would need authorising before the pre-election restriction period arrived, and that morning, the two had managed a good session of departmental business in the hour that he had before he needed to leave for the funeral.

He planned to just show his face out of politeness as the new minister but not stay long, but by the time the conductor called out the approach to Taunton, weary from a lack of sleep and unsettled by the problematic panini, Colbey was wishing he had not come at all. He was in half a mind to turn straight back for home, but he had come this far, so he might as well go in.

The widow's house was a ten-minute walk from the station, an over-extended rectory surrounded by rhododendron with a long gravel drive full of cars. Walking in and shaking the rain from his mackintosh, he saw that the wake had become an impromptu meeting of the tenuous network of influential individuals who seemed ever to have their hooks in the party leadership, and he became more resolved than ever to give his condolence to the widow as quickly as he could and be off. Hopefully he might make the express that returned to London via Reading in twenty minutes' time. He thought once again of settling down to snooze in the comfortable seat of a first-class carriage. If he missed the next one, he would be back on the old rolling stock again.

The house was full of Dvořáček's friends and neighbours and his local party volunteers as well as the MPs of his network and their partners. This was not a clique that Colbey was a member of; he chose to move in very different circles, so he shook a few hands in a friendly manner where politeness caused him to but moved off before they might try to enrol him into their fusty little groups. Through the vestibule window, he saw a knot of senior party leaders gathered on the side lawn, and hurried back into the centre of the room. There the widow was discovered, surrounded by a ragged queue of people with exactly the same idea as him, Kanha included, and he saw the chance for his express train slipping away.

'Yes, please,' he said to a passing waitress offering glasses of squash.

For a while he made polite conversation here and there, but after being cornered by the second wife of the member for Clevedon for longer than he could stand, he wondered if he might find an upstairs bathroom and take refuge until the rush died down, but he was not the first with that thought either. Turning from its locked door, he discovered the MP for Clevedon's wife had followed him and was making her way up the stairs. God, was he to be trapped in some hideous bathroom queue, to be further regaled with tales of her nanny's boyfriend's annoying habits? At random, he tried another door and, finding it to be a little study, ducked into it and sank gratefully onto a leather chair, feeling all of a sudden horribly tired. The saying 'The paths of glory lead but to the grave' came to him, as it would on such occasions, along with a reflection as to whether he was living his life as well as he should.

He heard the current occupant of the bathroom open its door and share a few words with his stalker, after which the two must have gone their separate ways, and the MP for Clevedon's wife must have gone in for her turn, because there was silence again. He would wait to hear her leave and be away downstairs before venturing out to take refuge in the more appropriate room to kill a few more minutes. But who knew what women did in such places? Five minutes passed. Then another five. He thought of her applying make-up to those puckered lips, adding rouge to those round cheeks.

There was a box on the table in front of him. It was the same sort he had used to collect up his things and bring them with him to the new office. For a moment, he thought it was his box, the one that he had carried from his beloved parliamentary office just two days ago, and wondered what it was doing there. But at the same time, he knew it wasn't.

Beside it sat a few items that had been taken out and put on the otherwise empty desk. There was a framed photo of Dvořáček and his wife. There was an ashtray made by a child – a misshapen circle of plaster painted an odd green with random yellow stripes. He thought of his plaster rabbit. These were the personal items of Dvořáček, taken from his desk. In the centre of them was a black notebook. He thought of his prime minister's instructions.

The toilet door opened, but another woman must have slipped quietly up the stairs and been waiting, for the two started talking and laughing and then, remembering where they were, hushing each other.

He didn't quite know why he did it. Perhaps it was because the box was the same as the one he had put his own precious possessions in, or perhaps because he was an obliging sort of chap, but he reached out and picked up the book, wondering whether he would need to ask the widow's permission to take it, now that it was hers. As he considered, he started to absent-mindedly leaf through it.

On many of the pages were the names of women and the dates and times of Dvořáček's meetings with them. So this was why the PM had wanted it and had told him not to look at it. He realised he was being inappropriate, but then he turned a page and saw the word 'Alcheminna' – the company or system that Tom had named as being behind Voter Services.

He heard again the voices of the women in the hall.

He traced his eyes down the page, not believing what was written there, trying to read as quickly as he could. A rage filled him such that he had not felt before. He had been used and most horribly deceived, he saw at once.

The voices outside were joined by others. Colbey froze, but before he could put the book down, before he could even close it, the door was opened. He looked up to see Dvořáček's widow and Kanha looking down at him, surprised to find him sitting there.

He experienced the greatest shame he had ever felt in his entire life. The widow stared, first in confusion, probably wondering who he was, and then, as she saw what was in his hands, in a form of horror. Her horror was matched by his at his blinding realisation that he had been caught snooping. That he was not to become known for his protection of privacy, but for his disregard for it. For even a child knows, even a child is taught...

He closed the book and started to apologise, some rambling excuse about how he had felt ill and come to sit down, and had mistaken the box for one of his own. Such nonsense it all was and such nonsense it sounded. The widow stepped forward and plucked the notebook from his hands. She went and stood in the far corner of the tiny room. It was as if she wanted the walls and the cluttered bookshelves to physically support her, as if the untidy jumble of her and her deceased husband's life could give succour at this moment. Or perhaps it just was because she was swooning and Colbey was in the room's only chair. He leapt out of it and indicated that she should sit. He could hear himself apologising still.

Kanha had not spoken throughout, but stood, carefully watching the widow. Colbey felt her stiffen as Mrs Dvořáček opened the book and looked at the first page. He wondered if he should go to her and wrench it from her hands, but there turned out to be no need. The widow suddenly flung it towards them. It hit the door jamb by Kanha's head and fell to her feet.

'There,' said the widow bitterly. 'That's your important government document, Esme. Take it away and do what you want with it.'

Kanha picked it up. Colbey felt her trembling beside him, and even in the horror of the situation it occurred to him to be surprised that Kanha could be shaken, that she was human after all.

'Did you think I didn't know?' Sarah said, the tears flowing already. 'Just don't rub my face in it was all I asked him. Just don't let there be a scandal. But you lot wouldn't give him that, would you?' And with venom she added, 'You hounded him, tortured him. Well, you can't do him any more harm now.'

'Sarah, I—'

But the widow raised a hand. 'Just leave,' she sobbed.

By now there were concerned murmurings from the hallway, people trying to push in and calling to understand if everything was alright.

Kanha put the book in her handbag and looked at Colbey. The two turned and with as much grace as they could muster walked down the stairs and out the front door. Nothing was said between them, but Colbey walked next to her, the inscrutable Kanha, who had trembled beside him. He didn't know where they were going as they went across the road but they stopped at a car parked on the other side. The cold rain drizzled on incessantly.

Kanha went to the driver's side and signalled for Colbey to get in. Even in his state of misery, he saw that the car was not one that even the poorest mums at his children's school would have driven.

They sat for a moment inside in silence and Kanha seemed calmer, but now it was Colbey's turn to shake. Suddenly that awful panini threatened to return. He opened the door and threw up on the grass verge. When he closed it again, he found Kanha holding out a bottle of water, and he gratefully took it and swilled out his mouth. The rain fell heavier and Kanha clicked the ignition on, so that the heating cranked up and blew hot air onto their feet. Kanha opened the voluminous bag that sat on her lap, took out the black book and placed it on the flat section between them. They sat like that for a while, their breath and the moisture lifting from their coats, causing the windows to mist up, each waiting for the other to speak.

2.8

Kanha didn't know what to say or do. She had waited while Colbey was sick, then taken the book out of her bag and put it on the division between them.

At last he spoke. 'Are you part of this?' he said and his words hung in the damp air of the car. Thinking of Tirrell and his grin, Kanha raised her forefinger and placed it on his lips. It felt strange to touch someone and she realised how long it had been since she had done so. After his surprise turned to understanding, she pulled her finger away and curled it inside her palm, as if to hide the importune appendage.

Kanha took her phone from her bag, placed it on the dashboard and made a signal that Colbey should do the same, which he did. Then gently removing his fingers, which were tugging at the corner of the book, she opened it and pushed it further up the central division. Their heads bent together as they came closer to page through – it contained untidy lists of women's names, along with telephone numbers, dates, times and locations. The hotel Kanha had visited was mentioned often. As she turned the pages they travelled through the sorry tale of Dvořáček's amorous adventures, the months falling by. Kanha was about to give up when Colbey took over the turning of the pages and led her to a different section hidden in the centre of the book.

Here again it was dates, times, meetings, attendees, but now of a different sort. The PM's club was mentioned often, as were the names of Anthony Tirrell and Henri Lauvaux. With Colbey so close, she could smell the musty scent of a man that usually came only with those first few moments of intimacy, before his essence became mingled with that of her own: his hair, the damp wool of his suit, the gabardine of his raincoat.

Gesturing at her phone, Kanha said loudly, 'It's nothing but a book of his conquests. No wonder Sarah was angry at you for picking it up.' But as she said it, they continued to page through and found some pages with scrawled notes and diagrams with arrows pointing between words such as *quantum computing, offshore unicorn, mezzanine debt, data parsing, individual profiling, multi-source data*, as well as between the names of companies, countries and politicians, *Alcheminna, France, USA, New Zealand*, this senator, that senator. Throughout it all were comments and wild exclamation marks. Words were underlined once, twice, thrice.

Colbey stabbed at the name that appeared over and over: *Henri Lauvaux*. He pulled a pen from his jacket pocket and then rooted around in the passenger door until he found an old parking ticket. He placed it on the book and wrote: 'The PM has agreed to pass a version of the privacy bill that best suits Lauvaux. In return our party get to use their Alcheminna system for the election campaign. Possibly more.'

Kanha felt a rising panic. She should persuade Harry Colbey that this was not something they could do anything about.

'Come drive with me?' she wrote, taking the pen. 'We can talk.'

'OK,' he wrote back, but out loud he said, 'Gosh, look at all the women he was seeing. This must be a gold mine for a chief whip.'

'Not really,' Kanha said, equally loudly. 'Not now Dvořáček has passed away. I'll destroy it.'

A thought came to her. 'Say goodbye,' she wrote.

Colbey smiled as if they were children hiding while their mothers called them in for tea. 'Well, I'd better be off, or I'll miss my train. Goodbye. I'm sorry for the scene with Mrs Dvořáček. It was entirely my fault.'

Kanha held Colbey's arm to signal he should wait while she reached across him and opened his door, and then after waiting a second or two slammed it again. She rubbed a small gap in the condensation in the windscreen. Elliot and Tabitha were among some of the guests leaving the wake. They would be getting the train back to London.

She turned the ticket over and wrote: 'Trust me.'

At Colbey's shrug, she picked up their phones and ran off into the rain.

'Hey, hold up, Elliot!' He turned and waited. Tabitha, under the same umbrella, her legs pressed tight together as her skirt blew about in the cold wind, was reluctantly forced to do the same.

'Good news, Elliot. There was a bit of a scene, but I got Dvořáček's little black book back. Let Paddy know, would you?'

'Thank god.'

'Colbey had picked it up. What an idiot.'

'Is it bad?'

'Just a diary of the women he was meeting. You know, the usual.'

'What will you do with it?'

'I'll destroy it when I get home. I wouldn't want it falling into the wrong hands.'

Elliot looked relieved and Tabitha gave a theatrical shiver, along with a disdainful glance in the direction of Kanha's car, its windows well enough misted to hide Colbey. She tugged at Elliot's sleeve and as Kanha went to turn away, she said, 'Oh, I nearly forgot. Colbey left his phone behind in the confusion. He must be ahead of you. Would you give it to him if you see him on the train?'

Elliot took the phone and slipped it in his pocket while Tabitha was already walking away.

When Kanha got back to her car, she opened the boot and put her own phone in the tyre-well, stuffing a high-vis jacket on top of it. Colbey was engrossed in the book when she got back in, and didn't speak as she drove off, so after a while she turned the radio on, dialled to a classical station so as not to interrupt him and Colbey read, every now and again frowning and shaking his head.

'Well?' she said eventually, turning off the radio, no longer able to stay quiet. 'What does it all mean?'

'It says...' Colbey flicked back and forth a few pages. 'Hang on...'

Ahead of them was a makeshift sign for a pit stop in a lay-by.

'Shall we stop?' he asked, looking up. 'I suddenly feel lacking in breakfast.' The rain seemed to have ceased for a while, though the sky was still overcast.

It was just a mobile burger stand with a few picnic tables on a grassy bank at the side of the road. Colbey clutched the black book tightly in his arm against his chest as if he thought the burger man was going to reach down and grab it from him as she ordered them both a coffee. He asked for a bacon roll, having to raise his voice over the intermittent roar of passing cars and lorries, and feeling hungry herself now she asked for one with a fried egg. The roll was soft and processed, and the egg's yolk started to leak out into the bottom of its paper bag as soon as she took it. She turned it the other way up as they walked over to the picnic tables, choosing one as far away from the lay-by as possible. Here, with their backs to the road, they discovered a surprisingly idyllic view down to a wooded valley, a patchwork of striped brown fields on the rising slope in the distance.

As she ate her egg bun and his bacon roll sat growing cold, Colbey told her what he had read, turning the pages as he did so.

'It seems Dvořáček has been working with this Henri Lauvaux for quite some time, working on a draft of the bill that would appease privacy campaigners yet still suit Alcheminna. It's a tech company based offshore. I don't think Dvořáček knew who the owners were.'

'And what does the system do?'

'Dvořáček's notes suggest it gathers all the data it can get hold of and then uses machine intelligence to sift through it and create artificially intelligent profiles of people.'

'Of which people?'

'Of everyone.'

'I see. And in return for assisting with that, we get help with the election?'

'Yes, that was the promise in any event. Voter Services is a front. It's a small Swiss-based campaign resourcing company that looks harmless enough, but in the background it runs off the Alcheminna system. Lauvaux had agreed with the PM and Dvořáček that they should trial it at the next by-election.'

'Which ironically—'

'Which ironically turned out to be Taunton. But there's more.'

'Tirrell?'

'Yes. Tirrell was given access to the Alcheminna system to try out its anti-terror capabilities.'

'Ah... so?'

'Precisely. Alcheminna must have been the source of his intel for yesterday's raid. And still there's more.'

Colbey was quiet for a while and Kanha thought he was being remarkably calm, but then he said bitterly, 'I can't believe he was using me all along.'

Kanha looked up from her coffee and saw he was possessed by a silent fury. She put a hand on his arm. 'That's how he operates.' How might she persuade Colbey to forget he had seen any of this?

'How can you work for the man?' Colbey said even more bitterly, and dumped the book in her lap. 'Look for yourself. So getting me, the next patsy, to sign off the bill was only the first stage.'

Kanha looked at a meeting note that he was angrily thumbing, which read: 'PM convinces home secretary to send Alcheminna all citizen data plus set up live feed.'

Kanha felt the jigsaw coming together, but she didn't like the picture that was emerging. She had a feeling it might be better to put all the pieces back in the box and put it on the fire, along with the bloody book.

'To do it without people knowing. To not even ask them,' he said.

'But think of our need to protect them,' Kanha muttered.

Colbey huffed angrily. 'That's exactly what he said to me, but I wasn't being told the full story. And neither is the House. We're being asked to debate a bill that's supposed to protect their privacy but which instead deliberately allows him to give away everything we know about them, and for what?'

'For protection, but also for—'

'To keep him in power. Us in power. Don't you believe in democracy?' he said, grabbing her by the elbow and shaking it in his anger.

Kanha pulled her arm away. 'Yes, I do as it happens.'

'Did Dvořáček? Is that why he did what he did?'

Kanha scraped the last of her egg out of the bottom of the paper envelope. 'Perhaps, but more than anything I think he was just tired of being pushed around, and maybe if they blackmailed him it was the last straw. I think he was out for revenge.'

'They blackmailed him?'

'Yes, I think so. Or kept dirt on him, to keep him co-operative at least.' She told him everything she knew, including her suspicion that Dvořáček had been videoed in the hotel room with woman after woman. As she told him about Dvořáček's voicemail begging for her help, complaining that 'they' were in his head, she found the words caught in her throat, and she thought again of the widow holding on to her children at the front of the church, swaying as if they were the only thing keeping her upright.

Colbey nodded slowly. 'Dvořáček wasn't trying to push the bill through early, he was trying to get a different version of it debated – one he drafted that would deliberately put a spoke in their works. I guess he planned to use his speech to be transparent to the House, to let the members of all sides debate the issue and vote on it.'

Kanha dug into her bag and pulled out Dvořáček's bill. 'Now it makes sense. So the extra clause in Dvořáček's bill explicitly made it illegal for companies to use artificial intelligence to pick through our citizens' private data and create digital profiles of them.'

The sound of the cars thundering by went on unabated. Finally she said, 'So the government bill does the opposite. Any AI system can sift through our emails, our texts, our conference calls, phone calls, app data – anything it can get its hands on – and use it to build profiles of us...'

'And from the looks of Dvořáček's notes, it's trying to get its hands on pretty much everything.'

'Governments can use it to predict who might be a terrorist...'

'Or to help a party stay in power.'

'Or come to power...'

'Yes, and god knows what else once they're in power.'

Colbey frowned. 'Ewan said if I were a member of the National Security Council, I'd understand what they were really up against.'

For the first time since the day started, Kanha laughed. She thought of all the arguments they'd had in the National Security Council meetings: her supporting the bill, Tirrell against it, saying the security teams' hands would be tied by it, but then giving in and conceding to her. She thought she had scored a point over him, that the PM had supported her view over his, when all along...

'Don't bet on it,' she said.

For a long time they lapsed into silence, lost in their thoughts. She was still confused about many things.

'Do you think the GCQH system that Tirrell has access to can see when I'm in your car?' he said. 'Surely they can't look at everything.'

Kanha watched the cars streaming by. 'People can't, but an AI with facial recognition that knows who everyone is can.'

She dipped her finger in the bottom of the paper bag but found nothing left as finally Colbey picked up his bacon roll and bit into it.

'You've let it get cold.'

'Better that way,' he said, eating it with relish as if he had not just thrown up on the verge an hour or so before.

Kanha shivered in the cold and Colbey offered her his coat.

'I'm scared,' she said, ignoring his offer. 'Let's just burn the book and pretend we never read it.'

'I don't think I can do that. I'm going to speak to Ewan in the morning. You don't have to be part of it. We can just pretend we never sat in this pleasant corner of England.' They turned their backs to the litter-strewn verge and looked out over the harvested fields, the winding country lane, the hawthorn and whitethorn hedgerows.

What a fool he is, she thought bitterly. But even as she thought it, she knew the bigger fool was going to be her. She was going to let him drag her down with him.

'It's not a good plan,' she said. 'You have to be smarter. There are ways to do these things. Honourable and transparent isn't going to cut it.'

'Mmm. I could really do with your help.' He wiped the last of the ketchup from the side of his mouth. 'You're better than me at being... dishonourable. But if you want to keep out of it, I'm happy to go it alone.'

'Like Dvořáček did? That didn't end well for him.' She thought for a minute. 'Did you sign off the bill yet?'

'Yes, I'm sorry, I—'

'Don't worry. It would have seemed odd if you hadn't.'

Damn it, she thought. *Damn it.* It was her job to look after the MPs. It was the MPs' job to do what the electorate voted them in for. Yes, she wasn't always the straightest; she cut corners, schemed along with the best of them, but mostly to keep herself on the way up so that she could do the good she wanted to do. Always her Machiavellian ways were to protect against those who would seek to unseat her, tread on her for the purpose of their own climb to the top. She did believe in democracy because without it, where would they be? She knew damn well where. She had come to this country as a small child, but she had memories. But there might be danger involved, not just her career...

Damn it, she thought again. She could see from his face that there was no doubt in his mind.

So with the traffic thundering past and the dregs of their coffee going cold, she made a plan. She told him what they would do. They would get Dvořáček's clause through to the House so that it could be debated just as he had wanted. But they would have to do it without the PM or Anthony Tirrell seeing what had been done, at least until it was too late for them to stop it.

At the thought of Tirrell, Kanha remembered Dvořáček's suicide. 'I think you should know—'

'That it's a foolish thing to do?'

'Foolish, yes. It will likely be the end of your career. But perhaps also—'

'You think dangerous?' Colbey bit his lip and looked away in thought. 'Surely you don't think that—'

'I don't know what to think.'

Colbey said nothing for a while, then he suggested they could pass messages back and forth by putting sealed notes into their lobby pigeonholes. That would not be traceable. 'Off the grid,' she joked, smiling again at last.

Handing her the book to put in her bag, Colbey said, 'Are you sure you want to keep it? Doesn't that put you in danger?'

Kanha ignored him. What could be said, in any event?

Later, as they sat with the car parked on a quiet street across from a small countryside train station, him wearing an old baseball cap she had found in the boot and her sunnies from the glove compartment, she felt calmer. She pulled her scarf from the back seat and wrapped it around his neck, pulling it up above his chin.

'Hurry,' he said as the lights of the level crossing gates near them started to flash red and the warning sounded as the barriers came down. He got out as soon as the train came crawling into sight, growing without seeming to move as an approaching train can.

She wound down the window. 'We mustn't look as if we are...' What were they? Fellow conspirators? In cahoots? She settled for, 'Friends.' Then she added, 'And we mustn't tell anyone else any of this, do you agree?'

'I agree,' said Colbey.

'Not even your wife,' Kanha said.

Colbey pulled a strange face and said, 'Definitely not my wife.'

'We need to know we can trust each other.'

Colbey put his hand through the open window, his little finger extended. 'My daughter always believed in the power of the *pinky promise*,' he said.

And smiling despite herself, Kanha linked her little finger with his, and they both promised. 'That's it now,' she said. 'It's a *pinky promise*.'

Colbey ran along to the station gates, hurrying onto the platform as the train pulled in and, with one last glance behind him, disappeared from view.

*

Although there was still half an hour to go before sunset, it was dark on the narrow lanes north of Marlow by the time Kanha reached them, hemmed in as they were between a brooding sky, copses thick with pheasants escaped from the shoot, and the banking flint escarpment of the hills.

Soon she would be there, in the cottage where she had once felt like an exile, but which these days could always provide sanctuary. At the peak of the ridge, she turned into her village as the dying rays of the sun fell below the line of clouds and lay flat on the fields before giving up and allowing darkness to gather.

The house she rented was at the far end of the village, the last before the dwellings petered out and fields began again. Kanha turned onto the blocked studded patch of grass that served as a driveway and saw Maximillian waiting for her by the front door. As she got out and fumbled for her keys in the dark, the cat curled around her leg. 'Well, you are a very welcome welcoming party,' she said and bent down to slip her finger gently around the cat's ear – but already he was off, away down the side path.

The cottage was old, she didn't know how old. Its front door opened directly into a sitting room, beyond which was a little hallway with a set of stairs twisting up to a couple of bedrooms and a bathroom. Beneath the staircase, Maximillian was waiting for her, having come in through the cat flap in the back door. He was stretching up from his cushion on the bench there, demanding another petting. She threw her keys in the pot, chucked him under the chin, and went through to the kitchen. Such was their routine.

Kanha put a bagel on to toast, laid some cat food down and, going to the back door, tossed her phone onto the wooden bench outside, closing the door after it with a feeling of grim satisfaction. She wondered what Colbey was doing and whether he was home yet, then took Dvořáček's book out of her bag and put it on a tray with a pot of jam. What fools they were, she thought. How could it be worth the risk? Then she smiled. Life had been dull of late.

It was cold in the cottage, so she went and started a fire in the wood burner by the sofa in the sitting room, then went upstairs and changed into thick woollen pyjamas. Maximillian, his dinner quickly scoffed, was pattering along at her feet and talking to her in his nonsensical way. Perhaps he was telling her about his day. Was she allowed to tell Maximillian about hers? Was that covered in her pact with Colbey? They hadn't discussed cats, only wives. She wondered what his look had meant when she had mentioned his wife.

'We found a book today, Maximillian,' Kanha said as she went back into the sitting room to see with satisfaction that the kindling in the stove had caught. She watched the flames gather strength, then put a log on. 'You wouldn't believe what was inside it.'

As Kanha closed the door of the stove, her eye was caught by the green light of her smart speaker, its plastic tower rising up on the mantelpiece behind the spider plant. 'Nothing that a cat would be interested in,' she said as she got down onto her hands and knees and followed the lead of the speaker under the coffee table and behind the sofa to where it was plugged in.

'Just the romantic affairs of a horny old rotter.'

With great satisfaction, she pulled the plug from its socket.

Then she looked around her. There was nothing else in the room, no television, no other speaker, no cameras or alarms. It was an old-fashioned place. Her phone was out back; her laptop was in a drawer upstairs. Without the smart speaker, downstairs was now a safe space.

Kanha carried it into the kitchen and put it on the counter just as the bagel popped up. She smothered it liberally in butter, poured herself a longed-for glass of wine and took the bottle and tray with Dvořáček's book into the sitting room. The fire was roaring away nicely.

It was good to see what Harry Colbey had described with her own eyes, to follow Dvořáček's convoluted notes and diagrams. She thought of searching for more information about it on her laptop, but realised that would be foolhardy. It would be easily traced back to her.

The more she read, the faster her heart beat, and her head spun from it all. She drank the wine until the fear softened. A drop of butter fell from the bagel onto one of the pages, melting quickly to a transparent stain. 'Damn it,' she said, cursing her impatience. Her fingers were messy with melted butter. She should have waited until she had eaten before opening the book.

Suddenly she wondered, would someone know the smart speaker was unplugged? She wasn't sure who 'they' were, but she and Colbey had agreed not to do anything different from before, not to react in any way that a system that monitored such things might pick up.

Yes, a system, she thought. As if Ewan or this Henri Lauvaux themselves were sitting somewhere with headphones, listening to her moving, to her stroking the cat and opening the vent on the fire to make it roar higher and warm her. Would they wonder why their hotline to her thoughts was severed?

Perhaps she should plug it back in, just in case. Let the kitchen be the room where she might be listened to. Keep everything as normal as possible as she had agreed with Colbey.

'Remember we don't get on,' he had said. 'You don't like me.'

'That's not true,' she had replied with a laugh. 'The press made it up.'

Colbey had looked charmingly relieved. 'I wondered if it was that.'

Gently pushing the cat off her feet, Kanha went into the kitchen. She would turn that thing on in here, and just remember to be discreet when talking to Maximillian, or anyone for that matter, in its earshot. But as she put it down, she jumped, and a scream escaped her mouth. There was a face looking in the window over the sink. For a moment she was afraid. Was it a burglar or an angry constituent come to attack her? These things happened. But the features came together in her mind as someone recognisable.

Fuck, she thought. For a wild second she wondered whether it was because she had unplugged the smart speaker and they had already come to see why, but that was irrational. He must have set off ages ago to have arrived here now.

He saw that she had recognised him, and a hand rose into view and gave a weird little wave. It was Tirrell.

Kanha mouthed at him and made a signal of a key, shrugging to suggest it was locked. What was he doing here and why was he at the back door? 'Let me find the key,' she shouted through the glass. She ran into the sitting room. The cat, wondering what was going on, followed her. As quickly as she could, she did what she could with the book and, opening the little door, threw it onto the fire and closed the door again. Then she hurried back through the hall and into the kitchen and made a show of finding the back door key, playing for time as much as she could, but eventually she was forced to unbolt the door.

'Anthony. What the hell are you doing here?'

He looked up for some reason at the top of the door frame and then back down at her and said, 'Just passing through.' He was holding her phone in his hands.

'Through Littlest Fingle? Don't talk nonsense.'

'Right you are as ever, clever Kanha.'

She wondered if she might be able to leave him there on the doorstep.

'Came to talk to you. Aren't you going to ask me in?'

Kanha stepped back, allowing him entry. 'There is such a thing as a telephone, you know.'

'No good if you leave it outside, though, is it?' Reluctantly taking it from him, she saw his missed calls as he ho-hummed a comment of sorts and stood in the kitchen as if waiting for her to start the conversation. He was acting a little like someone who rings you up only to ask you what you want.

'Would you like some coffee?'

'Any whiskey?'

'Sorry. Gin, vodka?' She was damned if she was going to offer him any of her wine. That would seem like an invitation to settle in for the evening.

Tirrell rubbed his hands and sucked at his teeth in a disconcerting manner. He was wearing a blue anorak over a grey suit, and it hung off his shoulders.

'Vodka will do. Though it always reminds me of my time in the gulag.'

She poured him a short measure in a glass, then a larger one when he gestured she had stopped pouring too soon. 'I thought you were imprisoned in Iraq.'

'Yes, there too.'

'Anything in it?'

'Just like that will be wonderful. Used to rougher than this. Did I ever tell you about that time? Cold, bloody cold. Was six months before the boys managed to break me out. Came disguised as Chechens. Terrible thing. Lots of bloodshed. Never drink vodka without thinking of it.'

As he gave this speech, he looked at the smart speaker.

'Put out by our talk yesterday? Thought you'd unplug it, eh? In case those Ruskies are listening in, I suppose.'

Reaching over, Kanha plugged it back in. 'I'd been thinking of cooking, needed a recipe, but...' She stopped abruptly in case it sounded like an invitation. 'But I was tired, so I just had a little supper instead.' She followed him as he went into her front room and looked down at her plate of crumbs, her half-empty bottle of wine. Then he gazed about him with a look of bemusement.

'All rather cute. Wouldn't have put you down for the cosy cottage type, Kanha. Imagined you somewhere with steel surfaces and a lot of chrome. Never assume, though, that's my motto.'

'Anthony, it's quite late and I'm tired. What is it you want to talk about that's so urgent?'

Tirrell bent down onto his haunches and stared at the glass door of the wood burner. 'Heard there was a little scene this afternoon, at the Dvořáček funeral.'

'You have your ear to the ground, as usual.'

'Not really. Everyone's talking about it. Not very discreet, your lot, are they?'

Kanha silently cursed her team. 'Bloody Colbey,' she said. She picked up her glass and poured some more from the bottle. Better to do something with her hands, so he wouldn't see they were shaking. 'What an idiot he is. I don't know what Ewan was thinking, promoting him to the cabinet.'

Tirrell put his glass on the table; the vodka was gone, she realised, as she watched him fingering the little knob of the stove's door.

'What happened exactly?'

'Nothing with any lasting ramifications, just a bit embarrassing.' She was slurring a little. That was good. 'I'd realised Dvořáček's famous black book might have been in the box of belongings sent to his widow. What a bloody day.'

'That *you* sent to his widow,' Tirrell said.

'Yes, fair enough, that I arranged to have sent to Sarah, but I had it under control. I just told her there were some confidential papers sent accidentally and could I go through the box and take them back. She took me to the box, and there was—'

'Yes, there was Colbey looking through it.'

'Well, she wasn't very happy. She saw at once it was her husband's little black book, and that I was trying to retrieve it. There was a bit of a scene, that's all.'

'And the book?'

'I took it, of course.'

'And it was exactly that, was it? The details of his dalliances with the fair ladies of Westminster?' Tirrell nudged the handle of the door of the wood burner and pulled his hand away, finding it too hot to touch. 'So what did you do with the book?'

'I burned it. No use to us now.'

'In here?'

'Yes, in there.'

Tirrell looked around and found the padded glove that was kept in the basket on the shelf of the coffee table; using it, he opened the fire. With the tongs he lifted the smouldering book out. Kanha looked around the room. Should she grab the book from him and have it out with him here and now? Accuse him of being a part of it? She had a wild impulse to take the poker from the set in case she would need it to protect herself. There was something about Tirrell she found very unpleasant, and she had invited him into her home and given him a drink. She imagined how that would come across, should he do anything untoward. It would be her word against his.

Stepping closer, she saw that what he had put carefully down on the granite slab was hopelessly charred. Kanha held her wine glass so tightly, she wondered whether it might crack and shatter in her hands.

She peered over his shoulder. It was too far gone. Was it too far gone? Tirrell gingerly reached out and turned over a page. Even as he looked, the smouldering red edge seeped across the blackened tome, overtaking names of women, dates, phone numbers, black ash following in its wake. He turned another page and then another, and the whole thing began to crumble. He could turn no more. Tirrell sucked some air in through his teeth. *Those terrible teeth,* was all she could think.

He stood up and beckoned her closer. Like some puppet jerked around by its master, she found herself obeying. He put his hand on her shoulder and, leaning on her, ground down the pages of the book with his foot. His fingers dug into her clavicle and she could smell him, that stale odour of mothballs and disinfectant, plus something uncertain and pungent like lavender or hyacinth or dank earth. All the while the fire door stood open, its heat roasting them. It took just a moment or two until all the book was dust, then he took his shoe off. There was a hole in the end of his sock, his big toe poking through. Kanha looked away, not wanting to see, and finally the hand was off her shoulder and she could stumble back. She deliberately swayed, so as to make it seem as if her manner, her confusion and inability to speak was down to the wine.

Tirrell now used the brush from the little iron set to clean the sole of his shoe, and the pan to hold the ashes that he swept up and tipped into the fire. The poker, the only tool in the set that he did not use, still hung there. He closed the door of the fire, put his shoe back on and put the padded glove neatly back in its basket under the coffee table.

'Very good, Kanha,' he said like a headmaster addressing a wayward child who has finally managed to do her sums. 'I will let you get back to your –' he glanced at the wine glass in her hand '– supper.'

She followed him out of the room, back towards the kitchen. Why he had to leave via the back door, or even why he had arrived that way, she decided not to ask.

Maximillian was in his basket under the hallway stairs, curled up on his cushion. Treacherously, the cat stretched up and took a petting from Tirrell's hand.

'There were cats in that gulag, you know,' he said. 'They lived from scraps that the guards used to throw to them.' He brushed his knuckle over the cat's jowls, held its head cupped in his hand. Maximillian purred. 'They used to throw the scraps into a yard that we were not permitted to enter. It was a form of torture, you see, so we could see all those delicious treats, but not reach them, be forced to watch the cats enjoy them while we lived on... on less pleasant victuals. But later, when the guards were drunk, we'd call to the cats. "Here, kitty kitty." And a cat might climb into our enclosure, slipping between the bars, thinking that we might also have some tasty titbits. And what do you think we did then?' Tirrell grinned as he turned his head to Kanha.

Giving the cat one final rub of its ear, he went on his way through into the kitchen, to the back door and away. Kanha turned the key in the lock behind him and shot the top bolt home as quickly as she could as Tirrell disappeared off around the side of the house. She pulled the kitchen curtains closed, making sure there were no chinks. Then she went back to the hallway.

'Maximillian,' she said, picking him up and holding him close to her chest. 'What a cool cat you are, my darling.' She was slurring heavily now and the room was spinning a little. She lifted the cushion he sat on and pulled out all the pages of Dvořáček's book that she had managed to tear out before she had thrown it on the fire. Then she put Maximillian back down, went into the sitting room, made sure the curtains there were tightly closed, too, and fell onto the sofa in relief.

PART THREE

3.1

'Yes,' said Clarissa. 'It's going to be fine.'

She and Colbey stood beside the pavilion, his hand around her waist, watching a steady stream of visitors making their way from the far gate, along the edge of the cricket ground towards them.

Those fickle gods who play with the English weather the way a child messes about with its paint set had indeed been kind. After a week of rain, although there was still a blustery wind, the sky was blue and the fat cumulonimbus adorning it were sparsely spread out. Down below everything was green and pink and bursting with spring prettiness: the regimented grass of the pitch, the newly lush horse chestnuts that ran along the wall by the churchyard, even the first little daisies that dotted the longer grass outside the boundary rope.

The prime minister was not due until later and, they had been warned, would only stay a short while, but the fundraising push would continue throughout the game, a quick twenty overs each side. Colbey had considered pulling out when he'd heard the PM was going to grace them with his presence, the thought of shaking hands with Ewan MacLellan being distasteful to him now, but he and Kanha had agreed not to raise suspicion in any way, so he had pretended to be delighted with the news. Clarissa had not needed to pretend but, he thought, wanting to be generous to her, she didn't know what he knew. Perhaps he should tell her? But even if he wanted to, which he didn't, he couldn't; he had made a *pinky promise*, after all.

Clarissa looked up at him. 'What's making you smile?'

'Just pleased how well everything has been arranged,' he said, improvising.

Earlier that week, from Sunday afternoon through Tuesday, Wednesday and Thursday, the rain had continued interminably, a fine drizzle from a low-lying bank of clouds that darkened London, while he and Clarissa had worked their way through a few strained phone calls for the sake of nothing but marital civility. He only saw Esme Kanha once during that time, when a vote was called. She had nodded to him as he moved into a division lobby. To anyone else it would have appeared the polite nod of a whip seeing their MP voting as he should, but for Colbey it was a signal to him to stay firm, and that she was doing likewise.

On Thursday night he had returned to Gloucestershire, to a frosty reception from Clarissa who was glued to the weather reports and complaining he had avoided all the work by staying in the city – an unfair complaint as his agent Tilly had arranged most of it – but by the next day, the forecast had turned favourable, and they woke Saturday morning to a warm spring day, the now thinned cherry blossoms in the garden popping out against the blue. Some tasks were discovered to have been forgotten and Colbey was dispatched to remedy them – floppy garden refuse tubs hosed down to be used as drinks buckets and a frantic drive around the local supermarkets for ice, all of which seemed to put Colbey back into his wife's favours, so that when they drove with Chloe over to the Oxfordshire village, an amicable peace settled upon them.

Now, nothing was left to be done. Scones and thick slices of malt loaf were arranged upon foil-covered platters on the trestle tables, rows of finger sandwiches made by an army of volunteers were stuffed layer upon layer in the pavilion's tiny fridge, and bottles of Pimm's, white wine and orange juice were chilling in the four improvised buckets. Left to Colbey was just the task of mingling with a gentle chit-chat accompanied by a steer to the booth for a donation, the purchase of a raffle ticket, or even better a monthly subscription to the party's recurring lottery.

Chloe came bounding up, her eyes wild with excitement. 'What time is he coming, Daddy?' Colbey glanced at the gaggle of gawky young men who had relinquished her from their midst and to whom in a moment she would return with the news.

'Ewan? Probably not until tea,' Clarissa said. 'And tell your friends not to take too many pictures of him. Or of Zandra.'

Chloe giggled. 'Ewan and Zandra, is it?'

'He's only a man,' Colbey found himself saying, 'and not even a good one.' But on seeing the confused faces of his wife and daughter, at last he agreed out loud that the day would indeed be fine. He still had one arm around the waist of his wife, and tried to put the other around his daughter's, but she squirmed away and looked at her friends. 'Not now!' she said.

Colbey already wore his flannels, newly delivered by the sports shop on Turl Street. His pads and bat leaned against the steps of the pavilion. He was a terrible player and would not last long on the field, so Clarissa had discreetly arranged for their team to bat first and for him to be last in play. That way he could work the spectators in the fresh hope of his whites, rather than what he would inevitably become – a sweaty, middle-aged man who had not raised willow to leather since his son left primary school fifteen years earlier, and even then only as a game of twos on the sands at Walberswick.

Several of his teammates had been briefed to say 'Bad luck, old man' when it came to his early retirement as if Harry were a team regular scorned by misfortune, rather than a hopeless star parachuted into a hastily put together rabble of correctly leaning village players.

The local party volunteers were standing by in a loose row behind Colbey and Clarissa, clinging to the safety of the pavilion, and nearby a few supporters and families of the players were milling around. Soon even they were lost in the growing crowds.

Tilly, a formidable old dear who had run the local office for forty years with a combination of matronly cunning and a personal address book that read like a who's who of the western counties, came out of the pavilion. She scooted through the volunteers and shook them off the wall as the PA system launched into a garbled version of a dance classic. After her, down the steps, came the fielding team. The babble of the crowd rose as they strolled out onto the pitch and started throwing a cricket ball around to warm up. Words of encouragement rose from the families of the players.

Tilly came up to Colbey and Clarissa and breathlessly said, 'Well done, Harry.' He knew that she was referring to the imminent appearance of the prime minister. So did Clarissa.

'Let's stage a photo of you both as soon as he gets here,' she said.

'Yes, of course,' said Colbey.

'Before you bat, preferably.'

'Good idea,' said Tilly and she sallied forth towards the throng. Her striped beige dress and rather over-the-top feathered hat could be seen momentarily here and there until the whole of her popped back out of the crowd, dragging a slightly reluctant-looking chap by the sleeve of his pale blue shirt. 'Do come and meet Harry,' she was saying.

It couldn't be put off any longer. Hand held out like a bayonet, Colbey stepped forward, his battle cry not so much a roar as a muttering to the volunteers of 'Alright. Let's go, then', and in he went, towards Tilly.

Time disappeared as it did at such things. Colbey became lost among colourful coats and wedge heels, blazers and loafers, children in cotton A-line dresses and padded little jackets. Knee deep in the welly brigade as he and Clarissa used to dismissively call it before they succumbed themselves: Range Rover, check; two public-school-educated children, check; black Labrador, check – or so their running joke went. Now Colbey might cynically add: sex only on birthdays, check; extramarital affair, check – but not out loud of course. Somewhere off to his right came the first satisfying thwack as the game began in earnest, ignored by the tight rings of Pimm's-clutching locals.

He clapped when he heard others do so, occupied as he was by complaints of roadworks and supermarkets with empty shelves, of poor teachers and a lack of gym facilities, of GPs who wouldn't answer their telephones.

Colbey absent-mindedly heard the calls of 'Come on, lads, good running' in the air above them, and the intermittent chant of the opposition's team captain: 'Impetus! Keep going!'

Here, among the voters, Colbey was at home. He mollified, he noted, he typed reminders to himself, he took phone numbers, he shook hands and promised to do what he could. 'Vote me back in,' he told them explicitly and without shame. Then I can fix all of those things, but do visit the tent, the little one with coloured flags, just a small amount to help our campaign, something larger if you'd like.

He felt a slight tension at the thought of his approaching turn at bat, but other than that, it was a perfect day and the duplicity and corruption in which he had become mired seemed miles away. He loved to see the relief on people's faces when he said, 'Yes, I can try to do something about that.' But, in the joy of it, he had forgotten about their coming guest.

'He's just arrived,' Tilly said gleefully in passing.

Clarissa coming up at that moment said, 'Isn't it wonderful?' She took off her sunglasses and polished them before putting them on again. 'I do think it's a sign, don't you? You're being groomed.'

Colbey shushed her.

'And the other day, Zandra mentioned Bequia again. I know you keep saying no, but I think it would be foolish not to go, after this. You do see that, don't you?'

Colbey looked at his wife and in a flash of understanding realised she would never be happy and that whatever she had, whatever they had, it would never be enough. If he were made prime minister tomorrow, she would find some other reason to be dissatisfied: that they didn't have the money to keep up with the new circle it brought them into; that they weren't young any more; that she had wrinkles on her face. What we have is not enough for her, he thought. I don't make her happy, that's the reason. Does he make her happy, he wondered, whoever *he* is? And if he does, why doesn't she just leave me for him?

'Well?' said Clarissa, impatiently. 'You do see that, don't you?'

Colbey felt his good humour and happiness flush away. How little she thinks of our life, he thought. After I worked so hard, all those hours, all those years, all those late nights at the bank, to get those promotions. All so that she could have the lifestyle she wanted. Wasn't a beautiful house in the Cotswolds, great schools for the kids, a tennis club, and at least two holidays a year enough? *Damn it*, he thought. And seeing how his thoughts ran, for both sides of this argument had been voiced enough times in the past for them both to be able to recite it as some sort of shared monologue, Clarissa flushed red too.

Were they to have a row here, right now? In the middle of their joint success? How hopeless it all was. But they were saved by Chloe who came bounding up and said, 'Daddy. Don't you think you should be getting ready?'

Agreeing, he went with her over to the pavilion steps where he found Tom standing with two glasses of wine in his hand. He offered one to Colbey.

'Rather have a juice if there is one,' Colbey said. 'I'm up to bat in a minute.'

'Right you are,' said Tom and disappeared into the pavilion to reappear moments later with a paper cup of squash. Colbey downed it in one, so Tom went and replenished it.

'Thirsty work, eh,' said Tom. 'Never gets any easier, does it?'

Colbey nodded. 'Good turnout. Reckon we might clear a few thousand at this rate.' Then he added, 'They're all talking about the by-election. Well done.' As he said it, he wondered what Tom would say if he told him everything he now knew. How much had Tom guessed?

Tom grinned. He was wearing a tweed jacket that would be better suited to Cheltenham on a winter's day, and looked uncomfortably hot. He dabbed at some sweat on his forehead with a cloth, then laughed at his discomfort. 'Bloody British weather,' he said. 'Impossible to dress for.'

'Daddy, your side's doing very well,' Chloe said. He glanced across at the scoreboard and saw that it was true, and then saw that Clarissa was coming over to join them with the prime minister's wife on her arm.

'Look at these men,' she said to Zandra as she got close. 'Standing around talking and drinking as usual when there's work to be done.'

Ordinarily, Chloe would have leapt to her father's defence, but she looked shyly at Zandra.

'I'm up to bat in a moment,' Colbey said, downing the second cup of orange to make his point.

'Gosh, right.' Clarissa went and collected his pads. He thought about asking her to put them on for him, but then thought better of it and sat down on the step to do it himself.

'We were just talking about the by-election,' said Tom, loud enough for Zandra, who was standing serenely nearby, to hear.

'Extremely impressive,' Clarissa said and gave Tom a small hug. 'We're so proud of you. Biggest swing in a local since 1931. Isn't that right, Zandra?'

Zandra came over and put a gentle hand on Tom's arm and squeezed it warmly. 'Thomas. So lovely to meet you. I've heard such good things. We were all very impressed with the results. Well done you.'

'Well, it wasn't all me,' Tom said, and Colbey was forced to turn away so that his friend wouldn't see the expression on his face, which he feared might give him away.

He surveyed the crowds from his higher position on the steps and saw that the prime minister had also retreated from the fray and stood alone being harangued by one of their volunteers. He had to fight an urge to turn his head yet again, so that he wouldn't have to look at the man. He knew for a fact he would not be able to meet his eyes, not out of shame or embarrassment, but in case his anger showed. Damn all this. How was it to end?

The prime minister looked absent-mindedly about him and it was only when Tilly rushed out of the pavilion and down the steps with a scotch and soda in her hand that it became clear what it was the PM was hanging about for.

Tilly spoke to the volunteer to shoo him away, but delighted with this sudden opportunity, he proved sticky, and being called off herself to deal with some difficulty with the laying out of the tea, she shrugged her shoulders and left the PM to find his own way out. Colbey reflected with a smile that if the young man had thought this cornering of the PM was his way into a seat of his own, he couldn't be more wrong. Tilly could make that happen with a snap of her rheumy fingers, whereas the PM's recollection of this conversation would be gone by the time he had finished the scotch and soda that was now clutched in his hand and rapidly disappearing.

'Why don't they do something?' Clarissa said to Zandra, looking at the PM's security detail, who stood nearby and also warily watched the pair. 'Shouldn't they intervene?'

Chloe giggled and found her voice at last. 'What? To save the prime minister from being bored to death?'

To Colbey and Clarissa's relief, Zandra laughed, and the two glanced at each other. All was forgiven for a moment in the love that they shared for their daughter.

'Tom. Go and rescue him, for god's sake,' Colbey said.

Tom did as he was told, trotting down the steps two at a time. 'Prime Minister! Sir!'

The PM turned and was extraordinarily happy to see them all there. At that moment, he looked no different from any ordinary Joe lost in a sea of strangers who suddenly turns and sees the safe haven of friends is just a few paces away. Colbey wondered if he had misjudged the man. There was much at stake, after all.

But then Colbey shook his head to see that the PM, his escape route identified, cut the young man off mid-sentence, taking his hand before hurrying off to meet the oncoming Tom.

Chloe's chatter fell silent again as the PM returned with Tom. Colbey could see that she was uncertain whether to stay or flee, so he stood up, his pads fixed in position, and put an arm around her shoulder, and this time she let him. 'Ewan, have you met my daughter, Chloe?'

Ewan gave a formal nod of his head and said, 'I have not had that pleasure until this moment.'

'We were just talking about the by-election,' Zandra said. 'What a fantastic result. Gosh, we're going to show them, aren't we?'

A yell rose in the field, which meant there was just one more down before Colbey was in to bat.

'All that fancy new data Tom has, I suppose,' Clarissa said, and once more Colbey looked about for his bat rather than meet Tom's eye. How did Clarissa know about that? But the PM didn't seem to notice. He complained that there was too much soda in his drink.

'Darlings, we probably won't stay much longer,' Zandra said.

'Oh, but there are scones with jam and cream,' said Clarissa and then bit her lip. The nerve of trying to tempt a prime minister to stay at an event with scones with jam and cream, Colbey thought.

'Made by Tilly herself,' Clarissa added quickly and Colbey had to hold back a laugh when he saw that her ploy had worked.

The prime minister raised his eyebrows and said, 'Clotted cream?'

'Of course.'

'Any pudding wine in that little black hut of yours?'

Clarissa, her organisational skills not to be put to the test, said, 'I'm sure we do. Might just take me a minute to unpack it.'

Colbey wondered which poor volunteer was going to have to run off to fetch a bottle from the local Co-op.

There was another shout from the crowd. Picking up his bat, Colbey said, 'This won't take long.'

'Good luck, Daddy,' Chloe said. Tom and Zandra patted him on the back, and as he walked down the steps he shook hands with the chap coming in off the field. He realised then he had been secretly dreading his time in bat, and was glad that in a few minutes it would be over and he wouldn't have the worry of it hanging over him. That was one of the good things about time. It did move forward whether you wanted it to or not.

Colbey decided that after the tea was served and the PM was safely away, he would feign some urgent ministerial issue that needed his attention and request a substitute stand-in for the second innings. Tilly might be cross, but really his work here was done. He wasn't going to be of use to anyone standing around for hours, a poor fielder hidden in a fine leg position. He could better serve his country as well as their game from back home with his feet up, a welcome mug of coffee in his hands and his red boxes lined up before him.

In the end, Colbey didn't do as badly as expected. Four byes off his pads from a ball he played and missed followed by another from an outside edge that beat the slip field. Even his dismissal wasn't his error. Anxious for a few more runs, his partner at the crease had called for a quick single, which Colbey hadn't a hope in hell of making. His desperate dive rewarded him with green badges of honour on elbows and pads. Run out, innings over, but the shame was with the other fellow.

As he walked back, everyone patted him on the back for real, not needing to use the staged response that had been prepared.

He returned to the pavilion to find the little group dispersed. Clarissa and Chloe were over by the trestle tables helping the volunteers serve tea to the line of visitors that was gathering. He went and found Tilly and told her of his plans to step out as soon as the PM was gone. She thought it was a good idea, patted him on the chest and said, 'Well done, Harry, the tally's looking very good. I think your work here is done. I'll let the substitute know they'll be standing in.'

Over beyond the far end of the pavilion, Ewan and Zandra looked as if they were preparing to leave, and he felt relieved, for he could not leave before them. They stood with their security unit by the edge of the green, presumably waiting for their car to return from whatever errand it had been sent off on. The prime minister was stuffing his face with scones from a paper plate.

Colbey went into the pavilion and through into its small kitchen. There he found an abandoned jug of squash, the remains of which he poured into a teacup, as well as some uncut malt loaf from which he tore a chunk. Balancing the two in one hand, he went out the back door in the hope of finding somewhere peaceful for his impromptu picnic. He found himself between the back wall of the pavilion and a hedgerow that ran along the bottom of a row of gardens. It was shady and cool here, but there were children playing a noisy game that involved running round the pavilion and catching each other up with a yell, so he took his squash and cake and walked along the hedge towards a wooden bench that was shielded from everyone's view by a sight screen. There he could have a moment to himself.

It was a relief to sit down and cool off. He felt the strain in his shoulders from the unaccustomed exercise. He was a runner before anything else. It was a long time since he had used the muscles of his arms in that way. He would hurt tomorrow, he mulled.

At his feet came a couple of sparrows who tripped around in the dust, snapping at the crumbs he dropped, flitting off and then returning for more. The chatter of the crowd came to him occasionally, but he was quite far from them here, and louder was the sound of the wind blowing through the great chestnuts above him. His mind wanted to dwell on his problems, marital and otherwise, but instead he watched the leaves dancing on the tree, the candle-shaped blossoms swaying up and down, and just enjoyed the beauty of nature's chaos.

The peace was broken by the sound of a one-sided conversation, a man on the phone approaching, who like him had come over for a little quiet away from the crowds. He realised almost immediately that it was Ewan MacLellan. The security detail would be watching their prime minister take himself off alone, not knowing that Colbey was behind the screen. *If I poke my head around the corner now and spook them, might they shoot me? Perhaps I ought to call out?* But seeing the PM's black Range Rover enter the far corner of the field and start making its way slowly over the grass, he thought the PM might not be long on his call. Soon, no doubt, Ewan would walk back to where Zandra and his security team were waiting for him.

The prime minister gave a loud harrumphing noise, and Colbey tensed. The PM was just inches away on the other side of the screen.

'Nonsense,' the PM was saying. 'Colbey? Nothing wrong with the man. Safe as houses, I tell you. We've checked up on him. Yes, I know he's nearby, we're all at some god-damn awful charity match.' Colbey knew there was no turning back now. He could not be found. He sat with the malt loaf pressed to his lips afraid to even move. He looked down at the sparrows hopping about at his feet, searching for his dropped crumbs. *Stay there, little things,* he willed them. *Don't go under the screen and give the game away.*

The PM scoffed at what he heard next. 'Of course he's behaving out of character. He's just been given the biggest promotion of his life. Look, I've said it already – who I have in my cabinet is my business. I won't have you trying to dictate that.' There was a pause, and then he said angrily, 'Of course we want to be in the club. We're doing everything that was asked, aren't we? What I want to know is why we haven't got access to the system yet?'

Colbey strained his ears and sat rigid.

'We've promised you a tap into everything we have, past and present. Health, immigration, criminal records. The listening eyes are in place. None of them, not a single one will be able to break wind without you boys knowing about it, and the bill is going through next week, I tell you. I'll make sure of it. Just give Tom the access he needs to the system and leave me to take care of Colbey. He's my honourable member, after all.' Then the prime minister cursed and Colbey realised the call had been ended. He sat for a long time, uncertain whether Ewan McLellan had walked off or not, and it was only when he saw the Range Rover in the distance driving out of the field that he finally relaxed and put his arm down. Delicately, he crumbled the malt loaf and fed it to the growing collection of sparrows and a pigeon that had gathered, his mouth now too dry to swallow.

He thought of Clarissa's insistence that they go to Bequia. It wasn't just that she didn't know. *If I tell her that the man is corrupt*, he thought, *I don't think she would care.* She would choose to be 'in the club', whatever that meant. As he dropped the last of the malt loaf, he decided that he didn't care what he lost. He would never be one of them.

3.2

The next week passed without incident, and although the PM's words *leave me to take care of Colbey* came to him now and then, he tried to put it out of his mind as he worked with Mani through the array of documents that needed to be completed before the election was upon them.

A few days earlier, Colbey had found a note in his pigeonhole from Esme Kanha warning that the PM was suspicious and he was reminded of exactly what was at stake. What had caused the PM's suspicion, he wondered. Was he behaving so out of the ordinary? He had tried hard not to, but his watch monitored his sleep, which had been disturbed of late, and tracked his heartbeat, and he knew his watch was linked to his phone, which was linked to god knew who and god knew what.

Even now as he sat at Dvořáček's desk with its scrawled words hidden beneath the lamp, picking through Dvořáček's bill to extract its additional wording, Colbey heard the blood pounding in his ears, felt a throbbing at his temples and, as seemed to happen quite a bit these last couple of weeks, he looked down to see a slight tremor to his fingers. How far might he end up treading in Dvořáček's shoes?

With half an eye on the door, Colbey copied Dvořáček's clause and all its associated definitions, pasted them into the official version of the privacy bill, and scheduled the document to go live later that night.

The first reading of the bill, a simple formality where the Speaker would read out its title to a hopefully empty house, was due in an hour's time. He and Kanha had plotted exactly what order to do things such that his changes to the bill might not be noticed until it was too late. It wouldn't be until its second reading in two days' time that Colbey would be called upon to give an introductory speech, after which the House would debate the bill and vote on whether it should proceed or not. Between then and now, it would likely be scrutinised by many parties and his additional wording spotted. It was only a matter of time before his addition was discovered, but by then it would be too late for anyone to do anything about it. And the cat would be out of the bag, so to speak.

Mani knocked at the door and came in just as Colbey pulled a memory stick containing the amended bill out of his computer and slipped it into his pocket.

'Everything alright, Minister? Need anything else this evening?'

'Thank you, Mani. All is well.'

'I've called the car to ferry you to the House for the first reading. Are you ready to go?'

Colbey went and took his coat from the rack and agreed that he was. 'Mani...'

'Yes?'

'You know that I was on the backbenches for a long time, don't you?'

'Yes, Minister. I hear you crushed it there.'

Colbey smiled. 'Kind of you to say so. Only... I'm not sure if I'm cut out for the front bench. If I don't last long... you'll be alright, won't you?'

Mani held open the door for him. 'Don't you worry about me, Minister. I've lots of options.'

In the car, as his driver turned through the gates into the parliamentary estate, Colbey prayed that the afternoon's debate on sheep farming was not well attended so that the first reading of his bill might slip by unremarked upon. Kanha had said that she would keep away from the session and he felt a little sadness that he would not see her – his partner in crime. He had spotted her once or twice in the last week, but not spoken to her. He thought sometimes of the delicacy of her fingers that shook as she turned the pages of that book, her lips that teased with the edge of the cardboard cup as she told him of her plan. Of their plan. It was like they were having an affair, a ridiculous *amour fou*. But it was not an affair, he reminded himself. It was a foolhardy scheme they had embarked upon. At least she should be safe, her career not be affected. That had been important to him.

As he got out of the car and headed into the parliament building, Colbey wondered for the hundredth time what had she done with Dvořáček's book. Hidden it somewhere safe, he hoped. They had agreed they would destroy it together at some point, but not yet, not until it was safe to do so. For a wild moment he wondered if she were double-crossing him, but he didn't think so.

Later that evening he would deliver the memory stick with the amended bill to the clerks, after which he was to leave a note in her pigeonhole to say it was done. The message was already written. As per their agreement, he had typed it onto a pink slip of paper and put it into an envelope with the House of Commons stamp upon it. The note sat now, already prepared, snug beside the memory stick in his pocket. When the time came no one would remark upon him walking up to the panel of pigeonholes, running his finger along the array of boxes until he found her name, the coloured sticker of their party beside it, and slipping his note inside.

He remembered the trepidation he had felt when he had seen the light underneath his name lit up and an envelope waiting for him a few days earlier. It had turned to excitement when he pulled its flap open and saw the slip of pink paper inside. His joy had not even been diminished by those few words of her message, warning him that the prime minister was suspicious, because of course that much he already knew from the PM's overheard phone call.

But his thoughts of Kanha were interrupted. As he neared the central lobby he could hear how busy it was, and arriving he found to his dismay that it was full with members. What on earth were they all doing here? For a mad moment he thought they had come to hear the reading of his bill, but the fact that nobody paid any attention to him as he edged his way in and stood in nervous confusion under the great chandelier dispelled that notion. He made his way through into the members' lobby. It couldn't possibly be the debate on sheep farming that had brought them all out. There was a tension to the air, a movement of members from one group to the next, voices pitched overly high, animated expressions.

He went over to the pigeonholes, but this time his was not lit, and he jumped at a hand on his shoulder.

'Looking for love letters, Colbey?'

It was the member for Southampton East, a friend of many years' standing, with grizzled jowls and unruly white eyebrows.

'Philip. What the hell's going on?'

Easterly laughed and raised his wild eyebrows. 'You don't know?'

'No, I've been locked away, rustling up a speech for my bill.'

The member came closer and whispered theatrically, 'There's going to be a crossing of the floor.'

So that was it. There was to be a defection. A member swapping sides, physically as well as nominally, walking from the benches of one party, across the floor of the House, to join their party's opposition's benches.

Colbey groaned. Why today of all days?

'Yes, terrible isn't it,' Easterly said, though Colbey felt nothing but annoyance at whoever it was for bringing out the crowds.

'Who is it?' he said. 'One of ours or one of theirs?'

'One of ours. Monty West for sure. Perhaps another.'

'Another?' No wonder the world had turned up, he thought. 'What's the opposition offering all of a sudden that's so attractive?'

'Not the opposition. God, no. They couldn't tempt a worm out of a hole. It's the Whigges Monty's going to.'

'Who's the other?' Colbey said, trying to feign the appropriate interest but feeling this little drama was not a match for his own.

'Don't know. Perhaps it's you...?'

Colbey quailed for a moment. Could there be such a rumour because of his wife's nephew?

But Easterly's eyebrows danced and he smirked. 'Or perhaps it's me...'

Both men laughed half-heartedly, although the sound was swallowed by the din of the room.

Colbey watched as the groups around him gathered information, sifting this and that for truth, swapping theories, testing rumours; members of all sides of the House as well as the lobby press were mingling freely in their greed for titbits. Colbey checked the Mouth of the Mob site on his phone. Defections to the Whigges was trending on the political pages. And the answers came: Monty West, William Barr, then a host of other names, his own and Easterly's included. He gave another hollow laugh and showed his phone to Easterly, who turned to the member behind him. 'Definitely not me. Definitely not Harry Colbey,' and they watched the ripple go through the room.

'Not us,' Easterly said again and again as they made their way through the members' lobby towards the doors of the chamber.

Colbey wondered if it might mean Kanha would be there; he could not see her. When present she usually hovered near the thin, curtain-covered door of the whips' little lobby office, as much a pantomime-like malevolence as all chief whips before her, but she was not there. Instead her team was making their presence known so that all must pass by them to reach the chamber or a division lobby. It was a brave party member who could walk past the whips without a quiver if they intended to vote against the party's directions, let alone defect to the other side.

Suddenly the noise in the members' lobby fell in volume and another ripple, of silence this time, followed in the wake of Monty West as he walked through the room and faced the whips. Nothing could be said. Their jurisdiction would soon be at an end for him, Colbey thought.

West was close enough that Colbey saw him swallow, saw his Adam's Apple ducking up and down and felt some comradery with the man. Both of them had made a choice to work against their party leaders, something they might come to regret and which they now must act upon. With what looked to be false bravado, West walked under the eyes of the whips and into the House. Behind him came a gaggle of Whigges. They were twenty young men and women, and with their silly trousers and little topknots they were the laughing stock of the House. Not a party to be taken seriously, representing just those few overly trendy parts of the country: Hoxton, Brighton, West Worthing, Edinburgh Central and so forth – at least until now. Monty West was Cheshire. Did he think the footballers' wives and monied Manchester folk would back him in this decision? Obviously he did.

And the other? Who was the other? If there was another, he or she was keeping their move hidden. The Whigges went through and turned to the right, to take their place on the minority benches. Already their numbers with those of the other independent parties filled them to capacity.

Easterly and Colbey waited until most were through before they followed in and parted, Colbey making for his place on the front bench and Easterly his on one of the back benches. The envelope containing the note for Kanha was still in his pocket, along with the memory stick. Nothing was irretrievable at this stage. He could still go back to the office and cancel the midnight amendment, he thought.

Taking his seat, Colbey was relieved to find the first reading of his privacy bill by the Speaker was largely ignored by the full but distracted House. Across from him, the members of the opposition had their heads in their phones or their noses in each other's ears, and he suspected if they were to look up, they would see it was the same on the benches of his side of the chamber. As soon as the Speaker had called out the title of his privacy bill and ordered it to be printed, Colbey slowly breathed out and looked up at the little microphones and cameras that hung like floating candles in the lofty panelled room.

So that was the first part done, the easiest part, he thought as the member for Strathclyde passed by on his way to the dispatch box and started to stumble through his opening speech. The member looked resolutely at his papers as he muttered about Leicester Longwall, talked of the importance of the Dorset Horn and Whitefaced Woodland, rather than look up at the hordes before him.

Those who had been in the know early enough had been able to place their prayer cards in time to reserve a seat on one of the back benches. Colbey saw that every space there was now taken. Those who had, like him, been slow to the gossip were perched on the steps between the benches on both sides of the House, or stood crammed together by the doors to the chamber. There, the Whigges had somehow managed to cram themselves onto their short benches. Colbey looked around for Kanha, but she could not be seen. Nor the prime minister, but then why would he come to watch a traitor make a fool of him and his party?

Colbey thought of leaving – now that the reading of his bill was over, he had no stomach for all this – but he didn't dare. What if they misunderstood as he got to his feet, and thought he was the as yet unnamed second traitor, making his move to cross the floor? All eyes would be on him. That would be a disaster, exactly what they didn't want; he could not leave now until it was all over.

As the poor member at the dispatch box plodded on, the flock about him lounged and chewed the cud, always with one eye to the bench off to Colbey's right, where he guessed Monty West sat. Colbey sneaked a look for himself and saw that the soon-to-defect member had placed himself at the end of the row, presumably to make his passage easier when he chose his moment to cross the floor. He was being polite enough to let the member finish his speech first, it seemed.

Just as the member for Strathclyde was coming to a close, Colbey saw Kanha slip through the door of the chamber, looking harassed. So the crossing must be about to happen. The member for Strathclyde sat down. Colbey thought of what would happen in two days' time when it was his turn to introduce his bill. What would the reaction to his speech be?

As was due, the Speaker called out the name of the MP who would ask the first question, but at the moment the questioning member stood, a shout arose across the room. Colbey knew that West had taken to his feet also. He looked to the floor as hoots of derision came from the opposition ranks and calls of 'shame, shame' arose from the members around him.

Usually Colbey would join in the fun of it all, but today his conflicted heart didn't know which way to turn or what it was his place to call out. He saw through a sneaked glance that Kanha had no such qualms. She glared directly at West as he made his way down the steps to the floor. Colbey thought of her trembling beside him in the doorway of Sarah Dvořáček's study.

Members of both sides of the House called out and the noise in the chamber rose to deafening levels. Allowing himself to look at last, Colbey saw a smug smile of satisfaction on the face of Monty West as the Whigges arranged themselves to allow him entry to the middle of their gaggle. Who knew what slights festered in the man that had made him decide to abandon his friends and colleagues of many years, and that he now must feel were paid back in full?

Colbey suddenly knew this was never going to be an option for him. Though his leader and perhaps others of the party may be corrupt, he still had faith in his fellow members, his friends and colleagues of many years.

There was a collective gasp and another roar from the House. Colbey couldn't help but look this time. Behind him the member for Nottingham West was on her feet.

It was true, there was to be a second member crossing the floor. The member for Nottingham West was seated in the centre of a bench and now she started to make her way towards the end of it. In their surprise, the first few members had let her pass but as she progressed her colleagues, soon to be ex-colleagues, made the way difficult for her. Knees refused to yield. The excited line of her mouth hardened, and a frown appeared; would they let her pass? She was as if stuck in brambles – more force was needed, more determination. Her seat, now vacant, could not be returned to. It offered no safe space to her now; the moment she had lifted her yellow-suited behind from its green leather, she had forsaken it. She could go neither forward nor back. Colbey felt her pain. She was trapped by a gnarly old backbencher, a sneer on his face while her own turned to fear. What hubris it had been to choose the subterfuge of a centre seat, Colbey thought.

But the next member on, a woman of obviously softer heart, whispered in the member's ear and the gnarly gentleman yielded, passage was allowed, and finally the member reached the end of the row and with obvious relief hurried down the steps to her new team, seemingly anxious now for it to be over. Now the Whigges could no longer even try to squeeze themselves onto the minority benches. With a grey-haired man and a middle-aged woman in their ranks, for the first time they looked to Colbey like a party that had a more general offering, and Colbey joined in the anxious mutter that took hold of both sides of the rest of the House.

'Order, order!' called the Speaker, and along with his colleagues, Colbey remembered that a question for the member for Strathclyde had been asked. It was duly repeated and the member for Strathclyde rose to his feet to reply. Although the debate was now to begin, the circus was over. Members slipped out of the chamber in twos or threes allowing him to leave at any time without shame, but he felt as if he could not stand. By the time the debate came to a close, the House was nearly empty. Colbey, in his misery at the sight of two other treacherous members, stayed where he was. How would it work out for them? He suspected that was the end of their careers. How foolish they had been. For a few minutes of fame, for a principal that he couldn't even understand, they had thrown away everything.

He could not bring himself to speak right now to another member of his party. The member for Strathclyde thanked Colbey and those who had remained until the session's end and made his own way out. Eventually only Colbey was left, sitting alone on the benches of his party. The doorkeeper called out to him to say he was turning off the lights and, in the darkness that fell, the only glow being that cast by the silhouette of the open door, he felt calmer. Colbey put his hand to his chest where a pain had gathered and he wondered again who else might know how he felt at that moment. He took off his watch and tucked it into the crease of the bench behind him. He had promised Esme Kanha not to do such things, but he couldn't bear the thought of them following the beating of his heart, seeing what made it speed up and what made it fall, some system somewhere tracking delta waves and REM patterns and sending little warning flags off somewhere to be checked out. He couldn't bear the touch of the watch on his skin any longer.

So, Colbey thought. There was no more putting it off. Now that which could not be undone must be done. Was he a traitor too? Or was he saving his party from falling to the depths of evil?

*

The corridors of power were empty, with the evening's work of the House over. Most of the MPs had taken themselves off to drinking establishments around Westminster or to their grace-and-favour flats and whoever might be waiting there. A few might have retired to their offices to work late into the night, and perhaps a few more might even have taken a long train ride or driven home to spend the night under the same roof as their families. As Colbey walked down the empty corridors to the clerks' office, the memory stick heavier in his pocket than its true weight, he thought there was still time to pull out, to return now to his office and reverse his amendment to the bill.

At the sight of the clerks' counter, his throat became dry. It seemed impossibly far away. He thought of the phone in his pocket. Did he normally walk like this? Was this slower than his usual pace? Perhaps he should speed up. Passing through an archway, he saw one of the cameras that were dotted about the place, its dark globe sucking in the world like a black hole. He sped up, then a moment later, he worried he was walking too fast. He thought of the gyroscopes in his phone that tracked his movements, sensors that could tell a gait out of odds with his usual one. Walk normally, he thought. But was what normal? He suddenly couldn't seem to remember.

Damn it, *acting out of character* indeed. He had tried so hard not to. What were the ways in which they might know that he might be acting out of character? His choice of words, his movements, his sighs? Or the fact that he could no longer sleep? That he woke at one in the morning, then at three and five, and finally again at six filled with relief to see a chink of light between the curtains. Did the system listen to his breathing as he tossed and turned?

To his right was a stairwell that led up to the gallery. He felt like running up there, taking his phone out of his pocket and throwing it into the Thames, shouting 'Is that out of character enough for you?'

By the time he had thought all this, he was there at the counter and soon it would be done. The clerk turned and came towards him. It was not the same clerk as the one who had given him the copy of Dvořáček's bill. It was an older lady with a moon face, eyes sunk into bags upon bags, but a friendly smile.

Time, Colbey thought, has no master. It trickles on in its fashion, a co-conspirator, if you will. Through the putting of his hand into his pocket, through the seconds it took him to give the stick to the clerk, during the time he needed to tell her to use this copy of the bill rather than the one on the system, through all of that, time flowed unstopped and unstoppable, even as he mumbled his prepared reason – the breach of an inbox capacity, an email account out of action, a techy on the case.

There was nothing before his eyes except the round face of the clerk. He didn't see his hand dip into his pocket, or feel her take the stick, but it must have been done, because now the stick was in her computer and then it was back in her hand again, and now back in his, and behind her a printer was already spewing out paper. The seconds clicked along in time with its automatic mechanism, its double siding and sorting and stapling. Colbey was unable to take his eyes from the machine, the flicking back and forth of the House of Common's paper with its green gated logo at the top, copies of Dvořáček's bill in duplicate, triplicate, quadruplet and so on and on, until there was one for every single member of the House, should they be bothered to collect it. Colbey realised the clerk had said something to him, and he asked her to repeat the question.

'Your first one, isn't it?' she said.

'Yes,' he said. 'My first one.'

And likely to be my last, he felt like adding as they both stood and watched the copies of the bill as they came and came.

'Something to be proud of,' she said.

He smiled at her and felt a swell of elation. Soon they would be ready for collection by the members of all sides of the House, and nothing could stop the debate of Dvořáček's clause after that. His little additions to the government's bill would make life difficult for certain players in this great game called life. He suddenly understood what Kanha had said about Dvořáček. That was all he had wanted, she had thought.

Hopefully, by now, Kanha would have found a way to leak the news of Alcheminna's dealings with the party to the press, so that all eyes would be on the debate. So long as the PM didn't find out too soon, in his speech Colbey would be able to tell the House why the clause mattered so much, why it was essential it remained, and how important it was that they keep Dvořáček's clause in the bill. Then it would be up to the House to decide. He could return to his constituency and his voters and spend the rest of his life working for them – at least until they decided they no longer wanted him. Ewan and his lot couldn't easily disenfranchise him, he didn't think. And if they did? Then at least he could retire with his head held high. There were plenty of other things to do in this big wide world.

He thought of Clarissa. It was harsh on her. He had not confided in her. He had not shared the decision to do what he had done with her.

Was there anything they could use against him? He racked his brain, but he had always lived a simple, perhaps rather dull life. *Leave me to take care of Colbey*, the PM had said. But what did they have? He drank a little too much at college, but who didn't? He had tried the odd puff of this and that, but that was long ago, before there were phones that took pictures. They had nothing on him.

He went back to the members' lobby and without lingering, slipped his note into Kanha's pigeonhole. Its little light, feeling the weight of his missive, switched on. Inside it were written just two words: *It's done.*

His part in the play was nearly over. All he needed to do now was to stumble through his speech as the member for Strathclyde had done through his, and then it would be up to the House to decide – to debate it and then pass the bill to its next stage or refuse it. Colbey told his driver to take him back to the flat where Clarissa would be, and there, beside her slumbering form, and for the first time in weeks, he slept through the night.

*

The next morning, Colbey woke with a feeling that there was something that should be on his mind. Seeing how light the room was, he realised he had slept in for the first time in months, and with a sweeping sense of joy, mixed with trepidation, remembered what he had done. Clarissa was already up. He followed the smell of ground coffee through the open bedroom door to find her at breakfast.

'I might work on my speech here this morning,' he said and kissed her.

She looked briefly up from her paperback novel. 'Mmm, OK.'

He felt a sudden urge to confess. 'Good book?'

'Mmm.'

So it was to be the backbenches again – what a relief. Clarissa would be cross, he thought as watched her, but it was his life too and for her nothing would change, not the book clubs or gym sessions, not the dinner parties with the neighbours, not even their financial security. It would just be her prestige that might take a knock – and was that not something worth sacrificing for the right cause?

He retreated to an armchair for a few hours and pretended to work on his speech, but in reality it was written, so he fell instead to dwelling on who might discover what he had done and when the axe might fall. It was most likely to be the shadow team or a lobby journalist. His phone rang and he jumped, but it was just his driver asking when he wanted to be picked up. He looked at Clarissa curled up on the sofa, still with her book, and a stab of guilt made him think of booking them a surprise trip to Paris, ready to soften the blow. He worked through his plan to pass the whole debacle off to her as incompetence. I'm too old for this, he might say. Look what a mess I made, but these things happen, my love. Perhaps we should just admit we're beyond all that.

After their late breakfast, Clarissa didn't mention lunch until mid-afternoon, when he offered to make her a salad. As she sat down, triumphantly turning the last page of her book, she said, 'You were late last night.'

He laid the table around her. 'The system crashed. I had to wait for them to restore it before I could give the bill to the clerks to be printed.'

'Chloe's up this evening.'

'Shall we take her for dinner? Somewhere nice? I'll book something if you like and treat you both.'

Clarissa gave him an odd tentative look as he put the salad in front of her and she started picking out the hazelnuts. He had forgotten she was off nuts with whatever diet she was on now. For once she didn't complain and he wondered why.

'Thank you, darling,' she said. 'But she's got a new boyfriend and I expect she'll be up to go out with him and his friends.'

'Who's that?'

'And if it's all the same to you, I'm going to go back home today. It's my book club this evening.'

'Can't you skip it? Who's the new boyfriend?'

'I could but I don't want to. Look, for once I've read the book, and it was Zandra's pick this month.'

'The boyfriend, Clarissa. Who's the boyfriend?'

With relief, he heard it was the son of one of their friends, who was sweet but a bit wimpy.

His driver pinged to say he was downstairs waiting for him. He had thought he would go into his office and see if he could chase for Mani's role to be made permanent before it all came out. Colbey said goodbye and kissed Clarissa on the top of her head.

On the way down to the car, he searched and found the hotel in Paris they had once stayed in when they were younger. Years ago he had promised her they would return, but they never had. He found the bookings page and got it teed up, then he logged into their banking system to transfer the money for the room from their savings account, but found it empty.

He flicked over to the screen that showed the summary of all their accounts in case the bank had moved the savings elsewhere for some reason, but they were all at the level he would expect.

In a panic he told the driver to wait, and rang Clarissa.

'What?' she said defiantly, when all he had said so far was her name. He heard her spoon clattering down, coffee splashing on the table. She had taken the money. He knew at once. That bloody Bequia trip. Yes, he was going to do the same for Paris, but just a weekend in a hotel, just a small amount. She had taken all of it. For what? All their savings for one stupid week with a bunch of entitled crooks.

For a moment he was speechless. Finally he said, 'Did you move our savings to another account?'

She started talking, all sorts of things, snippets of which he understood, much of which he didn't. Mostly it was justification, about her rights, the fact that it was her money too, that he should trust her, that she was fed up with his always deciding how they should spend their money. Some of it was fair, but most of it was a dressing up of half-truths.

'So you haven't spent it?' he said at last. He had been harsh on her. She hadn't bought the trip to Bequia against his wishes.

'No,' was the reply. She had invested it. And why shouldn't she? It was as much her money as his.

'But that's a shared decision,' he protested, and she pointed out that he moved the money around all the time without speaking to her. 'But that's because I look after the money,' he said, being foolish enough to add, 'and you don't know what you're doing.'

Now her fury was huge. How dare he? How dare he? Colbey said nothing, so she repeated again, 'How dare you?'

Colbey stood by the car, gripping the phone in his hand, and said nothing for a moment. He knew his wife's anger was a front and he knew her stance was a lie. That was the thing about living together for thirty years. You knew all their tells, all their little feints and ways of lying. He had looked after their money for their entire marriage and not once had she shown the slightest inclination to get involved. She'd always seen it as a boring chore. 'Sad old Harry,' she joked on many occasions when she found him knee deep in bank statements and fund prospectuses, 'counting his money.' Her new-found feminism was as false as her outrage. He got in the car as the silence between them stretched on.

She was in there; he watched her come to the window and see that his car was just below her still. She disappeared from the window once more. She spoke to him, fast, tense words that caused a cold feeling in his stomach. He imagined her pacing up and down the wooden flooring, phone in hand, or perhaps sitting back at the lunch table, her leg swinging furiously back and forward in her outrage.

'So where did you decide to invest the money?' he said, suddenly nervous.

She spoke of Zandra, the PM's wife, of a private investment that was going to make them very wealthy. That they would be able to *buy* a house in Bequia by the time it was done. A unicorn stock, pre-IPO. He didn't know she even knew those words. The company was private, the investment was invitation only. And they had been invited, think of that! Zandra had spoken up for them, lobbied for them to be included. And she had spoken to a... a friend who knew about these things. He had said he thought it was a great opportunity.

'Did you see Zandra invest?' Colbey asked, logging away the mention of the unknown financial advisor to pick at like a sore at a later date.

Clarissa faltered. He could hear now in her voice that already she was having doubts, that her certainty and boastfulness was turning through bravado into fear.

No, she had not seen Zandra sign the same forms.

'What forms?' he asked. 'What forms did you sign?'

Share subscription, an exception... no, an accession to a share-holders' agreement, a bank transfer for the funds. A power of attorney.

'A power of attorney?' he repeated, but she didn't hear the echo.

'Did I do wrong?' she asked him, and now there was the edge of tears.

'Do you have copies of the documents?' he asked.

'No,' she told him. 'Was it a silly thing to do?' There were tears now. He heard them catching in her throat.

'No,' he said. 'I'm sure if Zandra recommended you sign, it can't be anything too bad.'

She giggled, her relief radiating across the kitchen, through the glass pane of the window and down to him in the car. She was giddy with relief. He wondered who else might be listening to them share this strange moment between husband and wife. *The lies we tell each other.*

She said it was a shame they couldn't take Chloe to dinner that evening. That it had been a nice idea.

'Yes, we don't have much longer with her before she goes to study abroad,' he said. Then he brought himself to ask the question, 'Clarissa, what was the company called?'

And she told him.

'I might be late for dinner tonight,' he said. 'But I'll definitely come home to Gloucestershire.'

She said she'd double-check with Zandra that her and the PM had also invested as Zandra had said they were going to, and she would ask for a copy of the documents. It must have just been an oversight that she hadn't been given them.

Colbey told his driver to take him to the House as fast as he could, but he knew it was already too late. As soon as he entered the central lobby he saw members with the bill in their hands, folding it into bags, stuffing it into folders. He followed a stream of them back to the source, the little clerks' window in the members' lobby.

In his desperation, he felt like charging at the honourable members and snatching the papers from their hands, but even as he watched, a couple of lobby journalists passed by, the bill pressed to their chests.

He went back to the cold quiet corridor between the lobbies, sat on the bench beneath the painted scenes, and put his head in his hands. *Leave me to take care of Colbey.*

Colbey and his wife were now shareholders of Alcheminna. Willing or not, they were signed-up members of the club, whatever that entailed.

Filled with a rage he had not felt before, Colbey ran through the Great Hall, not caring who was staring. He found a black cab and told the driver to take him to St James's. By the time he was at the PM's club, he could think of nothing but his anger. The audacity, the good-for-nothing nerve of it – to use their wives in that way.

He stepped through the door, but the same young receptionist as before nervously told him he was not on the guest list. He insisted a message was put to the prime minister, and after a phone call he was told the PM was not available and was asked to leave. The doorman was called in. A scene was made. The doorman took his arm in a rough fashion, and Colbey knew at once that although dressed in a fancy suit this man had thrown far angrier and more dangerous men than he out of all sorts of places.

At that moment, the door opened and Anastacia came in. The little lobby that stood apart from the club with its impenetrable velvet curtain now seemed very crowded.

'Mr C,' she said. 'Whatever's going on?'

'I need to see the prime minister,' Colbey said miserably. 'He's hiding in there like a coward and refuses to see me.'

'There's some terrible misunderstanding,' Anastacia said to the doorman. 'This is a minister.'

The doorman relaxed his grip on Colbey's elbow ever so slightly, but the guest list was his only master.

'Why do you need to see him?' she hissed.

'I just do,' said Colbey.

Anastacia and the receptionist exchanged glances. 'Let me speak to him,' she said and hurried off through the black curtain and into the interior. They stood a while, the doorman refusing to relax his grip any further. The receptionist disappeared into a back room to hide. It was only when the phone rang that she returned, and with a faint nod to the doorman said, 'He's allowed in.'

Colbey shrugged the man's hand from his arm and the doorman pulled a face to show he couldn't care one way or the other. Through the curtains he went, tracing the path he had followed the previous week. The receptionist trotted behind him, but she turned back when he reached the lounge where the prime minister's security detail sat languishing untidily on chairs, not bothering to rise or even turn their heads, just watching him cross the long room. There was no sign of Anastacia.

The PM was in the same room as before, at the same table, which was once more full of the detritus of a meal, a last granary roll in a wicker basket, a half-drunk bottle of claret, the same pink-silver tea set and stains on the table.

The PM stood and smiled. It was the smile of a man who is used to winning. It was the smile of a man who has just won. There was another at the table with his back to Colbey.

He turned and Colbey saw that it was Henri Lauvaux.

'Join us?' the PM said. Then he gave an even broader smile and said, 'Why, of course, in some ways, you already have.'

3·3

Kanha was sitting in one of the many nondescript rooms of Number Ten waiting for something that was labelled a committee meeting, but which was really the true cabinet meeting for the inner-circle ministers and their advisors only. It was all about clubs within clubs, with this PM.

Around her were the supposed big guns: foreign secretary, home secretary, chancellor and so on, as well as several pale old men with one foot lingering in the Commons and the other softly working its way towards the Lords. They had been called into a meeting early on a Saturday morning for no reason other than that the PM liked to keep them all jumping to his tune. A few special advisors were dotted about, young assistants who acted like spare brains for those no longer able to have the facts at their fingertips. Kanha had often, after a few drinks on the terrace, spoken scathingly of such antics, but she hoped to follow when her time came, with her own young assistants to steal ideas from and her own merry tap dance into the Lords.

The PM was late.

In her bag, which felt as if it burned hot against her right shin, were the pages torn from Dvořáček's book. She had thought about hiding them in her house or in one of those dusty filing cabinets in her office that no one had opened for a hundred years, but after Tirrell's late-night visit, she'd decided it would be safer to keep them with her at all times.

The PM breezed in, his young diary secretary, Anastacia, pattering along at his elbow, an e-pad in her hand.

'Then you're over to Oxfordshire for Harry Colbey's cricket match,' she said, coming to an abrupt halt as he came into the room and pulled the door to behind him.

Kanha cursed inwardly. She was fluent in the PM's body language. The meeting was off. She thought of the warm bed she was missing, the stack of pillows and newspapers, Maximillian curled up under her arm.

'Sorry, everyone,' the PM said. 'Change of plan. I expect you've heard the news about the by-election. Well done, Tom.' There was a moment for all in the room to publicly congratulate their special guest, the party's new Head of Campaign, and although Tom nodded in a humble but slightly over-the-top fashion, his moment of glory didn't last long.

'We're going to reschedule this meeting to...' The PM turned to Anastacia.

'To be determined, Prime Minister,' she said.

'Yes, we'll let you know.'

Kanha pursed her lips. She'd had to get up at five that morning to make the meeting on time.

'I've to head down for a photo op with the new member for Taunton,' the PM said. 'Shake the hand, pap, pap, you know. Congrats all round – then I'm over to Oxfordshire for some local cricket match with Harry Colbey.'

'Are you playing, Prime Minister?' asked the home secretary.

The PM mimed hitting a cricket ball with a bat. 'Used to be quite good in my day, if you must know. Once hit a 112 at Lord's back when I got my blue for the University Match.' He paused with a glassy look in his eye. 'So next time, then. Election strategy, that's what we've all got to start thinking about. We're going to go with *In Safe Hands*. I want everyone's thoughts on how best to promote that.'

There was a murmur of agreement in the room.

Kanha felt a flush of annoyance. 'Why *In Safe Hands?*' she said.

The PM was already halfway out the door but turned back. 'Because we *are* a safe pair of hands, Esme. Don't you agree?'

'I do,' Kanha said, realising she was tapping her pen on the tabletop and forcing her hand still. 'But that's a *More of the Same* strategy. Shouldn't we debate whether that's the best approach before heading off down that route?'

The PM nodded as if giving the idea some consideration. 'I'd have thought, with the by-election we've just had, that a *More of the Same* strategy would be a given.'

'Not necessarily,' she said. 'The by-election success might have been down to other factors. The Whigge candidate split the opposition's vote, but what if they split ours next time?'

The home secretary squeaked a view that sounded like it might be in agreement, eliciting a frown from the PM.

The PM took the e-pad from his secretary and looked at it. 'We've had a remarkable run of it the last few years, and not changed a thing since the last election, so I can't see how anything except a *More of the Same* strategy would make any sense, don't you agree, Tom?'

'Oh, without doubt,' said Tom.

Arse-licker, thought Kanha.

'But the Whigges *are* gaining in strength,' said the foreign secretary. 'There's a groundswell of discontent they're feeding on – their three-day working week, a national fifty-mile-an-hour speed limit, free money left right and centre – it's striking a chord with the voters.'

There was a *pshaww* noise from Tirrell at the end of the table, along with a few other words of dissent.

The business minister said, 'Ridiculous. If you offer to give people money, of course they'll vote for you. There's a word for that.'

Kanha spoke over them. 'What I'm saying is that we may not have changed, but that doesn't mean people haven't. The world never stands still. There's a current out there that we're not speaking to. The Whigges, the anti-green, the Mouth of the Mob—'

'Don't talk to me about that dirty rag,' the PM interrupted angrily, and Kanha cursed herself, seeing that because of it, her chance was gone. In the last week its editorial content had definitely drifted towards the new politics of the Whigges.

'Thanks for your input, Chief Whip,' said the PM, 'but the strategy is *A Safe Pair of Hands*. Thoughts and ideas for how to support that at the next meeting everyone, please. Tom, I'll see you later at the cricket match. Thank you, everyone.'

Kanha put her best blank face on to hide her anger. It might be nice for once, she thought, to have a meeting with those who really set the party's strategy.

'Walk with me, Esme,' the PM called back as he set off down the corridor, and Kanha was forced to scrabble to collect up her pen, notepad and bag, and chase after him.

*

Kanha dutifully walked behind the PM and through the corridors of Number Ten as he was briefed on the security arrangements for the day's travel to Oxfordshire. With the meeting cancelled, Kanha had an unexpected free window and knew it was time to progress her side of what she and Colbey had agreed to do.

Outside on the pavement of Downing Street, the PM shooed his security detail out of earshot, and asked her in sibilant undertones, 'Do you have anything in your little chief whip tool bag against Harry Colbey?'

The PM's Range Rover pulled up, followed by the escort vehicle, and then a pool car to ferry her back to the Commons.

'Colbey? I'll check with the team, but I don't think so. As far as I know, he genuinely is as dull as he appears.'

The PM grunted his agreement.

'Why, what's wrong?' she asked, trying to keep her voice curious but not overly so. 'Are you still worried about his honest politicking?'

Kanha opened the door of the PM's car for him.

'You know, you might be right about the campaign direction,' he said. 'I'm going to give it some more thought.'

'Thank you,' she said, thinking, In other words you're going to go back to the party leaders and pretend this was some inspiration of your own.

'I'm not going to be around forever, Kanha. Succession planning is an important consideration. Some think Colbey might have it in him to go the whole way.'

'Really?' she said, genuinely surprised to hear this.

'When I go, we might need someone who is, how might you put it… steady…'

'Dull?'

The PM smiled. 'Traditional, respectable… to stop any more sliding towards the Whigges. They're a temperate bunch, after all.'

'Temperate? Colbey's not teetotal, as far as I know.'

'But he's a family man, isn't he? Even you, Kanha, even you have to admit you haven't anything on him.'

Kanha allowed herself to frown. 'Then I don't understand. Why are you looking for dirt on him?'

The PM put his hand on hers, which rested on the frame of the open door. 'I'm thinking of you, Kanha,' he said, and she had to fight the urge to pull her hand away from the touch of this deceitful man. 'He's not in my camp, like you are, though I have to admit our wives are friendly.'

As he said it, a thought seemed to occur to him, and the PM nodded to himself and muttered, 'Now there's an idea.'

Concerned, Kanha closed the PM's door after him, and later, alone in her own car, she fretted about what he might be up to. She didn't believe for a minute he was looking to shore up Kanha's position. What sort of a fool did he take her for? She resolved to write Colbey a note of warning.

Kanha pulled a pad of pink notepaper from her bag, along with a HoC envelope, wrote the note of warning quickly, glancing up at the driver to be sure he couldn't see as she dropped it inside the envelope, and then into the pocket of her coat, ready to be discreetly slipped into Colbey's pigeonhole in the members' lobby. It sounded like he was to be at a cricket match all day, so unfortunately he would not get it until Monday, but there was nothing she could do about that. She didn't know what he could do with the information anyway; she just felt better for warning him.

Putting the notepad back in her bag, she saw the ripped-out pages of Dvořáček's book, the soft black folds of her improvised hijab, and next to them the thing she had bought but not yet used. She felt the hard plastic edge of its box. Why was she stalling? Was she getting cold feet on the matter? She hadn't done anything too illegal so far, not even anything dangerous.

She had taken some cash out, but what of it? She often did that. She had pulled apart a skirt and sewn it into a hijab and matching niqab. Then she had gone to the ladies' toilets in John Lewis a chief whip, and come out a devout Muslim. *Can't a woman experiment with her lost heritage?* She had walked over to the Edgeware Road and bought a pay-as-you-go phone from one of the telecoms stores there. A *burner phone* as she and Colbey had laughingly called it when she had told him of her plan, but there was certainly no crime in that, even if she had given them a made-up name and address – there was no legal requirement to register a phone, at least not yet. She could have just refused, but that would have raised the salesman's curiosity. The only real law she broke was that she had left her own phone behind in the Commons so that her movements couldn't be tracked, which meant she was without an ID app; if she had been stopped and searched, she might have been arrested for that.

Through the whole expedition to get the burner phone she had felt more alive than she had for a long time. So why was she stalling? Or was she just teasing herself, enjoying the thrill of it all? With the phone acquired she had walked back through the streets of the West End and revelled in what she had done. She'd thought the bravado of her youth was behind her, all those high jinks with Mani, but the phone was there in her bag, waiting for her to act, and there she was walking in the shoes of a different woman, someone she might have been.

'We're here, Chief Whip.'

Her driver was tapping on the window. Kanha dragged her mind off the past with a nag of doubt about what she must do, but she was committed now. It was a *pinkie promise*, after all.

Kanha made for the terrace café, ordered some coffee and a croissant and found a seat in a corner.

This was not a hastily made plan. She had done her homework – figured out where the CCTV cameras were, and worked out that this part of the cafeteria was not covered by them, yet it had good access to the parliamentary Wi-Fi that hundreds of people used every day.

She took the burner phone out of her bag, unpacked it and taped two small pieces of paper over its cameras. Then she plugged a portable charger into it. The phone had no sim, so neither she nor Colbey thought it would be traceable at this stage, but what did they know?

As soon as it was a tiny bit charged, she turned off all the tracking settings, logged onto the Wi-Fi, went onto a free email service, created an email account with one firm, used that email account to create another with some other firm, and then for good measure used that to create a third. From that she sent a message to Woodward, one of the highest-ranking Mouth of the Mobsters to ask if he was interested in a leak from inside the House of Commons. He replied immediately.

She looked around, but no one was watching.

How do I know you are inside HoC?

Kanha took a discreet snap of the day's menu and sent it to him.

Send me anything you want, came back the reply.

Soon, she typed back.

Afterwards, she surfed random newsfeeds on the phone until its battery died, and put it back in her bag. She went over to the central lobby and from there into the members' lobby and slipped the envelope with her warning note into Colbey's pigeonhole. Now she just needed to wait until Colbey told her he had amended the bill to include Dvořáček's clause and it would be time for her to do what couldn't be undone.

*

Over the next week, Kanha didn't see Colbey other than once, which was again in the circus of a cabinet meeting. She had spoken to him, asking him to move aside so she could pass, and their eyes had met. What a strangely intense form of communication that was. There had been no smile of recognition from either of them, yet in that moment it was as if some magic of the air between their eyes created a physical connection between them.

Throughout the meeting she'd had to resist the urge to look towards him and after it was over, at last she was able to turn to the person beside her and sneak a glance in his direction. Colbey was making his way to the door talking animatedly with another minister. He looked well, but tired, she thought. There were bags beneath his eyes that had not been there before. As she sat waiting for the rescheduled committee meeting from last Saturday, which was in reality the true cabinet meeting, she wished she could just ring Colbey up and talk to him, like any other friend or colleague.

The PM was in a foul temper. The fact had been apparent to Kanha as soon as he came into the room, though he had hidden it well during the wider cabinet meeting. Now that there was just the inner circle, he was no longer bothering.

Those with keen antennae like Kanha had picked up on the fact, but not all had yet. The home secretary started in on the first agenda point, noticing the PM's mood only partly way through, after which she was forced to soldier on with her update of the true immigration figures, while the PM's thin, lined face turned to a scowl. The secretary of state for health, distracted, had still not noticed, and was stupid enough to interrupt with news of a rumour that she saw on her phone that Monty West was going to defect to the Whigges that afternoon, which both Kanha and the PM already knew.

'We're aware of it,' Kanha said as the room fell to gossip, the immigration figures forgotten.

'It's more than a rumour,' the secretary of state for health said. 'Woodward's confirmed it.'

'Woodward?' said the PM sharply. 'Who the hell's that?'

'A reporter at the Mouth of The Mob,' she replied, to which the PM became exceedingly angry and railed at her for the suggestion that anyone at Mouth of the Mob could confirm anything about anything.

'Why don't you speak to Monty?' the foreign secretary asked Kanha, whereupon the PM shouted at the foreign secretary and called her a bloody fool.

'Of course we've thought of speaking to that traitorous weasel,' he said. 'Now's that enough of the matter. There's to be a crossing of the House and talking about it will only draw attention to the fact.'

Kanha didn't like to point out the obvious fact that the rumour was already well and truly spread by the Mouth of the Mob, so she tried to calm the situation – the home secretary's bottom lip was wobbling – by confirming that she had spoken to Monty West for an hour that morning in an attempt to dissuade him, but that he was bitter over some issue about funding that had not gone his way.

'Who the hell is this Woodward anyway?' the PM asked the room in general.

'It's a pseudonym,' said the minister of defence.

'I figured that out,' barked the PM, 'but who the hell is he? Haven't you tried to find out? What about your lot?' he asked the home secretary. 'Can't they work it out?'

The home secretary told him that they had put some people on it.

'And?' said the PM.

'He's well encrypted,' she replied. 'We think possibly Russian.'

'Russian?' the PM erupted, and he turned to Tirrell. 'Russian?'

Tirrell quietly cleared his throat. 'Russian? I don't think so. We thought more likely Chinese.'

'He's a civil servant,' the secretary of state for health was brave enough to squeak. 'Or so I heard off the grid...' Her voice trailed away as the eyes of those who ran MI5, MI6 and the nation's defence turned on her.

'Off the grid!' said the defence minister.

'Do you mean on a private messaging service?' Tirrell asked icily. 'What are you, a government minister, doing on the dark web?'

The secretary of state for health looked like she might be about to cry.

'For goodness' sake,' said Kanha. 'She means she heard it in the pub.'

'Yes, the Red Lion,' Health managed to squeak out, visibly trembling.

'I hate to interrupt all this fun,' said the foreign secretary, who was still looking at her ministerial e-pad. 'But Woodward is confirming—' she saw the PM look at her sharply '—is *rumouring* that there's another one too.'

'What?' said Kanha, signalling the foreign secretary to pass her e-pad over, a request that was ignored.

'Well?' barked the PM.

'Woodward's claiming there'll be two crossing the floor this afternoon,' she said.

'Who?' said the PM. 'Who is the other one?'

Kanha guessed that the secretary of state for health was going to point out that the PM himself was now looking to the Mouth of the Mob to confirm which of his party members was planning to defect, so she glared at her until the woman thought twice.

'Doesn't say. Just says another's confirmed, who prefers not to reveal their identity for now,' she read out.

Kanha was on her feet gathering together her things even as the PM was rising and ushering her out of the door, the two of them already on their phones. The meeting abandoned, the next hour was spent in an empty office that she found in Number Eleven ringing round all the MPs she knew to be disaffected, and coordinating her team to do the same, but the task was hampered because the phones were starting to go unanswered one by one.

She rang Elliot who was on the ground to find out what was going on. He told her the terrace was empty, everyone had gone to the House for the first reading of the privacy bill and the evening's debate because no one wanted to miss out on witnessing a crossing. He called back a few minutes later to confirm the chamber was full. Kanha's first thought was of Colbey. A full House would be an unpleasant surprise for him and his first reading of the bill – they had wanted it to slip by unnoticed. Admitting defeat, she made her way back through the connecting corridor between Number Eleven and Number Ten to the prime minister's office and Anastacia waved her in.

'Any luck?' he said.

'None. You?'

The PM shook his head. 'Either it's someone surprising, or someone lying.'

'Or there isn't a second one,' she said.

'Unlikely, if Woodward has it,' he said, and she realised the display in the cabinet meeting had been put on. He knew perfectly well that Woodward was a high-ranking Mobster, with his ear to the ground like no one else.

The PM looked deflated, and for a moment she felt sorry for him. He looked like a man who had bumped into some friends off to the wedding of an ex-wife. He was too old and too withered, and looked at that moment as if he would rather be anywhere in the world than standing there in Number Ten with the weight of the country on his shoulders. Kanha brushed a little dandruff off his jacket and straightened his collar, and felt a pang of guilt at her own treachery. Even as they stood there, her handbag with the torn pages from Dvořáček's notebook and the phone on which she had sent her own messages to Woodward was lying at his feet.

'You go, Esme. Ring me after and tell me who it was,' he said.

On the way over she urged her driver to hurry and when at last she arrived, she trotted through the central lobby, aware of the national television cameras following her progress, arriving only just in time. The House was full, so she was forced to stand by the door. Monty West went first. She had never liked him. She gave him a look that told him so. Then came the second, someone who had told her only half an hour earlier that it wasn't her. What a treacherous snake. Kanha didn't stay to watch her trip smugly down the stairs. Those are your two minutes of fame, Kanha thought, but also a career over. She wouldn't retain her seat as a Whigge, come the election. That was the only satisfaction that Kanha could find in it and she sighed. They still had a strong majority, but it sent a dangerous signal to the public that the Whigges' policies were viable, respectable even.

Kanha went out to the empty lobby and called the prime minister to let him know. He had little to say and as she ended the call the chamber started to empty around her like a West End theatre when the show is over. She had seen Colbey sitting on the front benches, but for most of the time she had been there, his eyes had been fixed on the floor. She thought of waiting for him to come out, so that at least they could pass by each other and perhaps lend one another some support with an accidental brush of the hand in passing. But he didn't come out, and realising she was being foolish, she drove home and went to bed.

*

The next morning, Kanha went straight away to the pigeonholes in the members' lobby and found a note from Colbey to say the first part of their plan was done. She looked at the clerks' window, where copies of the bills were neatly stacked ready for collection.

Picking one up, she resisted the urge to flip it open and see Dvořáček's clause in black and white with her own eyes, knowing she stood under the watchful eye of the CCTV camera. She stuffed it into her bag as nonchalantly as she could as if it were any other bill.

Now it was her turn to act. First, she went back to her office to deposit her official government phone and pick up the burner phone. She didn't want hers to be in the same GPS position as the burner when she turned it on, but when she got there, she found that there was a lot going on in the office, and she was waylaid by work, so it wasn't until mid-afternoon that she finally managed to get away to carry out the next stage of the plan.

After returning to the members' lobby on the pretext of picking something up from their little office there, Kanha went upstairs to the same bathroom where she had sat and wept after hearing of the death of Dvořáček, the same cubical even. Just as then, she chose this bathroom because it was rarely used, being tucked away at the top corner of the House. Her heart was beating fast as she flipped through the bill and read Dvořáček's clause. *Well done, Colbey,* she thought. And then she whispered to the empty stalls, 'Well, he did you proud, Dvořáček.'

As soon as the burner phone had a little juice from the battery charger, she took Dvořáček's notebook out of her bag, peeled the paper off the back of the phone's camera lens, then took a photo of the page where Dvořáček had listed all the meetings that had taken place between his department and Henri Lauvaux of Alcheminna, which detailed the company's request for access to citizens' data in return for use of the Alcheminna system for anti-terror purposes. She put the sticker back in place. She sat for a moment with her hand hovering over the send button. She thought of Ewan. He had been her boss for a long time, they had been through many campaigns together. But then she thought of how even the country's National Security Council meetings were a joke. He, Tirrell and god knew who else were running the country like a fiefdom. She thought of how he had lied and said he wanted dirt on Colbey to shore up her candidacy for promotion, when really he planned to ruin him, perhaps just as he had with Dvořáček. She thought of what they had driven Dvořáček to even though he was a long-standing friend of theirs – or perhaps what even worse thing they might have done. She thought of the world they were nudging everyone into without their knowledge, without their agreement.

She pressed the send button. Then she logged onto Woodward's Mouth of the Mob page to see if anything would happen. At first there was nothing. How long might it take? Maybe he wouldn't post at all. Maybe this was all pointless. Maybe he didn't trust her as a source.

Then...

Breaking news Priority One.

She clutched the phone and waited. And waited and waited. Then...

Snooper's Charter. Previous minister for Department of Personal Information met with Silicon Valley start-up Alcheminna to discuss getting access to Brits' records to feed its cutting-edge AI systems.

The comments started to come, one, two, ten, fifty, eighty. Oh, what had she done?

Then came more…

In return, Government offered access to the system for anti-terror purposes.

Then something happened that confused her. The phone flicked itself back to the photo she had taken of the page. She frowned and clicked to go back to the page on the Mouth of the Mob website, but her phone flicked itself back to the photos again. Then it was onto the search engine, the empty email window, the unused text service. She dropped it in her lap. It was flicking through all the newsfeeds she had randomly searched the first time she had used the phone. Someone else was in the phone. Someone else was using it.

Kanha panicked, realising she had no idea how to turn it off. It was not the same as her usual model. It didn't turn off in the same way. Damn it. She thought she had been so clever. She pushed every button and combination of buttons she could think of. How had it all gone so wrong, so quickly?

Suddenly she realised the camera light was on and the screen had flicked onto messages. Someone was typing a message.

Hi.

She stared in horror.

Are there any more pages?

She stood up, lifted the seat, and threw the phone into the toilet.

The bathroom door outside opened. Kanha froze. Should she sit down and lift her feet? Would they hear the noise of it?

Go into a stall, she silently begged. But they weren't here to use the facilities. They walked slowly along to the far end of the row of cubicles, and then back again. Could it be a security guard?

The footsteps came closer and paused in front of the cubicle she was in. The toes of a man's shoes could be seen under the door. It was too late to sit down and lift her feet now. Then she saw a black tie fall and be pulled back. Whoever it was had just bent down, had already seen them.

She didn't dare move.

Then the person spoke.

'I recognise those shoes,' he said. Then he added, 'You might as well come out, if you've finished having a leak, *ha ha*, naughty lady. What an amateur you are at all this.'

She put her head against the wall. It was a voice she knew well.

3·4

The Frenchman Henri Lauvaux stood up from their lunch table, lifting his napkin to his lips and then putting it down on the table. He held a hand out to Colbey, and when it was not taken, used it instead to pull out the chair next to him.

'Please,' he said, 'let's be civil about this. Nothing can be gained from anger.'

Colbey had to admit it was true. A row here, possibly in the hearing of others, would not help his cause. What he needed was to understand how badly he was compromised, and what their intentions were. He sat at the table, followed by the Frenchman, and nodded at Lauvaux's offer to pour him a cup of coffee.

Lauvaux lifted the milk jug towards him and Colbey poured and stirred, wondering what he should say. Why had he not considered that on the way over? What was his plan? It was unlike him to be hot-headed, but then this Lauvaux chap and the PM had used his wife in the most despicable way.

'I'm glad we have this opportunity to talk,' said Lauvaux. 'I do find you most interesting.'

The PM took a slurp of his tea and snorted. 'Lauvaux finds everyone interesting,' he said. 'He's what you might call a people person.' He staggered to his feet. 'I might go and visit the little boy's room. Leave you two shareholders to your meeting.'

When he was gone, Lauvaux smiled and tugged at his open collar until it sat straight and symmetrical around his neck. His fingers were long but not as tanned as his face, and there were red veins across his cheeks. Colbey wondered whether Clarissa would find Lauvaux attractive and decided she probably would. He could imagine her laughing a little too loudly and playing with her diamond pendant, running it up and down the chain around her neck as Lauvaux said the pleasure was all his.

'You tricked my wife,' Colbey said. 'That wasn't very noble.'

'Nonsense,' said Lauvaux. 'We gave her an opportunity few ever chance upon.'

'An opportunity to ruin me?'

'An opportunity to be exceedingly wealthy.'

'We don't want to be exceedingly wealthy.'

'*Non, non*, Mr Colbey. That's not quite right, is it? It's you who isn't tempted by the thought of becoming exceedingly wealthy. Your wife's secret desires are entirely different...'

Colbey couldn't argue with that. Now that his temper had cooled, he wondered how it would look if it were reported that he was here, meeting alone with Lauvaux.

'What is it you want?' he said.

'Yes, we'll come to that,' Lauvaux replied. 'But I really would like to get to know the real you a little better. I've been talking to... to the other one quite a bit since you became someone of importance to us. As I said, I do so enjoy your company.'

'The other one?'

'Yes.'

'The one in the Alcheminna system?'

'Yes.'

'Tell me,' Colbey said. 'It's big data, big tech, is that what you've signed me up to? Storing everyone's personal data?'

'Big data, you could say that – it's an important element to the process. But it's not really what we do.'

Lauvaux got up and went over to the window. 'Tell me, Harry, do you know the difference between data and information?'

'Data and information? Of course, I'd say one is—'

'If I said your tie is red, that would be a piece of data, wouldn't it?'

'Yes, data. I guess this is what you guys are good at.' Colbey wanted it to sound sarcastic but it came out reverential.

'Indeed. But who cares, eh?'

'Sorry?'

'Who cares if your tie is red? Knowing that you have a desire for red ties, I could offer you another red tie the next time you go shopping. But that's rather old hat, isn't it?'

Colbey looked down at his tie. It was one of his favourites. When he looked back up again, Lauvaux was staring at him with slightly wild eyes.

'Now what if I said I hate men who wear red ties?' Lauvaux hesitated again for effect and stepped forward. 'Now that's information, isn't it? That's much more interesting. Do you see the difference?'

'That's your speciality is it, then? Information, not data?'

'Exactly. You have got it in one. Imagine being on the ground floor of that. It would be like being one of the early investors in Google or Facebook. Can you imagine it? No, of course you can't.'

'But Clarissa could.'

'Yes, your wife is a smart woman. I agree with her thoughts that she's wasted as just an MP's wife.' Colbey decided he would not be drawn on that, and Lauvaux smiled as if the conversation was going exactly as he expected it would. 'But for you, think of what you could do for your nation with access to the Alcheminna system.'

There it was. The system, the Alcheminna system. Did he really understand what it was?

Lauvaux laughed and came to sit down again. 'I'm sorry,' he said. 'Sometimes I forget you and I have not had all the conversations that the other you and I have had.'

'The avatar?'

'No. That's not the right word. An avatar is a representation of you in another environment. Do you know where the word comes from?'

'It means God made in man's image.'

'Yes, very good. It comes from the concept of a god placing a mortal version of himself into the world. As the god, you control your own avatar. But this is entirely different. The other you, the one in Alcheminna, is a discrete and separate version of you. Based on you, yes, but not controlled by you.'

'Controlled by who, then? By those who own Alcheminna?'

'*Non, non,*' Lauvaux said crossly, wagging one of his long fingers at Colbey. 'You are missing the point. Nobody needs to control them – they are just there! They are a source of information. What we control is access to the information they provide, do you see?'

Colbey was starting to see, and the more he saw, the more horrified he was.

'Of course you're horrified,' said Lauvaux. 'That was to be expected. But you do come round to it, once you realise how inevitable it is. You can't stop progress, you know.'

Colbey needed to get away from this magician, this Wizard of Oz, who seemed to be inside his head. 'What do you call it, then?'

'We call them our AI-generated simulations of individual units living or dead, but,' he chuckled, 'if we're in a hurry… just *digital replicas.*'

'So Alcheminna is a world of digital replicas.'

'That's right, and the more data we have, the closer the digital replicas behave to their earth-bound versions.'

It sounded like a game, but of course it wasn't.

'And whoever has access to Alcheminna…' Colbey said.

'Exactly,' said Lauvaux jubilantly. 'Your coming election, for example. We conduct the opinion poll not on the people, but on their digital replicas. We ask all the replicas, who will you vote for? And then we ask them, what if that person changes their policies to this or that, and we ask them again – now who will you vote for? It's much more reliable, you know, than asking the real things. People are such dreadful liars.'

Colbey took a sip of his coffee and found it had gone cold. 'Or perhaps, what will you buy if I show you this?' he said sarcastically.

'Yes, yes, of course there is a little commercial element to it, for those who wish for riches – your wife, for example.'

Colbey ignored the obvious needling. 'Surely it's illegal?' he said.

'Not at all,' said Lauvaux. 'Alcheminna is a respectable company. We only ever act within the law. And all the data we feed into the system has been freely offered up by the people of this world.'

'If that were true you wouldn't be trying to get me to change the law, would you?'

Lauvaux smiled. 'Your replica said just the same thing. But of course we're not asking you to change the law, just to ensure it doesn't get changed into something that might cause us difficulties.'

Colbey thought of Dvořáček's clause that was even now sitting on desks and in briefcases across Whitehall. Neither Lauvaux, nor his Frankenstein version of Colbey knew that.

Lauvaux frowned. Had he read Colbey's mind? This flesh and blood one?

'You are very confident,' Lauvaux said. 'I have these rather clever contact lenses. And they are suggesting to me that you know something I don't. They look at your eyes, the muscles in your face, that slight twitch that you have in your upper lip when you are nervous. What is it that you've done?'

For a while Colbey didn't speak. Perhaps he should just walk out, but he was tied to all this now, whether he wanted to be or not.

'When you asked me,' he said at last, 'the digital me, that is. How did it say you should influence me?'

'It said we couldn't.'

Colbey smiled. He felt a little warmth towards his digital self.

'Yes, I was surprised by that too,' said Lauvaux. 'An honest politician. Who'd have thought it.'

'So you thought of my wife instead?'

'Yes, well, actually, he did.'

Colbey felt less favourable towards it.

'He told us she was your weakest link. Who knows your life better than you, eh?'

Colbey thought of asking what his wife's replica had said, but decided he didn't want to know. He could take a wild guess.

'Yes,' said Lauvaux. 'Information, you see. So much more useful than data.'

The two men said nothing, then Lauvaux said, 'She has dreams too, you know, not just of that beach in Bequia that she endlessly looks at. Her affair is not leading where she hoped it would. Would you like to know—'

Colbey stood up abruptly. 'No! Thank you, but no. I'd rather not know, as it happens.' He knew his colour was rising, but what did that matter.

What made him angry was not that this man, this perfectly dressed, smiling know-it-all should have this information about his wife, have used it to trick her into something she most certainly would regret, but that he felt like he had betrayed Clarissa and that it was there for all the world to see. He thought of her searching for cheap ways to get to Bequia, how she must have hidden it from him. The thought made him want to curl up into a ball and do nothing but cry.

At that moment, the PM returned to the room and stood looking at Colbey. 'So you're up to speed then, are you? I hope you see now how important it is that we have access to the system.'

Lauvaux flinched at the PM's indelicate approach.

'And that we must change the law to help them?' Colbey said.

'Exactly,' the PM said.

'And give them whatever data they want to feed the system?'

Lauvaux and the PM looked surprised.

'How did you know about that?' the PM said, his face turning to a look of worry.

Colbey considered how these men who wanted everyone to surrender their privacy seemed to think they should still keep their own. 'There is no privacy any more, remember?' he said.

'Oh, fiddlesticks,' said the PM. 'Any fool can see that the system is only as good as the data you feed it with. Cut off the data and this future will belong to the Chinese. And the system already has so much, anyway. No one cares. You think anyone cares? They'd give open access to their souls for a free messaging service, for a game to distract them on the Tube, for something that will let them send round silly pictures of their supper to strangers. That's the stuff the system feeds on. Not just the words and pictures, but how you say them, where you took them and so on. How you respond to an answer, are you nice? Friendly? Abrupt? Factual? Do you put kisses at the end? Who to? Close family, friends – when does someone become a friend? What does someone have to do to convert you from someone you know to someone you trust? How can I get you to put kisses on any texts you send to me?'

He turned to Lauvaux, suddenly jovial. 'See, I have been paying attention.' Then he turned back to Colbey. 'Emails, videos, heart rates, lies, affairs, illnesses, humour, proclivity to speed, what makes you annoyed, cross, furious – the more it has, the better it is. You can't stop the joining up of the dots.

'Does it scare you?' he continued. 'Well, it should. But what should scare you most is that the Russians can do this too. And the Chinese. And our friends over the pond… well. It's a race to who gets the data. Who can scrape the most. Who can stop the other side joining the dots. That's today's cold war. Show him some more.'

Lauvaux picked up his e-pad, held it in front of his eyes to unlock it, and typed in a password being sure the others would not be able to see it. Then twisting the screen to face them, he swept through a ring of the heads of the cabinet. Kanha went flying by, a grimace on her face. Each said a few words as they passed. Lauvaux stopped the spinning carousel, and flicked back a few places to settle upon the prime minister's replica.

'Well, you are a handsome chap,' Ewan MacLellan said to the screen.

'And so are you,' came the reply, and both versions of the prime minister laughed a little too loudly. Colbey turned his face from the future, so he was not sure which of the two continued to say, 'Think of where we are going, Harry. Who do you want to have access to this technology? Your government... or the Chinese?'

Colbey turned back and saw that it was the digital replica speaking.

'You can't hold back progress,' it said. 'At the industrial revolution, people thought that trains going too fast would kill passengers, mush up their insides. You have to move with the times. Now...' The digital replica gave a lusty groan. 'Where's that sexy secretary of mine?'

The prime minister frowned, and Lauvaux quickly moved to a menu screen, so that the carousel of cabinet members disappeared. 'Still some glitches to sort out,' he said.

The PM took over from his replica's speech undaunted. 'We've got to work with these big tech boys, don't you see? It's the new future. Most of the Five Eyes nations are on board. Everyone's giving them what they have. Everyone – think about it. We're either in or we're out.' He got up, went over to a side table and picked up a bottle of brandy. Shaking it and holding it to the light, he grunted and wandered off out of the room with the empty bottle.

Colbey wondered if it were true about the other Western nations being signed up to this. He knew well enough now that the PM was a liar. As a member of the Security Council, Kanha would have known if it were true. Lauvaux turned the pad towards him again, and Colbey saw that an image of Clarissa was on the screen.

'You can ask her anything,' Lauvaux said. 'We bypass her discretion traits by making her think she is talking to herself.'

Colbey put out his hand and pushed the tablet away. 'While there is democracy, there is still hope,' he said.

Lauvaux put down the pad and flipped its cover over. He looked disappointed in the way a father looks at a son who has been sent down from college.

Nothing could be done now to change the fact that Dvořáček's clause was within the government's bill. Even now, Colbey thought, Kanha might be leaking Dvořáček's notes to the press. He felt tired. There was only one place he wanted to go, only one person he wanted to talk to who would understand.

The prime minister returned, a full bottle of brandy swinging from his hand.

'Enough of this cosy chit-chat,' he said. 'Here's where we're at. Lauvaux here has a signed agreement from your wife buying a small stake in Alcheminna. It's a private company with shares issued on an invite-only basis, so you can't sell them. He's going to hold on to that agreement until you've passed the privacy bill and we've discreetly given these chaps a feed to the data they need.'

Colbey nodded. What else could he do?

'After that you'll have a choice. Either you can resign as a member of parliament, and ask Lauvaux to take the money sitting in escrow and register the share agreement to make it official. You can make your wife exceedingly happy and, as the years go by and Alcheminna goes from strength to strength, obscenely rich. The two of you can waltz off to Bequia or wherever else you want to live happily ever after.'

Colbey nodded again.

'Or, if you're determined to ruin your wife's chances for happiness, then stay in my cabinet, be a good boy and do as Kanha and I tell you, and I give you my word, we'll bury the share agreement somewhere safe until you're snoozing in some back row of the Lords, by which time its power of attorney will have naturally expired. There! I can't say fairer than that, can I?'

Colbey looked from the man who was consumed by greed to the man who was quite mad. Or perhaps it was the other way around.

'Which did the digital me choose?' he said.

'What does that matter now?' said Lauvaux. 'What does the real you say?'

Colbey laughed at the fact that it was too late for him either way, and neither of them realised it, and the two men looked at him. Perhaps there was hope. Perhaps the world and real people were too chaotic for their game.

'I need to think about it,' he said.

Lauvaux looked disappointed, but the PM said, 'Show him something. Show him something that will impress on him that he can't fight it.'

'Must I talk to myself?' said Colbey sarcastically.

'Not necessarily,' said Lauvaux. 'The system has other facilities. A conversation is only one interface, but we can get close to someone's thoughts in other ways. We are inside people's heads, remember.'

Lauvaux lifted the pad again. 'Close your eyes and think of something random. Don't cheat. Tell me the first image that comes.'

Colbey did as he was told. He wanted to see if this was real so he didn't chop through a hundred images and settle on one – he went for the first that came to his mind. It was of a table laid for two, lunch in the lavender fields of Provence, a hotel with green shutters and a gravelled drive. There was bread and cheese and wine. The sky was a perfect blue with just one wispy cloud on the horizon. The top of Mont Ventoux stood out in the distance. The table was laid with a white cloth and the sun was making the glasses and the cutlery glint and shine. Coming up the drive, in the distance, was a woman in a flowing black dress.

He opened his eyes and was faced with the e-pad. He tried not to gasp. The hotel had a different kind of shutters, but the table, the wine, the gravel, the bright sun, the woman and even the distinctive grey-topped mountain were all there.

'Was it right?' asked Lauvaux a little too eagerly, and Colbey realised that Lauvaux's party trick didn't always play out. For a moment he fought the impulse to tell him that the woman wasn't right. In the picture her hair was blonde, whereas in the image in his head...

Lauvaux flipped the lid of the e-pad over for the last time and tucked it into a bag at his feet. 'When the computer knows everything,' he said, 'then it becomes the god. And what are you if you own a god? Well, that is the metaphysical question of the day, isn't it?'

Colbey was saved from answering by the PM's phone ringing at the same time as Lauvaux frowned and looked down at his watch. The PM looked up sharply. 'Our deal's been leaked,' he said, his mouth falling open.

He turned to Colbey and said angrily, 'Is this your doing?' Then he pressed his lips together into a thin line. 'You had better go, Lauvaux. Take the back entrance. And you, Colbey, I'll get someone to escort you out. I expect those Mobster rats will be waiting out there for you, though it's exactly what you deserve.'

Lauvaux was already lifting his bag onto his shoulder, a phone suddenly in his hands. He stopped and looked at Colbey and a crooked smile crossed his face, then he gave a slow nod and, reaching out, he patted Colbey on the shoulder, rustling the collar of his raincoat as he did so. 'Bravo, Harry Colbey,' he said, his eyebrows lifting in surprise. Then he hurried out of the room.

3·5

Kanha leaned her head against the wall of the cubicle and reached out for the door handle. Her hand was shaking, and she realised her entire body had become damp with a cold sweat.

'Come on. Open up.'

She paused for a moment, delaying the inevitable.

'Come on. I know it's you.'

Although he was trying to disguise it, she recognised the voice; how could she not? It was Mani.

Pulling herself together she swung the door open and said, 'You utter shit. You scared the life out of me.' She didn't know whether to punch him or hug him, but she didn't have to decide because as soon as the door was open he pushed her aside, one hand over her mouth, the other grabbing at her arms to look for the phone.

'Where is it?' he hissed in her ear, and she pointed at the bowl. Shaking his head he whispered, 'And where's *your* phone.' She told him it was in her office. He looked again at the phone at the bottom of the pan and said out loud, taking his hand from her mouth, 'Jesus, Esme. You could have just turned it off.'

'I couldn't figure out how,' she admitted.

He fished the phone out of the toilet and used the nearby china holder of the sanitary brush to smash it into several pieces, a few of which went into his pocket, and the rest he took with him out of the cubicle and dumped them into the waste bin there.

She followed him out of the stall. He scanned the ceiling and seeming satisfied that there were no cameras in the bathroom, stood waiting while she washed her face in one of the sinks, being kind enough not to comment on her still shaking hands. When she felt composed enough, she said, 'So you're Woodward?'

'I certainly am. Nice to make your acquaintance, and you must be the mystery Westminster leaker. Come on, don't be sore.'

'You nearly gave me a heart attack.'

'You always were a wild one, Esme. Want to explain why you're trying to leak a tech scandal that's going to embarrass your party?'

'Want to explain how you hacked that phone and found me so quickly?'

'OK.'

'OK.'

He leaned his shoulder against the main door of the bathroom to ensure no one would come in. 'You first, then.'

'It's a long story,' she said.

Mani slid down to sit with his back against the door and patted the marble floor beside him. She wondered what someone might say if they tried to come into the ladies to find her and Mani pressed up against the door so that it couldn't be opened – they would probably come to some conclusion, but she doubted it would be the right one – and joined him on the floor.

'How do I know I can trust you?' But even as she said it, she knew the answer.

'Remember that time we broke into the senator's office to take a picture of the contents of his drawer?'

Kanha nodded.

'Remember who got busted in the corridor keeping watch and lost his job?'

'I got you another,' Kanha said. They both laughed. 'Hey, we were wild then,' she said.

'Seems we still are. So, are you going to tell me what you're up to?'

'Am I talking to you, or to Woodward?'

'Talk to me. I'll only tell Woodward what you want me to.'

Kanha took a deep breath. 'What you leaked is only the tip of the iceberg,' she said. 'I don't quite know who's in on it, but MacLellan is planning to give Alcheminna all of our citizens' data, if we don't find a way to put a stop to it.'

'And in return they get to use the system for anti-terror leads?'

'And for election campaigning.'

'Even now, they would try that? After the last scandal? Did cabinet sign it off?'

'No, this is what I'm telling you. No one's signed it off. Not cabinet, not the national council, certainly not the House.'

'But the home secretary surely knows?'

Kanha laughed. 'She's a fool who wouldn't know her own arse if she saw it.'

'Foreign secretary? Can't get much past her?'

'I think they've worked hard to keep her in the dark. The PM's been working on it with Anthony Tirrell.'

'So who else is in on it? Anyone from the party leadership?'

'No idea. Dvořáček was, certainly, but I'm not sure how much of a willing participant he was.'

'And you?'

'I would never have agreed to it!'

'Because...'

'Because it's wrong. Anyway, so that's where I am. And you? You haven't entirely given up your sideline in hacking then, I see?'

'Not entirely. I do it for fun now. Got to do something to keep the blues away.'

'No wonder you're the top-ranking Mobster.'

Mani pulled a phone from his pocket.

'Hey! How come you're allowed your phone?'

'Because mine has the camera, microphone and tracker removed.'

'It's a good job I trust you. Thank goodness it was you.'

Mani laughed and tucked a leg under him. 'Actually, you didn't do a bad job. You just didn't know you were up against the best. I liked the piece of tape over the camera.'

Kanha punched him on the arm. 'How did you find me so easily then, and how did you get into that phone?'

'The first was easy after the second. They're easy to hack, those phones. I have a piece of Israeli software in my bag of tricks that can get into most phones.'

'And finding me?'

'Actually, that wasn't so easy. I could see you were using the Commons Wi-Fi but couldn't pinpoint it. So I listened to the microphone and heard a dripping noise that sounded like a leaky cistern. Then I looked at the phone's orientation, figured out you were sitting on the john, took a look at a plan of the Commons, figured out which one it must be – there's only one on that alignment – and there you were, sport.'

'There I was, sport. Mani, can I ask you a question?'

'Go right ahead.'

'What exactly is it you've been doing these last eight years?'

'Well, that would be telling.'

'So tell. I told you mine.'

'I got caught hacking into the White House catering system.'

'Jesus.'

'It was just for a bet. Me and a few others in the collective were debating how much the president drank.'

'I told you to stop messing about with those guys.'

'Next thing I know the FBI are at the door. One of the collective, total weasel, I won't name him – actually I guess he's a colleague now – was a rat.'

'Mani...'

'I know. You told me. I was given a choice between eight years in prison or a job.'

'So you took the job.'

'Right.'

'Are you still working for them?'

'My eight years are up.'

'That didn't exactly answer my question. So?'

Mani didn't exactly answer that one either. He looked at his phone. 'It's going crazy,' he said. 'A world of hacks are turning their eyes to Alcheminna. It's like a company no one ever heard of is suddenly trending on every site there is.'

'I'd better go,' said Kanha. 'Any minute now the PM is going to be yelling at anyone he can get hold of and my phone's back in the office. I don't want to be unexpectedly absent.'

They said their goodbyes and she hurried away. When she got to the whips' office, Paddy said, 'There you are. Everyone's been looking for you. Tirrell's in your office.'

She approached it warily to see Tirrell was at her desk, sitting in her chair.

'Wondered where you were,' he said. 'Kanha's phone is here. But not Kanha herself. How strange, I thought. And how very illegal.' Tirrell was twirling Kanha's phone round on its back. 'To be without your ID app. Tut tut, Minister.'

'What do you want?' she said.

'Haven't you heard the news?'

'No, what news?'

'There's been a scandal. Dvořáček... remember him... discussed giving a company, Alcheminna Systems, access to national data in return for access to their system. You wouldn't happen to know anything about that now, would you?'

Kanha forced herself to frown and look surprised. 'No. Is it true?'

'Maybe,' said Tirrell. 'Maybe. Though I don't know who could have told that nasty hack, whoever he is, other than Dvořáček, but of course he's dead.'

'Is that so?' said Kanha, taking her phone from between Tirrell's fingers. 'I'd better call Ewan. Where is he?'

'Unless he wrote it in that little black book of his, of course. The one you threw on the fire.'

Tirrell got up and stood beside her. 'Maybe someone tore a page out and sent it to the hack.'

'And you think that's me, do you?' said Kanha. The one thing she was good at. The one thing she learned at that bloody sadistic school of nuns was how to lie with a straight face.

'Was it?'

'No.'

'Well, who else could it be?'

'I don't know, Tirrell – you're the national security advisor. Why don't you figure it out and advise us?'

He seemed uncertain. 'I suppose it could have been his widow. Or Colbey. He had the diary before you, didn't he?'

'Or it could have been any number of people who saw it before I had it, or after when my team had sent it to the widow.'

Tirrell frowned. 'Mmm. You're right. That's quite a few people.'

She saw all the missed calls on her phone. 'Was there anything else, Anthony? Because it looks as if the PM is after my advice right now.'

'Right you are.' As he passed her, he said softly, 'I hope it wasn't you, Esme. Would have been a very foolish thing to do. I'd have to act.'

'You can't act, Anthony,' Kanha said. 'You're just an advisor, remember?'

'At the moment.'

Kanha dialled the PM's number and turned her back on the man. When she turned back, she saw him disappear at the end of the long room. She closed the door and prepared to face Ewan's fury, but he didn't answer. She left a message to say she had her phone and to call her if he needed her. When he didn't call, she decided to head over to the Department for Personal Information. She couldn't speak to Colbey, but there was something she needed to find out.

On the way there, Kanha called the PM's chief of staff to find out what was going on over at Number Ten. He told her, without telling her directly, that she was under suspicion for leaking the information, and that Tirrell was pointing the finger at her.

'We all know it's nonsense, Esme,' he said. 'And there are half a dozen other people under suspicion. The PM'll calm down and see sense soon, trust me. It's just Tirrell whispering in his ear.'

'Well, call me if you need me,' she said.

It suited her to have this time to follow up on something that had been nagging at her for a while. She came into the DoPI building just as most of the staff were clocking off for the evening, and had to wait for a door bubble to be opened for her direction of flow. Her phone was buzzing with calls, so she switched it off and went around the corner to knock on the security guards' office door. When she asked to see the CCTV footage of the night that Dvořáček ended his life, the guard let her in and sat her in a little swivel chair while he flicked through the files.

Then he turned and said in surprise, 'It's gone! Everything from that evening has been deleted.'

'Can you get it back?'

The guard scratched his head and confessed that was a bit beyond him and maybe she should speak to someone good with computers.

'Good idea,' she said.

Back outside, she called Mani. They'd agreed it was fine to communicate with each other, so long as they didn't act as anything other than just old friends and colleagues who had recently been reunited.

'Hey, buddy,' she said. 'My day's been pretty shit. Do you fancy a drink?'

'I'm already home,' he said. 'Come on over, I've got some grog in the fridge. Don't forget the house rule.'

'Nope.' Kanha dropped her phone off in her office, and then took a walk over the bridge to Vauxhall. The wind coming off the river was cold here. It skimmed over the water, travelling in the same direction as her, but was pulled up short by the line of newly built skyscrapers, creating an eddy that lifted her coat-tails and swirled around her as she came into the development. Mani's flat was in one of the two big towers there. Bridged between them was a swimming pool, a surreal strip of turquoise suspended many storeys high. The gap below was like that of a whistle, and the cold wind howled past her and off through it as she reached the lobby of his tower. It was a relief to be inside and taking the lift up to his floor.

Mani opened the door and she followed him into his sitting room, where a beer stood waiting for her on the table.

'Oh, I shouldn't really have a drink,' she said. 'I need to drive home.'

'You're welcome to stay.'

It was a tempting offer.

Mani sat at his computer where he was looking through the comments on his Mouth of the Mob page. She went and stood behind him, looking over his shoulder to read them. A little mermaid appeared on the screen. Mani gave it a wave, and it waved back at him, then dived into the page and disappeared. Kanha raised her eyebrows questioningly, but Mani said, 'Best you don't know.'

He made her a cup of coffee, and she said, 'So, how should I have sent you the information then, if my burner phone wasn't the best idea?'

Mani turned to her. 'You should have used a VPN to mask your location. Then you should have found a third party to ask me for my encryption key, encrypted the message, and sent it to me using a private email system like TOR.'

Kanha looked at him blankly and then laughed. 'Whatever,' she said.

She picked up the coffee and blew on it as Mani smiled and turned back to his computer. 'I've got to make a phone call. Don't talk, OK?'

Kanha went and looked at the river and the dotted strip of street lamps on the other side. Now that night had fallen, the

Houses of Parliament were a dark block of nothingness in a city studded with lights. She listened to Mani as he gave someone's secretary IT support for a kid's malfunctioning e-pad.

'Another sideline?' she said, when he was done. 'So you still never sleep, huh?'

After he joined her on the sofa, she explained about the missing security footage.

'It's never completely gone,' he said and went back to the computer while she made herself another cup of coffee. By the time she returned, the warm mug in her hands, he was spooling on his PC through the department's CCTV footage of the evening Dvořáček killed himself.

'How the hell?'

Mani didn't answer, so she leaned over his shoulder and joined him to watch Dvořáček staggering into the reception area and through the security tubes. He caught his coat in them, and the security guard had to open it twice to let him through. Mani speeded up the footage, and then paused it again.

'Now see what I found. Only one more person comes in after that.' He froze the screen on the man's face.

'Tirrell,' muttered Kanha. It was what she had dreaded seeing. 'When does he come back out?'

Mani spooled through. 'About ten minutes later.'

'And Dvořáček?'

'No, only Tirrell.'

'One thing I found out, after a bit of digging around,' Mani said. 'Did you know Dvořáček was a member of a vintage rifle and pistol club?'

'Yes, Morland told me. It's how they think he got the shot in for the pistol.'

'But do you know who else was a member of the same club?' he said, flicking into another screen, which seemed to be a members' area for the club.

'Let me guess, Tirrell?'

Mani nodded and Kanha put the coffee down; she decided to drive home. She needed a night away from this place of festering rot. This hall of robber barons, thieves and murderers.

'You want me to send this video to the police?'

Kanha sighed. 'Can you do it anonymously somehow?'

'Sure thing,' said Mani with a grin.

Kanha put her coat on. 'At some point, Mani, you're going have to come completely clean with me.' He agreed it was true and showed her to the door, handing her two phones as he did so.

'They can't be traced by anyone other than me,' he said. 'One for Colbey and one for you, and both have fake ID apps on them.'

Walking back across the river, the freezing wind in her face now, she wished she had driven over. She thought about leaving her phone in her office, rather than having to sit with it in the car. It would feel as if Tirrell were in the car with her, but that wasn't what they had agreed. She must act as normal. After all, Colbey would be losing much in order to ensure her part in all this was not discovered.

She thought of the prime minister who had refused to take her calls. Well, perhaps it was as it should be. She had betrayed Ewan, after all, but then he had betrayed her. Not only her. He had betrayed his position and the oath he had made when he became a member of parliament.

She felt an unexpected prick of tears in her eyes. Unexpected, but she had been one of his loyal lieutenants for several years now. Yes, he had always been a canny politician, and all that went with it, all that she admired and emulated – together he had taught her the games of playing this one off against another, of cajoling, of inventing half-truths to appease or manipulate a member on their side, on the other side, or a member of the press. But always with the right end in mind, always to allow them to be there to lead and look after the nation. Yet this, now. She saw that she had been a piece he had played all along with all the rest. She had not been within the circle. Angry with herself that she had so misjudged him, she realised that the old Kanha would have called him again by now. So as soon as she got back to the office and collected her ministerial phone she rang, and, disguising the reason for her anger, left a message to ask why he wasn't taking her calls. Was it true about Alcheminna, and had he known about it?

It was like demanding of a partner whether he was really having an affair, when you've already broken into his email and seen the traitorous messages back and forth with his lover arranging their dirty weekends.

Ewan called her straight back. 'Of course it isn't true,' he said, and it astonished her that even though he sounded tired he could lie so competently. 'It was Dvořáček acting outside his remit. I admit to you, yes, I knew he'd been approached, but I told him not to agree to anything until we'd all had a chance to discuss it at the next Security Council meeting. Then, of course, he...'

'Yes,' said Kanha, and she listened to the lies and allowed the PM to think he had talked her round, just as a woman might listen, nodding, to her partner's lies while really thinking of how to discreetly see a lawyer and plotting how to get the house, the car, how to screw his fucking cheating arse to the wall.

'I'll be in early,' Kanha said. 'So call me if you need me.'

'Wonderful, Esme. What would I do without you? The home secretary is causing a terrible fuss, you know.' So she had not known about it, Kanha mused, which meant MI5 had not known. So the PM would most definitely be in trouble with one of those factions who wielded power in their party.

'What about the foreign secretary?'

'Oh, don't worry about her. Anyway, look, I'd better go. Let's speak tomorrow.'

As she drove home, Kanha cogitated. There had been rumours for a long time that the PM was plotting to give Tirrell the top job at MI6, but was being blocked by those whose man was already in the job. Tirrell was a tiger, a bear, aggressive, combative. The current head favoured a diplomatic approach to international relations. The minister for defence, though it would be expected to be the other way round, sided with the doves.

Kanha drove up onto the escarpment to her village and the temperature outside fell below zero. Whatever she did with the dials, she couldn't get the clapped-out heating to blow in the right direction. Her feet were cooking but her nose was freezing. It was as she was fiddling with the dials that she realised. Getting access to the Alcheminna system was Tirrell's coup de grace in his attempt to take over MI6. He would walk in a man who appeared to know everything, the senior team would be forced to concede to him, and by the time it was discovered where his knowledge came from, his position would be secure. The nation would have become reliant upon the Alcheminna system and it would never be uninstalled, at least not until something even worse came along.

As Kanha turned into her driveway, she called for a takeaway. When had she last eaten a proper meal? She needed food, and a lot of it. The curry house was busy. It would be over an hour before they could deliver, but quicker if she could collect. She agreed she would come, and she thought of a hot bath in the meantime.

Maximillian was asleep on her bed and as Kanha ran the water into the bathtub he leapt up onto a stool and purred while she rubbed her fingers along his jowls. Then he watched as she let down her hair from its rigid bun, gave it a shake and tied it loosely again on the top of her head. When the bathwater was as deep and hot as she dared, she stepped gingerly in. Maximillian tucked his paws beneath him and settled down facing her, his nose just a few inches from hers as if ready for a chat. Kanha sank gratefully into the water.

'What a day, Maximillian,' she said. 'You wouldn't believe it if I told you.'

The cat responded with a sustained purring.

It was a relief to know that here, in her bathroom, there were no phones or TVs, no microphones, no cameras. There was so much inside her head that she wanted to put into words – it would be the only way of making sense of it, of finding ways through the myriad mess of uncertainties and connections. She used to do that in the car on her drive home, but now she realised those thoughts were possibly shared with others, so this evening she hadn't dared do it while her ministerial phone was beside her in her bag in the car. She thought of the kids in her office using bubble wrap to encase the phones, and wondered whether there was still a roll of it in the cupboard under the stairs. She couldn't keep leaving it out on the back porch.

She was about to speak when it occurred to her how easy it would have been for Tirrell to arrange for someone to break into her house and hide listening eyes about the place. Now that the thought had occurred to her, she was afraid to speak, even here in her own home, in her own bath.

She talked some nonsense softly to the cat for a while until her fingertips wrinkled, then she lifted a hand out of the water, and when it was dry, softly chucked him under the chin. The cat looked up at the little bathroom window.

'What do you hear?' Kanha said. 'Some nasty tomcat prowling on your patch?'

She wondered what the time was and craned to see the clock in the bedroom. 'Shit,' she said, getting up so suddenly that Maximillian jumped off the seat and went away to sit on the bed in disgust.

'Sorry,' she called out to him as she pulled on some jeans and a jumper, but he didn't seem too bothered, engrossed as he was in licking one of his hind legs.

Hurrying out of the house and into the cold air, she had a sudden feeling there was someone there in the dark with her. As she double locked the front door, she stopped still, though she hadn't heard anything. She cursed her stupidity in not turning the outside light on and stumbled her way to the car, her nervousness turning to a feeling of panic. What had made her think someone was there? Had her ear detected a movement, a footfall at the side of the house? Was it the recollection of the cat looking sharply up at the window as if he had heard something outside? Or was it just a muntjac or a fox, stalking through the undergrowth?

'You're being stupid,' she told herself on reaching the car, which was already covered in a soft sheen of ice crystals, but still she got in hastily and slammed her hand down on the toggle to lock the doors. Inside it was like the interior of a silk cocoon, with the windows to the front and sides frosted over.

The windscreen wipers came on with the engine and they staggered over the white frost. She turned the blowers on to their maximum level and watched the pathetic whine of air drift onto the frozen glass.

Then her heart was in her mouth. Someone was trying to open her passenger door handle. She thought of driving forward, but it would be madness. She was completely blind to the front, disorientated already as to which way was straight. She would be as likely to drive into a tree as along the driveway. A small hole appeared in the glass in the centre of the windscreen, growing too slowly, millimetre by millimetre, inch by inch as the wipers scraped back and forth.

She sat, terrified, trembling, and for a moment she was that five-year-old child again, hiding in a basement while the men with guns went from house to house. She fumbled in her bag, but that dratted phone was sitting in the back porch as was her new habit.

The wipers went back and forth, back and forth. She could see the end of the driveway, a patch of the road ahead; was it enough to drive? It was enough, she decided, and put her foot on the accelerator just as a figure came to the front of the car.

Jesus, fuck, what a cowardly idiot she was being. She opened the door and pulled herself out.

'Who the fuck are you?' she shouted, but even as she said it, she saw who it was. 'Jesus fuck,' she said again. 'Jesus fuck. Would everyone please stop creeping up on me like this?'

Poor Harry Colbey looked very crestfallen. 'I'm freezing,' he said. 'Didn't want you leaving without letting me in. I was just hiding my bike round the back and came back to find you about to go.'

Kanha felt the relief course through her as a laugh. 'You wouldn't believe the day I've had,' she said.

'Mine's not been a picnic, either,' he said, and she realised he was shaking from the cold.

Kanha gave him the keys to the house, warned him to unplug the smart speaker in the kitchen, have a good hunt for any listening eyes that might have been hidden in her sitting room and then to make himself at home. She was off for a curry and would be back before he knew it.

*

Kanha came home to find Colbey fast asleep on the sofa, his head back, his mouth open and a little snore coming from between his lips. Plates, cutlery and a few place mats were neatly arranged on the coffee table before him. He stirred at the sound of her laying the takeaway dishes out and looked about him in a confused manner. 'Gosh, I'm sorry.'

'Don't worry,' Kanha said. 'It must have been a long way to cycle.'

'About fifty miles.' Stirring and sitting up, he said, 'I've got to ride back yet.'

She fetched them some wine and sat at the opposite end of the sofa from him, her toes nearly but not quite touching his legs as he helped himself to the food. She couldn't help looking around the room, and seeing that she did so, he said, 'There's nothing here. I had a good look. Was this all for you?'

'No,' she lied. 'I added to the order.'

He ate like a man who had cycled fifty miles in the cold after a hard day and while he did so, she marvelled at the fact that Harry Colbey was in her home. It felt odd, like the room had been changed to be someone else's lounge, in someone else's house. Her own hunger had evaporated, so she picked at her plate and watched him. He had stumbled upon a chilli and looked up at her as if suddenly remembering that she was there.

'Oh.' He breathed in. 'You like it spicy, huh.'

'Jalfrezi.'

'Certainly is. Speak to me. Tell me everything that's happened since we met.'

So she spoke until she ran out of things to say and, when he'd had his fill of the food and she had said all she could, he lay back into the crook of the sofa, leaned his head against the wall and closed his eyes.

As the cat jumped onto his lap and took an absent-minded petting from him, she wondered if he might just fall straight back to sleep, but then he stirred and said, 'So you think Tirrell killed Dvořáček?'

'It's a strong possibility, isn't it?'

'That ups the stakes.' He sniffed. 'Are you coping?'

'Just about. It would be better if my comrades didn't keep sneaking up on me.'

'And Mani can be trusted, can he?'

'I think so.'

'I think so too.'

'What about your campaign manager, Tom?'

'Do you know, I'm not sure. I worry that... I might try and speak to him tomorrow.' His words trailed off, and realising he really was falling asleep, she pushed her toes into the side of his leg, and he started and shook his head. 'They tricked my wife into buying shares in Alcheminna,' he said.

Kanha thought for a while, but nothing seemed to be the right thing to say. She remembered seeing his wife in the lift lobby of the hotel where Dvořáček had holed up. She had forgotten the fact until now.

'I think your wife might—'

'I know,' he said, closing his eyes again. 'Everyone seems to want to tell me that. They said we can keep the shares if I resign, or they'll put the subscription agreement in a drawer somewhere for safe keeping – unsigned that is – if I stay and behave myself. Do as I'm told. Do as you tell me, in fact.'

'What do you think they'll do when they find out it's too late for any of that?'

'I suppose they'll make my wife's share purchase public, and I'll be forced to resign in disgrace.'

Kanha bit her lip. 'How can we undo what we've done?'

But Colbey shook his head. 'We can't.'

'Then we need to think of a way for you to not own the shares.'

She leaned over to the table and started to clear the dishes onto a tray.

Behind her, he said, 'There's only one way out of that problem. And it's something that's long overdue. I just don't know how to… how to go about it. I don't think either of us do.'

Kanha paused, uncertain if she had understood him right, and turning she saw that she had.

His eyes were open, but he didn't really see her. His own sadness was all he saw.

'It's like that song,' she said. 'The one that says there are fifty ways. Believe me, I've been there too. In fact, there are a thousand ways. You just have to pick one.'

He looked at her and saw her finally, and she felt a rush of emotion; not knowing what else to say or do, she leaned forward and kissed him. It was all she could think of to offer and she realised suddenly it was what she wanted.

It made him smile and he said, 'You're probably right about the fifty ways. I think she feels that way too.'

By the time she came back from putting the dishes in the kitchen, he was snoring heavily. She sat back down next to him, and the next thing she knew he was shaking her awake.

'I have to go.'

'Already?'

'It's four in the morning. I want to get on the road while it's still dark so the CCTV cameras can't pick me out.'

She nodded, sleepily pulling herself up. 'Wait, I have a phone for you from Mani. It can't be tracked. I can use it to get hold of you when you need to disappear.'

They talked for a while of his plan while he pulled his cycling layers and gloves back on, and then she said, 'Good luck with your speech today.'

'If I make it that far,' he said.

Kanha walked with him to the back door and waited while he found his bike where he had hidden it in the bushes. His breath was cold in the icy air as he came back to say goodbye, and standing with it between them, he kissed her properly and then left.

*

After Colbey had gone, Kanha knew there was no hope of getting back to sleep. So she fed the cat, freshened up, found new clothes, a dark trouser suit, her high-heeled shoes – her usual armour – and wound her hair up into a bun that was so tight it pulled at her temples. Even as she was driving down an empty Pall Mall at five thirty, with the sun only just rising, the PM was ringing. She paused with her hand on the button before answering.

'Where are you?' he said gruffly. 'This Dvořáček leak is proving to be a total disaster.'

'I'll be there in ten minutes.'

'No, don't,' came the answer.

Kanha's heart skipped. 'You don't want me to come to Number Ten?'

'No.' In the background she could hear Tirrell talking. 'I'm not there, anyway, I'm at my club.'

'Is that wise?' The old Kanha, the one who was loyal to the crown, would have said that.

'Don't question me. I'll meet my cabinet members wherever I want.'

So he was discreetly seeing his cabinet one by one before the day started, was he? It was exactly what she would have advised him to do.

Kanha said nothing in reply, and with his voice softening, Ewan said, 'You'll be more use to me in your office.'

'If that's what you want.'

'Yes, it is. Get the whips out into the breakfast rooms. I've put my chief of staff on this mess of Dvořáček's, so get them to feed anything they hear back to him.'

She agreed and he rang off. So it was Dvořáček's mess, was it?

By six o'clock Kanha was walking into the whips' office to find several of her senior staff already there. She called them together for a briefing and arranged for one of the assistants to chase the rest in. She thought how ironic it was to be managing the fallout from her own leak.

Paddy was in her private office on his mobile, pacing back and forth, the door closed. When he left it to hurry over to them, he was red in the face. The PM or someone from Number Ten must have called him, readying him to step in if needed. *And so it goes. Divide and conquer.*

'Everything alright, Paddy?' she said, and he swallowed and said everything was fine. 'Attention, everyone. Gather round. I want you to get on the phones, out to the terrace and into the tea rooms to find out what the sentiment is on this Dvořáček business. Call me as soon as you hear of any groundswell one way or the other.'

'Should we get the team to call me?' Paddy said. 'I can collate and feed back to you – that is if you're needing to get out and about yourself?'

Collate for the PM, more like, Kanha thought.

'Thanks, Paddy, I'm not going anywhere for the minute.'

One of the whips asked, 'Is it true Dvořáček agreed to give a Silicon Valley company access to citizen data?'

'No idea. Number Ten are investigating. I'm sure we'll be briefed when they've got to the bottom of it.'

'Is the PM in on it?' asked another.

To which Paddy said, 'Of course not.' Then he added, 'We know as much as you do.' The whip was not the only one to ask the question. It was being asked all over Whitehall.

Kanha took herself off to the privacy of her office, the better to make her own calls, but her door opened and closed on a regular basis as the whips trotted in and out with updates. She revelled in every rumour of dissatisfaction in the PM, but there was plenty of apathy out there too. Turning on the television in the corner of her office, she saw masked protestors had gathered in Parliament Square, but there weren't many of them. Kanha felt bad for Colbey that the general public and the newsfeeds weren't picking up the outrage they had hoped for. And, of course, the Mouth of the Mob – now that it had come out in support of the Whigge party – was pushing the line that it was a storm in a teacup. The editorial of its top hacks suggested the masked protestors needed to get real and face the future, or else take themselves off home to their allotments. 'The times they are a-changing' was the site's headline. Woodward's column had disappeared from the leader tables. She was desperate to call Mani to find out what they had said to him, but didn't think it would be a good idea right now. In any event, he was busy with his own part of their scheme.

Elliot brought her a cup of coffee. 'Do you think he'll go?' he asked.

'Who? The PM?'

'Yes. They're saying the heads of MI5 and MI6 are plotting to oust him. That the defence minister is ringing around trying to encourage letters of no confidence.'

Kanha already knew it was the case. Just moments before, the defence minister had called her to ask if he had her support. He had heard a rumour that Kanha was out of favour, and wanted to sound her out for a possible stand against the PM. Not as a candidate, he had let her know, but as a stalking horse.

'A stalking horse?' she had said. 'How stupid do you think I am?'

To Elliot she said, 'Yes, so I hear. They're pretty pissed off that Dvořáček was working on intelligence leads with a tech company behind their back. They don't believe the PM didn't know about it.'

But without Dvořáček there to defend himself, the PM's press office was beginning to win the PR battle. The old privacy minister was being painted by Number Ten as a lone wolf, acting outside his pay grade. Unnamed sources were providing quotes to speak to his increasingly erratic behaviour towards the end, suggesting he had become mentally unstable. The official line ran that the PM was shocked that Dvořáček had agreed to give out citizen data without proper process.

Still, Kanha mulled, at least the distraction couldn't have been better timed. With all the lobby press busy working up their own spin on the scandal, no one was paying too much attention to the fast-tracked privacy bill that already had support from both sides of the House. Perhaps they might even make it through to that evening, when the bill was due to be debated, before Colbey's addition of Dvořáček's clause was spotted. It was a miracle it hadn't been already.

Elliot said, 'I heard the home secretary is crying in the tea room.'

Kanha looked at him. The young man was so excited, he could hardly sit still, and she smiled to think of how she used to be when she was his age.

'What's your opinion on it all?' she said.

Elliot blushed, surprised to be asked the question. 'I think anyone who doesn't think that the PM orchestrated the whole thing is deluding themselves.'

Kanha laughed. 'I think you could be right.' As she said it her phone rang. It was the defence minister again. Was she interested in being the one behind the stalking horse, then? he asked. There were certain people who wanted to know whether she had an interest in taking the top job herself. She looked at Elliot sitting across from her. He must have heard, because he raised his eyebrows in excitement.

'That's more appropriate, William,' she said into the phone, 'but I'll pass for now, thank you.' It was good that the gossipy Elliot had heard that last part.

Kanha rubbed her bottom lip with her fingers in thought as Paddy came into the room.

'Is the home secretary still crying in the tea room?' she asked.

'Yes,' said Paddy.

'Do we know why?'

'Yes, apparently she was waiting for a call from the PM's chief of staff. I think she knew what it was going to be.'

'And is it done?'

Paddy leaned against the glass partition. 'Yes, I just spoke to her. She's been fired.'

'For?'

'Plain incompetence. They're not even going to dress it up as a resignation for personal reasons.'

'Is she playing along?'

'She kind of has to. She'd told so many people she had no idea her department had agreed to use Alcheminna's app for collecting citizen data or send files to them for their system. She sort of shot herself in the back with that.'

'So who in the Home Office did know about it?'

Paddy shrugged his shoulders. 'Can't seem to get any sense out of anyone on that score.'

Kanha waved them both out of her office. Turning her back to the glass screen, she pulled the pages with Dvořáček's notes out of her bag, and discreetly paged through them. She felt certain Dvořáček had written that he had been meeting with someone in the Home Office to arrange the app and data dump. Hah, there it was: the name of a Home Office junior minister who had met Dvořáček and the PM in his club a month ago.

She found his mobile number on the system and rang it. His voice shook even at Kanha's first gentle probing. In the background, she could hear the noise from one of the parliamentary bars. It sounded like the Stranger's Bar, but it could have been the Pugin Room.

'I knew you guys would call me eventually,' he said. 'What a fucking cock-up this is. I'm not going down for it, I tell you.'

As chief whip of many years' standing, Kanha knew how to use silence as the most effective tool of interrogation. And sure enough, the junior minister couldn't help filling the one she gave him.

'I said, I'm not going down for it, I tell you. It was the PM himself who told me to approve the use of the new app. He can tell you that's true.'

Kanha knew the young minister was staring at the prospect of what he had hoped would be a long and illustrious career potentially over already.

'He told me Alcheminna was going to give us the app for free, and that it was a great benefit to our party. It was going to secure us the election because the voters would be so impressed,' he said. 'You lot told me not to ask too many questions. And I arranged whatever I was told to arrange.'

'Of course you did,' Kanha said. 'You're not to blame. In many ways, the PM should never have put you in that situation. It was unfair of him.'

The junior minister faltered and said, 'But didn't he get you to call me?'

'He didn't, Oliver. I'm calling because I want to make sure you don't get made a scapegoat in all this.'

'A scapegoat? Do you think that's likely to happen?'

'Haven't you heard about your home secretary?'

'No... what about her?'

'She's just been fired.'

Oliver was silent, and then he said, 'OK, Kanha, tell me what to do.' But just as she was about to explain, he said, 'Hang on. Anthony Tirrell's here to speak to me. I've got to go.' And the line went dead.

Kanha opened her office door and waved Elliot over. 'See if you can find out where Oliver Whisty usually takes his lunch. Do it quickly, mmm?'

A number of the team looked in her direction as she stood there. Either Elliot had told them of her call from the defence minister, or the rumour that she was out of favour with the PM had already spread further. She realised that now she was outside the PM's camp and her trusty deputy Paddy had been recruited into it, there was no one left she could trust, other than Colbey and Mani.

Kanha was sure it had been the Stranger's Bar she had heard. Going back to her office and grabbing her bag, she hurried over there. Oliver Whisty was sitting on his own at a table in the corner, and the barman had just delivered a baby bottle of champagne.

'Something to celebrate?' Kanha said, unable to keep the sarcasm from her voice.

'You were wrong. They promoted me,' he blurted out. Kanha sighed and sat down. 'To a ministerial post in the Department for Work and Pensions,' he continued.

'So I suppose you don't remember what you just said to me on the phone.'

'Oh, I remember,' he said, pulling the foil from the bottle. 'But I've since realised I was confused. It was Dvořáček who told me to approve the app. He said he'd checked it out and it was fine under data privacy law.'

'So why did you say it was the PM?'

Oliver Whisty offered to get a glass for her, but she eyed the tiny bottle, hopefully with a look that showed her derision, shook her head, and repeated her question.

'I made that up,' he said, leaning forward as if sharing a secret with her. 'I wanted to sound important, but it wasn't true. I never met with the PM in his club.'

Kanha stood and said, 'I never said that you had.'

The junior minister, soon to be senior minister, frowned, realising his mistake, then let his eyes slide off to his left. Disgusted, Kanha left him to his celebratory drink. It was like the past was shifting even as she stood there.

Back in her office, she dwelled on what else they might have as proof. There was the fact that the party had used Alcheminna's system for the by-election. It was something that could not be changed. Were the party leaders aware of it? Had the PM kept even them in the dark, such was his greed to ensure his comfortable retirement, or were they all complicit? But she and Colbey had been over that as he was getting ready to leave that morning. They had no proof that the shell company Voter Services was connected to Alcheminna. The e-pads had been collected back from the volunteers at the end of the day's canvassing. There was just the presence of Lauvaux at the meeting and the fact that Tom was told by that American VP that Alcheminna was involved. But if she denied it, which she would, it wasn't really proof of anything.

Kanha's phone rang. It was Number Ten, telling her to come over at once. She called out to Elliot to find her a pool car, picked up her bag and, making sure those pages of Dvořáček's were safely tucked away at the bottom of it again, headed out.

*

As Kanha was ferried over to Number Ten, she caught up on the wider newsfeeds. The press pack had pitched their tents outside Ewan MacLellan's house in Carlton Gardens before dawn that morning to start their day's work of chasing him around. They wanted to be able to know where he was at all times, in case it looked as if the scandal would endanger his position as PM. None of them seemed to know that before they filmed him leaving for Number Ten, giving reassurances as he got into his car that the privacy of the public was his utmost concern, he had already been over to his club to meet his cabinet members one by one in secret. How had he got from his club back to his house without anyone spotting it?

Perhaps the rumour that there was a tunnel between Carlton Gardens and his club was true. As an image of Ewan making his way along a sewer, a lantern held up in his hand and rats at his feet, came to Kanha, she couldn't stop a giggle escaping her mouth. Did he do that every day? Just so that he could eat his meals at his favourite club without the public knowing. She thought of him coming up out of a cellar in the old gentlemen's club, patting cobwebs and dust off his clothes as some lackey there held the trap door open for him. Suddenly she couldn't seem to stop laughing. If it were true, it really was time he retired to that place in California he loved so much. Let those who wanted to tackle the serious work take their turn at the helm. The more she thought of it, the more she laughed. Kanha realised the driver was looking at her in the rear-view mirror.

'You alright, Esme?'

'Holding on, Mick.'

'Everyone else I've ferried around today has either been raging, sobbing or terrified, but here's you in hysterics.'

She thought about trying to explain, but didn't know where to start, and as they pulled up in front of Number Ten, the driver started laughing too.

Hers had been a laugh born from frustration, but she used it to give her the energy to walk into Number Ten with a relaxed look on her face. Outside the press pack across the street had shouted out to ask her what was going on, but she had ignored them. Just inside the door, she found the other members of the inner circle gathered, and with surprisingly mixed emotions she realised she was there for a cabinet meeting, not to be fired. At least not yet.

In the cabinet room, the PM was in good spirits. He thought he was winning. Already seated around the table were those ministers unaffected by the storm: business, farming, energy, treasury and so forth. They were acting as if it were a day like any other, a small scandal to be managed by the press officers and the PM's chief of staff.

'Ah, Kanha,' the PM said, looking up. 'There you are. We were waiting on you. Where have you been?'

There was no answer that could be given to that.

Tirrell sat in the seat to the PM's right, with no further pretence that he wasn't the PM's new right-hand man. *So I'm back in the snake pit*, Kanha thought as she looked around the room. Tirrell gave her a quixotic smile, the PM's chief of staff a weary one. The absence of the home secretary and the defence minister, his failed attempt at a coup exposed and abandoned, was not mentioned.

To Kanha's relief, she saw that the foreign secretary looked as Kanha herself felt – like a cheated-upon lover. The PM and the foreign secretary treated each other so politely that it was apparent to all that there was nothing but irreconcilable differences left between them, and that each was just biding their time.

The chief of staff cleared his throat for attention and said, 'Just a few words, everyone, about the Dvořáček issue. I think we're winning there. The liberal press will linger on it for a few more weeks, but in general, privacy issues bore much of the public, and Dvořáček's death makes it difficult for the broadsheets to dwell on it, so we think the storm will blow over pretty quickly.' Kanha pulled some blank sheets towards her from the stack and pretended to make some notes.

After that the PM trotted through a few mundane items, just to solidify the show of solidarity, and then the cabinet was dismissed. The meeting was a sham, just something to let the press see them all gather, and amicably all leave again. For them to see who was out and who was still in.

Before she could get away, the PM indicated for Kanha to follow him to his office. Without anything having been said, Tirrell came along behind. The two really were as thick as thieves now, Kanha thought, and she was glad she had chosen a side that didn't include Anthony Tirrell.

'Esme, what do you think Tirrell and I should do about Colbey?' said the PM, closing the door behind him.

'What do you mean?'

Tirrell showed his yellow teeth. 'It was him. He was the source of the leak.'

Kanha walked over to the window and turned her back to them so that her anger might not show. 'What makes you think that? Yesterday, you thought it was me. Even this morning, you didn't trust me to be here.'

'Yes, yes,' said the PM. 'I'm sorry about that, Esme. Difficult times, you know. Let's put all that behind us, shall we?'

Kanha said nothing and after a while, the PM rushed to fill the silence that hung in the room. 'Tirrell knows, you see. Has some intel, haven't you, Tirrell?'

She continued to feel a strange mix of emotions. She knew she ought to keep quiet, play the game, that was what she had agreed with Colbey, at least until the bill's debate that evening, because then they would be done and there might be no more pretending. But however things turned out, her time with this man was over forever. She suddenly knew she couldn't keep up the pretence any more. She couldn't be that false, couldn't pretend to be in cahoots with these two for even five minutes. She smiled at the realisation. What had Colbey done to her? He had made an honest woman of her.

'That is his job, you know, Esme,' said the PM softly, coming up behind her. 'It's his job to worry about security and advise me. We all make mistakes, don't we?'

'Advise *us*,' she said pointedly and turned to face him. 'Advise *us*, the members of the National Security Council.'

'Yes, good point, Esme.' The PM laughed as if it were a joke she had made. 'But tell me, come on now, I need your clever brain – what do you think I should do about Colbey?' The PM paced the length of the room. 'Should I fire him? Remove his whip? I mean the second reading of the bill is this evening, you know.'

As she thought of what to say, the PM's chief of staff came in and signalled to the PM that he needed a word. It looked, of course, as if she were thinking of a way out of the PM's predicament for him. 'You can't remove Colbey's whip,' she said slowly. 'And you've no cause to fire him.' But Tirrell looked up sharply, while the PM continued pacing in thought, ignoring the presence of his chief of staff, who stood in the doorway uncertain whether he had been seen or not.

'Yes, you're right. I can't fire him right now, can I? Thank you, Esme. I've made my bed and I need to lie in it, at least for the minute. You always help me to see straight.' He paced back to them. 'If it comes out that it was Colbey who leaked Dvořáček's diary to that blasted Mobster and I've sided against the man, it will look like I'm siding with Dvořáček. And we've just spent all day making it clear that Dvořáček was deranged. Let's wait until after this evening's debate and fire him then. The bill will have passed its second reading and we can get in someone dull to replace Colbey and shepherd the bill through its committee stage.'

Unable to stop, Kanha said, 'But you thought Colbey was dull enough for the job. I wonder what will happen to your next minister?'

The PM saw her mood at last, and she bit her bottom lip, but the words were out.

'Now, Esme, don't be like that. It was a confusing situation yesterday and we made an honest mistake. I've said I'm sorry, let's move on, mmm?'

'We?'

'Tirrell and I.'

Kanha saw Tirrell give the PM a little frown of warning, but the PM either didn't see or didn't care.

'Lots of people were under suspicion, not just you. Now that's all over because Tirrell knows for a fact it was Colbey.'

Tirrell shook his head and went to interrupt, but so did Kanha.

'And how does he know that?'

'Now don't you worry about that,' said the PM.

'I will worry about that, and I do worry,' Kanha said. 'Are you tracking your ministers now? Are you spying on your own cabinet with their phones?'

'Oh, do grow up, Esme,' Tirrell snapped.

Kanha turned slowly to him. 'Chief Whip. It's Chief Whip to you, *Advisor*.'

Forgotten by all, the chief of staff still stood, embarrassed, and coughed. 'Prime Minister...' he said.

'For goodness' sake, Esme,' the PM said angrily. 'It's a matter of national security.'

'Oh, that old one,' said Kanha. 'That gives you the excuse to do anything, does it? Spy on your citizens and even your ministers night and day wherever they go? Have you never read your Orwell?'

The chief of staff was still trying to interrupt. 'Prime Minister, sir, I think you should know...'

'What?' said the PM to him.

'I really am sorry to interrupt, and I don't know if it's important, but I wanted to let you know that Harry Colbey just announced that he and his wife divorced this morning. A fast-track decree absolute from a Rio de Janeiro court. It's all over the newsfeeds. Just thought I'd better let you know because I understand he's speaking in the House tonight and leading the debate on the privacy bill.'

The PM looked puzzled for a moment, then he shouted, 'Jesus fucking Christ.'

He turned to Kanha. 'Enough of this nonsense. I haven't time for it. Are you in my camp or not?'

So it had come to this so soon. Kanha straightened the tails of her jacket, and said, 'Actually, I don't think I am. I don't like what you're doing here. And I fear for where it's taking us.'

The PM looked at her, his expression hard to read as the chief of staff tried to interrupt again. 'And there's something else, sir...'

'What on earth else could there be?' the PM exploded.

'The lobby press are asking us about the new clause in the bill.'

'What new clause?'

The PM looked at Tirrell with a face that was crumpling, and Kanha felt a confusing stab of guilt. It was as if she were standing there plunging the knife into his back with her own hand, as if he were turning and looking over his shoulder at her to say, *'Et tu, brute?'*

'They're calling it Dvořáček's Clause, sir.'

'Dvořáček's Clause?'

'Yes, Dvořáček's Clause. Apparently, there's an extra clause in the bill that wasn't in earlier drafts. One of the lobby press has spotted it came from the private member's bill that Dvořáček tried to pass a couple of weeks ago. They want to know what's the thinking behind it. They seem to think it will cause quite a stir with the tech companies.'

The PM muttered. 'That bastard.'

He turned to Kanha. 'Again? How could your team let it get through for a second time?'

'I've no idea what you are talking about,' Kanha said icily, her ability to lie returning in force when she needed it.

'Strange,' Tirrell said. 'That lightning should strike twice.'

'I don't know what's going on with you, Esme,' the PM said, 'but you're either incompetent or corrupt.'

For a moment, Kanha remembered it was true. 'But who corrupted me?'

The PM turned away, and barely audibly said, 'Go to your office, Esme. Collect your things. We're through.' Then he roared, 'Anastacia!'

After leaving the room Kanha stood swaying outside the PM's office as Anastacia leapt up from her desk and hurried past. When the secretary opened the door to enter, she heard Tirrell say, 'Enough of this ballyhoo. I said it wouldn't work. Let me do it the old-fashioned way.'

And then, as the door swung shut, she heard the prime minister's reply: 'I agree. Get hold of Lauvaux and tell him you're going to sort it this time.'

3.6

Colbey stood outside the doors of what was, for the moment at least, still his department. Today the street was empty, and above the buildings he caught sight of a sky laid low. It looked like it might snow, but he had to be mistaken since none had been forecast and a snow shower in the centre of London was always a rarity. He turned the collar of his raincoat up against the cold and shivered.

There were still a couple of hours to go until he had to give his speech for the bill's second reading, which would open the debate, and he was uncertain what to do or where to go. Someone somewhere must have spotted Dvořáček's clause had been added to the bill, because his phone was ringing non-stop. As soon as he had seen it, he had fled the building. They had agreed that from this point on, he was to keep a low profile so that he wouldn't bump into anyone who might be able to fire him.

Colbey saw that his phone was flashing, and looking down he realised it was a video call from Tom, responding to his missed call of earlier that morning. He thought he had better take it.

'Hey, everything OK?' Tom asked.

Colbey gave a hollow laugh. 'Well, I've had better days.'

'Yes, I'm sorry to hear about you and Clarissa. That was quick – I didn't know you guys were at that point.'

'I guess we have been for a long time. We got an online divorce this morning. It suited us that way, to get it over with.'

'Do the kids know?'

'Yes, we rang them a few hours ago. Chloe cried but Sebastian was pretty matter of fact about it. Clarissa wants to travel. She has some friends and family over in Europe.'

Tom was silent for a minute, then he said, 'God, I'm so sorry, Harry. I just didn't think it would turn out this way.'

'What is it you want, Tom?'

'Right, of course. It's about Alcheminna. I have some proof they're behind Voter Services. Do you want it?'

Colbey frowned. 'What is it?'

'I can't say over the phone. Come and meet me. I'll drop you a pin.'

Colbey looked at where the pin had dropped on the map on his phone and considered that Tom was the last person he wanted to meet right now.

'Can I trust you?' he asked, and saw his friend frown.

'With your life,' Tom said, and despite everything Colbey believed him. Hanging up, he walked down the street and in passing, threw the ministerial phone into a bin. From his other pocket, he pulled out the one Kanha had given him but, remembering her instructions, didn't turn it on until he had crossed Trafalgar Square and was far away from the last location of the other, hurrying along Pall Mall. Realising he was getting dangerously near the PM's house, he ducked into St James's Square to head north to Piccadilly.

Crossing the little park there, Colbey looked up at the branches of the plane trees. It seemed as if the very sky now sat upon the tips of their top branches; that it was going to snow there was now no doubt.

Colbey thought of the time he had spent that morning with Clarissa at the family lawyer's office. Without a tear, they had signed away the last thirty years of their marriage. It had been a long time coming, and it hurt him to see how relieved she had appeared to finally have it out in the open.

At least she was safe from their schemes this way. If they registered the share agreement now, the holding would be in her name alone since she was the only signatory on it. She had asked whether he thought they would do so, and he had said bitterly that he had no idea what *they* might do. Then he had relented and told her that he doubted they would, and despite everything, she seemed disappointed at the fact.

Colbey looked up again at the trees as a first snowflake landed on his cheek. What might it be that Tom had for him? And why a hotel in Piccadilly? On instinct he reached for his phone, surprising himself to find the odd little one that Kanha had given him there instead. He hadn't much time if he was to find out what Tom had and yet be back in time for the debate, and putting it back in his pocket, he hurried out of the Square and towards Piccadilly.

3·7

Lauvaux sat in the back of his car as it drove up Haymarket towards Piccadilly Circus, and reached for his ringing phone. His daughter was beside him and kicking the back of the driver's seat, not that the driver had acknowledged the fact.

'Yes?' he said. It was Anthony Tirrell, and the man was ranting. 'Calm down,' Lauvaux said. 'I can't help you otherwise.' Then he said, 'Wait a second.'

Reaching down to his overnight holdall, and at the same time putting a warning hand on his daughter's leg, Lauvaux pulled his e-pad out of his bag. Tirrell wanted to know whether the Alcheminna system had made the deep fake call to Colbey yet. He logged into the system and found Tom's digital replica who reassured him that it had called Colbey just as they had asked it to. The minister was in all probability making his way over to the hotel in Piccadilly now as per the request, and Lauvaux told the PM's advisor so. Tirrell, sounding panicked, said that they had lost him.

'Calm down,' Lauvaux said again. 'I put a tracking strip on his coat yesterday.' Lauvaux logged into the system and used it to locate the GPS strip he had patted onto Colbey's mackintosh at the prime minister's club.

The new minister was not far away, just a few streets in front of them in fact. 'He's on Jermyn Street,' Lauvaux said, 'heading towards the hotel.'

Tirrell let out a series of expletives and Lauvaux said, 'Well hurry up and get your team ready, then.'

Looking at Colbey's progress on the map, Lauvaux frowned in thought, then he told the driver to turn into Piccadilly, but to be ready to stop as soon as he gave the word. Turning to his daughter, he said, 'Now, be a good girl and I promise we have just one more thing to do, then we can go home.'

'Mother is going to be cross with you. We won't be back in time for tea,' she replied.

Lauvaux tapped his fingers on the armrest and realised it was true. The UK situation was a disaster. The British prime minister did not have order in his house as promised and the feeling of a situation being out of his control was not something Lauvaux enjoyed; it was causing him to be more impatient with his daughter than he would usually be, and that in its turn was making her play up. She continued to kick the back of the driver's chair, despite the firm hand he had once again put on her leg.

'If you don't behave,' he said finally, 'I won't pick you up from your dancing lessons again. Next time it will be a driver and Nanny.'

The girl's leg ceased jerking. 'But I'm bored,' she said and slid down onto the floor of the car to twirl her broken e-pad on its corner.

'If you treat it like that, it's no wonder it broke.'

Lauvaux watched Colbey on the screen of his e-pad as the minister approached the Piccadilly Arcade on the other side of Hatchards and disappeared into it.

'Stop outside the bookshop,' he said to the driver.

Lauvaux saw that the sky had fallen lower, a grey smothering layer, within which his mountain goat's nose smelt snow. He hoped it would not be heavy, which might delay his plane from taking off. His daughter was right; her mother would be cross with him if they were late once again for dinner.

'Can I use your e-pad?' his daughter said and tugged at it. Absent-mindedly, he handed it to her, relishing the sudden peace that descended as she found and returned to the game she had been playing before.

How strange that such a nobody could be so disruptive, he thought. Lauvaux felt a little antipathy towards the man, but then he considered it was himself who was to blame. If the system had had the data they needed, he wouldn't have misjudged how the man would act. It only went to show how right they were in what they were doing, how essential it all was. They had to understand. They had to understand everything. The man had just behaved as the sum of his parts caused him to behave – his nature, his nurture, how fate had intervened, the connections he had made along the way and the influences of those people: *their* nature, *their* nurture. Everyone considered themselves unique, but it wasn't the case; most people were just shades on a spectrum.

Lauvaux knew that even he was a product of his own nature and nurture, and his product craved a little revenge. Tirrell's plan was a little old fashioned, but it would probably be effective. The British did so love a scandal, and it was one he was going to enjoy reading about in the papers tomorrow morning. *Know thyself* was his motto.

But though he may know himself, there was no version of him in the system, of course. For who watches the watchers? No one, in this case, he thought gleefully and got out of the car telling the driver to lock the doors.

'Stay here and behave yourself,' he said to his daughter. 'I won't be long.'

3.8

In the time it took Kanha to walk down the stairs from the PM's office to the front door of Number Ten, she had been taken off the list for the pool cars. *Hell,* she thought. *Bloody Colbey.* Why had she listened to him when they sat at that picnic table and he had swayed her with his fancy speech about the honour of being a member of parliament? Look at what he had reduced her to with his honourable ways.

As she stood searching on her phone for an app to dial a black cab to come to the gates of Downing Street, she thought with irony of that morning when she had watched him through her car's tinted windows peering gingerly out of them. But she was not down and out yet, she thought with a smile as her earlier pool car pulled up beside her and the driver wound down the window.

'Hey, where's that infectious laugh gone?' he said. 'I told them I need to get petrol. Hop in and I'll ferry you down the road for old times' sake.'

'Thanks, Mick,' she said. 'And I can promise you, it won't be the last time.'

'Good for you,' he said.

On the way, she received a negotiating call from the PM's chief of staff.

'Sorry, Esme, to hear the news. Just wanted to agree a statement.'

'Personal reasons?'

'Personal reasons, it is,' he said and hung up.

It was the best solution for all. They wouldn't dare do anything else. After the years she had worked for the PM, particularly as chief whip, they knew enough dirt on each other that a conscious uncoupling was the best outcome for all. Besides, he still had nothing to point to her having any involvement in the leak. He just thought she was being overly emotional at having been suspected of treachery. If only he knew. For a wild moment, Kanha thought of ringing him to tell him she knew everything, but that would be foolish. Better an eye to the long game. She thought of her nest egg. It would not get added to for a while now.

It was just a shame that the story had not caught fire. Already, it was falling down the rankings, its salt and pepper only the salacious connection to an MP who shot himself in his office.

She found that news of her 'resignation' had not yet reached the Commons. As she walked into the whips' office, there was no stir of excitement, just a team going about their usual business, but Paddy knew. She found him in her office finishing off a call. He smiled weakly when he saw her and she went in and joined him. They talked for a while as she gathered her personal things together and put them into a box.

'God, don't do that,' Paddy said. 'Don't walk about the halls of parliament with a box.'

'You're right,' she said, opening a drawer. 'Fuck knows what any of this is anyway, but I guess it's all your problem now.'

He was alright, Paddy. He'd been an OK deputy and she'd been an OK boss.

'I reckon you'll be back again soon, in any event,' he said.

'Not to this office. It's a bullshit brief.' They both smiled and she added, 'Sorry.'

'Tell me,' he said, laughing, 'what we do, eh? Say, did you know Tom Caldicott has been promoted?'

Kanha couldn't help frowning. 'Really?'

'Strange day of changes. What the hell's going on, eh?'

She handed him her official phone knowing the one Mani had given her was in her handbag.

Paddy sat down at her desk and logged into the office system. 'In lieu of a leaving present, based on the short notice, here's a little something for you, my love.' She came round and looked at the screen. 'I'll get one of the kids to take your box over there right now. It's a cracking piece of real estate – overlooking New Palace Yard. Inner and outer office. I was saving it for the right person.'

Kanha laughed and Paddy looked at her. 'The girl's hysterical.'

Kanha shook her head. 'It's Colbey's old office,' she said.

'And long may you be happy there,' Paddy replied.

On her way out, Kanha gathered together those of her team who were in the office and told them she had resigned for personal reasons and that Paddy would be stepping up.

Next stop was the Commons Lobby to check her pigeonhole for any messages from Colbey, but there was nothing. She went up the little staircase to the bathrooms above and, in her usual cubicle for such activities, turned on the phone from Mani to see if there were any messages from him. A text came through from Colbey to say that he was meeting Tom at a hotel on Piccadilly, but that he would be back in plenty of time for the debate. Kanha frowned. She had just passed Tom in the corridor downstairs. So who was Colbey meeting? She rang the phone she had given him, but there was no answer.

Kanha felt a jolt of worry and called Mani.

'Hey, I'm pretty busy,' he said.

'It's important. Harry has gone off estate to meet Tom Caldicott, but I just saw Tom here a moment ago.'

Mani told her to wait, then he said, 'The minister's just moved from Jermyn Street into the Piccadilly Arcade next door to Hatchards.'

'Sounds like he's nearly at the hotel, then.'

'Esme, I need to go.'

Kanha hung up, dwelling on the fact that Harry Colbey was heading for the hotel where Dvořáček had been caught in the sting, and it couldn't be Tom who was meeting him there. Putting the phone in her bag, she hurried downstairs, through the Great Hall, and out the gates of New Palace Yard. It was snowing. Thick flakes drifted down and the green of Parliament Square already had a dusting of white. As ever with the first bit of inclement weather, there were plenty of black cabs to be found, but all were taken. She waited hopefully for a few minutes on a deserted corner, empty of even the last of the protestors and Mobsters who had obviously taken themselves off into the warm somewhere, but the sight of a little orange taxi light was elusive. Worrying about the time she was losing, and unable to stand there doing nothing, Kanha determined it would be quicker to walk and retrace the path of her return from the hotel of a few weeks ago across the park.

It too was empty; gone were the tourists, the joggers, the picnicking office crowds sneaking over hooped black fences in search of a private patch of grass. Even the geese and ducks had taken themselves off to some warm reed bed or rose bush under which to curl up and wonder whether they had just dreamed of spring.

The snow fell heavily down through the branches of the trees, and as she hurried along, Kanha saw for the first time how beautiful the park was, with its lake with Buckingham Palace at one end and Horse Guards Parade at the other. For a moment she looked up at snowflakes tumbling down from the void, because there was nothing to compare to that, but only for a moment; then she put her head down, wrapped her coat around her, and with her court shoes slipping on the wet gravel path, pressed on as quickly as she could.

3·9

By the time Colbey reached the Piccadilly Arcade, the snow was falling heavily. Stepping into its dim interior, he dusted off his coat even though he would be out in the weather again in just a moment's time. Snow in London in April, thought Colbey, unable to stop himself smiling at the joy of it as he hurried along between antique barbers, gentlemen's outfitters and shops selling antiquated maps. Like a moth to the light he was drawn towards the arch at the far end where the chaos of Piccadilly could be glimpsed in all its raucous glory.

There he recognised a shape silhouetted in the archway and realised that unless he turned around and walked away in a cowardly fashion, he would not be able to avoid meeting the Frenchman. The two stood in the entrance of the Edwardian colonnade and watched the snowflakes fall on Piccadilly.

'What do you want?' Colbey said at last.

'Nothing, really,' replied Lauvaux. 'I was just curious to speak to the real you one last time.'

Colbey felt dizzy with tiredness. 'There is nothing you can do now,' he said. 'Dvořáček's clause will be debated.'

He went to move off, but the Frenchman put a hand on his arm.

'It's too late, Harry. We are the future, you know.'

'No,' said Colbey. 'You may want to be the future, and you and whoever else you represent may be doing all you can with your wealth and influence to make it so, but you don't get to decide. We do.'

A flash of annoyance crossed Lauvaux's face. 'You? Who are you? We're not building a world for the likes of you. Your time will soon be gone.'

'Who are you building it for, then?'

Lauvaux looked out at the passing crowds. 'For them, to make their lives better. We know what's best for them. Not you lot, with your laws that say you can do this and you can't do that. If it came down to it, which it does every day, which do they choose? Us, who bring them friends, family, entertainment, pizza, transport, fun? Or you and your associates, who bring them rules and tax them and dictate what they must and mustn't do?'

'But they do choose us, Mr Lauvaux, or at least people like us. We may err, we may be human, we may sit a little to the left or a little to the right, but we all believe in one thing that's important, and that is democracy. They trust us to put rules in place to protect them from people like you.'

'Look at them, Harry. Look at them,' Lauvaux said, but even as they stood there, they watched many look up from their phones and electronic devices into the sky to enjoy the sight of the snow-flakes falling.

Lauvaux looked at his watch.

'Snow in April,' thought Colbey again, saying it out loud this time. 'It wasn't forecast, was it?'

He looked up into the sky himself to watch the flakes fall, and when he looked down again the Frenchman had gone. He was a little way down the street, outside Fortnum's, climbing into the back of a black limousine.

Colbey hurried away, dodging between the taxis across the road, and went into the hotel. There was no sign of Tom, so he ordered a screwdriver from the waiter at the bar. One wouldn't hurt. It would carry him through to the speech and settle his nerves after his encounter with Lauvaux. There was an old man at the bar, drunk, who wanted to show him a picture of his granddaughter. Colbey looked at it politely, saying all the things he should in such a situation, before leaving to find a table by the window.

The bar became busier as a few people came in at once. Two women arrived and sat across from him. Attractive, he thought. I bet Tom will try to chat them up when he comes. Thinking of Tom, Colbey looked at his watch.

He shouldn't be here, he realised. Why was he not at the House? If Tom were not there in the next two minutes, he would leave and hurry back for his speech. He felt tired, so tired, dizzy with tiredness. He looked down at his half-empty glass, wondering for a moment whether he had not already been there all afternoon, drinking with Tom. Colbey shook his head, trying to clear his thoughts, but the room was sliding off to the side. He stared at his drink in amazement. The table was not level, which happened, of course, but then why didn't the glass slide off? And why wasn't the liquid in the glass level, that was unusual, surely? It seemed like an impossible puzzle, but he felt sure there was something more important. Wasn't there somewhere he was supposed to be? He shook his head again, but couldn't seem to remember. One of the girls opposite stood up and came to sit beside him.

'You alright, love?' she said, brushing her hand over his forehead.

*

As she hurried along, Kanha rang Colbey again and again, and the fourth time he answered.

'Harry. It's me,' she said. 'Where are you?'

'Esme! I'm so happy you called. I was wanting to ask you something.'

'Are you OK?'

'Yes, I'm lovely.'

'Harry, where are you? You sound drunk.'

Harry Colbey said maybe he was a little drunk, and what of it. Then he told her he thought she was pretty. A frown crept onto Kanha's forehead.

'That's nice of you to say—' she said.

He interrupted. 'Not you. *Her*. She's very pretty.'

Kanha picked her pace up as much as she could in the snow. 'Who? Who is that you're talking about, Harry? And where are you?'

'I don't know. It's a bar. A fancy pants bar. I must have been here a long time, but I can't seem to remember.'

'Is it the hotel bar where you were going to meet Tom?'

'Yes, that's right. I must have got squiffy somehow. Oh, hello.'

'Who's that? Who are you saying hello to? Harry, I'm going to—'

'She's a remarkably pretty girl too.'

'Harry, will you stay there, where you are?'

Kanha cursed her shoes as they slipped about on the sleet. She heard him say to someone, 'I'm a minister, you know.'

'Who are you talking to now?' Kanha said, feeling the panic rising.

'You're pretty too. I really like you.'

'Who? Harry, who is that you're talking to?'

'You, I'm talking to you.'

'Harry, can I speak to them?'

'Let me ask. No. They don't want to talk to you.'

'I want you to sit tight. I'm coming now. OK?'

'OK.'

'I mean it, Harry. Stay where you are.'

'OK.'

Kanha went onto the grass to see if she might get by quicker there, but her heels became bogged down in the mud. Twice she slipped and nearly fell to the ground. God, what had she been thinking? What had they done? They had ruined him, his career, his reputation, everything good he had done in his life, it would all be swept away.

She pulled her shoes off and, cradling them in her arms, started to run on the grass beside the path. Up ahead was the bridge that crossed the lake and led through gold and wrought-iron gates onto the Mall. Reaching it, she started to make a little better progress as she ran up the centre of the royal street, Buckingham Palace ahead of her. Just one lone black cab crawled along in the same direction, otherwise the Mall was hers. In her mouth came the metallic taste of cold air and desperation. Turning into Green Park, she could hear the horns of Piccadilly up ahead and knew she was nearly there. *Hold on,* she thought. *Hold on.*

3.10

At Piccadilly, as she came up beside the underground station, Kanha paused. Was it right towards the Ritz, or the other way? She started off in one direction, realised it was wrong and turned back the other way. The pavements were busy here and the pedestrians parted for her, turning with surprise to see her run in her stocking feet.

'Please be there,' she chanted silently, but when at last she reached the hotel, he couldn't be found. She hurried through to the back, damp footprints in her wake. The same receptionist was there, and she looked up at her with an odd expression on her face.

'Have you seen the minister?' Kanha said between gasping for breath. 'I think he's here.'

The receptionist put her nose in the air, and said, 'Sorry, who?'

'The minister. The new minister, that is. Harry Colbey.'

'He's drunk,' the woman said, sniffing, 'and with a couple of girls. The papers are right, you lot are a real disgrace.'

'Where? Where is he?'

The woman sniffed again. 'I'm not allowed.'

'Please,' Kanha pleaded, and finally the girl relented and told her the room number. It was an agony of time waiting for the lift, following the little arrows down the endless corridors that seemed to go round in circles. She banged on the door but there was no answer.

Banging on it again, she said, 'Open up, I'm a member of parliament.' She could hear movement inside; someone was standing on the other side of the door, peering at her through the spy hole. Lowering her voice, Kanha hissed, 'Hey, it's *The Sun*. They sent me over.'

She heard a chain slide across and the door opened. The lady behind it was buxom and down to her underwear. She frowned at Kanha, trying to make up her mind whether it was true, but when Kanha pushed past her and into the room, she said, 'Hey!'

Colbey was shirtless and propped up at the end of a bed in the arms of a half-naked woman. For a moment Kanha wondered if she shouldn't be here, whether in fact she had him all wrong, but then she saw that the girl was supporting him, that he looked in Kanha's direction with unseeing eyes.

Looking about her in desperation, Kanha spotted the coverlet from the bed lying on the floor, and keeping to the side of the room, picked it up and threw it over the television.

'You're not from *The Sun*,' said the one who had opened the door.

'Get out!' Kanha said.

'It's our room,' protested the one holding Colbey.

'Get out, I said,' Kanha repeated. 'You think I don't know what you did?'

'Not us,' said the one on the bed, but glancing at the other, some silent decision was made between the pair; she released Colbey and he slid to the floor.

Even as Kanha was hurrying over to him and trying to prop him up, the girls were grabbing at their clothes. They skulked out of the room, slamming the door behind them. Why had she ever agreed to this? Look at what it had come to. He had been ruined.

'Colbey,' she said and patted him on the cheek. 'Harry, say something.'

God, should she call an ambulance? Or the police? Would that make things worse? To her relief he groaned and said, 'Shit, I feel weird.'

'How did they spike you?' she said, but he closed his eyes. Patting him on the check, she said, 'Harry, how did this happen?'

'My drink,' he muttered. 'Man at the bar.'

'Come on, on your feet.' Kanha pulled off her coat and half cajoled, half dragged him over a detritus of bags and make-up and knickers to the room's little bathroom.

Propping Colbey up in the corner made by a tiled wall and the bath, and holding him steady with one hand as he opened his mouth to groan, she moved in and plunged her fingers to the back of his throat. Automatically turning his head towards the toilet bowl, Colbey threw up, spattering his chest and her shirt with vomit as he did so. He gasped, and Kanha went to do it again, but he waved her off. Putting his own fingers down his throat he made himself sick a second time. Then he slumped back against the bath gasping.

Kanha went into the bedroom and pulled out the plugs of all the electrical devices she could find including the television. On the floor beside Colbey's discarded mackintosh her sharp eye caught the glisten of a listening eye strip. She nudged it under the leg of a bedside table, using the weight of the furniture to crush it, then swept up a bottle of water which sat wobbling on top and brought it in to him; she watched, satisfied, as he drank it greedily down.

When he had drunk it all, she soaked a towel in the sink and handed it to him. He used it to wash the sick off him; she stripped off her shirt, got into the bath and washed her arms and hair and then rinsed and wrung out her shirt.

When she was done, she looked and saw that Colbey's eyes were focusing properly again, and felt the relief gush over her when he smiled weakly at her. She helped him back into the bedroom and sat him on the bed. Then she collected up all the chocolate, peanuts, water bottles and soft drinks she could find in the mini bar and threw them onto the sheets next to him.

Colbey looked around him. 'What a mess those girls made,' he said, and she could have kissed him.

'Were you in time?' he asked, but Kanha couldn't bring herself to answer. They both looked at the TV with the bed cover over it.

As he forced the food and drink down him, she found a hair-dryer and dried her hair and then her shirt. When she turned it off, she looked up to find him limping about, looking for his shirt. He started to put it on in a clumsy manner.

'I don't suppose it matters,' he said. 'Just another dirty old MP, eh.'

She didn't know what to say. 'I'm sorry,' was all she could think of.

'Is there any news from Mani?'

Kanha pulled the phone Mani had given her out of her bag and smiled. 'It's a thumbs-up emoji from him.' They smiled at each other.

'What time is it?'

'A quarter to six. But are you well enough?' Colbey staggered to his feet and she came to help him.

'Come on,' he said. 'There isn't much time.'

3.11

Lauvaux sat on his plane as it levelled out from its ascent, and looked at the images of the new minister and the two prostitutes that he had just received from Tirrell. The man was unpleasant, but his methods were effective, that had to be said. He looked across at his daughter who was still gripped by her game on his e-pad and frowned.

'What's that?' he said taking hold of the corner of it.

'My mermaid.'

He tried to tug the e-pad from her hand, but she held it firmly.

'But what is she?' he said.

Looking up at him, his daughter said, 'I help her find treasure.'

Lauvaux pulled the e-pad out of her hands. 'But what are you doing in the Alcheminna system?' And there she was, the little mermaid, swimming through carousels of the famous and not so famous, diving in and out of friendship groups, work teams, government departments, faces flicking by faster than a human finger could arrange, while the little mermaid spun through the screens.

As he stared, the mermaid appeared once more as if she had just swum out of a page. She turned and gave him a wave, holding a colourful shell in her other hand. Then she dived back in.

'How did you—'

Lauvaux gave a sudden howl of rage. He had handed his e-pad to his daughter without shutting down the system. They must have had access for hours. He fumbled to turn it off and then, thinking better, leapt to his feet, threw the pad on the floor and stamped on it, shouting, '*Non. Mon dieu. Non, non.*'

His daughter stared at him, her mouth falling open in amazement.

3.12

Kanha hurried out onto Piccadilly half dragging, half supporting Colbey and was overjoyed to see the orange light of a cab. The snow had stopped and a ray of sunshine fell onto the slushy pavement. She bundled Colbey in and said to the driver, 'The House of Commons as quickly as you can.'

The cabbie didn't try to even surreptitiously eye them in the rear-view mirror as they usually would, but turned and stared. 'Aren't you Harry Colbey?' he said.

'Yes, yes,' said Kanha, 'and he's due to give his maiden speech to the House any minute now, so please, please would you hurry.'

'I'd say,' said the driver.

As he drove off, he flicked his eyes to the road and then back again to his rear-view mirror. 'It's all over the news, you know.'

'What is?' they both said together.

The cabbie replied, 'People don't understand, you see. But now they do. That's for sure. Now they do. You want me to go down Horse Guard's Parade or take Whitehall?'

Kanha fumbled for the phone in her bag as Colbey fed M&Ms into his mouth and swayed with every turn of the cab.

'I don't do apps, you know? Drives my kids mad. I tell them, don't bring your phones into my house. But you can't stop them, can you? Glued to their phones, I mean look at them all. Do you know, I've been driving a cab for thirty years in London and every change they ever make makes it worse not better? But it's how they interact, isn't it? Pressure on these young kids, but they don't understand the cost. I say to them "look at all the apps that are listening to you" and they say "come off it, Dad, no one's listening" and then I show them all the apps that can access their microphone and they're panicking cos of what people might have been hearing going on, you know what I mean. Anyway, it's all out there now, isn't it?'

'What is?' said Kanha.

'The embarrassing moments hack? You not heard? Some hacker broke into that system that dead minister was in cahoots with. You know, that Dvořáček chap. The one the PM's advisor is wanted for his murder.'

Colbey looked up from his water bottle. 'What hack?' he said, his voice a dry croak still. 'What advisor?'

'Eh? Oh, you not heard. Thought you was the new data minister?'

'Please,' said Kanha. 'We've had a busy afternoon. Tells us what's happened.'

'The Alcheminna hack! I mean, I don't know much about this stuff, but I know what's wrong. And what these guys are doing is wrong. So this company, right, has a system with all of us in it. And they can ask it questions. So this hacker hacked it, right, and asked a bunch of people to confess their embarrassing secrets. It's hilarious. The link is all over social media. The internet people keep shutting it down, then it just comes back up somewhere else. Celebrities telling their secrets, but ordinary folk too, you know? Everyone's logging on to see if they're on it. My daughter's best friend's boyfriend is on it admitting he does you know what to videos of Beyoncé. And my wife's sister is on it confessing she piddles in the shower. And apparently the PM has the hots for his secretary. I mean, really, she's young enough to be his daughter. Disgusting. Anyway, all very funny, but now they know, huh?

Now they know what I've been telling them. You want me to drop you outside? Only they're pretty slow at the gate these days and...'

Kanha already had her hand on the handle of the door, her bag on her shoulder, Colbey's sleeve in her other arm. 'Who?' she said. 'Who's wanted for Dvořáček's murder?'

'Anthony Tirrell. He's gone on the run. A fugitive from the law. Says they won't catch him alive, not this time, whatever that means. Oh no, look, the gate's empty. I'll drop you by the door of the Hall. Get you there quicker.'

'There's no time to pay you.'

'Don't you worry. No need. I'm gonna park up here and come into the visitor's gallery and watch this speech of yours, Harry Colbey.'

*

Kanha pulled Colbey by the arm through parliament's Great Hall – a pigeon flitting about on its ancient great beams far above them catching her eye for a moment – into the central lobby, and from there to the members' lobby. The doors of the chamber were open wide and clogged with members. She knew that every bench must be full, every staircase tread taken for an impromptu seat, every camera turned to the dispatch box. The noise of the babble spilled out of the door. Here they all were, Dvořáček's dirty geese, squawking and squabbling. And above it all, the *bang bang* of the Speaker's gavel and his call of 'Order, order.'

The members' lobby was empty, other than of those still trying to squeeze their way in and of a few lone lobby journalists who had not yet made their way up to the press galleries – the BBC cameras stood abandoned; the whips must already have taken their places in the House. Only the doorman stood calmly with his back to the circus, giving Kanha a slight nod of respect as she came running over. Colbey came up behind her. She felt him shaking.

'Esme, Esme,' she heard, and saw Paddy standing within the group in the doorway.

'Do you know what's going on?' he hissed to her. 'They made me change the privacy bill to a three-line whip against.'

'What?' Kanha said. 'They made you tell the MPs to vote against the government's own bill?'

'It's a shit shower. The PM rang me himself and told me to do it.'

As he said it, a lobby hack looked up from his phone, spotted Colbey and came flying across the room.

'Why is there a three-line whip against your own department's bill?' he asked urgently, phone in hand, but Kanha and Colbey turned their back on him to confer. Behind him they heard him say to the camera: 'Well, what a turn up for the books. First the data privacy legislation's in a private member's bill and they have a one-line whip against it. Now the legislation is in its proper place, a government bill, and there's a *three-line* whip against it. Never heard of a government whipping against its own legalisation before. Meanwhile the opposition have a three-line whip for it, and who knows what those Whigges are up to. And all on the day on which the country is torn apart by revelations of a super computer holding secret versions of all of us. What is going on? You may well ask.'

Kanha looked at the order paper she had tugged from Paddy's hand. 'Hell. It's true. Our members are being told to vote against it. You're going to have to give the speech of your life. How are you feeling?'

She looked up at Colbey and to her surprise found that he looked to be calm.

'Do you know?' he said. 'Right now, all I want to do is try and do the right thing, and if that means after that I have to go and sit in that picture for the rest of my life, it wouldn't be a life wasted.'

Kanha looked at him. She had no idea what he was talking about, and hoped it was not still the drug in his system, but she squeezed his arm. It didn't matter if it looked like they were in cahoots now.

'Good luck,' she said and they pushed through the crowd in the doorway just as the foreign secretary stood up at the dispatch box, the PM at her side. When she saw Colbey coming, the foreign secretary made to yield and there was an awkward moment when the PM obviously whispered at her to stay, but she seemed to whisper back that she didn't want to, and this continued until Colbey arrived and she yielded the place to him, to the apparent annoyance of the PM.

The uproar in the House drowned out the Speaker's call for order, but he kept banging his gavel until he had quiet.

'Order, order,' he repeated. 'I had been led to understand that the foreign secretary was to introduce the second reading of the Personal Information Bill, but it seems that she has given way to the honourable member, Mr Harry Colbey. Mr Harry Colbey.'

'Hear, hear,' the House called on both sides accordingly.

All eyes turned from the PM's glare to Colbey, and Kanha heard someone ask in a whisper whether he wasn't swaying a little.

What shall I do if he can't speak? she thought. *After all this? Should I step in?*

Colbey came up to the dispatch box and silence fell on the chamber. Should she step in? What would she say?

Colbey's voice rang out loud and clear in the large room.

'I beg to move that the Personal Information Bill be now read a second time.'

The House erupted again, and the Speaker was forced to call the room to order several times before Colbey could continue.

'Mr Deputy Speaker. We are in the best of times. We are in the worst of times. We stand at the brink of unprecedented change. We stand at the brink of unprecedented challenges.

'But before I go on to that, I want to take you back, back to the early nineteenth century.'

Colbey most certainly swayed and looked for a moment as if he might fall. He put his hands onto the despatch box in front of him and shook his head. Kanha could only watch, but after a moment of horrid silence, he looked up and his voice came out into the chamber loud and clear again.

'1802, to be precise – a time when we in this land were at the forefront of human development. For it was here in this country that the invention of steam-powered motive force was first applied on an industrial scale. I'm speaking, of course, about the industrial revolution. It brought vast wealth to some, as well as many benefits to the populace, and seeded the life that we all have today: affordable clothes, shoes, household goods, a transport network that can swish us from one part of our land to another, modern health provision, labour-saving devices freeing us up for leisure time.

'Where am I going with this? Bear with me, please, for that is only half the story. For at that time, 49.9 per cent of mill workers began their working life under the age of ten. Yes, Mr Speaker, ten years old. And not only that. After the industrial revolution, children in the mills worked an average of fourteen to sixteen hours a day, Monday to Saturday, crawling beneath the dangerous machinery, eating the scraps that the mill owners provided. Many were orphans given free board by the mills in return for labour. And why is that no longer the case? I'm sure I do not need to tell the honourable members – it was because of the Health and Morals of Apprentices Act of 1802 when this House first moved to protect the rights of those children. For that, of course, is what we are here for – to temper those who would put greed and financial gain ahead of the rights of our citizens.

'What has this to do with data privacy, the honourable members may well ask? I would argue it is this.

'We are once again at a point of extreme advances. Of societal enhancement, of geographic expansion, of industrial revolution, of rapid technological advancement. Although sometimes we may not see it, so caught up are we in our daily lives, we are in the midst of a data revolution. And in this revolution, just like the last, there are sections of society who need the protection of this House and there are sections of society who would work to take advantage of those who have not the power to protect themselves.

'We all want the benefits that come from modern technology, but currently we are not allowed to use them unless we give everything of ourselves in return. Is this a fair exchange? As the leaks we have read about today show, modern technology is able to join up the dots of everything that makes us *us*. To get inside our very heads.' Here Colbey tapped his head and leaned forward, and Kanha couldn't help but smile. 'Is this a fair exchange for a free messaging or connecting service? For a game that distracts us for a few minutes on the Tube?

'It is not,' he roared triumphantly.

'And has anyone explicitly agreed to it? No. I would say not. I'm sure there are lawyers out there who would argue that we have. That if we look at the small print of this and that, it was made perfectly clear that our behaviour would be analysed. That there was nothing illegal in joining the dots. There was no law against it. Just like there was no law against making a child work sixteen hours in a mill and crawl underneath whirring machinery where he or she might lose a scalp or an arm or a finger. At least not until this very House brought laws into existence to make it illegal and to start the work of regulating the impossible.'

Kanha looked across at the faces in the House.

'Now a new dilemma falls to us. Do we want to allow such systems as those exposed today? Will we want to facilitate them, use them? Will we spy on our citizens, get inside their very heads? Watch them, listen to them, track them. Control them...

'Many of you have talked of a clause that is in the bill. Some have called it Dvořáček's Clause. I think that is a fair epithet. Dvořáček wrote the clause himself. Was keen that the honourable members should debate it. And that is what I intend also. And I know that many in this House have a three-line whip against it. But I am asking you to consider why. And most of all, Mr Speaker, I'm asking the honourable members to consider what sort of a world they would want for their constituents, their families, their children. There is no easy solution to this – for like that Health and Morals of Apprentices Act of 1802, there is only a start.

'They say that regulators move three times slower than technological progress. And that big tech moves three times faster than normal tech. Well, here we all are. We slow folk, catching up.

'I'm guessing I won't be standing here as minister for much longer. But while I still am, I implore the honourable members not to vote *against* this law that includes Dvořáček's Clause, but to vote instead to pass this bill to the next stage.'

The debate raged until ten that night, and Kanha was near collapse when the Speaker finally stood and shouted the words she had waited anxiously for.

'Divide!'

Now it was up to them, the six-hundred-odd honourable members. She and Colbey had done all they could.

Provence, France

Three months later

Harry Colbey sat with his eyes closed, listening intently to the incessant rustle of the cicadas. In his mind's eye he saw an orange sun sinking behind the frothy tops of umbrella pines and a sky ready to be dipped into night. Behind him, he knew there was a house with bright green shutters tied back against white stone. Although he could not see it with his eyes so tightly shut, he also knew that beyond the courtyard in which he sat, shielded from view by thick hibiscus, was an old 1940s swimming pool of speckled marble with water too green to be real, and that his chair teetered on gravel before a wrought-iron filigree table.

How could a digital recreation ever compete with the real world? Could it mimic the breeze that kissed his face, first here, now not here, now here again, a breeze that was no part of man's doing? Could it mimic the patter of a dog's paws, the unexpected wet fingers, the first sounds of the happy chatter of those close to your heart returning from the village with bread and cheese and crisp, pinker-than-pink rosé?

Colbey opened his eyes and patted the dog, a black and white scrap of a thing that belonged to the owner of the house. Down the path he saw Esme Kanha and his daughter, Chloe, returning from the village, their arms full of brown paper bags. He put the pencil that was still clutched in his hand down on his sketch pad as his daughter came running up. She still had, even at twenty-five, the loping, gangly run of a teenager and her phone was, as ever, in her hand and held out for him to see.

'Daddy, you're trending.'

Colbey groaned and cleared some space on the table so that they could empty the bags and lay out the bread and cheese on the board he had already prepared. As he opened the wine and put it in the ice bucket at his feet, he said, 'What an earth could they have on me now?'

Throwing her phone on the table, Chloe said, 'You tell him, Esme, I'm going for a quick dip.'

It was not too difficult for Colbey to ignore the phone that fell in front of him. 'Don't be long, darling, we're about to eat.'

'You can start without me.'

'We could, but I don't want to.'

As she left, her flip flops scattering the gravel as she went, Esme Kanha pulled out a chair and sat down. 'It's *The Sun* again, but good news this time.'

He groaned. 'Hard to be worse than their last headline – "Harry Two Shags".'

'I told you not to worry about that – it was obvious you were barely conscious, and you got re-elected anyway.'

'Only because of the postal votes. So tell me.'

Picking up Chloe's phone, Kanha read: 'Escort admits she was paid to spike privacy minister Colbey's drink.'

He slowly smiled as he opened up the cheeses and laid them out. 'Is that your doing?'

'I couldn't possibly say.'

'Read it, then.'

'Page-three stunner Suzi admits she was paid to spike the drink of previous information minister by shadowy security firm. Rebel Colbey had led a revolt against the government in April that forced prime minister Ewan MacLellan to resign when Colbey's version of a privacy bill, whipped against by the government, was passed to committee stage with three hundred and two votes for and two hundred and ninety-nine against. It's not known who was behind the honey trap or what its purpose was. When asked for comment, Colbey's spokesperson said, "I'm glad for my friends, family and all those in the constituency who have supported me these long years that the truth is finally out. Although the progress of the privacy bill was terminated by MacLellan immediately calling a general election before resigning, and although we lost the election to the opposition and Whigge coalition, I will not cease to campaign to protect the privacy of our nation's citizens."'

'Very good, I like that.'

'You're welcome. Where's Mani?'

'Inside, on the computer, as usual. Here he comes now. Did you see there have been a few more Whigges stepping down?'

'Yes, the coalition might not survive much longer.'

Mani stepped out of the hotel door and sauntered over to them, an open laptop carried in his hand, just as Chloe returned, a huge white towel wrapped around her. Her hair was dripping all over the table. Colbey frowned and moved the cheese away.

'Everything alright?' he said to Mani.

Picking up a piece of Tomme à l'Ancienne and putting it into his mouth, he replied, 'Tirrell's been arrested. Someone sent them satellite footage of him camped out in a bothy in Scotland.'

'Was that *your* doing?' Kanha asked, and then replying to herself, in a mockery of Mani, said, *'Better you don't know.'*

Mani shrugged. 'We've been tracking Tirrell.'

'We?' said Colbey.

He smothered his bread with some cheese and shrugged. 'Interpol. Can't have people running around bumping off ministers, can we?'

'Oh my god. Give me my phone, Daddy, I need to post about it.'

'Oh, I'm not sure that's a good idea, are you, Esme?'

'Probably better not to.'

Chloe reached for her phone, but Colbey picked it up and put it in his pocket.

They spent some time after that berating Mani for not telling them sooner, until eventually Colbey said, 'So, it's Interpol, is it? Is there anyone you're not working for?'

'I couldn't possibly say,' Mani replied.

After they had discussed it and discussed it, and berated Mani some more, there didn't seem to be much else to do but pour the wine and have their supper. It was a relief to know that Tirrell was safely behind bars. Colbey tried to hug his daughter but she pulled away and said that she was desperate to post, but Colbey still refused to return her phone, so she said, 'Esme, could you get my phone and pass it to me, please?'

'Certainly not.'

'Well, I'll use my father's, then.'

Both Colbey and his daughter reached for his phone but Chloe got there first.

'You don't know my code.'

'Want to bet?' she said, grinning, but even as she said it, the phone rang and without hesitation she answered it. 'Harry Colbey's office. Can I help you?'

She made a few humming noises, dodging away as Colbey tried to take the phone from her.

'Just a minute please.' Chloe held the phone to her chest. 'Apparently the coalition is on the verge of falling apart, in which case you guys might become a majority again. They want to know if you'll stand for leader. No, wait, they said they're all agreed they want you to be leader.'

Colbey groaned. 'I really don't—'

'Not *you*. Esme? They said you've not been answering your phone, Esme. They've been ringing around everyone, trying to find you.'

All three looked at Esme Kanha who was concentrating on her cheese selection.

'Well?' said Colbey.

She looked up and said, 'Tell them I'll think about it and call them back.'

'They said they've got the US president on the line, and he wants to talk to you on the basis you're a shoo-in.'

'Tell them I'll think about it and call them back.'

Chloe relayed the message and put the phone down. In polite silence the cheese was passed around.

Esme Kanha looked at Colbey and said, 'I suppose you might make quite a good Minister for Personal Information.'

He licked some Brie from the side of his mouth.

She looked at Mani. 'And I suppose you might have just the right experience to be a national security advisor.'

Mani winked at her and took some more of the Tomme.

She patted her lips with her napkin. 'I'm just going to go into the house to make a phone call.'

To her retreating back, Colbey called out, 'Can I put through my Honest Politicking Bill?'

Disappearing into the house, she replied, 'Mmm... let me think about that.'

And somewhere in Provence, a yellow sun set behind a mountain topped with grey, where there really was a stone house with green shutters and chairs teetering on gravel.

Author's Note

All the characters, companies, political parties, websites and events included in *Dirty Geese* are entirely fictional, but the technology in the book is not – either it already exists or someone, somewhere in the world, is working to bring it into being.

www.lougilmond.com

LOU GILMOND
Palisade

WHAT CAN SEE WATCHES, WHAT CAN HEAR LISTENS,
WHAT CAN BE FOLLOWED IS TRACKED...

When opposition Chief Whip Esme Kanha is handed a secret
dossier containing evidence of government corruption, she suspects
its original owner, a top journalist, was murdered for gathering it.
Despite the danger, she feels she must investigate. Meanwhile, lowly
backbencher Harry Colbey is working his own leads. A known
campaigner against big tech, he is often sent data from anonymous
sources and this time round he has something truly alarming.

But both Colbey and Kanha must tread carefully in a world
dominated by AI, where 'what can see watches, what can hear
listens, and what can be followed is tracked'.

As Kanha and Colbey again join forces, they are locked into a
deadly race against political corruption, no matter what the cost.
But when an old enemy returns, it may already be too late...

*'The constant presence of AI creates a foreboding
atmosphere'*
—*CRIME FICTION LOVER*

ALSO BY LOU GILMOND

The Tale of Senyor Rodriguez

Kanha and Colbey Thrillers

Dirty Geese
Palisade
Divinity Games

For exclusive info and the latest updates visit:
www.lougilmond.com